I0771680

PORTSMOUTH
Fields
GREAT ROAD
Fieldstone
SEAPERCH
FARMLAND
TRADING OUTPOST
NORTH WINGLE
WEST WINGLE
EAST WINGLE
MEDOC'S MARSH
THE FOREST
HILL PEOPLE
FLUMIN RIVER
THE LAKE
KAVENLAND
ROCK HAVEN
THE WALL
GREAT ROAD
Fields
LAKETOWN
(FARMLAND)
MAPLETOWN
SOUTH ROAD
CRAB HAVEN
GLENSWORTH
CRUMBLES
THE POINT

The Door in the Stone

Book 1 of the Kavenland Series

Rob King

Four Monarchs Publishing

Pittsburgh, PA

Praise for *The Door in the Stone*

"An unforgettable tale... *The Door in the Stone* is a masterful exploration of the transformative power of adventure and self-discovery. Rob King is a remarkable author who has penned a truly compelling book that grips you from the very first page."

The Midwest Book Review

"A winning story full of heart and action... A captivating blend of fantasy, adventure, and self-discovery. Unexpected twists... keep readers involved until the very end."

The Prairies Book Review

"An enchanting adventure into a world filled with magic, danger, and friendship... *The Door in the Stone* is a highly recommended read that captivates both the imagination and the heart."

Readers' Favorite

To Meg, who steers the ship so I can lie on deck and look

up at the stars.

Chapter One
Vic–Our World

When the legend of Vic Blake, dashing figure of mystery and intrigue, was written—and it would be written one day—this was the moment they would say it began.

"There's something ticking in the movie theater!" a boy yelled as he shoved open the glass doors and burst into the street. "Somebody, help!" A low buzz emerged from the crowd of customers who streamed out behind the boy and spread out onto the sidewalk. Some looked nervously back at the movie theater while others edged away toward their cars. Grim-faced moms seized their children by their wrists and marched them off.

Vic's sister grabbed his arm. Her eyes stretched wide in alarm. He looked down at her with a sly smile on his face. Her eyes narrowed.

At times like this, Vic wished Emily spoke more. Her facial expressions could say more in a moment than a week's worth of words could from somebody else. Her look now mixed equal measures of accusation and disappointment. Her judgement sent a pang deep in his chest, but he forced himself to shrug it off. Legendary figures had to remain cool and detached. Rules were for others to follow, not for Vic Blake.

He winked back at Emily and ambled past the movie theater on his long legs. Em walked next to him, her flip flops slapping a rhythm as they moved toward the center of town. Vic passed the boy who'd yelled for help and slipped some cash into his hand.

Another little pang hit him. Food was running low at home, and he'd have to surrender the rest of their money before the evening was through. But he reminded himself for the thousandth time that it would be worth it.

"Good work," he whispered to the boy.

"There's something in the alley!" another boy yelled from a little further up the street. "Something ticking!"

One of the men who'd left the movie theater looked around frantically. "Is it a bomb?" he called out in alarm.

"Did someone say a bomb?" another man shouted.

"It's a bomb!" a woman echoed.

"Two bombs!" a man yelled.

"Run!" someone shrieked. "Run!"

Vic looked around and saw panic in people's eyes and heard the screams from their lips as they jostled each other. A woman snapped her head around frantically. "Jimmy!" she shrieked. "Jimmy, where are you? Has anyone seen my boy?" She was bumped from behind, and she sprawled onto the sidewalk. Vic stepped over her and kept walking. Behind him, he heard Em stop to help the woman up.

Good. He wanted to be alone for the next few minutes. The boy who'd yelled out about the ticking in the alley slithered toward him between the panicked people on the street, and Vic tucked some money into his hand.

So far, his plan was working just as he'd envisioned.

He paused on the sidewalk and eyed his destination.

Mr. Zipkoff's jewelry store.

Vic snorted. Zipkoff. "Ripped-off" was more like it.

Mr. Zipkoff stood in the doorway of his store. He held a meaty hand over his beady eyes to block out the setting sun as he looked out at the pandemonium on the sidewalk. Vic pressed himself against a storefront a few doors down. The sound of sirens approached, and Vic looked up to see two police cars screech to a stop in the street. Mr. Zipkoff stepped out onto the sidewalk to get a closer look.

Everything was going exactly as planned.

Two officers, armed with bullhorns, jumped out of the police cars.

"Everyone, stay calm!" one of the officers called out. Some of the people slowed down and looked around them.

"Now," Vic hissed underneath his breath. His pulse thumped in his ears. It had to be now!

From across the street, a small series of explosions rent the air. The police officers jerked around. There was another explosion. "Another bomb!" someone shouted.

Mr. Zipkoff took two more steps out onto the sidewalk. He stood, hands on hips, and stared over at the park from where the explosions had come.

Vic smiled grimly to himself. He crept quietly behind Mr. Zipkoff. He knew he wouldn't be heard.

He never worried about being heard.

With the diversion he'd created, he wouldn't be seen, either. He glided inside the jewelry store.

He'd been here before. He clenched his jaw at the memory. He pushed the thought aside. He knew what he was looking for and what he needed to do to get it. He figured he had a minute, maybe less. The store was air conditioned and cool, but Vic felt a trickle of perspiration on his forehead.

He went behind the counter and snatched the small key that hung off a hook on the back wall. He slipped the key into the lock and slid open the glass door. His heart skipped as his hand closed around a gleaming hair comb. It was the kind of comb that was worn to hold hair back, not the kind of comb that brushed hair. He pulled the comb out of the case and thrust it into his pocket. It was pure gold and heavier than it looked. He closed the door, locked it, returned the key to its hook, and looked up. Mr. Zipkoff still stood on the sidewalk, gazing out across the street.

Vic estimated that he'd been in the store no longer than 45 seconds. He walked out quickly and quietly, so close to Mr. Zipkoff that he could smell the man's cheap aftershave, and he melted into the crowd.

He let out a long breath.

He'd done it.

He bit his lip to keep from laughing out loud.

He'd done it!

Em appeared in front of him as if by magic. She looked around to make sure that no one was listening then turned back to Vic and wagged a finger in his face.

"You'd better have a good explanation for all this," she hissed.

He spread his arms out wide. "An old clock ticks in the movie theater. Another clock ticks in the alley. Some power of suggestion is mixed in. All my boys said was that they heard ticking—which was perfectly true. The police show up. Some firecrackers happen to go off across the street, adding to the suggestion that lives might be in danger. I did nothing illegal. I thought of everything." He allowed himself that wide self-congratulatory smile after all. "I thought of everything," he said again.

"What it the police were needed in a real emergency somewhere else?" Em demanded.

He hadn't thought of that.

"And you created a panic," Em added. "That is definitely illegal."

"To make an omelet," Vic replied loftily, "you have to break some eggs."

"You didn't break any eggs," Em said, "you laid them."

A dog walked beside Em. The hair on its back bristled and it bared its teeth. It let out a low growl.

"Rufus thinks what you've done is terrible," Em informed Vic.

Vic let a long breath to control his exasperation. This nonsense of Em thinking she could talk to cats and dogs had him worried. He sighed inwardly. At least she wasn't chirping at every bird she saw.

A cat meowed at his feet. When Vic looked down, the cat hissed at him.

Emily glanced at the cat then looked her brother in the eye. "Willow doesn't like what you did, either."

Vic shook his head. She'd begun saying she could talk with cats and dogs a few months ago, right around her birthday. Animals had always loved her, and she'd always loved them, but this was different. After all, he loved ice cream, but he'd never had a conversation with a bowl of mint chocolate chip.

He looked down again at Willow. The cat lifted its tail stiffly up, turned, and sauntered away, its pinkish-brown butt staring back at Vic like an evil eye.

That was something Vic didn't need Em to translate.

Vic grunted and guided Em away from the animals and through the traffic which had begun to calm down.

"I got the gold hair comb back, Em," he told her.

She whirled to face him. "What?" she demanded. Her eyes widened as she realized what he was saying. "You created all of that, you risked the lives of countless people..."

"No one got hurt," Vic interrupted. "A few bumps and bruises, maybe."

"You couldn't know that would be all that happened," Em snapped. "Someone could have had a heart attack for all you knew."

"But they didn't," Vic said. He flung his arms up in triumph. "I did it!" he exclaimed.

"What happens if the police figure out it was you?" Em asked quietly. "You've risked someone finding out about us."

Vic's elation slipped out of him until he felt as empty as a wrinkled balloon on a cold floor. He'd been so intent on revenge, and—if he were being perfectly honest with himself, on doing something big—that he hadn't properly weighed the risks. What if he were caught? What if he and Em were separated?

Icy fear gripped him by the throat, and he shivered in the warm summer evening.

They walked on in silence. Vic's gait went from floating on air to trudging through sludge. Ugly thoughts crowded his head. What if he and Em were found out? What if they were separated, strong hands pulling them apart, ushering them out of their front door, shoving them into different cars, driving them away to two distant destinations? Vic's mouth went as dry as a math class as he contemplated for the first time the most important thing he'd risked tonight.

Himself and Em.

They'd survived trouble at school—ok, his trouble at school— and the death of their parents. They'd survived it by sticking together. Had his actions tonight put that in jeopardy? He swallowed a lump the size of a rubber ball as he and Em walked along in silence.

In a few minutes, they were on their street, and a few seconds after that, they turned up their short, crumbling path and stepped onto their sagging porch.

"Beautiful house," kids would snicker. "How are things at Castle Blake?"

The taunts had turned Vic's ears red and made his insides feel like they were being devoured by a ravenous beast. He'd spent hours and hours dreaming of getting away from his parents, from this house, from this town and going somewhere with Em to start a new life. He'd had wide thoughts of a big world, but those thoughts had narrowed lately. Their parents were gone, and this house was home for him and Em. He'd do anything to protect that and to protect them.

Vic opened the drooping front door and stepped inside. He groped for the light switch and flipped it up. He took two steps into the room and stopped.

A few feet away, in the only chair in the room, sat a strange woman with her eyes closed. Deep creases lined her forehead. A hooked nose sat over a crooked mouth that perched upon a large, misshapen chin. She had boils and moles all over her face. Thick hairs sprung copiously from the moles as if eager to form their own ecosystem.

The woman was monstrously ugly.

Her eyes shot open. "Amazing," she said. "I really couldn't hear your footsteps."

"Who are you?" Vic demanded. "What are you doing here?" Vic looked at the woman. He looked at Em. Em's mouth hung open. She looked back up at Vic.

"She's..."

"Hideous," Vic finished.

"...beautiful," Em said.

Vic's eyebrows arched up. He looked back at the woman and recoiled. She really was hard to look at. He stared back down at Em. She looked enraptured as she continued to gaze at the woman.

The woman sprang to her feet. Her light movements surprised Vic. She looked like an ancient, gnarled oak tree, but she moved like a bounding deer.

"We can debate the various merits," she said to Em, "or lack thereof," she added to Vic, "of my appearance later. But right now, we don't have time. I need you to pack a change of clothes and come with me."

Vic's mouth dropped and he let out an incredulous laugh. "We're not going anywhere with you, lady. In fact, if you leave now, it's just possible that I might not call the police."

The woman shook her head sadly. "I don't think you'll be calling the police. Especially not with what you just pulled tonight."

Vic's armpits and brow were suddenly damp.

"The item you stole that's sitting in your front pocket?" the woman added. "That item belongs to me. Actually, it belonged to my sister, but since she died a thousand years ago, I think I can rightly say now that it belongs to me."

Vic stepped back. His hand shot into his pocket and closed around the heavy golden hair comb.

"How could you possibly know about that?" Em asked in a hoarse whisper.

"I told you, the item belongs to me," the woman answered. "I've been keeping an eye on it for quite some time."

Vic wasn't sure what that meant, but something about the old woman gave him the creeps. His skin felt like a giant dance floor for ten thousand ants. What she somehow knew that she couldn't possibly know, her ghastly face, her clothes—which he could only describe as Salem witch trial-chic—all added up to...

Vic gulped.

"Are you...are you some kind of a witch?"

The woman gave a laugh—a melodic laugh like tinkling bells, which sounded odd coming from between her crooked teeth.

"Am I a witch?" she mused. She tapped a misshapen finger to her cracked lips. "All things considered, I'd say no, although I can see why you'd think that."

"Well, you can't have the gold comb. It belonged to my mother and her mother before her. Mr. Zipkoff got me to sell it to him for four hundred dollars when..."

Images dashed through his head. Empty liquor bottles, his parents' gassy breath, their reaching for the car keys several months ago as they staggered to the front door. Hours later, the knock on the door, and grim news of a one-car crash being delivered by police officers. Then Vic was wearing a dark, itchy suit to a funeral no one attended. Later, a neighbor came by with a casserole. Embarrassed that there was no one else at the house, she'd made her apologies, said there was no need to return the pan, and bolted out of the door like a prisoner granted parole.

"When what, dear?" the woman asked softly.

Vic cleared his throat and wiped a hand across his eyes. He was surprised that his hand came away wet. "When we were vulnerable and needed the money," he said. Rage rushed through him like a thunderstorm, engulfing and consuming his sadness and self-pity. "Mr. Zipkoff gave me four hundred dollars!" He clenched the comb in his fist and brought it out of his pocket. The comb's clasps bit into his palm as he brandished it in the air. "It's got to be worth thousands!"

"It's worth a lot more than that," the woman answered. "Oh, maybe that's a good price for it in your world," she said, with a dismissive wave of her hand, "but I assure you that it's worth a lot more than that where I come from."

"Wait—what did you just say?" Em asked. "What do you mean 'in your world' and 'where you come from'? Are you telling us that you're not from this world? And did you say your sister died a thousand years ago?"

"Right on both counts," the woman replied in a cheery voice.

Vic fought back a wave of panic. He wanted to strike a bold tone, but his voice came out thin and weak to his own ears, like an off-key oboe.

"Who are you? What are you doing here? What do you want with us?"

"Ah, the questions you should have been asking all along." The woman stepped back into a long, graceful curtsey, then stood up again. "My name is Adelessa. I'm here because I've been watching your family for years. Centuries, really. Finally, the time has arrived." She pursed her lips. "As for what I want with you—I want you to come to my world and help to set it right."

"Why would we do that?" Vic asked.

Adelessa answered with a question of her own.

"Have you ever had the feeling that you don't quite belong, that you want something more from your lives?" she asked. She looked at Em, then Vic, then Em again. "You are more comfortable with animals than humans," she stated.

Vic watched in fascination as Em and Adelessa locked eyes. Em seemed to fall into a kind of trance. She stared vacantly at the older woman. Her breathing slowed and almost stopped. Vic began to feel his scalp prickle. He was just about to step forward and say something when the connection that held Em and Adelessa together was broken.

"Yes," Em whispered. "Yes, that's exactly what I want."

Adelessa nodded and turned her attention to Vic. "And you— you have footfalls so light that no one can hear you coming. You went into the staff room at school and stole a teacher's mug on a dare. No one heard you coming or going. Did that make you more popular?" she asked.

As Adelessa's eyes met his, Vic's mind tumbled back to the third grade. He remembered the mocking tone of one of his fellow students, Chip Newhart. Chip was one of the popular kids. He thought maybe Chip would like him if he did something crazy like steal a teacher's mug. It didn't work.

Vic remembered the ache of loneliness that he'd felt when Chip tattled to the principal. Like a projector set on fast speed, more scenes of rejection and ridicule flashed through his mind. He'd pushed and compressed those feelings down deep into his gut, but they'd grown into a great, gray pearl of resentment in the years since.

He found that he couldn't look away from Adelessa as she leafed through his memories like a shopper leafed through shirts at the mall. A group of kids tried to corner him in the playground. He'd fought kids before, but this time they were too big and too many to fight. He ran away as they tugged at his backpack and pulled it free. He snuck back later to find that they'd dumped out its contents. Some had been swept away by the wind, and he had to scour around for an hour, burning with shame, until he'd retrieved everything.

He tried again to stop Adelessa's probing but found that he couldn't. He felt naked and exposed. He saw himself through her eyes, and he felt abashed and angry at what he saw.

Even finding success running on the track team a year ago hadn't helped. He'd always been the fastest kid in school. But overnight, it seemed, he'd become the fastest kid in the district, and then the fastest kid in the state. Instead of helping him to fit in, it was just one more thing that separated him from everyone else.

Those thoughts melted away as soon as they'd come, and he saw only Adelessa's emerald-colored eyes. Then that green became the green of a forest, and Vic saw himself and Em walking with three other kids about their age who he didn't know. The scene shifted, and the same kids were crowded around a table in some sort of cottage. The five of them laughed and talked. They clearly had formed a bond of some sort. They were something Vic had never had.

Friends.

"Perhaps you need a fresh start," Adelessa said quietly. Vic shook his head as the images faded away. There was a tinge of pity in Adelessa's eyes. "Your parents felt the same way. And their parents, and their parents before them, and their parents before them…" Her voice drifted off. "You feel like you don't belong because you don't belong," she added.

"Thanks," Vic muttered. "I'd already figured that out for myself."

Adelessa frowned. "That's not what I meant. What I meant was, you feel like you don't belong in this world because you *don't* belong in this world. You belong in my world. That's where your ancestors are from. That's where I want you to go now."

A bright ray soared inside of Vic's chest, a long-lost emotion that he searched to identify. He finally found the word.

Hope.

Vic couldn't remember the last time he'd felt it. He wanted to believe Adelessa. He wanted to believe in another world where he could start over, someplace where he could feel like he belonged. But cynicism crept from the shadows of his mind and wrestled hope to the floor.

"No," Vic said. "I don't know what kind of tricks you're playing with us, but we're not going with you." He didn't trust this woman at all.

Adelessa looked up at the ceiling. "I don't have time for this," she muttered, more to herself than to Vic or Em. She turned to Vic.

"I've told you a little about why you should come with me," she said. "Let me tell you what will happen if you don't." She took a step toward Vic and stared up in his eyes. "You're going to get caught."

Vic swallowed. He hoped his voice sounded more confident than he felt when he spoke. "No chance," he said. "I thought of everything."

"What about all of the security cameras around town?" Adelessa answered. "Several of them probably recorded you going into the jewelry store."

He hadn't thought of that.

Adelessa shook her head sadly. "Amazing that you've stayed away from child services for so long," she said. "When the police find out that there is no aunt living here with you like you've been claiming, and that two children are on their own—why, I suspect they'll have something to say about that." She let out a theatrical sigh. "I doubt the two of you will be kept together. Such a pity. Of course, Vic will probably be in jail."

"That's blackmail!" Vic said in a hoarse whisper.

"If you come with me, I will give you the chance to return..." She looked around doubtfully and gave a vague wave of her hand. "...to this." She shrugged. "Or you can stay here and be separated, and Vic can go to jail."

Em looked at Vic. She nodded slowly.

"We'll come with you," Vic croaked.

Adelessa nodded. "I'll give you five minutes to throw your stuff into backpacks."

Five minutes later, with some changes of clothes in their bags, Vic and Em followed Adelessa out the door. She told them to leave their phones behind. Vic felt numb. They were leaving their home. It wasn't much of a home, but it was all they knew.

Vic looked down at his sister. Her flip flops smacked down on the sidewalk, like a ticking clock counting down the time that they had left to be around everything they'd ever known.

"I'd like to believe her," Em whispered.

"And I'd like to believe in the tooth fairy," Vic hissed. "The first chance we get, I say we give this Adelessa the slip."

But they never got the chance. They passed through the town and into its outskirts. Adelessa stumbled once, then again, but it only made her more determined to increase their pace. She stopped in front of a huge outcropping of rock and leaned against it for a moment.

In the distance, Vic heard police sirens wail. Adelessa looked around, then made a small gesture with her hand. To Vic's astonishment, a door in the stone, invisible just a moment ago, swung open toward them.

"This is how your ancestors came to this world long ago," she said. "Through the Door in the Stone."

Vic stood motionless and open-mouthed.

"In you go," Adelessa said.

Vic gulped. He grabbed Em's hand firmly and stepped into the cool, dark tunnel. After a few paces, he stopped. A dim light filtered in from somewhere, and Vic saw that the passageway split into several different corridors.

"The one all the way to the left," Adelessa ordered from behind him.

Vic followed her instructions.

"I think you can find who you truly are in this world." Adelessa said. "I won't tell you it will be easy, but I think you can do well for yourselves."

"What is this world called?" Em asked.

"You'll be going to a city called Laketown," Adelessa answered, "in a country called Kavenland."

"What's the world like?" Vic asked as he came to the end of the tunnel. "What do you expect us to do?"

Adelessa slipped past them. She pulled open the door. Vic threw his hand over his eyes. Bright sunlight temporarily blinded him as he stepped forward.

Then he felt a shove in the small of his back. A moment later, Em hurtled past him.

"The first thing I expect you to do," Adelessa answered, "is to survive." Then she slammed the door shut behind them.

Chapter Two
Larkin–Kavenland

Larkin felt his stomach clench.

Something was different. Something was terribly wrong.

He could almost smell it in the air.

Larkin tried to push the thought out of his mind. He grabbed his shovel, thrust it into a pile of manure, grunted slightly and lifted it and dumped it into his cart. He wiped his forearm across his brow, leaned the shovel against the wall, grabbed the two handles of the cart and wheeled it out of the barn. It rocked slightly as he pushed it across the yard.

There was certainly nothing different with his daily routine, Larkin thought. Collect the eggs first thing in the morning. Feed the pigs. Clean up after them. Shovel out the stalls that housed the horse and the cow. Dump the manure over by the garden.

"Larkin!" his Aunt Magdelina called out to him from their cottage, but he pretended not to hear. He wanted to get his chores done in case his uncle came back today.

A week ago, Larkin had been cleaning the barn on another typical morning when he heard the door of the cottage slam. His Uncle Dain had emerged from the cottage. He strode across the lawn and headed for the barn. He had a grim look on his face—even more grim than usual.

"I'm off to Portsmouth," he'd informed Larkin as he whisked past. "Urgent business. I'll be back in a few days." He'd swung himself up on his horse and headed north up the Great Road.

A few days had passed and then a few more. His uncle still hadn't returned. His aunt's normally tidy hair hung in scattered strands. She stood for hours at a time and stared out the window toward the Great Road while her fingers drummed along the countertop. This morning she'd cut flowers from the garden, walked past the vase on the kitchen table, and put the flowers in a cupboard.

Larkin pushed the cart over to the garden. The scent of jasmine wafted toward him, and his mind immediately hurtled him back to the lone memory he had of his mom. He couldn't have been more than two or three. She tossed him up in the air. He looked down at her. She smiled back up at him, a stem of jasmine tucked over her ear. She caught him as he fell, then, laughing, she tossed him back up again.

Larkin rubbed a hand across his face. Smells always did that to him. They could take him to a time and place that was so real it was almost like he was living through an event again.

He picked up the handles. The cart wobbled as he pushed it up the slight hill. He could smell a deep purple dread and a fiery red anger in the air as he trudged along. He turned the cart over and added the horse and cow dung to the pile. As he walked back to the barn, he stopped.

He'd smelled dread and anger.

He was sure of it.

But that was impossible.

You couldn't smell emotions. He blinked. This smell hadn't taken his mind anywhere. He was still right there, standing on the lawn.

He breathed in deeply.

The scent was still there. Deep purple dread and fiery red anger.

The gnawing feeling in his stomach returned.

He set down the cart in the middle of the lawn and walked over to the Great Road. He cupped his hands over his eyes to shield them from the late morning sun and turned his head to the north. He squinted.

He half-expected to see his uncle galloping toward him, but he didn't.

There was no one there.

"Larkin!"

He jumped at his aunt's voice.

"Okay, okay, I'm coming," he called. He went back across the lawn to the empty cart. He walked it into the barn and shoved it against the wall. He ran his fingers absently through his long hair, pushing it back, then brought his fingers back in front of his eyes and examined them. They were crusted with manure. Which was now in his hair. He blew out his breath. It sure seemed like the usual boring morning routine. Except for something in the air...

Maybe he was wrong. Maybe nothing was the matter.

But when he inhaled, he smelled dread and anger again.

"Larkin!" his aunt said, this time with an edge to her voice. "There's someone here to see you."

It had to be Ariana and Noll, he thought. They had their own chores to do, so they usually waited until after lunch to stop by on Saturdays, but maybe they were early today because it was his birthday.

And not just any birthday.

It was his coming-of-age day.

He had been wondering for weeks if something might happen to him like had happened with his two best friends. Something big and exciting.

Noll had always been the largest boy in the village, but since he'd come of age, he was now far larger than any *man* in Fieldstone, too. Ariana had always jumped in to try to protect kids who were being picked on, but now none of the bullies in town, even the older ones, would dare to cross her.

Larkin smiled at the thought of them. Noll remained a little timid. He still walked with hunched shoulders, as if trying to conceal his enormous size.

It wasn't working.

"You don't understand what it's like to be this big," Noll told Larkin. "Everyone says they want to be big and strong until they meet someone like me. I hear what the kids are saying when I walk by. 'Freak!' they'll say, always when they're in a group and when I can't really make out who said it.

"And the grown-ups are just as bad," Noll continued. "If something's stuck on the top shelf at the grocer's, don't bring in a ladder—just get Noll. If someone needs to move a boulder out of the way? No need to hitch up some draft horses—we can always use Noll. The kids treat me like a grown-up, and the grown-ups forget I'm still a kid."

"At least you have Ariana and me," Larkin answered.

"I know," Noll said. He dropped a huge hand on Larkin's shoulder. Larkin winced and his knees buckled. Noll still didn't know his own strength. "But remember this: no one roots for the giant."

"Everyone rooted for Beredor and Galeran," Larkin pointed out.

"Yes, but they had themselves and 48 other Protectors with them," Noll replied. He threw his arms out theatrically and looked all around. "I don't see anyone else like me. I'm a one-person circus. I don't know why I've been changing," he complained, "but I don't like it."

Ariana, meanwhile, was as outgoing as Noll was bashful. Enthusiasm bubbled out of her like water out of a fountain. She was always up for playing a game or climbing a tree. The younger kids in the village, especially, adored her.

Right after she'd come of age, a large boy in the village had made fun of a frail, friendless kid. She'd confronted the bully.

"Apologize," she'd demanded.

The boy had laughed at her. After all, he was at least a head taller than she was.

"What are you going to do about it?" he'd snarled and surged at her threateningly.

She'd knocked him down. More shocked than injured, the boy cried and ran away. A few minutes later, the boy had returned with his older brother, the biggest and meanest bully in town. He'd swaggered up to Ariana, full of bravado, but that swagger and bravado disappeared when she'd knocked him down, too. After that, every kid who felt like an outcast clung to Ariana whenever she walked through the village.

"Any time I see anyone getting bullied," Ariana had confided to Larkin, "I get this icy fire in me, like a steel flagpole on a winter's day. I feel an overwhelming desire to protect the weaker from the stronger. I don't know why I've been changing," she added, "but I love it!"

Larkin didn't know why his friends were changing, either. He really hoped he'd come up with some kind of special strength or power, too, although he hadn't heard of anything unusual happening to any of the other kids in Fieldstone on their coming-of-age days. Maybe it was just Noll and Ariana who were different. He hated to admit it, but he would be extremely disappointed if his two best friends were special, and he wasn't.

Larkin thrust his hands into his pockets, scuffed at a stone, and ambled toward the cottage. What a boring life. He felt suffocated. The north of Kavenland was so dull. Nothing ever happened here. He wanted adventure. His imagination took flight and swept him far away from the farm to battlefields where he fought side-by-side with his hero, Galeran the Great. He saved the Protector from certain death by plunging his sword into a hideous beast. Galeran thanked him and repeated the story at the victory dinner, where a modest Larkin shrugged off the praise from the grateful army.

"You saved us all!" they shouted. "Three cheers for the hero! Lar-kin...Lar-kin..."

"Larkin!" his aunt cried out again.

Larkin let out a long sigh as the daydream drifted away. He stepped inside the back door, took off his mud-caked shoes, and walked into the kitchen. A woman in a hooded, tattered old cloak was talking with his aunt. Larkin looked over at her as he washed his hands. He opened his mouth to speak, then closed it. He cocked his head to one side, then the other, leaned forward, and then stepped back.

The woman gave a light, silvery laugh.

"You can't quite make me out, can you?" she asked.

Larkin shook his head. It was like trying to focus on something that you saw out of the corner of your eye. He reached behind him and grabbed the countertop to steady himself.

The woman laughed again. "You'll see me soon enough," she told Larkin. "You must get past your coming-of-age day to start to see clearly." She turned to Larkin's aunt. "Today is his coming-of age day, correct?"

Larkin's aunt nodded. The woman turned back to Larkin.

"I hope to see clearly, too," she added. "It's part of the reason I've come today."

Larkin had no idea what that meant.

His Aunt Magdelina spoke. "Larkin, this is Adelessa. She lives in The Forest..."

"You *live* in The Forest?" Larkin interrupted incredulously. No one *lived* in The Forest. No one even went in there. Ever. There were Wolves, and bears, and boars, and Hudenpole. And worst of all, there was The Scourge of The Forest.

"You've heard of all of the terrible things that live in The Forest," Adelessa answered. "Well, some of them are dangerous, of course. But maybe not for me."

"What about The Scourge?"

Adelessa's answer was cut short by the door banging open. Ariana burst in, followed by Noll. Noll ducked, but not enough, and his head thudded off the top of the doorframe.

"Ow!" he said, rubbing his head. "Stupid size. Who wants to be this big?' He threw his hands out wide as he spoke. His left hand crashed into a cabinet, which folded inward under the force of his unintended blow. Larkin heard something that sounded suspiciously like plates breaking.

Noll turned to Larkin's aunt and began to stammer out an apology. Ariana stepped in.

"Happy Birthday!" she said. She grabbed Larkin by both shoulders and looked searchingly into his eyes. He shook his head slowly. She frowned. She averted her gaze then seemed to notice for the first time that there was a stranger in the kitchen.

"Who's your guest?" she asked. Without waiting for an answer, she bounded over to the cloaked figure.

"I'm Ariana," she said. She vigorously shook Adelessa's offered hand. "Pleased to meet you. We don't get a ton of people visiting around here. Too remote, my mom says. But it's nice to see someone make the trip here even though, of course, I don't know why you did. Still, I'd love to hear about it. My name's Ariana, by the way." She wrinkled her nose. "Or did I already say that?"

The woman smiled and pulled back her hood.

Ariana took a step backward. Her brown eyes widened. Noll's mouth sagged open. Ariana gave him a short, sharp elbow to the stomach.

"This is Noll," she said. "His mouth will close at any moment. He's just not used to seeing beautiful women around these parts. Like I said," she added with a shrug, "we don't get a lot of visitors."

Larkin squinted at Adelessa. He still couldn't make out what she looked like, and she was standing not more than ten feet away from him.

"You're both of age," Adelessa said to Ariana and Noll. It was a statement, not a question.

"A couple of months ago," Ariana answered. "Same with Noll."

"I've been to Fieldstone before," Adelessa said. "I've seen Noll's size since he was very young. It gave me hope. And you, Ariana—I've heard of some of your changes since you've come of age as well. And earlier today I was in Laketown, where I brought two other youngsters..."

Adelessa stopped talking as Magdelina raised her hand and looked toward the window. They heard a clatter of hooves. Then the door burst open for a second time that morning. Larkin's uncle strode in. His face was grimy, and his expression was grim. His aunt started toward him, a look of relief on her face. But he held up his hand, looked at her, Larkin, and Adelessa, and let out a long breath.

"Kavenland has been invaded. An army is coming this way as we speak. They'll be here in a few hours. We must evacuate immediately."

Chapter Three
Vic–Laketown

Vic whirled around. He'd expected to see some sort of door behind him, but there was nothing there except the side of a building.

He hammered his fists into the stone structure.

"Adelessa!" he hollered.

There was no answer.

He turned back around. A wave of noise assaulted him.

"Spices straight from Jadspur!" a merchant bellowed. "Just ten coins for the lady." The woman who'd bent down to smell the display straightened up and walked away. "Did I say ten coins?" the merchant called after her. "I meant eight coins, just for you." The woman kept walking. "Six?" the merchant wheedled. While his attention was on his would-be customer, Vic saw his chance. He drifted in, grabbed a loaf of bread from the merchant's table, slid it into his backpack, and slipped into the throng of people walking past.

"Feel the quality of this silk," another seller purred to man who rubbed a garment between fingers.

"If that's silk, I'm the mayor of Laketown," the man answered.

The seller huffed and pulled the garment away. As he did, Vic quickly and quietly helped himself to two of the seller's apples. He spent the next half hour gliding around, liberating a hunk of cheese and a dried sausage from their owners before he oozed back next to Em and gave her a wink.

"This Medieval mudhole is a thief's paradise," he informed Em.

"I'll bet Laketown has some lovely, rotting jail cells," Em shot back.

Vic scowled at her. "Did you pack any food from home?" he demanded.

"No," Em admitted.

Vic grabbed both of her shoulders firmly and bent his face down to hers. "Look, Em, I don't care where we are. I don't care what world we're in. I don't care who runs our world or who runs this one. All that I care about is you and me."

"And stealing things," Em added.

Vic huffed and tried to look indignant. Em's arched eyebrows told him that he'd failed.

"Look at these people," Em said. "They have almost nothing." She swept her hand around at the bedraggled people. Their clothes hung loose over their thin frames, and their eyes were sunken and defeated.

Vic shrugged and melted back into the crowd. Their misfortune wasn't his issue. Besides, "almost nothing" was more than he and Em had. After all, it wasn't his idea to dump them in a strange city in some weird world. How were they supposed to know what the Adelessa woman wanted them to do so they could get it over with and get back home? Instead of giving them guidance, the hag had abandoned them here.

"Make way, make way!" a voice yelled out. A horse clip-clopped by pulling a spotless carriage. Two armed men walked on either side of the carriage, and another man on horseback rode behind it. Everyone who'd been milling around in the street jumped out of the way.

The horse that walked behind the carriage lifted his tail. Without slowing down, he left a pile of manure in the middle of the street.

"Guess they can't even do that on the other side of the gate," a woman beside Vic said. A few people laughed. Vic followed the carriage with his eyes as it rolled up the hill toward a massive wall. A gigantic gate swung open from the wall, and a handful of soldiers trotted out and took up positions on each side of the road. Vic could see big homes and broad lawns on the other side of the gate. Far in the distance, a castle sprawled across the top of the hill.

Vic let out a low whistle. He rubbed his hands together and shot a glance at Em. She rolled her eyes.

The carriage passed through the gate and headed up the road. Several people in tattered clothes pressed forward to follow, but the soldiers hit them with fists and small clubs.

"Please!" a man wailed. "My family hasn't eaten in two days."

The soldiers said nothing. They drove the man and the rest of the crowd back. Then they pulled the gate closed from the inside.

Vic wiped the drool from his mouth. The other side of the wall was clearly the place he and Em needed to be. An image blossomed in his mind. He would sell the comb in his pocket. Adelessa said it was worth a fortune here. Then he and Em would buy one of those houses up on the hill. He could already feel the sun on his face, hear the birds singing, smell the scent of fresh bread from the corner bakery tickling his nostrils as he strode out his front door. He smiled and inhaled deeply.

He regretted doing it instantly. The stench of horse dung and rotting vegetables assaulted his nose and pulled his attention back to his surroundings. He sighed, let go of the daydream, and got to work. With everyone else staring up at the great wall, he swiped two large rolls and crammed them into his pockets. A mangy dog asleep under the bread seller's table woke up and bared his teeth at him, but he was evidently too weak and too tired to pursue Vic as he slipped away to rejoin Em.

"Not too much hunger going on up there," a man grumbled as he stared up at the wall.

"Probably ain't tightening their belts to hold their pants up," another agreed.

A woman pointed at the man's pants, which had lost their hems, and—judging from the worn patches that stitched everything together—most of the original material.

"Not sure those are worth holding up," she said.

"You said it there," the man answered. "The king taxes us so much that I can't buy no food or clothes."

"It's got worse since the queen died," the woman said.

"Well, it might have been a little better, but it still wasn't none too rosy when she was alive, neither," the man observed. "You never seen them around here, even when your precious queen was alive." The man shook his head mournfully. "Long as the king got that big castle down in Glensworth, he don't worry any about the likes of us." He paused as he spotted Em.

"Look at this one," the man grumbled. "You a rich girl from the other side of the gate?"

A dozen heads turned their way.

A woman tilted her head as she looked at Em. "What kind of clothes are you wearing?" she said. She turned her gaze to the people that had begun to gather around Em, looking for support from the crowd. "And who wears a number on their shirt?" she asked.

There were murmurs of agreement.

"What's '75' mean?" a man demanded.

Em looked down at her Steelers' jersey and looked nervously at the crowd around her. Vic grabbed her firmly by the arm. He was glad that his number 21 Pirates' shirt remained tucked away at the bottom of his knapsack.

"We're just going now," he announced. He felt a small wave of fear as he guided her through the crowd. It gave way grudgingly. He felt warm and acrid breath and saw a mixture of curiosity and hostility on the hard and dirty faces that stared at them as they pushed through.

Vic felt like a cork released from a bottle as they finally got free of the crowd. He sucked in the air and hurried his pace. It amazed him that the kids back home picked on Em and him for being poor, while the people in this world had singled them out because they thought they were rich.

But he didn't have long to think about that. As they went past the bread seller's table, the dog that Vic had awakened growled.

"Uh oh," Vic said.

The dog barked and lunged at Vic.

"Run!" he yelled. He propelled Em forward and ran after her. The dog followed. Vic grabbed Em by the arm as he shot past her. He was happy to see that his speed in this world wasn't diminished. Soon, the dog's barks sounded further away.

"I'm not as fast as you!" Em yelled. "You're dragging me as much as I'm running." Em pulled her arm free from Vic's grip.

"Why is that dog chasing us?" she demanded. "I heard him call you a thief."

Vic reached into his pockets and pulled out the two rolls. "He was guarding a bread merchant's table," he said.

"I thought stealing was going to be easy here," she snapped.

Vic shrugged. "I thought so, too. I guess I got careless."

Em pointed straight ahead. "You got careless with where you took us, too," she said.

She was right. Vic looked at the tumble of rickety wooden houses on either side of the alley. He and Em didn't exactly live in the best part of their town back home, but this alley was downright depressing. The slumping windows made the houses look like frowning faces that were on the verge of bursting into tears. Most importantly for now, though, was the line of ramshackle houses that cut across the end of the road.

He'd led them to a dead end.

"Let's get back to the main street," he urged.

"Too late," Em said.

The mangy dog prowled down the narrow alley toward them. There was no way they could get past him. He let out a low growl that made Vic's insides feel queasy.

Em raised a hand. "Now just hold on a second," she said to the dog. "You don't look like you're being treated all that well. What's your name?"

Vic rolled his eyes, but to his astonishment, the dog sat down in the middle of the alley and faced Em. As he did, Vic could see the outlines of its rib cage.

Em nodded at the dog. "Pleased to meet you, Canis," she said. "I'm Em and this is Vic. We're not from around here."

The dog looked at Em, then looked at Vic, then looked back at Em. Em snorted.

"Yes, he is very quiet when he wants to be," Em said to the dog. "But he can get a little cocky."

"Hey!" Vic said.

The dog let out a low series of sounds. It sounded to Vic like he'd just been laughed at.

Em leaned forward and put her hands on her knees.

"C'mon," she said to the dog. "Vic and I will try to help you if you can help us." The dog looked left and right before it scuttled over to her side.

Vic slapped a hand to his forehead. They were looking for help from a half-starved dog who his sister claimed she was talking to. He massaged his temples. Canis sat on his haunches.

"Is there anywhere safe for us to go?" Em asked Canis. Canis nodded his black and brown head and jogged back to the main street.

"Let's go," Em said to Vic. Vic grumbled but followed Em and Canis. The dog led them back to the main road, then along twisted, narrow alleys higher up into the town. The crowds thinned out, and soon it was just the three of them. Canis trotted up one more road and they came to the entrance of an overgrown graveyard. They were just below the wall that divided the city between rich and poor. Vic thought they could squeeze past the rusted, locked gate and into the graveyard, but Canis stopped instead. Vic tapped his finger on his chin. He had to figure out a way to get over that wall.

But he forgot all about the wall and everything else when he turned around.

The view was incredible. Laketown sat on an escarpment that rose above their surroundings. To their left, a thick blanket of green forest stretched as far north and south as he could see. A wide road ran alongside it. Something about those woods gave him a faint feeling of déjà vu and hope. He wasn't sure why. His mind went back to Adelessa showing him something positive that might await him in this world, but he realized that he couldn't remember what it was.

The only interruption in the forest was a river that ran through it and gushed into the large lake directly in front of and below them. Long docks extended from the edge of the city below out into the lake. Ships were moored at the docks, and Vic could see goods being loaded on and off the ships. Beyond them, small boats crisscrossed the lake, some with sails and some being rowed. On the other side of the lake were small farms and a few scattered houses set among fields of crops that disappeared into the distance. To their right, a wide river flowed out of the lake. Miles and miles away, it joined what looked to be a sea or an ocean. A line of ships stretched from the mouth of the river all the way to the sea. Probably waiting for their turn at the docks, Vic figured. Laketown looked like a busy place.

Vic began to rummage through his pockets. He pulled out a small loaf of bread. He broke it in half and gave one of the pieces to Em. Em, in turn, broke hers in half and gave some to Canis.

"I wasn't able to get that much, Em," Vic cautioned.

"Look at Canis," Em answered. She rubbed her hand over his thin chest. "He needs the food even more than we do."

Vic grumbled but tore off a piece of his bread and gave it to Canis. He withdrew a small piece of cheese and two apples from his pocket and handed half his food to Em. Em took them, but her attention was on Canis.

Em took a bite of her apple. She wiped her mouth with the back of her hand. "Canis says that Laketown is the biggest trading port in Kavenland. It's pretty much right in the middle of the country. Goods come here from all over Kavenland and from other countries as well." She pointed back to her left, in the direction of the woods. "They're then transported on the Great Road, which runs from one end of Kavenland to the other." Vic saw wagons, some horses, and a few people in the distance going up and down the Great Road. He was surprised that it wasn't busier, considering all those boats that were lined up in the river. They were going to need a lot of wagons to unload those boats.

Em stared for a long time at Canis then nodded and turned to Vic.

"Canis says that the woods to our left are just called 'The Forest.' He says that no one ever goes in there. He says that there are ancient beings who live there called Hudenpole that don't like people, and someone called The Scourge who is huge and kills anyone he catches in The Forest."

"Sounds great," Vic muttered. So much for the faint feeling of hope The Forest had given him.

"He says we should never, ever go in there," Em added.

Vic let out a long sigh. A couple of hours ago, he and Em had been in their own house after he'd pulled off his greatest theft. True, they were out of money and out of food, but at least they were home.

Now they were in a squalid city in some backward world hanging out with a half-starved dog who his sister said she could speak with and who told them that they couldn't go into the massive forest that took up half the horizon because some hideous ancient beings would kill them if they did. Vic felt his jaw tighten as he thought of the mean crone who'd dragged them here.

Adelessa.

He grumbled to himself and looked at his sister.

"You've got my word, Em," he said. "We won't ever go into The Forest. Promise." In fact, Vic thought they might stay awhile in this Laketown place. Sure, it smelled, and the people weren't very friendly, but they didn't know him here like they knew him back home.

Vic had worked at a hardware store after school for a little while, but the pay was meager. Items on the inventory list had shown up missing, and Vic was blamed for stealing them.

He had stolen them, of course.

He was fired.

Em was furious. "We could have gotten by on the money you were earning without stealing anything," she said.

Vic had tried to explain that she was wrong. Their parents had left them so little money, and bills kept arriving—for electricity and gas, for garbage pick-up and water usage, for TV and internet. Even when he'd cut out the TV and the internet, the money going out was more than the money that he'd brought in from his job at the hardware store. It was after he was fired that he'd sold the gold hair comb to Mr. Zipkoff.

His hand went to his pocket and clasped the comb. He felt reassured by its touch.

For the fourth or fifth time that day, he reached into his other pocket to pull out his cell phone, only to remember that it wasn't there, and it wouldn't have mattered if it was because there was no cell service. He couldn't play a game or check out social media or go to a website or anything.

What in the world were they going to do in this awful place? He looked around. He peered through the gate and into the graveyard. Gravestones had toppled over, and many were obscured by the long grass that grew everywhere. It didn't look like the cemetery was in use anymore. His eyes fell on a scrubby tree that grew at the base of the great wall that separated the two halves of Laketown. He wondered if he could leap from a branch in that tree to the top of the wall.

His thoughts were interrupted by Em's fingers digging into his arm.

"What's that?" she asked in a taut voice.

Vic gazed down to where she pointed. A dozen large ships had sailed into the lake. It was the beginning of the line of boats that he'd assumed were waiting for their turn at the docks.

But they definitely weren't waiting.

Some had stopped on the river's bank to their right, and Vic saw figures far below scamper out of the boats and fan across the wide plain that stood between the city of Laketown and the sea. Other ships continued to sail up the river and into the lake.

"It almost looks as if..." Vic started to say, but his voice trailed off. Several of the ships that had sailed into the lake had turned broadside to Laketown. There was a flurry of activity on the ships and then small objects hurtled through the air. They rapidly grew larger, and Vic saw them for what they were.

Huge boulders.

They smashed into the houses below them with a sickening crunch. Screams of pain and terror rent the air. Vic felt Em seize his arm. She pulled his ear close to her lips and bellowed louder than Vic had ever heard her.

"Laketown is under attack!" she yelled.

Chapter Four
Larkin

There was a brief, stunned silence and then everyone began talking at once.

"Quiet down!" Dain commanded. He turned to Larkin. "Take your friends and go outside for a moment. Let me talk to Adelessa and your aunt." Larkin wanted to protest, but his uncle's expression left no room for negotiation. Ariana grabbed him by the arm and pulled him and shoved Noll out the door.

When they got outside, she spun around to look at them.

"An invasion!" she said.

Before she could add anything else, Larkin's aunt scurried out the door.

"I'm going to go talk to your mother, Ariana," she said as she darted past them. "As Fieldstone's mayor, she should be the first to know. Then I'm going to warn the rest of the village." As she got to the Great Road, she called back over her shoulder. "Ariana and Noll—you should return to your homes."

Ariana and Noll fell silent. Larkin could hear his uncle talking with Adelessa inside the house.

"The Hill People are involved in this," he heard his uncle say. "We have to keep Larkin away from them. As you know, his mother and father…"

"Shhh!" Adelessa answered. "You don't want the boy to hear you." They continued speaking in hushed voices. Larkin strained to hear more but couldn't make out what they said.

What was there about his parents that they didn't want him to hear? That his father's body had been found in what looked like an ambush by the Hill People? That his mom had been captured or killed as well? He already knew that.

He'd vowed revenge one day on the Hill People. If they were involved in this invasion, there was even more reason to despise them. He looked down at his hands. They were clenched into fists. He forced them open. He needed to think clearly.

Noll cleared his throat. Larkin snapped back to the present.

"I think your aunt's right," Noll said. "Maybe we should head home." He turned to go.

"Wait," Larkin said. His mind whirled. "I have a crazy idea."

Noll raised an eyebrow. Ariana shrugged. Larkin motioned them over, then grabbed a stick and knelt in the dirt.

"We're here," he said, and worked a smudge into the soil with his stick. He reached far across his body and made two more marks. "Glensworth is here. King Tenney has the largest army in Kavenland. Sir Alymer is here, in Rockhaven." He pointed to the latter mark. "He has the second largest army in Kavenland. And even his army alone has more soldiers than all the north combined." He thrust the stick into the smudge that represented their village of Fieldstone to emphasize his point.

"And in between," he continued, sweeping the ground back and forth with his stick, "is The Forest. The Great Road," he added, "goes in a wide semi-circle from where we are, past Laketown and all the way to Rockhaven."

"Thanks for the geography lesson," Noll said dryly.

"What's your point?" Ariana asked. She squatted down beside him. She brushed her dark, tangled hair away from her face and examined his drawings. "I mean—I assume there's a point?"

"The point is this," Larkin answered. "If a rider left right now, it would take him maybe ten days to get to Laketown, then another ten days to get to Glensworth and Rockhaven." He tapped his stick at Fieldstone and traced a straight line across to Rockhaven. "But someone on foot could save a week or more by cutting through The Forest. That time difference could be vital."

"Yes," Noll said, "but who in their right mind would cut across The Forest? No one's been in there in centuries."

"How about us?" Larkin replied.

Noll began to laugh but stopped when he saw that Larkin was serious. He looked at Ariana. She had her forefinger curled around her lips and her thumb tucked under her chin.

"You're actually THINKING about this," he sputtered at her. "What about The Scourge? What about the Hudenpole? What about..."

"Larkin!" his Uncle Dain called from inside the cottage.

Larkin looked at his friends and motioned his head toward the door. "C'mon," he said.

"Larkin," his uncle began, as the three companions entered the kitchen, "I want you to pack your sword and some clothes. We need to move quickly. Your friends should go home and do the same. But before you go," he added, turning to Ariana and Noll, "I'll tell you what's happened. It's only fair.

"Adelessa is the reason I went to Portsmouth," he continued. "She passed along rumors of evil happenings there. When I arrived, ship upon ship had sailed into Portsmouth's harbor. They were from the Archipelago."

"The Archipelago?" Larkin asked. The legend of the ill-fated journey of the Protectors almost a thousand years ago spoke of a nation of islands way out in the middle of the sea called The Archipelago, but no one knew for certain if the stories were true.

His uncle nodded. "A myth has come to life," he said, then continued. "I helped organize some defenses to slow them down, but it only bought us a few days. They have big numbers and are led by some three-dozen silver-haired men who fight like demons. The Hill People have joined them and are serving as their guides."

Larkin felt his breath grow ragged at the mention of the Hill People.

"We have to make our way south and try to get word to King Tenney and Sir Alymer," his uncle continued. "We've been at peace for centuries. Now we're at war."

Adelessa nodded. "I'll go from here to King Tenney in Glensworth. I can get there quicker cutting through The Forest than a rider can on the Great Road." She paused before continuing. "It would be good if someone could get through The Forest and get word to Sir Alymer as well."

"Yes," Larkin's uncle answered, "but who would do it? No one ever goes into The Forest except you, and you're going to Glensworth."

There was an absolute stillness in the cottage. His uncle was still looking at Adelessa, but Larkin saw her head turned to him. He could feel his friends' eyes on him as well.

"We'll go," Larkin said. He looked at his friends. Noll's forehead was furrowed, and his mouth turned down. Ariana's eyes shone, and she had a huge grin.

His uncle spoke up. "Absolutely not. Too dangerous."

"This is Kavenland's darkest hour," Adelessa said as she turned back to Larkin's uncle. "The armies in the north are too small and scattered. We need to get word to Sir Alymer. Every day matters. A small party traveling through The Forest on foot could reach Sir Alymer much quicker than a rider going all the way around on the Great Road."

"That's exactly what you said," Ariana whispered to Larkin.

Dain started to object, but Adelessa raised her hand.

"I live in The Forest. I would never suggest this if I didn't think there was some chance of success."

There was something about Adelessa that made Larkin trust her absolutely. He felt a surge of hope that he and his friends might be able to pull his plan off.

"And," Adelessa added, raising an eyebrow meaningfully at Dain, "there's that other matter we discussed."

Dain beckoned Adelessa to join him in the corner. He tried to keep his voice down, but Larkin could still hear his words.

"Adelessa," he hissed. "Larkin is a capable boy, and his friends are good kids, but they'll never make it. Maybe my father when he was a kid, or my grandfather, back when kids were tougher..." He shook his head. "Kids today are spoiled and weak."

Adelessa said something that Larkin couldn't make out. His uncle paused, bowed his head in thought, then turned to Larkin.

"I don't like it." he said. Larkin started to object, but his uncle raised his hand. "I said I don't like it, but I won't stop you. What Adelessa says is true. If you can make it through The Forest and get word to Rockhaven, you can help save Kavenland."

They were going to do it, Larkin thought. They were really going to do it! No more shoveling manure and doing chores. They were going on an adventure that even the mighty Protectors would have found worthy.

The next hour was a blur. Adelessa left, saying that her path was different from the one Larkin and his friends would take. Larkin felt a twinge of disappointment. He thought he would feel safer in The Forest in the company of the mysterious woman. Ariana and Noll, meanwhile, rushed home to pack. Dain went with them to explain to Noll's mom and Ariana's parents what was happening. And then Larkin and his friends were throwing packs over their shoulders and picking their way through the town and toward The Forest.

His aunt had clearly gotten the word of the invasion out to the rest of the village of Fieldstone. Larkin was shocked by what he saw.

"I told you to just pack the essentials!" the grocer bellowed at his young daughter, who clutched a stuffed animal. She began to cry. Larkin had only ever seen the man smiling. When he'd been shopping with his aunt, the grocer would wink and sneak him a piece of hard candy when she wasn't looking. He was one of the nicest men in the village. Now his face was red and angry and bewildered.

An old woman was jostled by the crowd. She called out in panic as she was knocked to the ground. People stepped over her as they hurried on their way. Larkin leapt forward and helped her to her feet.

"Thank you, dear," she gasped. Larkin felt a lump in his throat as he saw the fear in her eyes and the scratches and bruises on her arms and face.

A small boy wandered through the crowd, his head turning one way and then another. Larkin stopped and knelt beside him.

"Tristan?" he said to the boy. Larkin looked up at Noll and Ariana. "He lives next door to me," he told them.

"Mom?" the boy called out. He wrapped his arms around Larkin. "I want my mom!" he wailed. A woman burst through the crowd.

"Larkin!" she called out. "Oh, Larkin, thank you! I lost him in the crowd," she said. She wiped a sleeve under her eye. She hoisted the boy up and pulled her to him. "Mom!" he said as he buried his face in her neck. Then they raced away.

Larkin and his friends continued past wagons loaded up and tied down, horses who bucked and whinnied, and people who strained under the weight of packs slung on their backs. Younger children cried. Older ones tried to look grown up. The kids in between—their age—looked stunned. Larkin, Ariana, and Noll nodded to their friends as they walked past. Some acknowledged them, while others seemed to stare right through them.

"It's awful, isn't it?" Ariana said.

Larkin felt numb. It was hard to believe what he was seeing. All his neighbors and friends, all the people who made Fieldstone special, were running for their lives. This was a village filled with farmers and shopkeepers—good people who wanted nothing more than to live their lives in peace. Who were these invaders? Why were they attacking?

He stared at The Forest, some hundred yards away to his right. He dropped his sack beside the Great Road.

"We've got to help," he said.

"What about our mission?" Noll asked.

"We'll see any attack coming down the Great Road. We can sprint to The Forest and take cover if we have to."

They spent the next two hours helping their fellow villagers. Larkin carried a box filled with yarns and a small loom out of a shop. A gnarled hand rested on his shoulder.

"But what about you, Larkin?" said the old weaver. "Shouldn't you and your friends be going?"

"Soon," he answered. He looked down and fingered the tunic he was wearing.

"You made this for me," he said. "It's my favorite."

She nodded. "I wanted to thank you for helping out when I'd hurt my hip."

"You didn't need to do that," Larkin said quietly.

Her smile forged through the deep creases of her weather-beaten face. She patted his cheek. "And you didn't have to give up your afternoons to clean up my shop for me," she said. She climbed onto her wagon, and Larkin watched her ride off.

It was the same everywhere in Fieldstone. Their friends and neighbors thanked Larkin and his friends for their help. Many cast longing glances back at their homes and stores before turning and trudging down the Great Road and out of town. Their expressions were full of doubt and fear.

Larkin understood, because he felt the same things himself. What would happen to their village? Would he and his friends ever return here? He realized that all the stories he loved so much about The Protectors going to war left out some vital details.

They didn't talk about abandoned villages and frightened friends. They didn't emphasize that war meant people being ripped away from their lives by strangers who wanted to take everything away from them. That win or lose, lives would be changed forever.

As the retreating caravan kicked up dust along the Great Road, Larkin, Ariana, and Noll went from house to house to make sure no one had been left behind. After they'd finished, Larkin looked south down the Great Road. The villagers were out of sight. As Ariana wiped sweat off her glistening skin, and Noll mopped his brow with a cloth, Larkin breathed out a long sigh. They'd done it.

A small group of people had decided to stay. They were milling about on the far edge of town.

"No one's chasing me out of my home," said the village tanner loudly. A few other men nodded grimly. They held rusty swords and old pitchforks and stood with their feet set wide in the middle of the Great Road. The tanner's two sons were friends of Larkin. They were twins—sturdy boys who were quick with a smile and a word of encouragement. They stood with the men, trying to look brave.

"We can't let them stay!" Larkin said to Ariana and Noll.

"We can't talk them out of it," Ariana said. She looked exasperated. "You know that. The tanner is the most stubborn man in town. Should we stay and try to protect them?"

Larkin stroked his jaw. He hated to leave them behind.

"We have to go," Noll said. "After all, Larkin, going through The Forest was your idea."

"I know, I know," Larkin said. He picked up his bag and walked over to the men standing in the Great Road. He asked if they wanted to change their minds. The men shook their heads. Larkin wished the tanner and the others good luck and angled across the field with Ariana and Noll toward The Forest.

When they were halfway there, he heard a swelling sound. He looked back.

The army came snarling and shouting down the Great Road. Some brandished swords, while others had torches that they thrust into the bases of houses, barns, and shops. The flames licked greedily up the sides of the structures and then the breeze did the rest, sweeping a roaring fire of destruction that smelled to Larkin of blue-black dread and sorrow.

Larkin felt numb. This couldn't be happening. Fieldstone—their village, their home—was being destroyed.

A group of strange, savage-looking men with silver hair led the marauders. The silver-haired men urged their horses through the conflagration as they sneered and howled in triumph. Larkin felt his chest tighten.

But the worst was still to come.

The silver-haired men dismounted and walked through the burning village. Larkin glanced back at the small knot of villagers who'd decided to stay. Most of them were running down the Great Road. Only the tanner and his two sons stood their ground.

One of the silver-haired men approached them, his sword drawn. He was at least as big as Noll. The tanner yelled and thrust at him with his pitchfork. The silver-haired man swatted it aside and drove his fist into the tanner's face. He dropped as if he'd been kicked by a steer. His twin sons stood behind him, frozen in fear. The silver-haired man sheathed his sword, grabbed the twins, and dragged them back toward the rest of the army.

He hauled the two boys to their feet as if they weighed no more than small children. They looked shockingly small and utterly defeated next to the huge, silver-haired man.

"Let them go!" came a cry. Their father had staggered to his feet. "They're just boys," he pleaded through his bloody mouth. "Show them mercy. Kill me instead!"

There was no response.

Larkin inched back across the field to get a better look. He crouched down in the tall grass. Ariana darted forward, and Larkin just managed to grab her by the ankle. She whirled around, hopping up and down on one foot.

"What are you doing?" she said. "We have to protect them!"

"There are too many," Larkin said. "Ariana, please."

Ariana reluctantly knelt beside him. They parted the grass and looked back at the scene in the village.

The knot of large silver-haired men stepped aside. A stooped figure rose slowly to its full height. Larkin gasped. The silver-haired men had to be seven feet tall, but this new being dwarfed them. He had broad shoulders, but the skin on his hands was papery thin and mottled with brown spots. He swayed unsteadily as he shuffled forward, and two of the silver-haired men leapt to his side to help him. There was something about the man that made Larkin's blood run icy cold in his veins.

"Bind them," he commanded in a raspy voice.

One of the silver-haired men took hold of the tanner. The tanner and his two sons were tied to a hitching post a few feet away. The silver-haired men gathered behind the huge old figure.

He raised his hands and let out a gasp of effort. The man and his two sons let out short shrieks.

And then they were gone.

Just—gone.

Larkin looked away. Everything swirled around him. He heard the shouts of triumph from the invaders. He could hear the fire as it roared through Fieldstone and smell the smoke and the destruction it bore with it.

From across the field, the chants of the invaders reached his ears.

"Kyn-was, Kyn-was, Kyn-was!"

"Keenwas?" Ariana said at his shoulder. "Is that some kind of victory chant?"

"I think it might be the name of that huge old guy," Larkin answered.

Noll grabbed his arm.

"Larkin," he hissed. "We have to go. Now!"

Larkin took another step forward then stopped. He nodded. He looked back over his shoulder as they crossed the field. Everyone's eyes, including his, were on the huge old man. He had slumped down and was caught up and carried off by four of the silver-haired men. Whatever evil power he had used to kill the tanner and his sons had completely drained him.

Larkin took one last look back as they entered The Forest. He wanted to remember what he saw.

The feelings of sorrow and dread left him. He had only one emotion now, and it welled up inside him like the fire that burned through his village.

Anger.

"We're going to get to Rockhaven," Larkin told his friends through gritted teeth. His voice sounded foreign and harsh to his own ears. "We're going to complete our mission, then I'm going to come back and find that Kynwas. I don't care how long it takes or what I have to do.

"And then I'm going to destroy him."

Chapter Five
Em–Laketown

The stress and pressure of everyday life brought different reactions from Em than they did from Vic.

Take cruel words from their parents or being ignored or ridiculed by the kids at school. Vic would hold in the anger until he was ready to burst, then he'd lash out, fighting back tears of rage as he shook his fists and bellowed at the night sky. Then he would draw the remnants of his despair back in, where they would roil and fester inside of him like an old pot of stew simmering on the stove.

From an early age, Em had built a protective layer around herself. Some of the hurtful words would filter through to her like rainwater on the ground, but it didn't hit her as a deluge like it did Vic. She lived with a dull, steady ache in her chest which only went away when she was with Vic or with cats and dogs.

But when she and Vic saw the scene below them in Laketown, they both had the same reaction.

They froze.

The big ships continued to fire boulders at the city. Small boats crammed with soldiers pushed off from the ships and were rowed toward the shore. When they landed, men leapt out and charged across the docks and into Laketown. Scores of others began to move along the shore of the lake and toward the Great Road.

"They're trying to surround the city!" Vic bawled above the shouts of panic, the crashing of giant rocks as they splintered apart wooden buildings, and the howls of pain and anguish from the injured and dying people of Laketown. "We need to run! Follow me!"

Vic dashed away down a busy street, where the tide of people swept them up the hill. Em saw people pounding on the gate that separated the upper part of Laketown from the bottom part.

"Let us in!" people howled. Some looked over their shoulders in panic at the death and destruction below, turned back, and slammed their fists against the wall.

Suddenly, the great gates opened, and the people in its way were flung to one side. A squadron of grim-faced soldiers in gleaming metal uniforms marched through the opening. When they were through, the crowd surged forward in desperation. Guards punched and clubbed and shoved, and the gate swung closed with not a single person slipping through.

Em yanked Vic to the side of the road as the squadron of soldiers marched toward them. To Em, their faces looked as frightened as anyone else's in Laketown as they moved in formation down the hill to face an army that outnumbered them by at least ten to one.

"Deblek!" a woman shouted to the commander of the soldiers. "Deblek! Why won't you let us in the gate!"

The man raised his hand, and the squadron of soldiers came to a halt. He stepped toward the woman and took her by the hands.

"Aunt Boyka," he said. His face looked sad. "I'm a soldier. I obey orders." He dropped his voice. "Please help my wife look after our children." He let go of her hands and surveyed the people who'd crowded around him.

"My friends and neighbors of Laketown," he said, in a clear, crisp voice. His mouth had hardened, and the sad look was replaced by the determined look of a warrior. "I cannot tell you what to do. But this I would urge of you: take care of yourselves and your loved ones. There seems little reason for hope but try hard to hang onto it."

"But where are you going? What will you do?" the woman named Boyka asked.

"I am a soldier," he repeated. He looked around as if everything he was seeing he was seeing for the first time. "Today, I am going to die." He stepped back into line, barked out a command, and led his squadron down the street.

Em flashed back to reports she'd seen on TV and the internet from a recent war in her world. The stories of bravery and sacrifice had warmed her heart and soul as they had for so many others. But now she looked around at panicked parents, wailing children, dead and dying people, and ruined buildings.

Her heart didn't feel warm.

It felt sick.

Vic tugged on her arm. He pointed ahead. "There's the place where we came through the wall with Adelessa." He dashed forward, stopped in front of the building, and began to hammer on the wall.

"Deal's off, lady!" he hollered. "Let us out of here!"

Em and Canis ran toward him.

"Adelessa!" Vic screamed, his voice rising in panic. "I don't care what happens in our world. Let us out of here!"

Even amid the chaos, people began to stare at Vic, no doubt wondering what this boy in his strange clothes was doing assaulting and verbally threatening the side of a building.

"I don't think Adelessa's there, Vic," Em said.

He spun his head back to her. He looked around wildly. "We're stuck here!" he exclaimed.

"Looks that way," Em agreed.

"We have to run!" he yelled. "This way!" He shoved his way through the crowd, found a side street, and sprinted away.

Em and Canis followed, with Canis barking at Em as they ran.

"I agree," she shouted to him. "Go!" Canis sprinted after Vic. Vic was way too fast for Em, but maybe Canis could catch him.

Em lost sight of Canis and Vic when they reached the main road. Em plowed into the street and ran into a teeming wall of pandemonium. People grabbed anything in sight—food, their children, precious belongings—and either rushed back into their homes or pushed their way up the hill toward the wall. The people moving toward the wall were in for a disappointment, Em feared.

As she looked up the hill, she saw the top of a huge catapult as it flung a boulder that soared over Em's head down toward the bay. Instead of landing in the harbor on one of the ships, though, it landed ahead of Em on the road she was running down. It tumbled through a knot of people and crashed through several houses before coming to a stop in a tangle of crumpled wood and stone.

The panic reached a fevered pitch. There appeared to be nowhere to go. The wall was barred up above. Enemy soldiers advanced from below. Giant boulders flew from both directions.

Em shook her head. They came through the Door in the Stone for this? She and Vic must have been crazy to listen to Adelessa. Adelessa had shown her something in her mind that made coming here sound wonderful, but what exactly it was had slipped from Em's memory.

She was sure this battle wasn't it, though.

A little way down the road, Em saw that Canis had caught up with Vic. The dog had sunk his teeth into the hem of Vic's jeans. Vic hopped around trying to free himself, but Canis wouldn't let go. They spun around in a circle like a demented Merry-Go-Round.

"Get this dog off me!" Vic howled, as he spotted Em moving toward him. Em dashed forward. She grabbed Vic by the wrist and looked at the dog.

"It's ok, Canis," she said.

"It's ok...Canis?" Vic sputtered, but the dog let go of his hem and sat on its haunches. He wagged his tail in nervous excitement as he looked back up at Em. Em nodded and cocked her head at her brother. His expression had changed. It was a look of regret that Em knew well.

"Sorry," he said. "I sometimes forget how fast I've become."

"It's ok," Em said. She squeezed his hand. "But if we don't keep our heads, we might lose them."

Vic nodded. Em set her jaw. She knew Vic wouldn't like what was on her mind.

"I think we should follow Canis," she said.

Vic's mouth dropped open. "The DOG?" he shouted.

Canis let out a low growl that managed to sound authoritative without sounding menacing. Em nodded.

"He knows his way around here a lot better than we do," Em said.

Em locked eyes with Vic. She let him run through his usual gamut of emotions. He was incredulous at first. Then he was skeptical. Em continued to stare at him with the blank expression she'd put on her face. She saw a brief flash of fear in his eyes—fear that Em might follow the dog instead of him. Vic wasn't afraid of much, but Em knew he was afraid of losing her. Finally, she saw that he was resigned to doing as she'd suggested. His shoulders sagged.

"Ok," he said, "we'll follow the dog." Then, under his breath, he muttered, "This better work."

Canis leapt up and trotted down a side street. Vic loped alongside of him. Em had lost one of her flip flops, and it made her gait awkward. She kicked off the other and ran after them in her bare feet. There were fewer people here, and the road was drier and stonier. The ball of her foot came down hard on a sharp stone that jutted from the road. She gasped in pain but continued to follow Canis and Vic, limping along as fast as she could and wishing she'd brought her sneakers along.

They began to work their way down through the side streets, moving left in the direction of The Forest. Without breaking stride, they grabbed a few loaves of bread and hunks of dried meat and cheese that had been abandoned by merchants. Em felt guilty doing it, but she knew they might need the food to survive.

As they ran, she caught glimpses of the battle through gaps in the houses. Below them and to their right, some of the stones thrown by the catapults above the wall found their mark, but for every boat they damaged, ten more pushed their way to shore. The first of the soldiers sent from the upper part of Laketown had engaged the invaders, but they were badly outnumbered.

When Em, Vic, and Canis reached the edge of the Lake, the noise of the battle was almost overwhelming. Swords clashed, boats crashed together, men roared and swore and cried out in triumph and pain. At the head of the invading army, a dozen or so tall, silver-haired men cut their way through Laketown's defensive forces.

Canis and Vic had stopped at the back of a house. Em slid to a stop beside them and peered around the house's corner. Her foot throbbed, but what she saw pushed the pain out of her mind. Her entire insides felt as cold as if they'd been dragged through a snowbank.

Up close, the strange, silver-haired men were enormous. Em had glimpsed some of the Steelers' players around town, but the silver-haired men were huge, at least a half-foot taller and broader than even the biggest and burliest football player she'd seen. Their shields moved in a blur, repelling sword thrusts and arrows shot at them from a distance. The men who bravely stood in front of them with weapons drawn were cut down easily, like sharp scythes slicing through a field of dry wheat.

Em was wondering if the silver-haired men were invincible when a lucky arrow struck one in the neck. He dropped his shield and sword, sagged to his knees, then dropped onto his face. The other silver-haired men around him bellowed and roared in rage. Their attack gained a new ferocity and level of vigor that horrified Em. They might not be unbeatable, Em thought, but they were close to it.

Their rickety house back on the other side of the Door in the Stone was looking better and better. Just a few feet in front of her, people were slashing and stabbing each other with swords. What had Adelessa gotten them into? Anything was better than this.

Then she thought of the threat Adelessa had made to separate her and Vic. No, that was worse. She looked at the battle one more time and shuddered.

This was still bad.

She'd seen enough. She ducked back around the corner and let out a shaky breath. Canis tilted his head and looked up at her. She gave a quick nod, and he started off again.

The dog led them away from the battle and along the shore, past ramshackle huts, and down rutted alleyways, until they reached the base of the escarpment upon which Laketown sat.

A field of wheat stretched out between them and The Forest, and Canis led them through it, giving them cover for a brief time. They burst through the other side of the field and kept running. Canis bounded over the Great Road. The Forest was rushing toward them. 100 yards away. Now fifty.

"What is he doing?" Vic shouted.

When he reached its edge, Canis kept going and disappeared into the trees. Vic stopped up short. Em crashed into him from behind. They went down in a heap, just yards away from The Forest.

Vic looked at Em. "I am NOT going in there!" he announced. "What happened to the Hudenpole and the crazy Scourge guy?"

Em looked at him then looked at Canis, who'd walked back out of The Forest.

"I didn't tell you this before," Em told Vic, "but Canis says there are giant Wolves, too."

Vic blew a breath up out of the corner of his mouth. His long, lank hair wafted up for a moment, then settled back over his eyes. He brushed it out of the way. "Great. Anything else I should be terrified of?"

Em started to answer, but Vic held up his hand. "I don't want to know," he said. "But I'm not going in there." He jabbed his finger at The Forest. "I mean, twenty minutes ago you made me promise that we would never go into The Forest."

Em realized that was true, but she also realized something that Vic might not have noticed.

He wasn't treating her like she was crazy anymore. Without thinking about it, he'd acknowledged that Em and Canis were, in fact, communicating with each other.

Canis cocked his head sideways at Em. "I agree," she told him.

Vic let out a groan. "Agree with what?" he said.

"That Laketown isn't safe. That the Great Road isn't safe." She jerked her head to the right. "You saw that soldiers are coming this way, didn't you?"

Vic bobbed his head once.

Em gestured to the left.

"Other soldiers are moving toward the road that way, from behind Laketown," she said. "They'll cut us off. We can't go down the road in either direction, and we can't go back the way we came." She looked at The Forest, then she looked back at Vic. "We have to go forward. That's into The Forest."

Vic ran his hand through his hair and let out a sigh of exasperation. Em put her hand softly on his forearm.

"I've never known you to be afraid of anything," she said.

He shook his head. "We must have been crazy to follow Adelessa here," he said.

"The same thing occurred to me," she answered.

He let out a low growl. "Alright," he groused. "The Forest it is."

Chapter Six
Larkin–The Forest

Larkin's heart hammered, and his blood pulsed so fast and hot through his veins that he barely had time to realize that he and his friends had done something no one in Kavenland had dared to do in hundreds of years.

They'd stepped into The Forest.

His hand went instinctively to his sword, but nothing leapt out and attacked him. His anger cooled but his heart thudded on. He tried to remember what Adelessa had said—that she thought they'd be okay in The Forest.

He shook his head. He couldn't get over the fact that his friends could see Adelessa clearly, but he could not. If somebody asked him, he wouldn't be able to describe anything about her physical appearance.

"What's that noise?" Noll asked in alarm, interrupting Larkin's thoughts.

Larkin heard the rustling sound. He pulled his sword. His eyes darted everywhere.

"Over there!" Noll shouted. He slunk back and pointed to a huge, rotted log.

"Stand back!" Larkin commanded, as he bolted in front of his friends. Whatever strange beast lay in wait would have to go through him first. That's what Galeran would have done—protect his companions. He crept closer. His heart darted like a scared jackrabbit. He peered over the top of the log. Whatever had made the noise lay in wait there.

His shoulders slumped. Ariana had nocked an arrow in her bow. She let her arms fall to her side. She gestured with her chin toward the sound that had alarmed Noll.

"Behold the mighty chipmunk," she said drily.

Noll turned red and stared at his feet.

"It sounded a lot louder than a chipmunk," he muttered. He shoved his sword back into its scabbard and stalked ahead with his head still bowed.

Larkin snorted. Some hero. He'd charged a rodent. He sheathed his own sword and took a deep breath. He smelled pine trees and decay and something else. A dark green suspicion, and a deeper feeling he couldn't identify.

He stopped. It had happened again. He'd smelled an emotion. How could you smell suspicion?

Larkin knew that smelling jasmine brought back the memory of his mom. Warm bread coming out of the oven brought him back so clearly to a picnic he'd once shared with Ariana and Noll that he could taste the sandwiches five years later. The smells coming from the tanner's shop transported him to a library in Portsmouth in such a lifelike way that he could almost feel the leather-bound books in his hands.

But this was different. Larkin thought back to the dread and sorrow and anger he'd smelled earlier today. He didn't know what was happening, but he began to have an uncomfortable idea.

Something that felt like a small, dark green creature burst to life in his belly. It gnawed at him in a strange and disagreeable way. He tried to ignore it. Nothing mattered except their mission: to survive The Forest and get word of the invasion to Sir Alymer.

They walked on under the towering old trees for another hour, each lost in his own thoughts. Larkin was aware that the muscles in his neck had bulged and tightened.

"This place gives me the creeps," Ariana said. "I mean, my older brothers locked me in a closet once and that was weird, and I used to think that Farmer McNatt was the creepiest guy ever, and I never really liked ghost stories around the bonfire, and I had this doll when I was younger that had swirly glass eyes that gave me the willies, but this place..."

Larkin agreed. His eyes swept all around. He was half-expecting something or someone to attack them at any moment. He looked down. He didn't remember pulling his sword out, but it was right there in his hand.

"I know what you mean," he said, as he slid the sword back into its scabbard. "I keep thinking that The Scourge or the Hudenpole or a bear is going to jump out at us."

"Don't forget the boars and the Wolves," Ariana said. "And all of this," she added, and waved her arms around. "I'd rather be in a cave full of bats than this place."

Noll, meanwhile, had forgotten the chipmunk incident and was whistling a tune as he ambled along.

"Why do you seem so comfortable here, Noll?" Larkin grumbled.

"You're the one who didn't even want to come," Ariana added grouchily, "and here you are, walking through The Forest like you're walking down The Great Road on a sunny day. That's like saying you don't want any popcorn and then eating it all after someone else makes it."

"I have to admit that I was nervous about coming into The Forest," Noll answered. "I mean—The Scourge, and the Hudenpole, and the bears and Wolves and boars."

"Thanks for reminding us," Ariana deadpanned.

"But then I remembered that the Nisser live here. And if the Nisser live here, it can't be all bad. If you look at it that way, without fear, it really is beautiful here. And then there's the Gwyllions, and they say that unicorns once roamed The Forest thousands of years ago, and..."

Larkin let out a sigh. Nisser, Gwyllions, unicorns---Noll believed in all the old fairy tales. Noll's voice slipped into the background as Larkin went back to what he'd smelled. Suspicion and something else, something deeper.

He stopped. What was he doing? Thinking about odors. Who cared what he smelled? He gave up and listened as Noll finished his thoughts.

"I think Adelessa is right," his friend concluded. "There are things to fear here, but is it any more dangerous than Laketown? Or the streets of Glensworth? Or sailing on the sea?"

Larkin had no answer for that. Ariana shot him a look. She wanted to believe it. So did he. But it was hard.

People lived in Glensworth.

Sailors roamed the seas.

No one came into The Forest.

He turned his attention to his friends. Larkin knew that they were hoping that he'd develop some sort of special ability like them. He'd hoped so, too. His friends were everything he daydreamed of being. The beast in his belly rumbled. For the first time in his life, Larkin felt left behind, and his insides were fiery and uncomfortable.

"What do you think about the Hill People helping out the Archipelagans?" Noll asked.

"Noll!" Ariana said.

"It's all right," Larkin said quickly. The sounds of The Forest melted away, and Larkin could hear nothing but his own blood rushing in his ears.

Thoughts from long ago tumbled around in his head. He was little. His parents had gone away and had not come back. A crowd of people gathered in their house in the village, a jumble of legs that he tried to weave through, an occasional grown-up's face dipping down to his, saying "I'm sorry, Larkin." The strangeness of it all made him know something was wrong, although he wasn't sure what.

And then he was whisked away from that house to his aunt and uncle's farm on the outskirts of Fieldstone. It smelled funny. It felt cold. Laughter and hugs were replaced by orders and rules.

He had never seen his parents again.

Over the years, he pieced together what had happened from overheard conversations that died on lips when people saw him coming.

His mother and father had gone on a trip out of town. They were waylaid by the Hill People. His father was now buried in the village graveyard. His mother's body was never found. He used to hope she'd show up one day, miraculously alive, but she never had. Not knowing for sure had made it hard, but he'd finally come to accept the truth: The Hill People had killed his mother as well as his father.

Larkin's eyes were hot, and his vision blurred. He wiped his knuckles under each eye. They came back wet. His jaw worked back and forth. He wanted revenge on the Hill People. He felt energy surge through his body. He quickened his pace.

After a few more hours of walking, though, Larkin felt like a great weight was pushing down on him, making his legs drag heavily. It had been a long day. The adrenaline of leaving, the fate of their friends and neighbors, the death and destruction in their village, the fear of The Forest—all of it together started to sap his strength. He looked at Ariana and Noll. Noll plodded along like he was wading through waist-deep water. Only Ariana, as usual, seemed fresh.

Finally, as the sun sent low slanting shadows through the trees, Larkin saw a small hill rising in front of them. It looked like the perfect place to stop for the night.

The three reached the top of the hill in a few minutes and began setting up their tents and gathering wood. Soon they had a fire going. They ate, but mostly in silence. Normally, they couldn't stop talking when they were around each other. Larkin wanted to say something, anything, to help his friends take their minds off their worries, but he couldn't think of what to say.

"How about a story?"

It was Noll who'd spoken.

"Great idea!" said Ariana. "How about one about Beredor and Galeran?"

So Noll told the story of how Beredor and Galeran, the leaders of the Protectors, set off to subdue the Frost Giants of the north who'd plundered Rockhaven. It was a familiar story. Rockhaven's great metal worker, Helidix, had armed the Protectors with specially made swords and shields. He'd labored day and night at his forges, literally working himself to death while completing Beredor's shield, which was so massive that only Beredor and Galeran could even lift it. Celerox the Swift, who had a footfall so light that he could run across the treetops in The Forest, figured into the story as well. But the true heroes were, as always, Beredor and Galeran.

Larkin always enjoyed the stories of The Protectors. He knew that most kids liked Beredor best, since he was the boldest and the best fighter, but he'd always admired Galeran. Galeran was a great fighter, too, and he was Beredor's best friend. He wasn't quite as big and strong as Beredor, but he was the better strategist. Larkin admired Galeran's brains more than he admired Beredor's brawn.

Noll was the perfect one to tell the story. He loved all Kavenland's history and its folklore, and he believed firmly in fairy creatures like the Nisser and the Gwyllions. Larkin's superstitious aunt was a believer, too. She left a plate of food out on the back steps for the Nisser each night, and it was always empty the next morning. That was proof enough for her. Larkin tried not to roll his eyes at that logic. He knew there were any number of animals that would be happy to eat the food that was on the plate. He didn't think for a second that there was any such thing as Gwyllions or Nisser.

Nisser, schmisser.

He watched Noll. His friend's face shone as he talked. Ariana lay on her back, with her feet crossed and her head propped up on her sack. She looked at Larkin and smiled. Larkin smiled back. He could feel a warmth spread over him. It pushed aside the jealousy that had crowded his thoughts all day.

Noll finished the story. Many of the Protectors had died during the savage fight with the Frost Giants, but Beredor had slain their leader, Oculus, and the Frost Giants had pledged to never enter Kavenland again.

How much easier things would be now if the Protectors were still around, Larkin thought. They'd have swept back the invasion, and Larkin and his friends would be sleeping in their own beds in their own houses instead of out here. He looked around. The trees seemed closer and taller in the dark, like judges looming over their benches, ready to render an unwelcome verdict. They felt menacing, like the silver-haired men and their evil leader.

He poked a stick into the fire. Could he, Ariana, and Noll really do what they'd set out to do? Could they cross The Forest, dodge all its dangers, and reach Rockhaven in time? It had seemed possible this morning. Adelessa had even endorsed it. In fact, Larkin felt like she was somehow expecting him to suggest it.

But all of that had happened during the day, in the familiar surroundings of Fieldstone. Here, alone in the gathering gloom in the middle of the forbidding Forest, the whole idea of three kids doing what no one else dared to do seemed ridiculous.

"Where are The Protectors now when we need them?" Noll said, as if reading Larkin's thoughts.

"My uncle always says that our generation is weak," Larkin answered.

"I heard him say it to Adelessa this morning," Ariana added. "And other grown-ups say the same thing. That our future looks bleak. And that was before the invasion."

Larkin tossed his stick into the fire. What had seemed like a great adventure this morning seemed like a great burden now. Who were they kidding? The three of them, on their own, trying to save Kavenland?

Impossible.

Or was it?

He thought again about Adelessa. She had faith in them. He wasn't sure why, but she did. He thought about the invaders and the huge old man, Kynwas, killing their friends and setting fire to their village. They had to find a way to stop him. He looked at Ariana and Noll. If they were going to try to do the impossible, he was glad they were with him.

He tossed and turned all night. He could hear Noll gently snoring a few feet away. He turned his head, and as his eyes adjusted to the dark, he could see the outline of Ariana, her body rising and falling slightly with the rhythm of sleep.

Larkin shifted slightly into a more comfortable position, although "comfortable" was a relative term. His lower back was numb from sleeping on a tree root, his legs ached, and his face was sore where it had been whacked by branches.

And the discomfort that felt like a creature in his belly was back. It felt demanding and hungry as it gnawed away at his insides.

His two best friends were special.

And he wasn't.

Another sudden smell interrupted his thoughts.

But this smell wasn't an emotion. It was food.

Their food.

He heard a sound and held his breath. Voices argued in loud whispers. Larkin slipped out from under his covers. His heart hammered in his chest as he strained his eyes to see who was talking. He slid his sword out of its sheath and crept toward the sounds.

"Run!" a voice yelled.

All around him, Larkin saw movement, although he had no idea what was causing it. His, Ariana's, and Noll's packs lay open, and their items were strewn about the ground. In a flash, whatever had made the noises was gone.

Except for a small shape that cursed furiously.

Larkin approached it, his sword raised.

Then his jaw sagged open, and his arm dropped to his side.

At his feet struggled a small, plump creature, no more than three feet tall. It was dressed all in brown, and its unkempt hair poked out from beneath a pointed hat.

Larkin could see the problem. The creature—whatever it was—had gotten its ankle stuck solidly in the gnarled roots of an old maple tree. It pulled at its leg in a vain attempt to free itself.

Larkin shook his head rapidly and looked down. The creature was still there. He blinked and rubbed his eyes.

Still there.

He crouched down to get a closer look, but to his surprise, the creature stopped tugging at his leg and socked him squarely on the shoulder.

"Ow!" he said, as much in surprise as in pain. Although, to be honest, it did hurt a bit. The little fellow packed enough of a wallop to knock Larkin onto his haunches.

He looked up to see that the commotion had awakened his friends. Ariana had grabbed her bow and scrambled to her feet. Noll's large form joined her as they stumbled over to Larkin. Larkin could see them looking around wildly. He pointed down to the small, bearded creature.

"Over here," he said.

Noll took a step forward. His mouth widened into a smile.

"Why, it's..."

"Careful!" Larkin warned. He ran his hand over his shoulder. Another ache to add to his list. "He's stronger than he looks," he added ruefully.

"Of course he is," said Noll. "He's one of the Nisser."

He and Ariana watched in fascination as Noll dropped to his knees in front of the Nisser.

"And how are you, my friend? My name is Noll."

"How do you think I am, you imbecile?" the Nisser answered. "I'm stuck. Why don't you put that hulking mass of yours—which is probably sitting under a great, big empty head—to some use, and get me out of here so I can be on my way?"

"What, and not get our three favors first?" Noll said calmly.

Larkin looked at Ariana in wonder. They had been sure the Nisser didn't really exist. After all, no one had ever seen them. Thank goodness Noll knew all about them.

"Cut me loose, Groll, and then we'll talk," the Nisser said to Noll.

"My name is Noll," he answered, "and that's not what we're going to do. You're going to tell us your name, and you're going to pledge to us that you'll grant us three favors, and then we'll cut you free."

"You will not have my name, Poll," the Nisser answered, "and I will not grant you three favors." He continued tugging at his leg and cursing. His face turned very red.

Noll moved closer—but not too close—to the struggling Nisser.

"My name is Noll," he repeated. He gazed up at the rising sun. "It looks like it's going to be a hot one. I'm sure that sitting stuck here all day will be uncomfortable and painful. The other Nisser won't come out during the day, and if we leave them a plate of food, they won't come rescue you tonight, either. You're stuck, and you're stuck with us."

The Nisser let out a small, furious howl of frustration. He then seemed to resign himself to his fate. He looked at Noll accusingly.

"If you'd left food out for us, we wouldn't have had to rummage through your bags. And if we didn't have to rummage through your bags, we wouldn't have woken that one up." He pointed at Larkin. "And if that one hadn't woken up, we wouldn't have had to run away, and I wouldn't have gotten stuck. This is your fault. I think you should call it even and cut me loose, and I'll be on my way."

Noll remained unmoved. He looked at the Nisser and slowly shook his head.

"Your name," he said, "and your pledge."

Some cursing followed and then the Nisser mumbled something under his breath.

"I didn't catch that," Noll said.

"I said my name is Gurn. And you can have one favor."

"Two," said Noll.

"Two it is," Gurn agreed with a sigh. "Although technically, they belong to that one over there," he added, waving vaguely at Larkin, "since he's the one who caught me. Now get me out of here, will you?"

Noll got up, went over to his bag, and pulled out a small hatchet. He carefully hacked the root in half, and Gurn popped up to his feet. He rubbed his ankle, tested it a few times, then looked at the three companions.

"Well, I've got Fole's name here. How about the rest of you?"

Larkin was still in a bit of a daze, and his voice sounded like it was coming from far away. "I'm Larkin," he heard himself say, "and this is Ariana."

"And you might as well be a bit more pleasant about things," Ariana added. "You're likely to be spending at least a little time with us, especially since you seem to have eaten quite a bit of our food."

"Can't blame that on me," said Gurn. "You didn't leave any food out for us. What did you expect us to do?"

"Well, we certainly can't make it across The Forest with the food we have left," Larkin grumbled.

The Nisser put his hands on his hips and looked at them all one by one.

"Just what *are* you doing in The Forest in the first place?" he demanded. "I thought humans were too scared to come in here."

"You might have asked that question before you stole our food," Larkin pointed out.

"I could teach you how to get more," Gurn offered.

"If that's the case," Larkin said, "why didn't you do that yourself, instead of taking our food?"

"You can't expect us to work for it when you've brought it right to us!" Gurn complained.

"Enough!" Ariana said. "Whether he took the food or not is now irrelevant."

Larkin began to protest, but Ariana silenced him with a look.

"We have an important job to do—more important than squabbling over what Gurn and his friends did..." Ariana said. Gurn smirked at Larkin, and Ariana continued, "...no matter how reprehensible it was to rob innocent travelers." Gurn frowned.

"We're in The Forest because we're trying to save Kavenland from an invasion," she said to Gurn. The Nisser's mouth dropped open.

Ariana turned to her friends.

"We can't make it across The Forest to Rockhaven with the food we have. If Gurn will promise to help lead us and re-provision us for the entire journey, I think it would be a smart way to spend a favor."

Gurn bowed low toward Ariana.

"The young lady is as wise as she is pretty," he said in a courtly manner. Ariana looked down quickly. Her mass of black, curly hair tumbled over her face, but Larkin could still see a small smile of pleasure poking through.

"But you'll never make it," Gurn added. "Bears, boars, Wolves, The Scourge, the Hudenpole. You don't stand a chance. The best thing for me to do would be to take you back to where you started."

Larkin shook his head. "We just told you that we've been invaded. We can't go back. We have to go forward."

"It's your skin, not mine," Gurn huffed.

"And our favors," Ariana reminded him.

Gurn stared up at her with his hands on his hips. Then he shrugged.

"All right, you louts," he said, turning to Larkin and Noll. "Pack up your stuff, and let's get moving." Larkin rolled his eyes and Noll snorted, but they moved to get their bags re-packed.

"One more thing!" Gurn called after them.

They stopped, swung around, and looked at him expectantly.

"Is there anything for breakfast? I'm starving."

Chapter Seven
Vic–The Forest

Vic grumbled to himself as he followed Canis and Em, who'd plunged into The Forest ahead of him. To their right, the river's waters crashed into rocks, churning and leaping in a mad dash to the lake. There was certainly no crossing it, not that they'd want to. They just needed to go a little way into The Forest to be safe.

"Canis says he doubts anyone will follow us in here," Em said. It was uncanny how she knew what he was thinking sometimes. "He says all we have to fear is being tortured by the Hudenpole, ravaged by Wolves, or worst of all, being captured by The Scourge."

Vic swallowed. "So being captured by The Scourge would be *worse* than being tortured or torn into pieces?"

Canis craned his head back and bared his teeth at Vic. Vic was pretty sure the dog was laughing at him again.

"Canis says that the less civilized people in northern Kavenland used to leave babies as a tribute to The Scourge," Em continued. "They'd set the babies at the edge of The Forest, and in the morning, the babies would be gone. Old stories said that travelers used to go into The Forest and never return, victims of The Scourge. It was even rumored that he ate his captives. The Scourge is the real reason why no one goes into The Forest anymore."

Vic felt like a hundred snakes were crawling all over him. He wasn't sure if he wanted to meet anyone in this country. The people up north sure sounded like a bunch of cowards and losers. Leaving babies at the edge of The Forest for some old guy to eat? What kind of world had he and Em been dragged into?

Vic glanced behind him. He could just make out the Great Road through the trees. He didn't want to go any further into The Forest than was necessary. And if it was true that no one wanted to go into The Forest, then Vic figured they must be safe right where they were.

"Em!" he whispered, as loudly as he dared. She heard him and turned around. "This is far enough, don't you think?"

She looked at Canis, who stared back at her. She turned back to Vic. She tucked her raven black hair behind her ear. Her eyebrows knitted together over her dark eyes. When she gave him that look, Vic knew she was serious.

"No," she said firmly with a shake of her head. "Canis thinks we need to go in a little further to truly be safe."

Safe from what, Vic wondered? He rubbed his hand over his face. They'd been in this strange land for not much more than an hour or two. They had already survived an invasion led by a handful of huge silver-haired men, but where they were going might be even worse than what they'd just left behind. And if that wasn't enough, they were being led by a mangy mongrel that only his sister could communicate with. He let out a sigh.

"Just hear me out," he said. "If we stay within sight of the road, and move carefully, we can make our way past these troops without getting lost. Then we can go back out onto the Great Road, head south, and see if we can find someplace safe."

"And maybe send out a warning to the rest of Kavenland, too—right?"

Vic felt his forehead furrow like a field that was ready to be planted. He waved his arms around him.

"Now why would we risk our necks for anyone in this place?" he asked.

"I've been thinking," Em answered. "Adelessa brought us here for a reason. It must be why we arrived right when this country is in the middle of being invaded."

"Right, sure, we'll try to help," Vic lied. He no longer cared what that crazy old hag wanted them to do, and he certainly didn't care about Kavenland in the least. There was no sense in bringing that up now, though.

"Canis thinks we're not safe this close to the road," Em added.

Vic felt like a thermometer that had been dropped into boiling water. He tried to master his rising anger. "Why don't you try listening to your older brother for once," he asked through gritted teeth. "I say we're far enough in, and if I say we're far enough in..."

"I see something in the woods there!" a man's voice hollered. "Let's have a look." A few other soldiers grunted their agreement, and to Vic's horror, they pushed back branches and entered The Forest.

Em's eyes widened. Vic grabbed her by the arm and put his finger to his lips.

"I see something too!" shouted one of the men. "After them!"

"Let's go!" Vic said and pushed Em ahead of him.

He realized that he'd gotten too far ahead of Em in the mob at Laketown. He'd gotten so fast so quickly in the last year that he sometimes forgot just how fast he was. Now he was going to make sure that Em stayed in front of him.

"Follow Canis!" Em called over her shoulder.

Vic needed no convincing this time. They ran, with Em using her smaller size to her advantage, darting in between trees and ducking under branches. Vic thought that her gait looked a little funny, like there was something wrong with her left foot, but she was moving fast enough. Vic could hear the leaves crunching under Em's footfalls as she ran. As usual, though, he heard the same thing he always heard when his feet hit the ground.

Nothing.

Behind him, Vic heard their pursuers tripping and grunting and swearing, but he didn't dare to look back. After half an hour, the voices trailing them grew fainter, but Em was noticeably limping. Vic grabbed her and swung her up on his back without breaking stride.

The ground before them began to rise. Vic leaned forward and hoisted Em higher onto his back. He staggered on, his legs screaming, as the sun dipped down to the horizon. He slowed to a walk and veered over to the bank of the river. He stepped his foot carefully into the water, feeling for the bottom. The river wasn't as fast or deep here. A short way upstream, an old bridge spanned the slower moving water. Vic saw no reason to cross it. That would have them headed north, which was where the barbarians in this place seemed to live, according to Canis. He crouched down, legs burning, and Em slid down from his back.

Vic knelt by the water and picked up Em's foot. She steadied herself with a hand on his shoulder as he examined it. It was bloody and swollen. He cleaned it as tenderly as he could, but Em still winced, and her hand squeezed his shoulder tightly as he tried to get the dirt out. The foot must have hurt all day, but she hadn't complained about it once.

They both cupped their hands and drank the icy water. Canis lapped away next to them, submerged himself, then jumped back on shore and shook the water off. He looked expectantly at Em. Em looked at Vic.

"What do you think?" she asked.

Vic shrugged his shoulders. "I guess we should find a place to lay down for the night. I've got a couple of small loaves of bread, some dried meat, some cheese, and a couple of apples that I grabbed as we ran through Laketown."

"I grabbed a loaf of bread and some dried fruit as well," Em answered. "It isn't much, is it?"

"We've both done with less," Vic said in a voice that he hoped sounded optimistic. But what Em said was true. It wasn't much. And they'd have to split it with Canis.

"We can make it through a couple of days, if we're careful," he added. "Maybe we'll find some berries or something. If we head away from the river for a day or two, then angle back toward the road, we might get past the soldiers. Then we can find a town or a farmhouse."

Em nodded. "I'm getting a little cold. Do you think we can build a fire? I brought some matches from home."

Vic shivered. His sweat had dried and he, too, had gotten cold. His thoughts turned to Adelessa, and his fists clenched. Why hadn't she told them what to pack? Some extra food and a blanket would sure come in handy right now. He decided to keep his thoughts to himself. It wouldn't do Em any good for him to say them out loud.

Vic thought they were far enough away that the soldiers wouldn't be able to see a fire, if they were still even following, which he doubted. They must be miles behind them by now.

"Sure," he said, "but let's keep it small, just in case."

As they scoured around for some wood, Vic noticed that Em now limped badly. He sat down beside her to examine her wounded foot again. He fought back a rush of bile in his throat. The cut was red and angry with black at its edges. It must be hurting her much more than she let on. A first aid kit was something else that he wished they'd brought.

As Vic sat back, he felt the heavy, gold hair comb in his pocket. It couldn't feed them or keep them warm—yet. But if they could somehow make it to a town or city, they could sell it. He and Em would be set for life if it was as valuable as Adelessa said.

He shook his head. He couldn't believe it was only a few hours ago that he'd stolen that comb. A few hours ago, *in a different world*. Their world. Not some crazy place with a war going on and with people chasing them through the woods trying to kill them and with a mangy mutt as their only friend.

He always liked to have a plan, but he had no idea what to do next. And what was Adelessa's plan for them? Her final words before she shoved them out on this side of the Door in the Stone echoed through his mind.

"I expect you to survive."

Gee, thanks, lady.

Vic let out a sigh of frustration. He rummaged in his bag and pulled out a t-shirt. He gripped the bottom of it with his teeth and ripped off the length of it. He tied it around Em's foot.

"It's not great," he said, "but it may help to keep the dirt out of it."

He avoided eye contact with her as he tied it on. He didn't want her to see his concern. Her foot would be much worse tomorrow. What were they going to do?

He felt Em's hand rest gently on his forearm.

"Maybe it would be best if you went on without me," she said. "Then at least one of us would be safe."

Vic shook his head firmly. "No way," he said.

"There's no sense in both of us getting caught."

"They're not going to catch us," Vic said. He sounded more like he was trying to convince himself than Em. He hoped she didn't pick up on it. His muscles felt sore from carrying her the past few hours. How much longer would he be able to keep that up if Em's foot continued to bother her? He grunted. Why had they even agreed to come here in the first place? Maybe it would have been better to be separated in their world than to be captured in this one.

He shook his head. No. Nothing would be worse than he and Em being separated. She needed him, he reminded himself. He set his jaw. They just couldn't let themselves be captured.

He gathered some more wood, and soon they had a little blaze going. They'd slowly eaten the dinner he'd rationed out from their meager supplies. Canis had dried himself and sat next to Em. Her thin arms encircled her legs, which she'd pulled up tight. Her chin rested on her knees, and her hair fell around her in long, dark strands that reflected the firelight. The flames danced in her eyes—eyes which watched him intently.

"Do you want to hear more of what Canis says about The Scourge?" Em asked.

"Sure," Vic said, though he felt anything but sure.

"Canis says that people used to go into The Forest all the time," Em said. "Kind of like in our world, where people play or go hiking, things like that."

Vic looked around at all the trees that towered above him and shuddered. "I can't see the attraction myself," he muttered.

"Anyway," Em continued, "it was said that people started to disappear in The Forest. They sent a few search parties to look for the missing people, but no one ever returned. They figured it had to be The Scourge. A few brave knights decided to bring him to justice, but no one ever heard from them again, either. So, people stopped going into The Forest."

"But that sounds like the end of the story, or maybe the middle," Vic said. "I mean, who is he? What's his real name? Where's he from? They must know something about him."

Em shook her head. "No one knows where The Scourge came from or exactly how old he is. They say he's hundreds of years old, maybe more."

"Like Adelessa claimed to be," Vic said.

"Right," Em said.

Vic thought about what he could do with hundreds of years of life. He'd finally stolen something and not gotten caught. Maybe he could get good at it. Maybe he could steal a fortune for himself and Em.

Vic shook off the image of chests filled with gold and silver and got back to The Scourge.

"But how could no one know anything about him?" he asked.

Em looked at Canis then back at Vic. She shrugged. "For one thing, nobody alive has ever talked to him. As far as Canis knows, we're the first people who've even been in The Forest for centuries."

Em grabbed a stick and poked at the fire before continuing.

"Some people say that he just appeared one day, that he was born from the earth with no mother and no father. Others say that he destroyed the last of The Protectors on their great voyage to the east and came to Kavenland on their ships. He claimed The Forest as his own and killed anybody who defied him."

Vic had no idea who The Protectors were, but another thought dawned on him.

"If that's true," he said slowly, "that he came from across the sea, I wonder if he has anything to do with this invasion? After all, the invaders came to Laketown on ships and not by land. Maybe he's on their side."

Em didn't answer. Canis sank to the ground and dropped his head into his paws. Vic shivered in front of their little blaze. "That wouldn't be good at all," he whispered.

He stared into the fire. The silence of The Forest seemed smothering.

A burning log popped, and Vic spasmed like he'd been zapped by a taser. He looked over to see Em leaning close to Canis. She nodded her head and turned to Vic.

"Canis says that the Hudenpole might be as dangerous as The Scourge," she said.

"As dangerous as the old guy who wants to eat us?"

"The Hudenpole were the first inhabitants of Kavenland," Em continued without answering. "Humans came along afterward. The two sides got along for a while, but then something happened that made them enemies. Luckily, there aren't a lot of Hudenpole. But some stories say they can make themselves invisible, and other stories say they can make the trees do their bidding."

Vic gulped and looked around him. They were surrounded by tall trees, all of which seemed to have grown larger in the dark.

He didn't say anything for a long time. As the fire's embers turned from orange to gray, he saw Em yawn and lay down. She curled up with Canis, and soon both of their bodies heaved up and down in sleep.

Vic thought about their predicament. Maybe they were deep enough into The Forest to avoid the men who were chasing them, but not deep enough to run into the Hudenpole, the Wolves, or The Scourge. Maybe their food would hold out long enough to slip out of The Forest on the other side of the invaders. They'd already avoided those enormous silver-haired men and the brutal attack on Laketown. Maybe they'd get lucky.

But as he laid down in the dirt and leaves and closed his eyes, a thought occurred to him.

Just when had he and Em ever been lucky?

Chapter Eight
Larkin–The Forest

Hopeful.

It came to Larkin in a flash so suddenly that it made him stumble. It was the emotion he smelled that he hadn't been able to put his finger on before. The Forest felt hopeful. A crystal-blue hope.

"Are you OK?" Ariana asked.

Larkin grunted and turned away. He didn't trust himself to speak.

When kids chose sides to play games in the village, he was always selected to be a captain. When Ariana and Noll wanted to get together, they let him decide what to do.

He was used to being a leader. Now he was being left in the dust.

The creature that had grown inside him over the past 24 hours gnawed at another chunk of his soul. His insides roiled with jealousy. He felt ashamed of that, which made him even angrier.

He didn't want to think about his feelings anymore. He rubbed his nose and thought instead about the emotion he'd smelled. Underneath everything, buried deep like a forgotten object in a long-lost corner of an old attic, The Forest held hope. Larkin had a vision of people walking through The Forest and having picnics, with sunbeams streaming through the branches and birds singing in the trees. He felt a latent joy in The Forest that he hadn't felt when they entered it yesterday.

Larkin shook his head to clear the vision from his mind. He looked around. He didn't feel much joy. He shifted his pack and strode on.

As for Gurn, Larkin and his friends soon became glad he was around. They explained to him about the invasion and why they needed to cross The Forest to get to Rockhaven. Gurn quickened his pace. They hurried along for two days behind him.

On the first day—without the Nisser—Larkin and his friends had blundered and hacked their way along in a straight line. But Gurn's eyes darted around constantly, and he'd find paths Larkin and the others couldn't see made by deer or other animals. The paths twisted and turned but allowed them to move quickly while still going in the right direction. Thanks to Gurn they were making much faster progress.

Even with the Nisser as their guide, though, they ran into some troubles. After hiking for hours at the bottom of a steep ravine, they found their path blocked by a huge boulder.

"We can't climb over it," Gurn said. "We're going to have to go back."

"But we'll lose half a day going back and finding another way forward," Larkin complained.

Noll stepped past them and heaved against the great boulder. For a long moment, nothing happened. Then it began to move. Dirt and sticks wedged between the boulder and the ravine showered down as Noll strained and pressed forward. Rivulets of sweat gathered on his arms and legs and poured down his face.

Finally, Noll pushed the boulder free, and it rolled a few feet forward.

"Great job, Noll!" Ariana cried out. "There's enough room for us to get by!"

Gurn shook his head in awe. "I've never seen anything like that," he said.

Larkin said nothing.

Later, as the sun began to set, Ariana threw her hand up.

"What is it?" Gurn asked.

"Coyotes," Ariana said softly.

"I don't see anything," Gurn said.

"If Ariana says she sees something, she sees something," Noll said.

Ariana unslung her bow and reached for an arrow. "I'm going to scare them off," she said. She sent an arrow whizzing through the dusk. It thunked into a tree trunk. They heard a coyote howl in fright followed by the sound of animals scampering off through the underbrush.

"Good going!" Noll said.

Larkin scowled and kept silent.

As the second day wore on. Larkin saw his friends have whispered conversations with the Nisser, occasionally glancing back at him. He wondered if they were making fun of him.

A small voice inside him said that was ridiculous—that there was no way Ariana and Noll would do that. But that was the Ariana and Noll from back in Fieldstone. Out here in The Forest, maybe they felt differently about him. Maybe they'd changed.

Gurn interrupted his thoughts. He said he was off to do some foraging and told them to follow a deer trail that lay ahead. A couple of minutes later, Larkin heard a voice cry out.

"Help!"

Larkin looked at Ariana.

She bolted off in the direction of the cry. Larkin and Noll followed, and they thrashed through the underbrush, trying to locate the Nisser. A few minutes later, they heard another cry for help coming from their right.

They plunged through the trees. Branches stung Larkin's face as the three friends tried desperately to find the Nisser. After a couple of minutes, they heard him cry out again, this time behind them and to their left.

"What the...?" Larkin said.

They once again headed for where they thought Gurn's voice had come from. They emerged into a small clearing but saw no sign of their new friend.

"Maybe we're up too high to see him," Ariana suggested. "Let's get lower and see if we can detect some movement."

That sounded like a good idea to Larkin, and the three friends crouched down. At first, Larkin huffed from the exertion of the chase, but as his breathing slowed, he became aware of an absolute stillness in The Forest. He swiveled his head around, trying to keep his field of vision wide. He saw no movement. The Forest was dead quiet.

"Boo!" said a voice directly in his ear.

Larkin had no idea he could jump so high. When he landed, he staggered backward, desperately struggling to pull out his sword.

"Whoa, whoa now!" a voice said.

As Larkin watched in amazement, he saw a little bit of Gurn appear, and then a little more. He was wiping something off that had made him invisible. What the Nisser didn't wipe off was the huge grin on his face.

Then he started laughing. He pointed at Larkin as if he were going to say something, but the words wouldn't come out. He bent over, gasped for breath, and finally composed himself.

"Well," Gurn began, wiping the tears from his cheeks, "that was a pretty good one. Not as good, mind you, as the old 'rainbow' trick, when we put a pot of gold at one end, then whisk it away when someone gets close. Now THAT's funny. But this was pretty funny, too."

Larkin looked at his friends in astonishment. But he detected a smirk on Ariana's face. He glanced over at Noll, who looked down at his feet, trying to hide a wide smile on his face.

"Don't tell me you two were in on it?" Larkin demanded.

Ariana broke off eye contact with Larkin for a moment and stared at the ground before answering.

"You've been so serious since we left." She looked at Noll, then back at Larkin. "We know you feel the burden to lead us. And I know," she said more quietly, taking a step toward him, "that you're disappointed about your coming-of-age day. But," she added quickly, "Noll and I don't think you need any special powers, do we?"

Noll nodded his head rapidly in agreement.

Ariana gave his arm a squeeze. "You're our best friend, Larkin," she said. She looked like she wanted to say more, but for once, she didn't. She stopped and shrugged instead.

Larkin's mouth sagged open for a second before he closed it. He'd been short with Ariana and Noll since they'd entered The Forest, but they'd chalked his behavior up to disappointment and pressure, not the bitterness and jealousy he knew was behind his ill temper. They'd thought the best of him when he was at his worst, and now they were trying to cheer him up.

Or were they? Maybe they just pitied him. A spark of angry indignation flamed in his stomach at the thought of it.

He didn't want anyone feeling sorry for him.

Larkin's insides felt like a kindergartner's fingerpainting project. Bright blue smears of love for his friends were mixed with the angry dark green and purple emotions that had been consuming him since his coming-of-age day.

He couldn't answer Ariana. He didn't trust himself to speak.

He was interested in what had made Gurn invisible, though.

"It's an ointment," Gurn said, opening a large tin and showing it to Larkin. "You put some on your clothes, then all over your exposed parts, like your arms and face. It works best when your clothes are brown or green—something that will blend in with the rest of the forest." He looked up at Larkin. "It would work perfectly with what you're wearing.

"Here," Gurn said, and handed Larkin the tin. "I guess it's the least I could do." He snickered again, then regained his composure. "I've got tons of it. We use it for fun, or if we need to, uh, liberate a few things from farms and villages. But don't try to use it on Wolves or any other animals. They don't need to see you. They can smell you."

Larkin thanked Gurn and put the tin in his rucksack. It seemed like something that could be useful.

Other than that dubious stab at humor, Larkin enjoyed Gurn's company. He tried to learn as much as he could from him as well. Gurn showed Larkin how to lay traps for rabbits at night and how to forage for wild vegetables. They'd regained most of what the Nisser had taken on their first night, and, of course, they'd been careful to leave a plate out for the other Nisser in the evening to protect their new store of food.

"What about the Wolves?" Noll had asked. "Shouldn't we worry about them eating our food at night?"

"There aren't any Wolves on this side of the Flumyn River," Gurn answered. "They're up closer to Rockhaven, so you'll want to watch out for them when you get near there. The Nisser might take your food, but we won't harm you in any way. The Wolves will. The biggest fear on this side of the river is the boars. Especially Scrofa."

"Who's Scrofa?" Larkin asked.

"The biggest, meanest boar in The Forest. As tall as you or Ariana."

Larkin doubted this. He figured that a lot of things seemed huge when you were only three feet tall. To be polite, he changed the subject.

"How about the Hudenpole and The Scourge?"

"They both live on the other side of the river. The Hudenpole are very mysterious. They stick to themselves. And, of course, they don't like your lot. I'd steer very, very clear of them if I were you.

And as for The Scourge—well, you've probably heard lots about him."

Larkin felt a prickle in his scalp. He'd thought that the Nisser were a fairy tale, but he'd obviously been wrong. He'd hoped that The Scourge was a fairy tale, too, but now Gurn seemed to be saying that the thousand-year-old terror really did exist.

"It sounds like this side of the Flumyn River is a lot safer," Noll observed.

Gurn nodded.

"There are all kinds of strange and dangerous things over there," he agreed. "Better to stay over here or follow the river down to the Great Road and go to Rockhaven that way."

"But we can't," Larkin answered. "Adelessa says this is the fastest way. And if we don't get there first, all Kavenland could be lost."

Gurn's head whipped around. "You know Adelessa?"

"Well, I can't say I know her," Larkin said. "We've all met her, though."

Gurn was quiet for a while. Finally, he spoke, and for once his tone sounded respectful.

"Adelessa is the only one in Kavenland that is of The Forest and also of the land of humans. She moves about freely in each. That's how it once was for everybody, I'm told. The Hudenpole, humans, and The Protectors all living in peace."

"You said The Protectors separately," Noll interrupted. "Weren't they men and women?"

"Well...not exactly. But that's another story. Adelessa is more like The Protectors than anything else. She's older than she looks."

"How old is she?" Noll asked. "40?"

Gurn burst out laughing. He laughed so hard that he fell over, holding his stomach. He struggled to his feet, and tried to talk, but started laughing again. Tears streamed down his cheeks as he bent over, breathing hard.

"Fa-fa-forty?' he finally managed to say. "You think that's old, do you? How old do you think I am?"

"I...I don't know," Noll stammered.

"Well," Gurn said, pulling himself together, "I've seen over three hundred winters come and go, and Adelessa is far, far older than I."

"You're over three hundred years old?" Noll exclaimed.

"Just a pup among the Nisser."

There was silence as Larkin and his friends absorbed what Gurn had told them. Larkin let his mind drift to what he could do with three hundred years. The heroic deeds he would perform, the adulation he would receive, his name in the minds and on the lips of everyone in Kavenland...

His thoughts were interrupted when Gurn continued in a more serious tone.

"The Hudenpole don't like humans, and I'm sure they have their reasons why. Our relationship with your lot is a little more complicated.

"We Nisser will venture out of the woods, but never too far anymore. We eat a lot, I won't deny it, but what we really feed on is the belief of humans. We were once far more numerous, but as people cease to believe in us, our numbers dwindle, and we grow weaker. Someday all the Nisser will pass from this world.

"But I fear that we'll pass a lot quicker if you're taken over in this war. There will be a new group of people with new beliefs and no time for the Nisser." Gurn shuddered and shook his head. "I believe this invasion could be as bad for us as it is for you."

The thoughts of the invasion, the threat to them and their families, their village being burned down and people dying all returned to Larkin and his friends. They walked somberly on before stopping for lunch. As they began to unpack their food, Noll turned to Gurn.

"What else can you tell us of the Nisser?"

"Do you know the story of how the Nisser came to Kavenland?" Gurn asked.

The companions shook their heads.

"We come from Thorthuil. It's a land of great, fertile plains, filled with winding rivers and creeks with trout so plentiful that it takes only a moment to catch your dinner. It's our true home.

"But many, many years ago, a group of Nisser were exploring a cave on a lazy afternoon. They went in deeper and deeper, and suddenly emerged into a forest. They were filled with wonder, for the forest seemed to be inside the cave. But when they turned around, the cave was gone, and the forest was 'this' Forest. Somehow, they'd passed from Thorthuil to Kavenland. No one is sure how. It's been over a thousand years now. We assume we're here for some purpose, but we're not sure what."

He let out a long sigh.

"We've looked for a way home ever since. We've explored every cave in Kavenland, every crevice, every city, town, and port, but we've never found a way back."

"That's awful," said Ariana.

Larkin looked at Gurn.

"You said the Nisser used to mix more freely with men. What happened?"

A cloud of anger passed over Gurn's face, and his voice rose as he spoke.

"It was the Nisser who taught humans the art of farming many years ago. We arrived just after Sendina had banished the Ancients and divided up Kavenland between Hudenpole and humans. We taught humans how to grow fruits and vegetables, how to tend livestock, how to build barns, and how to salt and can food so that they could stop scavenging and roaming and build homes and communities instead. And do you know what we got in return?"

No one tried to answer this time.

"We got the boot! Driven away! We helped them create better lives, but they got greedy and kept everything for themselves! We couldn't believe it! The old nomads, poor and living in the dirt, had been more generous with the little that they had. But we didn't go quietly."

Noll spoke up. "You stole chickens and eggs, and trampled through vegetable gardens, and created mischief everywhere you went."

"That's right," Gurn said. "Finally, we came to an agreement: leave us food every night, and we'll not only stop our mischief, but we'll protect your gardens and livestock as well. It's been a good truce.

"But over the years, men have stopped believing in the Nisser, and many have stopped leaving us food. And the Nisser have started slowly fading. We seem to just—disappear. No one knows why."

Gurn's voice caught as he said these last words. He looked down. When he looked back up, his eyes glistened. He cleared his throat and continued.

"Some hope that the Nisser who fade away go back to Thorthuil, but we can't say for sure that's what happens. All we can figure is that we somehow need humans to believe in us to survive. Some sort of magic brought us here long ago, and that magic, in some way, has tied us to you."

"Who did you lose?" Larkin asked quietly.

Gurn stared past him. His eyes grew unfocused. He shook his head and didn't answer.

"If you need our belief," Noll asked, "why don't you come out and show yourselves to us? If more people saw you, then more people would believe in you."

"Always the same with humankind. Seeing is believing." Gurn snorted. "And it's not like our last relations ended well for us."

"I didn't know about this part of our history," Larkin said slowly, "but there are still good men and women who would help you. Noll and his family believe in you strongly."

Gurn gave Noll a warm glance.

"I've put out the food," Larkin continued, "but haven't always believed. Now I do. When this is over, I'll do what I can to help you. I don't know what that is, but I'll do whatever I can." He looked at his friends. "We all will."

Gurn grunted, hoisted up his sack, and began walking again. The three companions had grown fond of him, and for all his blustering demeanor, Larkin could tell that Gurn liked them, too.

Ariana and Noll walked along beside Larkin.

"Can you imagine being in the company of one of the Nisser?" Noll asked. He shook his head in wonder. "I mean, what could be crazier than that?"

"I don't know," Ariana answered. "Maybe a talking dog?"

Noll laughed. "That would be crazier," he said.

After a moment, Larkin said, "Gurn obviously lost someone close to him."

Ariana nodded. "And you're right," she said. "We'll do everything we can to help him and the Nisser when all of this is over."

The three shrugged their packs higher up on their shoulders and followed Gurn.

"Are we going up?" Larkin asked several hours later.

Gurn nodded. "The river is at its fastest where we're going, but there used to be a bridge near here to cross it. It's the quickest way, but if the bridge isn't still there, there's no place to ford it around here. We'll have to march another half day to the north to find slower water."

Larkin, Ariana, and Noll looked at each other. They were all thinking the same thing. A half day up also meant a half day back down on the other side. One valuable day would be wasted.

"Let's hope that bridge is still there," Larkin said.

A half-hour later, Gurn called a halt.

"The river's just on the other side of that rise. You rest here, and I'll see if I can find the bridge."

Larkin and his friends sat down wearily. Larkin couldn't wait to get across the Flumyn River and camp for the night.

"Help!"

It was Gurn again. Larkin looked at his friends suspiciously, but Ariana was already on the move.

"This isn't a prank!" she called over her shoulder. Larkin and Noll ran after her.

In a few moments, they caught up to her. She stood stock-still, with her right hand up, the back of her hand facing them. Larkin understood. She wanted them to stop, and she wanted them to be quiet. One quick glance showed him why.

Thirty feet in front of them, an enormous, tusked creature snorted and pawed at the ground. Larkin had no doubt that it was a boar. And Gurn had been right. It was huge.

Larkin's aunt and uncle had pigs on their small farm. The largest male hog was big and strong and hard to deal with. The boar that faced them was at least three times bigger than that hog. It had tusks the size of small swords.

Larkin suddenly became aware of the blood circulating in his body. It felt as icy as his uncle's barn in January.

Gurn stood fifteen feet away, between them and the massive beast. Ariana's hand moved slowly up over her shoulder, toward her quiver of arrows. Larkin quietly pulled out his sword.

Suddenly, the giant boar let out a bellow of rage and charged. Larkin couldn't believe how fast it moved.

Gurn dove out of the way and rolled to safety. Ariana stood her ground and shot an arrow that hit the beast right between its eyes. It bounced off. She cursed and reached back for another arrow, but Larkin shoved her aside. He dodged to his left, and in one motion, swept his sword in a high arc and brought it down onto the back of the great beast as it rushed past. The sword bounced off, and the recoil almost knocked Larkin off his feet. Noll's sword also failed to penetrate the boar's tough hide.

"Climb!" Gurn yelled, scrabbling at the base of a huge maple tree. The branches were too high for him to reach. Larkin glanced over his shoulder and saw the beast slide and skid to a stop. Its momentum had taken it well past him, Ariana, and Noll and bought them a few precious seconds.

Ariana scrambled to her feet, and Larkin shouted and pointed toward the tree Gurn was trying desperately to climb. He saw her boost the Nisser and climb up after him. Noll was already navigating up a tree on his right. Larkin dashed to the next nearest tree, leapt for its lowest branch, and swung himself up to safety.

He climbed up a little way, then stopped, panting. Adrenaline still coursed through his veins. He'd never come that close to dying. He now fully understood why Gurn had warned them about boars.

"Is everyone ok?" he hollered.

They all were.

"Now what?" Larkin called to Gurn.

"I don't know," Gurn answered. "But that's Scrofa, and now that he's got us trapped, he won't leave."

Larkin looked down. It wasn't just a boar, although that would have been bad enough. They'd been trapped by the largest, meanest boar in The Forest. The massive creature stomped from tree to tree, emitting large snorts of anger. Larkin shuddered. He'd never seen anything as ill-tempered and menacing in his life.

He thought about what to do. They couldn't just sit in the trees for days until they ran out of food. He couldn't think of any diversion that would work, though. They could all climb down at once and run away in separate directions, but that meant that whichever person the boar chased would be doomed.

The great beast seemed impossible to defeat. Larkin thought back. He was astounded by how quickly the boar had moved. Ariana's arrow had bounced off it. His sword and Noll's hadn't even dented its tough hide. It was faster than they were, tougher than they were, and angrier than they were. The way the beast had skidded to a stop and then re-charged...

Skidded to a stop.

That was it! It wasn't the nimblest of beasts. Larkin climbed higher into the tree. He looked to his right. A mere thirty feet away was a steep bank which led down to the fast, frothy rapids of the Flumyn River. On top of the bank was a maple tree. Its lowest branch hung parallel to the ground, about eight feet up.

Yes, Larkin thought. It should work. He didn't have Noll's size and strength, or Ariana's protective ferocity, but he could still show them a thing or two. He could get all of them out of this mess by himself.

He could be the hero. He could almost hear himself shrugging off the praise of his friends as they thanked him. "It's nothing you wouldn't have done," he said modestly in his daydream. "But you're the one who did it," Noll said. "You saved our lives," Ariana added.

A strong scent interrupted his reverie. An ugly, blotched smell of pride and envy wafted to Larkin on the afternoon breeze. He inhaled and felt consumed by it. He fought against the feeling it put in the pit of his stomach. He exhaled and looked at the giant boar stalking around beneath them.

"Ariana and Gurn," he called out, as he climbed down. "Can you distract this monster for a minute."

"What are you doing?" Ariana asked in alarm.

"Trust me," Larkin answered.

"Larkin?"

"Trust me."

"Larkin!" Ariana said. "You don't have to do this!"

But this is what The Protectors would have done. Galeran would have found a way to be the hero, and now Larkin would, too.

Not Ariana. Not Noll.

Him.

He hopped down from the tree. He heard a yell of frustration from Ariana, and then an arrow whistled through the air and hit the giant boar in the rump. It bellowed in rage. Another arrow followed, and the boar galloped over to the base of Ariana's tree. Its great roar filled the air.

Larkin ran to the maple at the top of the ridge. In the distance, he saw Ariana scurrying down the tree as fast as she could. If he had his way, he'd have solved everything before Ariana even made it to the ground.

Larkin planned to whistle to attract the boar's attention but realized that he didn't need to. It had spotted him, turned, and charged.

Larkin positioned himself below the branch. It was a trifle higher than he'd guessed, but he thought he could just manage it. He knew that he'd only have one chance, and that his timing would have to be perfect.

Closer the beast came, and closer. Larkin crouched down, his arms at his side, his pulse pounding in his temples.

"Larkin!" Ariana yelled. She'd reached the ground and was sprinting toward him behind the giant boar. "What are you doing?"

Larkin waited. The beast was forty feet away and moving like lightning. Now it was twenty feet away. Finally, Larkin leapt up. His hands caught the limb, and he swung his knees up to his chest.

Larkin knew instantly that he'd jumped just a split second too soon. He saw rage replaced by bewilderment and then fear in Scrofa's malevolent eyes. More rapidly than Larkin could believe, it pushed down frantically on its front legs, trying to grind to a stop. When it did, its hind legs reared into the air, and its backside thudded hard into Larkin, knocking him from his branch.

He landed on top of the bank. Scrofa's panicked efforts to stop had failed, and he saw the great beast just in front of him, rolling and tumbling until it finally splashed into the river.

That had been Larkin's plan, but what happened next wasn't. He cartwheeled down the slope. He felt his sword tear free as he grabbed and clawed for something to hold onto.

There was nothing to grab.

Larkin felt himself ricochet off the banks, and he was catapulted into the river's fomenting rapids.

Chapter Nine
Vic–The Forest

Vic awoke to Canis licking his face. As he opened his eyes, he saw the dog frantically dancing about while letting out a low whine. Vic rubbed his eyes, sat up, then stopped. He held up his hand.

"Shhh!" he whispered. Canis sat still. In the distance, he heard men lumbering through the Forest's undergrowth. A cold wave of fear swept over him. He crept around the burned-out fire pit, put his hand over Em's mouth and gently shook her awake.

"We have to go. Now!"

Em made a muffled sound through his hand and her eyes opened wide. Then she nodded, and Vic withdrew his hand from her mouth. Em winced as she scrambled to her feet. They grabbed their knapsacks, and Vic knelt and motioned for her to get up on his back.

She shook her head. "You can't keep carrying me, Vic. You don't have to be the hero."

"Hero?" he said. "I don't want to be a hero. I just want us to live through another day. The best way to do that is to carry you. Otherwise, you'll slow us down and we'll be caught for sure."

She hobbled over and climbed on. Vic looked at Canis.

"Lead the way," he said softly.

As they set off, Vic felt stiff and sore. His mattress back home was thin, and the worn-out springs beneath it creaked and whined and bounced when he rolled over, but it was like sleeping in a palace on a featherbed compared to this. The ground in The Forest was lumpy. No matter how he'd twisted about, something had pressed into some part of his body all night long. Once he got loosened up, though, his legs felt strong, even though he'd run for a lot of the day yesterday with Em on his back.

He thought back to Em's comment about being a hero and laughed an inward, bitter laugh. Guys like him didn't save the day. They weren't called heroes, and they didn't get the girl in the end.

Guys like him stole things from stores in Pittsburgh and from half-starved merchants in Laketown. If he even dreamed of being a hero, he'd need to wake up and find someone to apologize to.

As the sun rose high in the sky, Vic felt his legs get a little rubbery. He hadn't seen or heard their pursuers for hours. He let Em down, arched his back, and stretched his legs.

"I think we should get as far away as we can. Are you OK to walk for a bit?"

Em nodded. He quickly unwrapped the makeshift bandage on her foot and examined her cut. It had grown an ugly dark red. He choked back a sob.

He'd learned about the dangers of infections at school. He had nothing to clean her wound with, though. His mind raced to get ahead of itself, to get ahead of horrible images of the infection spreading and gangrene and...

Stop. Breathe. Smile. Reassure Em. He plastered a smile on his face and looked at her.

"It's bad, isn't it?" she asked.

His face fell. Once again, he hadn't fooled her.

He nodded. He couldn't trust his voice. He wrapped up her foot, and he tried to wrap up his thoughts as well. He had to keep his wits about him.

But one thought seeped through. Vic had always looked out for Em. Their childhood hadn't been very happy. Their parents hadn't been very loving or very supportive. Neither he nor Em had any friends. Em was more interested in animals. As for himself...

Vic saw in his mind a younger version of himself. He saw his worn, cheap clothes. He saw bony wrists extending past sleeves that were too short.

"Flood pants!" one of the kids shouted, pointing at the pants that came up four inches short of his old sneakers. He felt his face burn in shame and frustration at the memory.

He remembered how Chip had goaded him into stealing the teacher's coffee mug, and how it had made him fit in less, not more. He grew desperate. He swiped candy bars and gave them to Chip and his friends.

It didn't help.

His behavior grew worse. He'd been rude to teachers, talking over the voice inside his head that told him it was wrong. He snapped at other kids, and he even got into a fight or two. A timeline of detentions, scoldings, and warnings from parents and teachers rushed through his mind. Those experiences had hardened on him like a second skin. He felt the layer of protective armor that they'd provided for him against the rest of the world.

He was an outcast? So be it. He'd be an outlaw, too. And a loner.

His fists had clenched as the unwelcome memories flooded his mind. He relaxed his hands and breathed deep. He looked down at his sister. Canis stood by her side, and the reality hit him.

Yes, he was her big brother. Yes, it was his job to look after her. Yes, in these past few months he'd had to steal food for them both. Yes, he'd have to carry her now through The Forest and somehow find help for her in the next couple of days.

He'd thought so much about how much Em needed him, though, that he hadn't thought about how much he might need Em. He gulped, then pushed the thought aside.

This wasn't the time to think about that. He had to stay focused.

He gritted his teeth, swung her up on his back again, and trudged on. For the next two days, they headed deeper into The Forest. When he needed a breather and set her down, Em could barely walk on her foot. Their food supply was almost gone. Vic's stomach gnawed at him and sent spasms of pain that made him gasp. Weakened by the lack of food, his legs now seemed to be made of concrete as he trudged on with Em on his back. He looked at Canis. The dog's back legs sagged, and his tail drooped.

On the first day of their slog through The Forest, a voice inside Vic's head had softly made a suggestion. "Give up," it had said. "This is too hard." As the journey continued, the voice grew louder. "Giving up would be easy," it said. "Besides, you don't really know what these men who are chasing you want. Maybe they mean you no harm. Maybe they're part of Adelessa's plan." But Vic ignored the voice, set his jaw, adjusted Em on his back, and kept going.

The sun faded on their third day in The Forest. They staggered up a small hill. When they reached the top, Vic set Em down and she threw herself on the ground. He half sat and half fell beside her. Canis flopped onto his side, his tongue out and his chest heaving. Vic looked down at Em, who fought to keep her eyes open. She couldn't go on like this much longer.

"Here," he said, offering her the last of his bread and cheese. "Have this before you nod off."

"How about you? Aren't you going to eat?"

"Already did while we were walking," he lied. She would need whatever food they had left to fight her infection. "Here. You've got to keep your strength up."

She took it gratefully. While she chewed, Vic outlined the plan he'd been working on throughout the day.

"Em, I'm going to sneak back when it gets a little darker and find the camp of those men. Maybe I can figure out why they're chasing us." She began to object, but Vic continued. "You know how quiet I can be. They won't hear me or see me."

And I want to steal some food, he thought, although he decided not to mention that. He was curious about who would chase them for three days through The Forest, but he also realized that it was no use getting away from these men if it meant starving to death.

A thought had pinged around his head the last few days like a rubber ball in an anti-gravity chamber. He'd finally stopped long enough to examine it, and the realization of what that thought was was horrible.

If he hadn't stolen the comb from Mr. Zipkoff, Adelessa wouldn't have been able to blackmail them. They'd still be at home instead of here, where Em was suffering from an infection so painful that she couldn't walk, and strange men with bad intentions were chasing them through a forbidden Forest where all humans feared to go.

The small rubber ball grew into a huge boulder of guilt that pressed down on him so hard that Vic thought it would crush him into the ground.

All of this was his fault.

He let out a shaky breath. He had to get out from underneath that awful weight. He had to for himself and for his sister.

He built a small fire and sat across from Em.

"I'm going to get Canis to tell us some more about Kavenland. What do you think?" Em asked.

Vic shrugged his sore shoulders. "Sure." Anything to take his mind off his own failures.

"So you have the Hudenpole and The Scourge," Em began to translate.

"Thanks for reminding me," Vic groused.

"But there used to be a group of heroes called The Protectors," Em continued. "There were fifty of them. They were led by great warriors named Beredor and Galeran. They kept Kavenland safe. Canis says there was one named Celerox, who was so fast and whose footfalls were so light that they said he could run on the treetops without falling through. Canis says you're like him."

Vic snorted. Protector? He couldn't even protect Em and himself.

"He also says there was one who talked with animals, like me." She rubbed the top of Canis's head. "Only cats and dogs for me, though," she said.

"What happened to these Protectors?" Vic asked. He wasn't really interested—it sounded like more hero nonsense to him—but he'd begun to fidget. He knew he had a tricky and dangerous plan to carry out. He wanted to get started, but he had to wait a little longer. He wanted the men to be asleep, or close to it, by the time he found their camp.

"No one knows for sure. The story is that they went exploring out in the eastern seas and never came back, but that was a thousand years ago. It was at about that time that The Scourge showed up."

Vic didn't answer. What a world this was. He tried to remember the vision Adelessa had shown him back in their own house, but he couldn't. He just knew that she'd given them some hope of a better life in Kavenland. He looked around him.

He didn't see any better life.

Chalk up Adelessa as someone else he couldn't trust.

Em stretched her arms above her head and yawned.

Vic stood up and walked around a little. He was tired and the fire was making him drowsy. He didn't want to fall asleep. The sun had long since set, and Em began to resemble little more than a shape curled up a few feet away, with Canis lying next to her.

He stopped pacing and stood very still. He heard Em's slow and steady breathing.

He left her with Canis and tiptoed away. A half hour later, he saw the orange glow of a campfire. Just as he feared, their pursuers had gained on him and Em in the last two days. Vic crept closer. Six large, dirty men with shaggy beards and tattered clothing sat around the fire. They gnawed on bones, tossed them into the flames, and licked their fingers.

"There's definitely a dog with them," said one. "I could see its tracks."

"Dinner tomorrow night," barked another. "I love roast dog."

There were a few murmurs of agreement.

"And if I'm not mistaken, one of the two is a girl."

"Could be a small boy," said another.

"Could be," the other agreed. "Either way, we could make a little money selling them. Though maybe it's not worth the trouble carrying 'em back to Laketown," he added.

The others laughed at this—a mirthless, unpleasant laugh that made Vic's insides feel like pudding. Vic now knew that he'd rather starve to death than be captured by these men.

"Why do you suppose the Archipelagans care about a couple of strays running around in The Forest?" one man asked.

"Guess they don't want no witnesses to warn of the invasion."

"And we got to do the dirty work, I guess."

"Better the dirty work for them than nothing at all. The Hill People's been disregarded for years. About time someone gave us something."

"The queen's making sure of that."

Vic had no idea what this last comment meant. He remembered what he'd heard on their first morning in Laketown. Kavenland had a king, and the townspeople said the queen had died. As for the Archipelagans, Vic guessed that they must be the ones invading Kavenland.

And who were these 'Hill People'? Maybe the Hill People were from here and had joined forces with the invaders. That's what it sounded like. Vic didn't much care, though. He just wanted to steal some food. He, Em, and Canis would need it to keep their strength up, or they'd be caught for sure.

He waited a long time until the fire died down. The men stretched and yawned and laid down on the ground. He waited a little longer until he heard their snoring. He took a deep breath. Now was the time.

But before he could move, a hood was popped over his head. A hand was clamped over his mouth, and his arms were pinned to his side.

He'd been caught.

Chapter Ten
Ariana–The Forest

Ariana watched in horror as Larkin and the boar tumbled over the embankment. She reached its edge and scrambled and skittered down the slope toward the river's frothing rapids. Her momentum carried her up to the tips of her toes. She flung her arms out wide and swung them in small, rapid circles. For a moment, she thought she might topple into the river herself, but her balance held.

"Larkin!" she shouted, but the river was so loud that she could barely hear her own voice.

"Ariana!" Noll yelled.

She looked up and saw him kneeling on the top of the bank, looking down at her. "Where's Larkin?" he asked. She saw confusion and fear in his widened eyes.

"He's gone," she yelled back. "Can you see him from up there?"

Noll stood up, faced downriver, and cupped his hands over his eyes to shield the light from the sinking sun. He shook his head.

"What's the use of having this power to protect," Ariana cried out, "if I can't even protect Larkin from some dumb beast!"

"Ariana!" Noll said. "You can't blame yourself for what Larkin did!"

But Ariana knew better. She'd been the first to get to Scrofa after Gurn had called out, and she hadn't been able to stop the giant boar. She hadn't been able to protect her friends.

She sprung lightly up the steep back. "Let's go!" she said, as she sped past Noll. Gurn had managed to drop out of the tree and was running toward her.

"Larkin fell into the river!" she called to the Nisser. "Come on!"

She didn't want to think about what a current that fast and that strong might have done to her best friend. Instead, she took off at a fast pace, as close to the riverbank as she could manage. She heard Gurn close behind her. She knew that Noll would never be able to keep up, but that wasn't her main thought right now.

"Oh, Larkin!" she thought. "Why? Why did you think you had to be the hero?"

Thoughts of Larkin flashed through her head as she thrashed through the underbrush. He wasn't the biggest boy in Fieldstone, but he was tough and smart. They'd played battle games growing up. She, Noll, and Larkin would take on her two older brothers.

"Hide behind these haystacks," he'd told Ariana and Noll one time. Then he'd lured her brothers past the hay piles and into a fenced-in enclosure. He'd shouted at them so that they'd keep their attention on him. She'd admired his acting. He'd looked panicked, and her brothers had fallen for it. They'd closed in on him, certain that they'd won—right up until the time she and Noll crept up behind them and pressed their wooden swords into their backs.

She smiled at the memory. Larkin always came up with something, and the three of them almost always beat her brothers. Larkin called it luck.

Her smile faded. She hoped his luck hadn't run out. They weren't in Fieldstone anymore. They were in the real world now. Decisions here could be a matter of life and...

Ariana cut off the thought. She glanced at the river every few steps as she ran. She knew Larkin. She knew there was no way that he wouldn't survive this. At any moment now, she'd see him drenched but alive, waving cheerfully as he climbed out of the river.

But she didn't.

Ariana's mind went back to when she first felt the surge of her new power to protect the weaker from the stronger. Her mom had issued words of caution.

"You can't fight every battle for every person," Ariana's mom had told her. "Sometimes people need help. But sometimes people need to fight their own battles. Learning to stick up for yourself is a part of growing up."

A couple of weeks before they'd left home, Ariana had caught a girl making fun of a younger boy. She'd demanded that the girl apologize. She had, although she did it with malice in her eyes.

"See!" Ariana had told the young boy after the girl had stalked off. "You don't have to worry about her anymore."

The boy shook his head in sorrow, his eyes cast to the ground.

"I won't have to worry when you're around," he said. "But when you're not around, her teasing will only get worse."

Ariana had started to reply, then she'd stopped. She realized that the boy was right.

This gift she'd been given—protecting the weak from the strong—wasn't always as straightforward as it seemed.

But this time, it was. She'd needed to protect Larkin, and she'd failed.

Ariana continued to run even after the sun had set and dusk had turned into darkness. Branches whipped at her face. Tree roots tripped her, and she sprawled on the ground.

"Ariana," said Gurn's gruff voice. She ignored him and ran on. She felt a tug on her sleeve and tried to pull away, but the Nisser's grip grew firmer and slowed her down.

"Ariana," he repeated softly. She stopped. He gestured at the darkness in front of them. "Another hundred yards and you'd have run right off a cliff," he said. "Stay here."

"Where are you going?" she asked.

"The cliff is a huge bowl," the Nisser answered. "There's a big waterfall that drops into a deep pool. It's the beginning of a long canyon. Maybe Larkin is in that pool. If not, he's going to have to float a long way down stream before he can get out of the river." He stroked his face. "Miles," he added. "If..."

He didn't finish his sentence.

"I'm going with you," Ariana said.

Gurn shook his head. "I'll find a way down. In the meantime, wait here for Noll. Build a fire. Maybe we missed Larkin in the dark. If we did, he might see the fire and come to us."

Ariana nodded reluctantly. It made sense.

Gurn jogged off. Ariana groped around for wood and built a fire. She sat down next to it to wait for Noll, and her thoughts turned again to Larkin. Something that had happened when they were younger popped into her mind.

They were back in their village of Fieldstone. Larkin, Ariana, and Noll had climbed onto Farmer McNatt's fences. Farmer McNatt was a big, gnarled, unpleasant man who scowled at kids when they went by his house. But he had the best fences for climbing in the village.

The three of them had been walking across one of the split rails, arms spread wide as they teetered back and forth, when Ariana heard a crack. She tumbled to the ground as the fence fell away beneath them. They leapt to their feet to assess the damage. The supports had caved inward on either side, dragging the next connecting rails with them. The fence sagged for twenty feet in either direction. It was a mess.

"Let's go!" Noll had urged, and they'd run away.

A few minutes later, they'd slowed to a stop. Noll was bent over, clutching his knees. Ariana put her hands on her hips and arched her head back, gasping for air. When her breathing finally slowed, she'd noticed Larkin staring at her.

"What?" she'd asked.

"I think we should tell Farmer McNatt what we did."

"Are you crazy?" Noll said. "He's the scariest man in Fieldstone!"

Larkin looked back at Ariana. She slowly shook her head.

Larkin hadn't said anything more, but the next morning, when she and Noll went to his uncle's farm to pick him up, he was gone. They searched the village for him, but Ariana already knew where he'd be. She and Noll crept up to a position across the road from Farmer McNatt's cottage. The surly old man glowered down at

Larkin, who nodded as the farmer wagged a finger in his face and then pointed at the fence.

She and Noll had slunk away. They'd gone back later in the day, and Ariana couldn't believe her eyes. The fence had been repaired, and Farmer McNatt had a hand on Larkin's shoulder. Larkin said something, and the man tipped his head back and laughed.

He'd laughed! Farmer McNatt!

After that, every time they'd gone by Farmer McNatt's, Ariana had a tight ball of fear in her belly, but Larkin's arms swung easily by his side, and he'd call out a greeting to the farmer, who always waved back. Occasionally, the old man would reach deep into a pocket and pull out three apples, which he'd toss over the fence to Larkin, Ariana, and Noll.

Ariana had felt guilty for several weeks. Then guilt gave way to shame that she'd never told Farmer McNatt that she and Noll had been involved in damaging his fence. She knew that Larkin hadn't told on them, but she'd wake up suddenly at night, heart pounding, dreaming that she'd been found out. During the day, she'd tried to avoid walking down his lane whenever possible. Finally, she couldn't take it any longer and she confessed to Farmer McNatt.

He'd squinted down at her. "I know, child," he'd said. "Larkin wouldn't tell me who else was involved, but it wasn't too hard to figure out." Her conscience had felt better after that, and she wasn't sure why she hadn't handled it the way Larkin had in the first place.

But that was Larkin. He always did the right thing and make the right choices.

Until now.

Her thoughts were interrupted by the sound of someone crashing through the underbrush.

She sprang up. "Larkin?" she said.

"No," Noll responded as he came huffing and puffing into view. "You didn't find him, huh?"

Ariana shook her head.

"Me either," came Gurn's voice from behind them.

Ariana whirled around to see the Nisser, his small shoulders slumped. Ariana's insides felt like a hollow log. This couldn't be happening. Not to Larkin. She looked at Noll. He stared into the fire with unseeing eyes. Gurn slung his pack down to the ground and offered everyone something to eat.

No one was hungry.

Not even Gurn.

They spent a restless night wrestling with grief and guilt. She knew that Larkin had been disappointed about not waking up with a special power on his birthday. She had tried to tell him he was special, but she saw the wounded look in his eyes.

She let out a deep, shuddering sigh. Here she was, with her fierce desire to protect, and her wondrous eyesight. There was Noll, with his enormous size and strength. But what did those things matter?

Where had her own powers gotten her? They hadn't helped her today.

Ariana had never quite realized just how much she and Noll depended upon Larkin until now. When decisions or plans had to be made, it was Larkin who made them. It was his idea to cut through The Forest to begin with. She and Noll had just followed along, like they always did.

Ariana was sure she'd able to sleep with all the thoughts that tumbled through her mind, but she must have, because Gurn's gentle shake of her shoulder woke her up.

All energy had been drained out of her. Noll rubbed his eyes and sat up. He looked stunned. Even Gurn's feet dragged as he packed for the day ahead.

The three of them picked at their breakfast before finally giving up and breaking camp. They walked single file along the river. In a few hours, they passed the spot where Larkin and Scrofa had plunged into the river. They said nothing. Noll saw

Larkin's sword lying on the top of the bank. He picked it up and tied it onto his waist.

They walked for a while longer in silence before they came upon two decaying posts jutting out of The Forest floor. Ariana looked to her left, across the river to the far bank. She could see rotted logs and two more posts sticking out of the ground on that side of the river as well.

The bridge Gurn had hoped to find was gone.

Ariana's hands went to her hips. She stared down at the posts. Noll let out a yell and kicked at one of them. A piece of wood flew off and sailed into the underbrush. If they'd known this bridge wouldn't be here, maybe they'd have veered further north, looking for a place to ford. Maybe they wouldn't have encountered Scrofa.

Maybe Larkin would still be with them.

Ariana shifted the weight of her pack, turned away, and began walking.

The land flattened out and the river became wider and slower as they continued to move north. With the sun creeping toward the horizon, Gurn stopped.

"This will do," he announced. He pointed toward the river. "It's still pretty fast here, but you should be able to wade across it. Hold your packs above your head so your food doesn't get wet."

Ariana stared at him.

"Aren't you coming with us?"

He shook his head.

"I'm not sure I'd survive over there. Men on that side of The Forest haven't believed in the Nisser for centuries. I'm feeling a little weak now, to tell you the truth. I've stuffed enough berries and wild carrots and parsnips and dried rabbit in your bags to hold you over until you get to Rockhaven."

He looked at them sadly.

"I'll have to owe you a favor. I'm sorry, but I can't go with you when you cross the river."

Ariana was stunned. They'd come to rely upon Gurn and needed him now more than ever.

Suddenly, the magnitude of what they were trying to do descended upon her. She sucked in air, but it didn't seem to fill her lungs.

She and Noll, alone in The Forest? With the Hudenpole, and the Wolves, and The Scourge, and who knew what else? And everyone in Kavenland relying upon them?

She remembered when they'd first met Gurn. She remembered the look on Larkin's face when the Nisser said they'd never be able to make it across The Forest. He'd been shaking his head before Gurn had finished talking. Larkin's expression was one of sheer determination. Ariana knew right then that if Larkin was leading them, they'd make it to Rockhaven.

But now Larkin was gone.

Ariana looked down at Gurn. The Nisser was staring at the ground. When he looked back up, his eyes were wet, and his lips trembled.

"Do you remember how I told you the Nisser are fading away, and we don't know why?" he asked. His voice was choked and raspy. "And Larkin asked who I lost?"

Ariana nodded slowly.

Gurn tried to speak, but he couldn't. He cleared his throat and looked off in the distance. Finally, he composed himself and looked back at Ariana and Noll.

"It was my wife," he said. "She grew ill, and she was bedridden, and one day, she just vanished."

Ariana felt a clutch in her throat, and she laid a hand on Gurn's small shoulder.

"That's awful," she said. "I'm sorry."

Gurn shook his head. "I didn't tell you because I wanted you to feel sorry for me. I told you because I know what you're feeling right now. And I want you to know how sorry I am that I can't come with you to share your burden."

Ariana felt the same. What had seemed a few days ago to be a thrilling adventure now seemed like a grim task. She and Noll would have to find a way to finish their quest, but even if they did—even if they could help to save Kavenland—it would feel empty with the loss of Larkin.

She felt a great reluctance as she and Noll said their good-byes. Soon, the two of them would be on their own. She watched as Noll gently placed a large hand on Gurn's shoulder. She bent down to give the Nisser a hug. As she straightened up, she saw a tear running down his cheek.

"Got something in my eye," he muttered. Ariana wasn't sure if he was sad about his wife, sad about Larkin, or just sad to be leaving them.

She and Noll waded into the current. Behind her, she heard Gurn call out.

"I'll keep an eye out for Larkin!" he shouted. "I haven't given up hope!"

Ariana nodded and turned back to face the far bank. After a few more steps, she heard the Nisser's voice again.

"Ariana!"

She turned. Gurn was standing just outside the canopy of trees.

"You're going to make it!" he said. "I believe in you!"

Ariana felt a small ray of sunshine pierce the shadow of sorrow that had descended upon her.

"Thank you!" she called back. Gurn waved in return.

Ariana and Noll sloshed across the river, careful to keep their packs dry, and clambered out of the water onto the far shore. They turned around. Gurn was gone.

She stared, unblinking, at the emptiness around them.

Noll spoke first.

"South and west, I guess."

She looked up and spotted a narrow path leading in the direction they were headed. She began to point to it, but she realized that Noll had seen it, too.

"Wow! Is that Gurn rubbing off on us or would we have seen that anyway?" he asked.

Ariana suddenly felt uneasy. The path was there, leading exactly where they wanted to go. But all the same, she got a tingling feeling in the nape of her neck.

"I can't put a finger on it," she said, "but I don't like it."

Noll looked at her, then gestured with both arms all around them.

"I don't like any of it," he answered. "I couldn't have imagined being in The Forest for ten seconds a week ago, much less for days and days. Larkin's gone. We're on the side of the river with The Scourge, and the Hudenpole, and the Wolves. and that's a path, and it's going where we're going, and if it gets us out of the woods and into Rockhaven five minutes earlier, I'm all for it."

She nodded reluctantly.

The two struck out along the path. A pricker bush grabbed at her and ripped off a small piece of her shirt, but other than that, the path was straight and wide enough to allow them to move quickly. They were heading more south than west, with the sun directly off her right shoulder, but as long as they were moving at this speed, that was okay. A path veered off to the north, but they clearly didn't want to go that way and so they kept on walking. A half hour later, with the sun sinking ahead of them, Ariana saw something fluttering a few feet off the ground on the left side of the path. She grabbed Noll's arm, pointed, and walked up to it slowly.

"Why, it's just a piece of cloth," she thought, but then stopped up short. It wasn't "just" a piece of cloth. It was the same piece of cloth that had been ripped off her shirt a while ago.

But that was impossible. That would have meant that they'd come in a circle, and they hadn't. They'd been going straight ahead. The sun had stayed in the same place, off her right shoulder, the whole time. She began to feel goosebumps running up her arms.

Ariana explained what had happened to Noll. His face turned white.

"I don't like this," he croaked. "I don't like this at all. Let's get off the trail."

Ariana agreed. "Let's veer a little to the right. That's due west. We'll at least be heading in the exact right direction."

They thrashed through the underbrush, keeping the waning sun directly ahead of them. After 15 minutes, they came upon another trail.

"Should we take this one?" asked Noll.

"It's heading north and west," Ariana answered. "It's not too far out of the way, and it angles away from that other path. Let's try it."

They moved down the trail. A few minutes later, Noll stopped up short. Ariana almost ran into him. He pointed a few feet ahead of him. Ariana followed his gaze. There, hanging from a bush on the left-hand side of the path, was the piece of cloth from Ariana's shirt.

"It can't be," she said in a hoarse whisper.

The hair stood up on her neck and arms. She felt as if she'd been dropped into the middle of a ghost story.

"There was a trail a little way up that led to the right," Noll said. "I know that's due north, but let's take it, and get off this trail, and find a place to rest for the night. We'll figure this out in the morning."

Ariana nodded. It was pitch dark by the time they found the path to the right.

"Let's just go a little way down and we'll find somewhere to sleep," Noll said.

They stumbled on blindly until they came across something solid that stopped them in their tracks. They couldn't see it, but it appeared to be a wall made of branches and vines.

"Why don't you go a few steps that way, and I'll go this way," Ariana suggested. "Let's see if we can get around this thing."

Noll agreed, and Ariana began working her way to the left, feeling her way along the wall. Suddenly, she realized that she couldn't move her hands. Then she couldn't move her legs.

"Noll!" she warned, at the same time he yelled out, "Ariana!"

"I'm stuck! I can't move!" Ariana said. She felt herself being lifted and spun slowly so that her back was to the wall. The more she tried to struggle, the tighter the vines bound her.

She was helpless.

"Are you ok?" Noll asked from a few feet away.

She started to answer, then she stopped.

Was she ok?

Everything she'd been fighting to keep out of her thoughts came flooding in now.

Larkin was gone.

She and Noll were stuck.

She'd failed to protect either of her friends.

Her country was in danger. She was separated from her family. Her village and her home had been burned to the ground.

Now, thanks to her failures, she and Noll could do nothing about any of it. All of Ariana's emotions rushed forth from her stomach like a hurricane, and she screamed in frustration.

Her voice was swallowed up in the immensity of The Forest. The night grew quiet, but only for a moment.

"Save your strength," a voice said from the darkness. "You're going to need it."

Chapter Eleven
Em—The Forest

A low growl from Canis woke Em up.

"Who's coming?" Em asked. She looked around. She must have nodded off by the fire. It was out now, and it was pitch dark. She saw no sign of Vic. She swung into a sitting position and winced. Her foot throbbed with its own painful pulse. But what Canis said next made her forget all about her foot.

"Hudenpole?" she hissed. "Are you sure?"

Canis whimpered.

"Go," she told him. "I can't stand up to run or fight. There's no reason for you to stay here."

Canis danced in front of her.

"I know," Em said. "I know you don't want to leave me. But we wouldn't have made it this far without you. Go. Maybe we'll see each other again."

Canis wagged his tail, slopped a wet tongue across Em's cheek, and bolted off.

Em sat and waited. She didn't have to wait long. She felt a presence around her before she saw anything.

"Child," a voice said. "You must come with us."

The voice was deep. Em remembered seeing fireworks displays back in Pittsburgh and how some of the big boomers rumbled in her chest. This voice felt like that. It wasn't friendly or unfriendly. But it also didn't leave any room for argument.

A large shape shimmered toward her. It was very tall and very thin. It held something in its hand.

"I am sorry, child," the being said. "But you must wear this."

Before Em could react, a sack dropped over her head.

She was a captive of the dreaded Hudenpole.

Em had one hope. Vic was very quick and incredibly quiet. She fervently hoped he'd avoided the Hudenpole. If he had, maybe he could somehow follow her. Maybe Canis would find Vic and they could somehow rescue her.

Vic would do all he could, Em was sure of that. He'd proven that these past few days. That was the stubborn part of Vic that was good. She wished he was like that all the time. Maybe kids would like him if he was. Maybe they'd be able to see past his threadbare clothes and his cocky demeanor if he let them see that side of him. But he never did. That was the stubborn side of Vic that was bad. He acted like being bullied and ridiculed didn't bother him.

Em knew better.

Her heart wrenched, and then it gave another twist as her mind flashed back to scenes of Vic trying to protect her from their parents. Her mom and dad hurled cruel words fueled by alcohol, and Vic stood in front of Em, arms stretched wide as if that could stop their anger from filtering through. The first time, the words stung beyond any physical pain she'd ever felt. By the fifth time, and the tenth, and the twentieth, the sharp pain became more of a constant ache, like standing too long in freezing weather in a t-shirt and shorts.

Em had turned to cats and dogs. Vic still hoped for acceptance from other kids.

It hadn't turned out well for him.

His air of cool indifference might convince some kids, but Em could see the deep pit of sorrow behind his eyes.

Em and Vic had gone to a traveling carnival once, and they had entered a fun house. She remembered seeing different versions of Vic in the mirrors—some clear, some close, some distorted, some far away. It was funny then. Now, though, Vic seemed further away and more distorted than ever. She thought that was the way he saw himself, too. If Vic didn't change, the close and clear Vic, the Vic she knew, might be gone forever.

She felt a cool trickle of sweat on her forehead underneath the hot and stuffy hood. She needed the good Vic now. If Canis was right about the Hudenpole, she was in big trouble.

Em felt herself being lifted off the ground and slung over a shoulder. As soon as the Hudenpole began to move, Em's heart sank. It felt like they moved at an incredible speed. She wasn't sure even Vic or Canis could keep up this pace.

That surprised Em, but it surprised her less than the smoothness of the ride. Vic had tossed her onto his back the past few days, and riding that way was at times bumpy and uncomfortable, even with Vic's light footfalls. This was like riding along on the currents of a wind.

But that was small consolation. Em was in the hands of the Hudenpole. According to Canis, the Hudenpole hated all people. And despite what some of the mean kids at school said about her because of her love of animals, Em wasn't an animal. She was a person.

As she glided along on the shoulder of the Hudenpole, Em thought again about Adelessa, and how the mysterious woman had brought them to this world. Why, if it were only for Em to be captured by the Hudenpole?

She'd seemed to have had a plan for Em and Vic. It seemed straightforward. If they did what they wanted, she'd let them go back home.

Em didn't care about going back home as much as Vic did. As long as they were together, she didn't care where it was or what world it was in. Either way, though, Adelessa hadn't done anything to help them once she'd shoved them out of the Door in the Stone and into Laketown.

There was a lot to think about with Adelessa. For one thing, she was a beautiful woman, even though Vic said she was ugly.

Em realized that so much had happened so fast that she'd forgotten about that. Why had Vic thought she was ugly?

She might never know the answer to that question.

Em still couldn't remember what Adelessa had shown her that convinced Em to come to this world. Whatever it was had filled her heart and soul with so much joy that it had almost hurt. She'd shown something to Vic, too, but it hadn't convinced him to follow her. They'd finally decided to come when Adelessa threatened to separate them. They'd followed her through the Door in the Stone so that wouldn't happen. But now, she and Vic were separated in this world.

In their world, being separated meant living with foster parents. In this world, it meant being captured by the Hudenpole.

After what seemed like hours, the journey ended, and the hood was whisked off her head.

"Wait here," the deep voice of the Hudenpole commanded.

Now that the hood was off, Em blinked and tried to focus her eyes. She was in a large clearing, with a fire in the middle that was waning. The sky was still dark, but it was getting close to dawn. Before she was fully aware of her surroundings, someone ran up and hugged her.

"Em!" whispered Vic.

"Vic," she whispered back. There was something about their situation that made her want to keep her voice down. "I was hoping that you'd gotten away."

"I was thinking the same thing about you," he said. "I was just about to steal some food from those guys that were chasing us when the Hudenpole grabbed me and threw a sack over my head." He glanced around and leaned toward her. "I don't think those guys who were chasing us are alive anymore," he said. He shuddered. "They were pretty foul," he added. "I overheard their plans for us. They weren't very pleasant."

Vic glanced around then looked back at Em.

"The Hudenpole and this place give me the creeps," he said. "But what's that old proverb? 'The enemy of my enemy is my friend'? Maybe taking care of those guys chasing us means the Hudenpole are our friends."

Despite the dire conditions, and the pain in her foot, Em smiled. Quoting some ancient proverb was typical of her brother.

Vic was smart, but he purposely did poorly at school. Em thought it was another of his sad attempts to fit in. Vic didn't want another reason to feel like an outcast, but Em thought that was silly. Being smart was nothing to be ashamed of.

Vic nudged her and pointed up. She squinted and saw faint lights suspended in the air. As her eyes adjusted to the dark, she realized that the lights were candles, and that they were beginning to go out.

"Look," Vic said. He pointed up. "There, in the first 'v' of that big elm tree. Do you see?"

Em squinted, then opened her eyes wide. No doubt about it. There was a house in the trees. She gazed right and left.

"There's another!" she said. "In that oak!"

"And another in that maple!" Vic exclaimed. "If I hadn't known they were there, I would have walked right through this clearing and never noticed a thing."

"We would have noticed you, though," said a sonorous voice directly behind them.

Em jolted so fast that she was sure she could have set the world's high jump record. How did these Hudenpole keep sneaking up on them? They might even be quieter than Vic.

"We move about at night, and rest during the day," the voice informed them. "I know that's not your habit, but it's nearly dawn now, and you're tired. Sleep. You're safe here, for now."

Em and Vic were handed blankets, and they laid down next to the fire. Em thought that being a captive of the Hudenpole, being so hungry that she thought about eating her blanket, and the throbbing in her foot would make it impossible for her to sleep.

She was wrong.

It was well past the middle of the day when she awoke. She groggily rubbed the sandy residue of sleep from the corners of her eyes. Her head felt like it was stuffed with wool.

Then she sat bolt upright.

Last night hadn't been a dream. She looked around wildly and saw the fire pit and the clearing. Vic was still asleep a few feet away. She exhaled slowly and tried to think of what to do. She gently shook her brother.

"Vic" she hissed.

Vic shook his head. He pivoted up to a sitting position. Em watched his eyes. She could see in them the same thought process she'd just gone through.

"Em," he said, in an urgent, hushed tone. "Let's go. Climb on my back, and we'll make a run for it."

She shook her head. "How far would you get? You haven't eaten in two days." Vic started to object, but she raised her hand. "I know what you did," she said. "I know you gave me your last ration."

"You needed it more than I did," he answered.

She nodded her head. "That might be true, but you can't go on like this, not with me holding you back." She swung her arm around. Beyond their small clearing was nothing but The Forest. "If you can get to the edge of the clearing, maybe you can get away. You're fast and resourceful. Maybe you could find some berries or something to keep you alive until you can get back to the Great Road. From there, you can get to a village…"

Her voice trailed off when she gazed into her brother's eyes. He would never admit it, but the look Em saw there was fear. Not fear of the Hudenpole. Not fear of The Forest.

It was the fear of not having Em with him.

Vic was her older brother. She looked up to him and loved him, and she knew that he felt protective of her. But she'd also come to realize something that she wasn't sure Vic had understood until right now.

Em loved being in the company of dogs and cats. They were like friends to her.

But Em was all that Vic had.

He shook his head. "I'd never leave you all alone," he said. He seemed to examine the words he'd just said, as if he could see them hanging in the air. Em saw his eyes harden. "I think that we need to stay here and see what happens," he said.

"Ok," Em answered.

Vic jumped up, all business now, and back in charge. Despite their problems, Em had to bite back a smile.

"Let's get a look at that foot," he said. He knelt beside her and untied the makeshift bandage he'd put there. He let out a choking gasp.

"That looks very serious," a voice said. Em lurched like she'd grabbed an electric fence. Vic leapt up, made a squeaking noise, and scuttled away like a crab.

"My name is Lyster," the voice said. Em saw something that shimmered in the air above her.

"Ah, let me try this," the voice said. Em saw a movement and then a hood fell back, and a cloak opened. Em had her first look at a Hudenpole.

Lyster was tall—as tall, it seemed to Em, as the silver-haired men she'd seen in the invasion of Laketown, though he was much more slender. But what really was unusual about him was his grayness. His skin was gray. His hair was gray—not gray like an old person, but gray as if that was its natural color. His clothes were gray. Even his demeanor seemed gray. He looked wise and grave and honest and—well—gray.

"We have brought you to our home," Lyster said. "This clearing is where we make our important decisions. We don't know quite what to do with you. It's been hundreds of years since we've had any interactions with humans. The last interactions did not go well. Did you not know this?"

Vic and Em stole a glance at each other. This didn't seem the time, Em thought, to volunteer that they were from another world and that their knowledge of this world had been learned from a dog.

"Hmm," Lyster said. He arched his eyebrows. Em felt sure that the Hudenpole knew that she and Vic were holding something back. "Very well," he said. "Please come with me."

Em stood up, took one step, cried out, and collapsed back onto the ground, gasping for breath.

Lyster bent down to examine her. "Your foot is bad, child, even worse than I feared," he said.

"Please, Mr. Lyster," Vic said. He licked his lips as if summoning the strength to address the Hudenpole. "We haven't eaten in two days. We had to split our rations with Canis..."

"Canis?" the Hudenpole interrupted.

"He's a dog," Em said through clenched teeth. Every beat of her heart sent a pulse of hot pain to her foot. "He's the one who told us to come into The Forest to get away from the attack on Laketown."

Em put a hand over her mouth. She hadn't meant to say that about Canis, but she found it hard to think with the pain in her foot and the angry gnawing of her empty stomach.

The Hudenpole's reaction surprised her.

"The dog told you to come into The Forest?" he said.

Em nodded.

"That is most curious," Lyster said. "And someone has attacked Laketown," he mused, more to himself than to Vic and Em. He looked back at them.

"Stay here," he commanded. "Your foot must be attended to immediately," he said, "and I will be back with food."

While they waited, they saw several of the Hudenpole glide through the clearing. Some had fish from the river slung over their shoulders, some had baskets filled with berries, and others carried firewood.

"I don't see any children," Vic whispered. Em realized it was true. She hadn't heard any babies crying or seen any children playing. Maybe that was part of why everything seemed so somber.

Darkness began to fall, and as it did, the candles began to flicker in the trees. It was like seeing stars come out at night, Em thought. First there were one or two, then a few more, and before you knew it, they were everywhere. Em saw shimmering shapes moving through the trees and climbing down the ladders.

Occasionally one of them threw back his or her cloak and became clearly visible.

Em thought about what Canis had told them. There were some who believed that the trees were controlled by the Hudenpole and would do their bidding. She felt a slow trickle of sweat roll down between her shoulder blades. There were trees everywhere, and they seemed to have grown taller as it got darker. Em could swear they were leaning toward her as well.

Lyster reappeared, carrying a small sack, a cup of water, and a pestle. He knelt beside Em, took a dry mixture from the bag, shook some into the water, and ground it into a paste with the pestle. As he applied the mixture, Em felt a white pain like a lightning bolt hurtle up her leg and into her brain. Her eyes throbbed and her foot jerked in pain, but she willed herself to be still.

Vic spoke up.

"Mr. Lyster," he stammered, "we've heard that the Hudenpole control the trees." His Adam's apple bobbed up and down. It looked like an egg on a string. "Is that true?"

One of the edges of Lyster's lip quivered for just a moment. It seemed to Em as if that was the Hudenpole's version of a laugh.

"We cannot control the trees," he said. "We could sooner lasso the wind or grapple with a sunbeam than control the trees. They are older than even the Hudenpole. No one controls them."

He stopped applying the paste. He looked at Em.

"You're a strong one," Lyster said. "That's good. That will help the healing process. Can you stand?"

Em raised an eyebrow. Already? No medicine moved that quickly. Vic gave her his hand, and she pulled herself up. She slowly put weight on the injured foot. She expected to feel the biting pain again, but it was almost completely gone.

"I can walk," she said. She could hear the note of wonder in her own voice.

"Come with me," Lyster said. "You will eat with the Hudenpole." They followed him to a long, low table set at the edge of the clearing. Other Hudenpole were already seated around it on the ground, and they ate from heaping plates of fish, bread, berries, and vegetables.

Em hadn't noticed much noise from the table as they approached, but what chatter there had been died to nothing as they sat down. Some of the Hudenpole nodded at them, and some regarded them with open hostility. Em's skin crawled, then stood-up, and then ran up and down her spine.

Lyster sat between them. He beckoned them to lean toward him.

"Remember what I told you about our last interaction with humans not going well?" he said. "Well, there are some like me who would like to try again."

"And the others?" Vic asked.

Lyster sat silent for a moment. Pinpricks leapt out on Em's scalp when he finally answered.

"I would advise you to enjoy your meal," he said. "It might very well be your last."

Chapter Twelve
Larkin—The Forest

Larkin awoke naked and shivering underneath a pile of leaves. His first thought was that he was alive. He couldn't believe it. The rocks had pounded him, and the river had sapped his strength, but he'd somehow survived.

He'd known the Flumyn's current was swift, but once he was in it, he realized that it was far more powerful than it appeared to be from the shore. He didn't see the giant boar again, but he hadn't exactly been looking for it, either.

He'd banged off rocks and been pulled down by eddies. His rucksack had dragged him down and he hadn't been able to shake it loose. He'd been lucky that his sword had come off somewhere. He'd plunged over a waterfall and been swept way downstream before he finally dragged himself to shore. At least, he thought wryly, he'd been able to get across the river.

Larkin's second thought was that he smelled something burning. He had no idea what it could be. He crept out from his little cave shelter to investigate.

A woman crouched over a small fire. He saw that his clothes hung on makeshift drying racks fashioned from branches. He rubbed his eyes, then suddenly remembered that he was naked. He scrambled back as far as he could into the stone enclosure.

"Who...who are you?" he called out.

"Why, I'm surprised," the woman answered in a silvery voice. "We met at your house such a short time ago."

He didn't recognize the woman, but he did recognize her voice. He peered around the corner.

"Adelessa?"

She smiled.

"I take it you can see me clearly now. I must ask you a question—do you find me pleasing or displeasing to look at?"

Larkin wasn't sure how to answer that. He didn't really think of her as either. He risked another peek around the corner.

She was very plain, he thought, but he wanted to be polite.

"Uh..." he said.

"Hmm," she answered. She tossed his clothes back to him. "Interesting."

Larkin snatched the clothes and retreated into the small cave. He quickly pulled his clothes on and came back out. He looked at her again. Ariana and Noll had described her as beautiful. He didn't see it himself.

"I don't have much time," Adelessa told him. "I'm cutting south now toward Glensworth to warn King Tenney of the invasion. But why are you way down here, and where are the others?"

Larkin quickly explained all that had happened. He told her about meeting Gurn and their encounter with Scrofa. He thought carefully about his next words.

What happened with the boar had been an accident, of course. He'd tried to save his friends. He HAD saved his friends. In fact, he'd nearly been drowned in the river, while his friends were safe and sound because of him. His chest welled up, but he tried not to let his pride show in his words.

"I almost made it," he said modestly, as he told her of his exploits. "If I'd just jumped a moment earlier..."

She tucked her chin down and looked at him through raised eyebrows. Larkin saw judgement in her eyes that held a verdict he didn't like. When he spoke, his words sounded defensive.

"What?" he said. "At least I acted bravely. At least I acted with honor."

"Honor?" Adelessa asked in a quiet voice. Larkin could hear nothing else but that voice. He couldn't hear the river, or leaves rustling, or birds singing—just Adelessa. "Honor for whom? For yourself?"

"What do you mean?"

"How do you think your friends feel when you always act 'with honor'? Doesn't their honor count? Are they also capable of acting with honor, or is it only you?"

Larkin opened his mouth to answer but slammed it shut just as quickly. He'd never thought about it that way.

"You thought you were being selfless," Adelessa continued, "but weren't you really being selfish?"

Larkin felt as if he'd been slapped. Anger rolled up his throat like a volcano. No one had ever called him selfish in his life.

"Don't you see," Adelessa said in a softer voice. "Your friends need you to lead them, and Kavenland needs you to get to Rockhaven. There is much more at stake than your honor."

The truth of what Adelessa said pushed the red ire back down inside him. He was quiet for a long time before he answered.

"You're right," he admitted, though the words tasted sour and stale in his mouth. "I'm separated from my friends because I wanted to prove to them that I was special, too." Larkin felt as if the beast in his belly had devoured all his insides so that his stomach felt like an empty box filled with angry tornadoes.

"Have your friends been treating you any differently lately?" Adelessa asked.

All the silly suspicions that Larkin had harbored about Ariana and Noll mocking him or ganging up on him over the last few days melted away. Larkin looked down at the ground and shook his head.

"Look at me," Adelessa said. Larkin reluctantly raised his eyes to hers. "Jealousy is a terrible emotion. It's even worse when it's something you feel toward your friends, and worse still when they've done nothing to make you feel that way. Jealousy is an emotion that you create, and which you must master, or it will consume you."

Larkin froze. That was exactly what it felt like his jealousy had been doing—consuming him. Still, the beast wouldn't give up.

"But they're superheroes," he complained, "and all I have is...is..."

"Is what, dear?"

Larkin expulsed a long breath of air. What he said next came out so grudgingly that the words almost hurt his teeth when he spoke.

"I smell things," he said. "Emotions."

Adelessa tapped her finger on her lips. She looked out beyond Larkin's shoulder.

"Hmm," she said. "Not what I expected. Not at all. But I can see the possibilities." She nodded her head "In fact, I'm sure of it."

She beamed at him.

"You've been given a great gift," she said.

"A great gift?" he asked incredulously. "Don't you mean a lame one?"

She shook her head. "Your gift is one that should set you on the path to wisdom if you'll let it."

"You mean like the wisdom to not leave a plate out for the Nisser?" Larkin sputtered. "The wisdom to separate myself from my friends and nearly drown in the river? The wisdom to put our mission to save Kavenland in danger because I wanted to be a hero?"

She smiled as he spoke, but then the smile slowly receded, and her mouth became tight. Larkin thought he could see a look of pain flicker in her eyes before she answered.

"The road to wisdom can be long and cruel. Along the way are many failures and disappointments. But the rewards are knowledge, insight, and truth.

"You've already learned one lesson and that's this—you don't have to try to be a hero. Everyone has strengths and weaknesses. If you can understand what yours are and understand the strengths and weaknesses of those around you, then together you can accomplish much more than you could ever accomplish alone. That is what leaders do and what their value is. You have good friends, and they look to you for guidance. With them, you can be very, very strong."

"You mean they can be strong while I sniff things with my super schnozz," he blurted out.

"Every child dreams of being a hero," Adelessa said, more to herself than to Larkin. She let out a long sigh. "I'm afraid you don't have that luxury anymore."

Adelessa was quiet for a moment, then she pulled an emerald pendant from inside the folds of her garments.

"Come here," she said quietly. Larkin stepped toward her. She began to pull the chain with the pendant over her head. Larkin could see a scar that circled her neck where the pendant had lain.

"I've never allowed anyone to put this on," she said. "I want you to see what the world of wisdom can look like. I'll give it to you to wear, but only for a moment. I can't survive long without it."

She slipped it over his head, and his eyes opened as a flash of pain seared his neck and throat. But as he reached to take the necklace off, he noticed that all the colors around him were brighter than any he'd ever seen. His hands fell to his side. He looked at Adelessa. She was so beautiful that it almost took his breath away. He continued to look around him. The richness of colors amazed him. The trees, the leaves, even the stones seemed to glow. He had an overwhelming sense of joy that made him feel like he'd never truly known joy before. He looked back at Adelessa, and concern grew on her face. She reached out her arms to him, and he understood. Reluctantly, he took the chain and pendant up over his head, and when it came free, he was shocked at Adelessa's appearance. She suddenly looked old and withered. He quickly slipped the necklace back over her head, and she reeled backwards a step. She hunched over, and then slowly began to stand back up straight. The years melted away, and the old woman became a young woman again.

"Well," she gasped. "That was worse than I thought it would be."

Larkin rubbed his neck. "The pendant burned me when I put it on," he said. "I almost took it off."

"It does that to remind you that the quest for knowledge can be painful. If someone of impure motives put it on, it would destroy them." She smiled. "I knew that wouldn't happen to you.

"The pendant teaches us that many things have beauty," she continued, "regardless of how they appear on the outside. Have you heard the expression that 'beauty is in the eye of the beholder?'"

"Yes."

"Well, that is what the pendant shows, and I am an extension of the pendant. If you're willing to look beyond the surface and see the beauty that's hidden inside so many things and so many people, then you will see beauty properly when you wear the pendant. That's the essence of knowledge—insight and truth."

Larkin chewed the inside of his cheek. "So are you saying we see you as we see the world? Or do we see you the way we see ourselves?"

She pursed her lips. "I think it is some of each. And the fact that your friends have seen me as beautiful means to me that there is still hope in this world. I think, as you grow, that you will come to see me as beautiful, too."

Larkin felt his face flush. He hadn't fooled her when she'd first asked him how he saw her. In truth, though, Larkin did see something more attractive about Adelessa already.

But what could Larkin and his friends do, he wondered? It was too bad for Kavenland that Beredor and Galeran and the rest of the Protectors weren't alive to fight this invasion.

"My uncle says that men were better in the old times," he said. "Is that true? I heard him say it to you right before we left."

"Better?" Adelessa said, frowning. "I think I'd be a good judge of that, and I wouldn't say they were better. People generally think that they had it tougher when they were growing up and that that makes them better. But they just have different problems than those who come after them. And besides," she added, "we're at war now, and you can't blame that on the younger generation.

"I believe that people are just as good and just as bad now as they've ever been," she continued. "That means that you're just as well-equipped to defeat this invasion now as those of past generations would have been. That's what I told your uncle."

Larkin clenched his teeth as he thought back to the army that had burned his village to the ground. He thought back to the enormous old man who'd wiped out the tanner and his sons.

"But how can we defeat someone like Kynwas?" he asked Adelessa.

Her eyes widened and her knees buckled as she staggered back a step.

"What did you just say?" she gasped.

Larkin registered the shocked look on her face. "You didn't know he was part of this, but you know who he is, don't you?" he asked.

She nodded once and cleared her throat.

"Yes," she said. "I know Kynwas. I can't believe he's still alive." She let out a long breath. Larkin realized he was holding his. Adelessa went so long without talking that Larkin thought she wasn't going to add anything else, but she finally spoke.

"Kynwas is from Kavenland," she said. "He lived here over a thousand years ago. He was the forbidden son of two gods. Sendina banished him, but he left Kavenland with Tyndella, the most beautiful woman this country has ever seen."

She exhaled a long, shaky breath before continuing.

"Kynwas swore revenge upon Kavenland before he left. He and Tyndella rode east across the vast wasteland. When Sendina heard that Tyndella had left with Kynwas, she sat down at the edge of Kavenland and cried for forty years. Her great, salty tears formed the eastern sea."

"And now he's back?" Larkin asked. "At the head of any army?"

"Yes, although some things happened in between that are important. Sendina left Kavenland, but not before she appointed a group of half-gods to look after her country."

"The Protectors," Larkin stated.

Adelessa nodded. "You've heard of some of their exploits, and some of them were good for Kavenland. But then Beredor got bored. He convinced the other Protectors to sail east in search of adventure. They loaded their ships with chests of silver and gold and cedar seeds. They thought they might use them to barter with if they were to come upon other countries on their journey."

"Did they?"

Adelessa shook her head. "They reached the end of the world, and there they were decimated by the Stone Giants."

"So that's what happened to them?" Larkin asked.

"Well, a few managed to escape to their ships. They came upon the Archipelago on their way back to Kavenland. Kynwas welcomed them as guests. But what he really wanted was the chests of cedar seeds from the trees used to build their great ships. The Archipelago has nothing but scrubby trees that are not adequate for true ship building. Then Kynwas killed the remaining Protectors, who were too weakened from their battle with the Stone Giants to put up much of a fight."

"So," Larkin said slowly, "he's used the years since to grow the cedar trees and build up a fleet."

"Very shrewd," Adelessa said. "Yes, that's what I think has happened. The silver-haired men are the sons of Kynwas and Tyndella."

"What happened to Tyndella?" Larkin asked.

Great pools of liquid formed in Adelessa's eyes.

"She died many years ago," she said. She wiped a sleeve across her eyes. "But her sons present the greatest threat that Kavenland has ever known. And with Kynwas still alive it's even worse than I feared. I must get to Glensworth to warn King Tenney. And you must get to Rockhaven." She gripped his arm with more strength than Larkin thought she could possess. "You must not fail," she said.

Larkin's head swirled with these new facts. "But if all the Protectors were killed by Kynwas, how did you learn of their fate?" he asked.

The look of grim determination left Adelessa's face and was replaced by a small smile. "That is a very astute question," she said. Her smile widened. "You were truly born to tread the path to wisdom. The reason I know is that one ship escaped from the Archipelago and returned to Kavenland."

She handed him a small sack with food inside.

"This should last you several days." She paused for a moment.

"There's one more thing. There are two others like you and your friends. They are part of a prophecy Sendina told me before she left Kavenland. Find them. I believe they'll help you if you can win their trust. Good luck, Larkin. I hope to see you soon."

She turned to go.

"Wait!" Larkin cried out. "Who are these two others? How can I find them?"

Adelessa pursed her lips. She gave a curt shake of her head. "Prophecies are dangerous things," she said. "I've already done what I can. I don't dare say or do more. It must be left up to you now."

"Please," Larkin said desperately. "One more question. About something else."

She tilted her head to one side and gave the briefest of nods.

"I overheard you talking with my uncle about something else. There was something said about my parents and the Hill People. I know they killed my mother and my father when I was young. What do the Hill People have to do with what's happening?"

Adelessa's smile ran away as she looked Larkin squarely in the face. "What's befallen the Hill People is one of the most misunderstood stories of Kavenland. Do you know their history?"

Larkin shook his head. All he'd learned about the Hill People in school, and all he'd ever heard about them from the grown-ups back in Fieldstone, was that they were lazy, untrustworthy, and bad.

"They aren't from Kavenland originally," Adelessa said. Her voice was quiet, but it throbbed with emotion. "They were caught up in the war in which the Southern Isles tried to invade Kavenland."

"The war the Protectors won," Larkin said.

"Yes," Adelessa answered. "The Hill People lived on an island between Kavenland and the Southern Isles. Their homeland was destroyed in the war. They had nowhere to go. They set sail and landed here. They settled by the sea, hoping for a new life, but the people of Kavenland never accepted them. They'd been at least partially responsible for the misery the Hill People had suffered, but they turned their backs on the Hill People because they looked a little different and acted a little differently than they did. They've always treated them badly, kept them down, and never given them a chance to fit in. Both people are the poorer for it, though the Hill People have had the worst of it."

This wasn't what Larkin expected to hear.

"Do you remember your uncle saying it was I who sent him to Portsmouth?" Adelessa asked.

Larkin nodded.

"I've been tracking the silver-haired men since I learned they slipped into Kavenland a year ago," Adelessa stated. "One of the silver-haired men went to the Hill People and offered them a better life if they joined the invasion. They took the offer. What did they have to lose?"

Adelessa shook her head. "They're desperate, but they're wrong. The silver-haired men won't keep their promise. I fear, win or lose, that life will get no better for the Hill People."

Larkin was silent. He thought back again to his uncle saying that his generation would be the downfall of Kavenland. It didn't sound, though, like the preceding generations had done very well for the Hill People. In fact, their failings had created a desperate enemy right in their own country.

Larkin thought he could understand a little about what they'd gone through. His village had been destroyed, just as the Hill People's home had.

He tried to imagine what it would be like now if there was nowhere to go. What if he and his family and friends were rejected, shunned, and made to feel inferior? It must be a lonely and frustrating way to live.

Larkin suddenly felt something he'd never imagined he could feel for those who'd killed his parents. He felt a twinge of pity for the Hill People.

"There is more to tell," Adelessa said, "but now we both must focus solely on our missions. If we fail, Kavenland is doomed."

And with that, she turned and strode down the hill.

Larkin's mind reeled. He gaped after her until she disappeared in the distance. Adelessa had told him so much, but she'd omitted a lot, too.

For instance, the lone Protector's ship that had returned from the Archipelago coincided with the appearance of The Scourge in Kavenland's history. Was it possible that The Scourge was somehow aligned with these invaders? He shuddered at the thought of The Scourge and Kynwas fighting together.

For another thing, who was Tyndella? Adelessa seemed sad when she mentioned Tyndella's name. It made Larkin think that Adelessa had known her personally. Had they been friends?

And what was this prophecy and who were these two others he had to find? And how could he hope to find Ariana and Noll in The Forest, much less these two other people?

He ran a palm through his hair. He had to clear his mind and concentrate on his task. He had to get word to Rockhaven, hopefully—somehow—with the help of Ariana and Noll.

He took a mental and physical inventory. Most of his body was sore, and where it wasn't sore, it ached. He was separated from Ariana, Noll, and Gurn by many miles. Wherever they were, he wouldn't be surprised if they thought he was dead. When he thought back to his ordeal, he couldn't believe he wasn't dead, either.

The Forest was turning out to be just as odd— and now just as dangerous— as he'd originally feared.

"Wisdom?" he thought, the word popping unwanted into his head. He thought again of the Protectors. Beredor was the person of action, while Galeran blended strength with intelligence. He wished he could be like Galeran.

He thought back to what he smelled when he'd climbed the maple tree yesterday afternoon. Pride and envy. It had consumed him.

So much for being wise like Galeran.

He exhaled. He had to think about his quest. The first thing he needed to do was to try to find his friends. He had no choice about which way to go. The river was calmer here, but it was still a tough place to cross, and even if he could get to the other side, the cliffs he'd tumbled over would block his progress. Besides, he knew that Ariana and Noll would need to get to this side of the river to cross the remainder of The Forest. He knew they wouldn't give up. He knew they would try to continue their quest without him.

He started walking, trying to ignore the way he felt. He knew he'd loosen up, and the pain would lessen. At least, he hoped it would.

Unfortunately, the terrain kept pushing him west and deeper into The Forest when he wanted to go north along the river. He tried not to think about how big The Forest was and how small he felt. Could he really find his friends? If he couldn't, could he make it to Rockhaven on his own?

Loneliness settled on him like a heavy and unwelcome garment. He had to find Ariana, Noll, and Gurn.

Larkin plodded on throughout the morning and into the afternoon. As the shadows around him lengthened, his legs felt weary, and his body ached. He knew he wouldn't find his friends today, and that made his legs feel even heavier. The only sound he could hear was his ragged breath and his feet as they scuffed The

Forest floor. He stopped and leaned against a tree. He reached into his bag, hoping that some of the food that Adelessa had provided would give him a second wind.

He pulled out an apple. He munched on it gratefully. He became aware of a very faint rustling noise around him. A little breeze would be welcome. He looked up at the trees but saw no movement among the leaves.

He frowned.

Larkin knew that the sound he'd heard was too faint to be that of an animal. He remembered back to how much noise the chipmunk had made when they'd first entered The Forest.

He listened, hardly daring to breathe.

The faint rustling noise was still there.

If it wasn't the wind, and it wasn't an animal, what was it?

"Who's there?" He'd wanted his voice to sound big and bold and unafraid, but it sounded small and thin and shaky to his ears.

Then, before he could move, strong arms grabbed him from behind. He was driven to the ground, where he was gagged and blindfolded. He was hauled up roughly and thrown over someone's shoulder.

Larkin wriggled around and thrashed his feet, trying desperately to free himself.

"Any more of that, and I'll kill you," a voice said in his ear.

Larkin fought to keep his panic at bay and forced himself to relax.

"That's better," the voice said. Whoever it was readjusted Larkin onto his shoulder and began to run. Larkin jounced uncomfortably. The wind was knocked out of him, and he gasped for breath around the gag in his mouth.

After what seemed like hours, the journey ended. Larkin was heaved onto the ground, and he pitched forward onto his face. A foot was placed on the small of his back, and he felt his binds being loosened.

"We have two more of you vermin as well," the voice hissed in his ear.

Emotions clashed in Larkin's chest. Whoever it was who'd caught him had obviously caught Ariana and Noll as well. He felt a pit in his stomach. That was bad news.

On the other hand, he hadn't been separated from his friends for even a single day and now they were going to be reunited. Maybe they could figure a way out of this together. He also knew he owed them an apology for the way he'd been behaving.

Larkin was hauled to his feet. As the blindfold was torn from his eyes, he blinked into a huge bonfire. He threw a hand over his eyes and forced a smile onto his face. He wanted Ariana and Noll to know that whatever had befallen them all, he wasn't afraid.

Two figures were led out from the other side of the fire. Larkin kept the smile pasted on his face. As the two were brought out of the shadows, he stepped forward, then stopped. The smile dropped from his face.

He'd never seen these two people in his life.

Chapter Thirteen
Ariana–The Forest

Ariana couldn't ever remember being so uncomfortable. Her arms were stretched out, although thankfully not all the way. Because the vines had encircled her torso, arms, and legs, her arms weren't holding up her entire weight. But her rucksack and quiver of arrows were still strapped to her back, and they pushed into her in ways that made it extremely uncomfortable.

The voice that had advised her to save her strength had startled Ariana. She and Noll hadn't seen or heard anyone before they'd been captured by the wall of vines. She was about to ask Noll if he was ok when she heard a noise below her and to her left followed by a shriek of frustration.

"I'm trapped!" the high-pitched voice said. Ariana recognized the voice as the same one that had just surprised her, and it was followed by movement and other voices coming from The Forest.

"Oh, no!" one voice said.

"What do we do?" said another.

"Lila!" said a third, and then Ariana couldn't make out anything more as a dozen voices started babbling at once.

"Be quiet, you fools!"

The voices subsided. Finally, one asked tremulously, "What shall we do, Lila?"

"Cut me down, of course," the voice from the vines answered immediately. This was evidently Lila.

The voices from The Forest all started speaking up again at once. "Oh, no!" and "But we might get stuck, too!" and "I'm afraid of heights!" they protested.

"Quiet!" Lila said again. Ariana could sense the vexation in Lila's voice. She decided to speak up.

"Who are you?" Ariana demanded.

The response was a dozen different yips of fear and the sound of whatever was below them running away through the underbrush.

"Come back, you idiots!" Lila yelped.

The noises from the underbrush stopped. Ariana could hear Lila let out a long sigh of exasperation. Then she answered Ariana's question.

"I'm Lila, queen of the Gwyllions."

"I should have known it!" Noll said from a few feet away.

"Should have known what?" Ariana demanded. "And what's a Gwyllion?"

"They're why we kept going around in circles," Noll explained. "Gwyllions can change paths in the woods to lead travelers astray." His voice turned accusatory. "Then they rob them," he added.

"But now I'm stuck, too," Lila said.

"Serves you right for wanting to rob us!" Ariana said. "And if it wasn't for you, we wouldn't be stuck."

"That's right," Lila answered, without the slightest bit of remorse in her voice.

Ariana was flummoxed. She had no idea what to make of Lila and these Gwyllions, although no flattering thoughts sprung to mind.

"Breckin!" Lila said.

"Here, your majesty," a voice answered from below.

"How do you plan to rescue me?" Lila asked.

"Rescue you?" said Breckin.

"Rescue me," Lila answered.

"We're not going to rescue you," Breckin said. "We're going to run away."

Lila groaned.

"But if we find anyone who can help, I promise we'll come back. Won't we?" Breckin said to the other Gwyllions.

There were a few half-hearted murmurs of agreement, and a great deal of whispers about running away. Now.

"And what kind of help do you expect to find out here in the middle of The Forest?" Lila said, the temperature in her voice rising.

"Why, we don't expect to find any," Breckin answered. "Do we?"

There was a lot of agreement about this statement. "Not a chance," said one voice. "Who'd be way out here?" added another. "I'm not planning on trying to find any help. I'm just running away," said a third.

Lila let out a squeal of frustration.

"So I guess we'll be off now," Breckin said. "Good luck!" And then Ariana could hear the scampering of feet as the Gwyllions ran away.

"A courageous lot," Ariana muttered.

"Believe me, they have more courage than brains," Lila answered. "There are root vegetables with higher IQ's than that bunch."

"Now what?" Noll asked.

Good question, Ariana thought.

"We've got to get out of here!" Lila said.

Ariana heard a sudden rustling of the vines below her, then a quick expletive.

"The more you struggle, the tighter the vines get," Noll warned Lila.

Another expletive.

And then silence.

They were stuck.

It was a long night. None of the Gwyllions reappeared. Ariana was exhausted. She dozed off a couple of times, but it was hard to sleep stretched out on the vine wall. She had no idea what to do.

She wished Larkin were here.

Finally, the sun sent its first, tentative rays out to greet the new day, but Ariana didn't feel the sense of hope and promise she usually felt in the morning.

Instead, Ariana could feel a red wrath spread from her head to her toes. They'd traveled with a Nisser and survived Scrofa the Boar. They'd lost Larkin in the Flumyn River. They'd crossed half of The Forest, a place no one in Kavenland had entered in centuries. And now their quest might end with them stuck on a vine wall, thanks to this Gwyllion.

She was about to share her displeasure with Lila when the vine wall shook. A door in it opened to her left, beyond Noll. An enormous figure emerged. It stepped toward Noll. Ariana let out a gasp.

Even with Noll being suspended a foot in the air, the figure looked down at him. It let out a grunt of surprise. It took a step to its left, then noticed the Gwyllion. It crouched down to examine Lila.

"Interesting," the figure said.

Then it stepped in front of Ariana.

The sheer size of him up close was terrifying. He had a scarred face, disheveled white hair, and a white beard. He stared at her through piercing blue eyes. His face twisted into a hideous scowl. Ariana was as sure of who he was as anything in her life.

The towering figure was The Scourge.

He stepped back and looked at his captives.

"What are you doing here?" he demanded in a thundering voice.

Ariana said nothing. A quiet fell like a metal veil over The Forest. Then Lila spoke up.

"I'm just here to rob them," she said.

"Silence!" The Scourge bellowed. His voice was so powerful that it blew back Ariana's hair.

"I know what you are. But what are you doing with them? And why are they here?" He jabbed a huge finger first at Ariana and then at Noll.

"Let us down, and we'll tell you all about it," Noll squeaked.

Ariana felt adrenaline course through her veins. This big bully was intimidating her friend. She didn't care how big The Scourge was. She had to protect Noll from him.

The Scourge let out a harsh, mirthless laugh. He bowed mockingly at Noll.

"Your wish is my command. Release them," he said. The vines slackened around Ariana, but didn't let go, like a mother reluctant to release her child's hand on the first day of school. Ariana's brain started working rapidly.

"I said 'Release them'!" The Scourge thundered. Ariana felt the vines let her go. They gave her a little petulant push as well, for good measure.

Ariana hit the ground and did a somersault. Fighting against her stiffness, she reached back for her bow and nocked an arrow. She came up pointing it at The Scourge.

The Scourge arched an eyebrow. The eyebrow looked like a giant white caterpillar. "Impressive," he said, "but ultimately fruitless."

She saw Noll unsheathe his sword behind The Scourge.

"Get behind me, Noll," Ariana said, keeping her arrow fixed on The Scourge's torso. She hadn't been able to protect Larkin, but she could protect Noll. She looked up at the giant. "I think we'll be going now," she said.

"I think not," he said, condescendingly. With breathtaking quickness, he lunged at Ariana, swatted the bow out of her hands with a stinging blow, and lifted her up by the front of her shirt. He pivoted and ducked under Noll's slashing sword. Ariana felt herself being dragged along the ground, then she was thrust hard enough into Noll's chest that it knocked the wind out of her. Noll's sword clattered to the ground. The Scourge pinned them to the vine wall with one enormous hand, then, with the other, snatched up the darting Gwyllion by the nape of the neck and held her aloft between two of his fingers, her legs still kicking.

"Well, well," he sneered. "Nothing like a little exercise to work up an appetite for breakfast."

Ariana's blood ran cold. The stories of The Scourge eating his victims came back to her in a flash. She did not want to be The Scourge's breakfast. She desperately thrashed out her legs but couldn't reach The Scourge with a kick. She did manage to hit Noll with her heels on her backswing.

"Oof!" Noll said, his voice muffled by having Ariana's back pinned into his face.

The Scourge sighed.

"Bind him," he ordered. Ariana could feel Noll become motionless behind her as the vine wall once again ensnared him. The Scourge tucked her under one enormous arm. She pounded at him with her fists, but it had as much effect as punching the side of a building. The Scourge transferred Lila to his other hand, pulled a length of rope out from his robe, and deftly tied it around both of their waists, pinning their arms to their sides in the process. He commanded the vines to release Noll, then quickly tied him to the same rope.

"Now, then," he commanded. "Through that door."

Lila was in the lead and had no choice but to comply with The Scourge's demand. She took two steps forward, but the rope jerked taut, and she fell onto her face.

Ariana had refused to move.

"I'm not going anywhere," she announced.

"You'll go this way, or I'll tie you hand and foot and sling you over my shoulder. It makes no difference to me. But I think this way will be easier."

Ariana had no doubt that The Scourge would do as he said. Reluctantly, she nodded.

"Lead the way," she told Lila.

Dawn began to spread its light across The Forest floor, and Ariana examined the bobbing head of Lila as she followed her through the door in the vines. The Gwyllion was certainly the strangest looking thing she'd ever seen.

Ariana's first thought was that she resembled a misshapen mushroom. Lila was about two feet tall and very thin. She had a knobby head and grayish skin. She walked with a stoop to her narrow shoulders, but she was light on her feet. A good trait for a thief, Ariana thought.

But there wasn't much time to think about the Gwyllion. What she needed to think about was escaping. She'd failed to protect Larkin, and now she'd failed to protect Noll. She had to find a way to escape from The Scourge.

They passed through the vine door, and Ariana was surprised to see a large clearing with a cottage situated in the middle. It was clearly where they were headed. That didn't give her much time to come up with a plan.

She searched her mind frantically for an idea. She couldn't think of anything. They were getting closer. Her panic grew. The Scourge's cottage loomed like a jail cell.

A jail from which they would never emerge.

It was just a few yards away. She wished again that Larkin were here. He'd think of something.

But Larkin was gone. And now she and Noll were walking into the one place in Kavenland no one ever wanted to go.

Ever.

They were going into the cottage of The Scourge.

Chapter Fourteen
Vic–The Forest

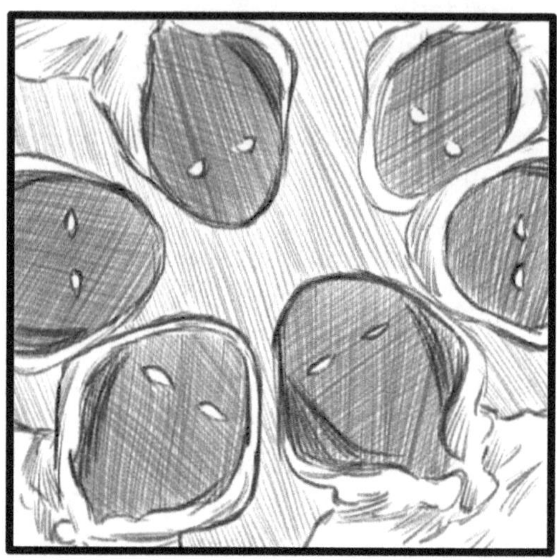

A Hudenpole whispered something to Lyster, and he led Vic and Em over to the fire.

Vic's mouth dropped open. Of all the things he might expect to see in The Forest, another boy was at the bottom of the list.

The boy had been grinning, but when he saw them, his expression turned to one of confusion.

"You're not Ariana and Noll!" he stammered out.

"Who?" Vic asked.

"My friends," the boy answered. He looked about wildly, as if his two missing friends would materialize from thin air. His face ran through a range of emotions—from joy, to confusion, to sadness, and finally to curiosity as he stared back at Vic and Em. "But what are you two doing in The Forest?" he demanded.

There was no short answer to this, so Vic said nothing.

Lyster glided past Vic. "Who are you?" he asked of the boy.

"My name is Larkin," he said. "My friends and I were traveling with Gurn of the Nisser. I fell into the river and became separated from them. I thought that must have been who you'd found."

"Why are you in The Forest to begin with?" the Hudenpole behind Larkin asked sharply.

"Sylba," said Lyster in a deep voice to the other Hudenpole. Vic thought he heard a note of warning in Lyster's voice.

"It is the right question to ask, whether you think so or not," Sylba answered.

All eyes swung to Larkin. The boy didn't flinch. He was about the same height but stockier than Vic, and he seemed to grow taller as he stood his ground.

Even in Kavenland, Vic thought, he could spot the cocky kids right away. This Larkin was a cocky kid, no doubt about it.

"I come from the north," Larkin said. "Kavenland has been invaded there by an army from the Archipelago. We wanted to get word to Sir Alymer in Rockhaven. There are riders from our village going down the Great Road, too, but my friends and I figured by cutting across The Forest, we could get to Rockhaven quicker than the riders could."

"That was a bold decision," Lyster said.

"It was foolish," Sylba snapped. He glared at Larkin. "Now you will pay the price."

"That hasn't been decided yet," Lyster responded.

There was an uncomfortable silence. Vic used it to examine Larkin.

He figured Larkin had two strikes against him. He was cocky, and he was from the north. The north, he remembered, was where all those loser barbarians put babies at the edge of The Forest for that Scourge guy to eat.

Em broke the silence by speaking up.

"We came into The Forest from Laketown," she said. "There was also an attack there."

"Laketown's been invaded, too?" Larkin exclaimed. "Rockhaven needs to learn of that attack as well."

He seemed to think for a minute. Then he groaned.

"Actually, it's worse than that. If Laketown's been invaded, then the invaders probably have control of The Great Road. That means that the riders my uncle sent from the north can't get through. My friends and I are it. We're the only ones who can warn Rockhaven of the danger Kavenland is in!"

Lyster pulled Em and Vic over to one side. "I must talk with the other Hudenpole. I would like to help you and Larkin. There are others who feel as I do. You can clearly see that Sylba does not. Many agree with him. I do not know what the Hudenpole will decide to do."

He left them alone for a moment. Em leaned toward Vic.

"Larkin seems like a very capable boy," she said.

"I don't like him," he said.

Em scowled. "Why not?"

Vic waved his hand dismissively. "I'll bet he's a spoiled rich kid. They're all the same. They act like they own the world."

"You can't judge kids until you get to know them," Em stated.

Vic snorted. That hadn't been his experience. Kids judged him all the time without knowing him.

"Besides," he continued, "he's from the north, and you remember what Canis told you about the people up there leaving babies out for The Scourge to eat."

As he spoke, Vic realized with certainty that he believed Em when she said she could talk with cats and dogs. The revelation jolted him. What a strange few days it had been.

"That baby at the edge of The Forest thing sounds like an old wives' tale to me," Em said. "I think you should give Larkin a chance. He's the only other kid we've met in this world."

Vic scoffed. If all the kids here were like Larkin, he'd be happy if he didn't meet any more of them.

"I can tell his type," Vic said. "Believe me, if he stepped on your foot, he'd expect you to apologize for putting it there."

Em rolled her eyes as Larkin strode over to them. "The Hudenpole told me to wait with you," he said. He looked them both squarely in the face. "I'm sorry if I was rude," he said. "I did something really stupid yesterday and got separated from my friends. The Forest is a big place, and I wasn't sure I'd ever find them again. When the Hudenpole told me they'd found two other kids, well..."

He shrugged. "Sorry," he repeated.

As Larkin apologized, Vic could feel Em's eyes boring into him, but he refused to look at her.

Larkin ran a hand through his hair. "Maybe my friends will still make it to Rockhaven, though. They might be the only chance to save Kavenland." He looked around. "Sylba wasn't too friendly. He was the one who caught me. If he gets his way, I don't think they'll let us go."

Larkin offered his hand. Vic took it reluctantly. Larkin's handshake was firm but not overbearing. He asked them questions about the invasion. He seemed especially interested when Vic and Em told him that the invaders mostly were heading south along the Great Road.

"That's good news, at least for now," he said. "If they were headed north, my friends and family would be caught between two armies." He rubbed his chin. "It also means that they're headed toward Rockhaven," he said. "Maybe Glensworth, too, to attack King Tenney." He stared off in the distance. "I wonder if Adelessa can get there first."

"Adelessa?" Vic said. The word was out of his mouth so fast that he didn't have a chance to stop it.

Larkin cocked his head to one side. "Do you know her?" he asked.

"She's the whole reason we're here," Vic said. He could almost taste the bitterness in his words. "Ugly old hag," he muttered underneath his breath.

Larkin's head jerked back.

"Ugly?" he said. He looked from Vic to Em.

"I thought she was beautiful," Em said.

Larkin's eyes narrowed as he looked at Vic. There it was again, Vic thought. Another kid was judging him. Typical. Larkin was just like everybody else.

"All three of us saw her differently," Larkin mused. "There's something I should tell you about Adelessa's appearance," Larkin began.

"Come with me," Lyster's voice said, interrupting Larkin and startling Vic and the others. It was hard to get used to the fact that the Hudenpole were quieter than a school detention hall.

Lyster threw back his hood, and Vic saw the Hudenpole's face. He didn't like what he saw.

"I am sorry," Lyster said. Vic's heart bungee jumped to his toes and stayed there. Lyster shook his head slowly. Two hands grabbed Vic's arms from behind. He saw a shimmering shape behind Em, and he could see that someone had seized her as well.

He turned to Larkin. "You may go," he said. "We know something of the Archipelago. We think we know why they have invaded Kavenland. If they defeat your armies, they could make war upon the Hudenpole. It would not do to have them running around The Forest." He looked sad again. "There are not as many Hudenpole as there used to be," he said. "At least the Kavenlanders have left us in peace. If the Archipelagans defeat Kavenland, what would stop them from bringing the war here in The Forest to the Hudenpole? Larkin, your mission is as important to us as it is to the rest of Kaveland."

Vic expected Larkin to slap Lyster on the shoulder—well, maybe not literally, but figuratively—and hightail it out of there. That's what he would have done. Instead, Larkin walked with his head down as they made their way over to the other Hudenpole.

"We will blindfold Larkin and take him to the edge of our land," Sylba announced. "We will release him there." His voice grew softer. "I am sorry Lyster, my friend. But humans cannot be trusted. We have given in on Larkin because his release may aid us. The other two must die."

Die? Vic's mouth suddenly felt dry, like it had been swabbed out with a giant Q-tip. He'd thought that maybe he and Em would be forced to live with the Hudenpole. One day, after they'd earned their trust, maybe he and Em could escape. Or maybe they'd like it here and decide to stay. Or maybe Adelessa would finally show up and help them.

But there were no "maybes" with death.

"I am sorry," Lyster said again to Vic and Em. "The Hudenpole do not agree about humans. I believe that we would be better off having dealings with you. At your best, you are many things that we are not—joyful, light-hearted, spontaneous." He paused before continuing.

"But at your worst, you are greedy and mean-spirited. You take and take. You will eat until you are sick, ignoring others who starve. You will chop down trees to make weapons to kill so that you may take land that you do not need. You build houses for a few that could provide shelter for many. You would leave behind a scarred landscape, little concerned with how it affects other creatures, or even future generations of men. The Hudenpole are not like that.

"Kavenland was once completely covered with forest. Many, many years ago—too many to count—there were just the Hudenpole and the trees and the animals and the Ancients. Sendina made it all, but she wanted more, so she created humankind. Sendina walked among us and was happy. But humans are never satisfied. Though they had all they needed, it wasn't enough. Humans pillaged the land and drove the woods and the Hudenpole back. One of Sendina's final acts was to divide up Kavenland as you know it now, with your people living in the fields they created and the Hudenpole living in The Forest. We do not mix."

"Adelessa told me that Sendina left Kavenland," Larkin asked.

Lyster stopped. "Yes, she rose to the sky herself and became the moon. It is why the Hudenpole move around at night, so we can continue to feel close to the one who made us." He peered down at Larkin. "It is interesting that you know Adelessa," he stated.

"She was the one who convinced my uncle that my friends and I could make it through The Forest safely. And I just saw her again this morning." Vic saw Lyster look at Sylba. Larkin noticed it, too. He snapped his fingers.

"I'd almost forgotten," Larkin said with excitement in his voice. "Adelessa told me that I needed to find two others to help me." He gestured at Vic and Em. "She must have meant them. If you're going to free me, you should free Em and Vic as well."

"Sylba?" Lyster said. Vic felt his heart rise.

"I don't like it," Sylba said. Vic's heart fell. He felt like he was watching a combination of a cage fight and a tennis match. Up and down and back and forth.

"Surely if Adelessa..." Lyster began.

"If these two knew Adelessa," Sylba interrupted with a dismissive wave at Vic and Em, "that might be different."

"But we do know her," Em said. "She came to our world and said that we were needed here. She led us through the Door in the Stone and dropped us into Laketown."

There was a long moment of silence. It felt like the entire Forest was holding its breath.

"Are you saying you're not from this world?" Sylba finally asked.

There was another silence. Vic knew that the truth wasn't a very convincing argument. He wracked his brain for a good lie, but Larkin spoke up first.

"The Nisser aren't from this world," he said. "Gurn told me that."

"That's true," Lyster said. "Come, Sylba," he said. "Let's examine them." Lyster put his hands on either side of Vic's temples and lowered his forehead so that it touched Vic's. He saw Sylba do the same to Em.

"I am searching through your memories," said Lyster's voice. It sounded as if it came from inside Vic's own head. "I will not hurt you."

Still, Vic felt as if he'd been thrust in front of a school assembly with no clothes on. He tried to squirm away, but he couldn't move. It felt exactly like it did when Adelessa had stared into his eyes.

Vic saw himself, pink with embarrassment, standing in front of the principal after Chip had turned him in for stealing the teacher's coffee mug. He heard the insults kids hurled at him as he walked down the school hallways. "Dork!" and a sarcastic "Nice clothes!" and the mocking laughter that pierced his heart like a knife.

"Ah, there it is," Lyster said. He examined the memory, then his voice saying the words "I'm sorry" echoed through Vic's head. He released his grip on Vic's temples and stood up. Vic gasped and staggered back as Lyster glanced over at Sylba. The Hudenpole had just finished his examination of Em. She didn't look nearly as shaken up as Vic felt. Sylba gave Lyster a brief nod.

"They are telling the truth," Sylba said. "Put food in their sacks, blindfold them, and take them to our borders with Larkin."

Vic felt light and heavy at the same time, as if he could sink to the ground and cry with relief, or float to the clouds and yell with joy.

Lyster shimmered up to them. "I am glad of the way that turned out," he said.

"*You're* glad," Vic muttered.

"Yes," Lyster said. His eyebrows knitted together. "I think you made a joke," he said to Vic. "I am afraid that the Hudenpole have an underdeveloped sense of humor."

That, or no sense of humor at all, Vic thought.

"I will put more of the medicine in your pack," Lyster said to Em. "I do not think you will need it for your foot, but it may come in handy in the future."

A few minutes later, Vic, Em, and Larkin were blindfolded. They were carried out by the Hudenpole, and a few hours afterward, they were set down on the ground and their blindfolds were removed. The moon was low and faint, and the sky was dark. Vic guessed that it was three or four o'clock in the morning. When his eyes adjusted, he saw that Lyster and Sylba were staring at each other. Lyster gave a slight nod.

"There is a Gwyllion here," Sylba said. "Show yourself!"

Vic heard a faint rustling noise below him, then watched in fascination as a small creature appeared. It was slender and perhaps two feet tall. Its skin was a grayish color. It had small eyes and a small nose, but its ears were enormous. It had exceedingly long, slender fingers, but its feet were small and wide. It was, without question, the oddest thing that Vic had ever seen.

The creature dropped to its knees in front of Sylba and Lyster.

"Please, sirs," it said in a wheedling voice, "can you help? Our leader, Lila, has been captured."

"These are the borders of our lands. Lila is not here, or we would have known it. We will not go beyond our boundaries."

The Gwyllion let out a pitiful wail. Lyster turned to Vic, Em, and Larkin.

"Are you familiar with Gwyllions?" Sylba asked.

Vic looked at Larkin. This was his world, after all. But Larkin shrugged his shoulders.

"The Gwyllions are a mischievous folk," Lyster said. "They can change the paths in The Forest. They usually do it to confuse travelers, so they can rob them."

The Gwyllion had stood up. He clasped his hands behind his back and looked at the ground.

"These three," Sylba said, gesturing to Vic, Em, and Larkin, "have an important task. They cannot be detained. Swear that you will not lead them astray."

The Gwyllion looked up at him, a puzzled expression on its face.

"But...but it's our nature to lead travelers astray."

Lyster rubbed the bridge of his nose. "Swear it," he repeated. He hadn't raised his voice, but there was no mistaking its tone. It was a command, not a request.

The Gwyllion recoiled in fear.

"I swear it," he stammered.

Lyster nodded. He turned back to the three companions.

"And now we must leave you. At first light, head due west. You should arrive in Rockhaven within a week. Good luck."

And with that, the Hudenpole were gone.

Vic and the others looked at each other, then back at the Gwyllion.

"What's your name?" Em asked the creature.

"I'm Breckin," the Gwyllion answered.

Larkin quickly made the introductions then turned back to Breckin.

"I'm not sure we can help you," Larkin told the Gwyllion.

Breckin sighed. "I'm not surprised," he said. "I really didn't expect to find any help. Lila got herself in her own jam. If she hadn't tried to rob those other two humans, she never would have been caught."

Larkin stiffened as if he'd been struck by lightning. "What other two humans?" he asked.

"Why, the girl and the huge boy," Breckin answered.

"Ariana and Noll," Larkin whispered. His voice grew urgent as he bent down to the Gwyllion. "Take us to them. Please!"

Vic put his lips down near Em's ear. "Us?" he said. "I just want to find the fastest way out of here. Let's go our own way. We don't owe this Larkin anything."

Vic felt Em grip his shoulder. Hard. "We don't owe him anything—except, you know, our *lives*," she hissed back.

Vic knew that Larkin's quick thinking about Adelessa had led to the Hudenpole letting them go. Still, his thanks could only go so far, and this kid rubbed him the wrong way. And he'd done lots of favors for lots of kids and never gotten any thanks. The sooner they ditched Larkin and struck out on their own the happier he'd be.

"Besides," Em whispered furiously, "look around you. Where else can we go?"

Vic started to answer, but he realized Em was right. He wouldn't give a nickel for this Larkin kid or his friends. But they were in the middle of a creepy forest in a strange land surrounded by Hudenpole, these weird little thieving Gwyllions, and--somewhere out there--The Scourge. They might as well stick with Larkin for now. If they came upon trouble, Vic figured he could swing Em up on his back and run away faster than Larkin.

"And Adelessa told Larkin he needed to find us," Em added.

Vic shook his head. Everybody in this world seemed to bow and scrape at the mere mention of Adelessa's name. All the ugly hag had done was dump then into some backward world in the middle of a war with a bunch of creatures that seemed all too happy to kill them. And her telling Larkin to find them was supposed to be a plus?

He looked down at Em.

She glared back at him.

He stared at her for as long as he could, then sighed and broke eye contact.

"All right, all right," he muttered.

He turned back to Larkin. The boy cleared his throat.

"I didn't mean to be presumptuous," Larkin said. "You don't have to come with me."

Vic shot Em a hopeful glance, but she gave her head a quick shake. Vic sighed.

"We, uh, owe you our lives," he said. "So if we can help you out..."

Larkin shrugged. "I'm sure you would have done the same thing."

Vic, to be honest, wasn't quite so sure. "We'll come with you," he said. Like they had any alternative.

Larkin nodded and turned back to Breckin. "What happened? Where are my friends?"

"They stumbled right into our lands," Breckin said. "As you can imagine, we haven't seen travelers in years and years and years. Lila couldn't pass it up. She led them to a great wall of vines. They were captured by the vines. Lila climbed up to liberate some of the contents of their rucksacks, but she was captured, too."

"So what did you do then?" Larkin asked.

Breckin looked at her blankly.

"Why, we ran away, of course."

"Remind me not to rely too much on the Gwyllions," Larkin said to Vic under his breath.

Vic averted his gaze and looked down. His foot drew a light semi-circle across the ground with the ball of his foot. He thought that Breckin had done the smart thing. Why should Breckin risk his neck just because this Lila had been careless enough to get herself caught?

"Can you take us to them?" Larkin asked the Gwyllion.

"It's not far," Breckin told them. "Follow me."

To Vic's amazement, as Breckin sprinted off, he left a path in his wake. In front of the Gwyllion was thick undergrowth. Behind him was a smooth, well-worn footpath. Vic shook his head.

This world just got more bizarre by the minute.

The darkness began to lift as they joined up with another, broader path. After a few minutes, Vic could see the large vine wall and two figures, clearly a boy and a girl, hanging suspended from the ground. As they drew closer, he gasped.

"That boy is huge!" he whispered.

"It's my friends," Larkin told him. "It's Ariana and Noll."

Vic thought he could see a small shape on the wall between them. That had to be Lila.

Larkin started to step forward, then stopped. He sniffed the air.

"Hmm," he said. But he shook his head and continued forward.

A few steps later, the vine wall shook. Vic grabbed Larkin and Em and hauled them behind a bush.

"What the..." Larkin started to say, but Vic pressed a hand over his mouth. He held up a finger and peered out through the bush toward the vine wall.

Suddenly, a section of the wall swung open. Through it stepped an enormous figure which approached the wall.

Even from a distance, Vic saw that Larkin's friend Noll, was huge—about the same size as the silver-haired men who'd been at the head of the attack on Laketown.

But Vic shuddered when he saw the hulking mass of this new figure. It made Noll look like a third grader standing next to a tenth grader.

At a command from the huge figure, the vine wall spit its three captives out. The girl reacted with stunning quickness and had an arrow pointed up faster than Vic thought possible, figure, but with blinding quickness, the huge figure disarmed the two kids and tied them up along with the bolting figure of Lila. In mere seconds, he had the three of them walking toward the door in the vines.

When Larkin spoke next, his voice was strangled and as coarse.

"It's The Scourge," he gasped. "My friends have been captured by The Scourge."

Chapter Fifteen
Larkin–The Forest

From where he crouched in the underbrush, a scent of dark purple anger with an undertone of violet blue regret wafted toward Larkin through the early morning light.

He shook his head in disgust. Smells again. Adelessa said they'd put him on the road to wisdom. Well, this road led him to hiding in a bush with two strange kids from a different world while his friends were captives of The Scourge.

He remembered smelling a yellow band of caution just before Vic had hauled him under the cover of the bush, but he didn't want to think about that.

What he'd wanted to do was to charge out to help Ariana and Noll, but Vic's firm grip on his shirt had held him back.

A brief daydream captured Larkin's thoughts. He saw himself pulling free from Vic moments ago and sprinting ahead. He saw surprise in the eyes of The Scourge. The Scourge lunged for him, but he dodged out of his grasp and swung himself up on the giant's back. He saw himself—armed only with a knife—holding that knife to The Scourge's throat. He saw The Scourge kneel on The Forest floor and beg for mercy.

The daydream drifted away, and Larkin watched in horror through the door in the vine wall as his friends and Lila walked through an open field, climbed up a set of steps, and disappeared into a cottage, trailed by the enormous figure of The Scourge.

"Well, I guess that's that," Vic said. He gestured his chin toward the cabin. "I don't see how we can get them out of there," he said.

Em appeared and tugged at her brother's shirt. She put her hands on her hips and stared up at him.

"No way," he said to her. He looked back at Larkin. "I mean, come on," he continued. "Did you see how big that guy was? Did you see how fast he moved?" He spread his arms out wide and jerked his glance from Larkin to his sister, to Breckin, and back to Larkin.

Em continued to stare at Vic.

"Wait—what?" Vic said. "You really think that..." His voice trailed off as he withered under his sister's glare. Em turned her attention to Larkin.

"How can the four of us rescue your friends and get away without being killed?"

Larkin had been wondering the same thing. He shrugged. "No idea," he admitted.

Em tugged Vic away and spoke to him in a hushed whisper. She'd shown some gratitude for Larkin saving them from death at the hands of the Hudenpole, and Larkin appreciated that. He had no idea why her name was a letter, though. Who would name their child 'M'? And why was she wearing a number on her shirt?

As for Vic, the first thing that Larkin noticed was how the boy walked on the balls of his feet so lightly that he almost floated. Even so, he had a cockiness to his strut. Larkin hadn't seen anything yet to back up that cockiness.

Quite the opposite, in fact.

Em and Vic walked back to Larkin. Vic cleared his throat. He looked at his sister, let out a deep breath, and looked back at Larkin.

"Uh, we'll, you know, be happy to help if we can," he said.

Vic, in fact, looked completely unhappy with his suggestion. A flicker of annoyance arose in Larkin. He'd never met anyone who could get under his skin as easily as this Vic kid could.

But there was no time to dwell on that. They had to rescue Ariana and Noll.

Larkin thought about their assets. For starters, they had a Gwyllion. Breckin might be able to help them escape if he could make a path through The Forest that The Scourge couldn't follow. But how could they get Ariana and Noll out of The Scourge's cottage, and how could they make sure they had enough distance between themselves and The Scourge to be able to use Breckin's abilities?

And what about his own gift?

They needed courage and bold action, not the feeble gift of smell.

"Adelessa said that you two were like my friends and I," he said to Em and Vic. "You've seen how big Noll is…" Vic gulped and nodded. "…and Ariana is someone you want on your side, believe me." He cleared his throat. What he had to say next wasn't going to be easy.

"I can smell things," he announced. He felt the tips of his ears grow hot and crimson as he spoke.

Vic smirked at Em. Em frowned back at him. Larkin gritted his teeth.

Em said, "I think that sounds very interesting," she said.

"But kind of useless right now," Vic offered. Em elbowed Vic in the ribs as Larkin's ire sparked once again.

Vic rubbed his side and turned back to Larkin.

"You probably noticed my gift," he said. "I can walk so quietly that no one can hear me coming. It's hard to describe it, but it's like my feet don't even touch the ground. It makes me really fast, too."

Much to his annoyance, Larkin thought that sounded like a pretty cool gift. He absently rubbed his nose.

"And I can talk with cats and dogs," Em said. Larkin waited, but that was all she had to say. He nodded. It sounded incredible, too, but—like his own gift—it didn't seem like something that would help them in their current situation.

"Too bad one of us couldn't use mind tricks, or fly, or become invisible," Vic said.

Larkin felt a jolt. Then his face spread into a wide smile. "Invisible," he said. He clapped Vic on the shoulder. "That's it! It would take too long to explain all of it now, but I have an ointment that Gurn of the Nisser gave me. It can make us invisible."

Em's face lit up. Vic frowned.

"That's great for getting us into the cabin, but how does it get your friends out?"

"We need to create a diversion," Larkin said, "something that will lure The Scourge outside." He began to pace back and forth. "How about you and Em put on the ointment and hide outside of his door. I'll put some on, too, and wait with Breckin in the woods. We'll lure him away, Breckin will lay down some false trails so that we can get away, and you and Em slip inside, rescue my friends, and run for it."

Em nodded. "That sounds like a good plan," she said.

"Good, but not great," Vic announced. A smug look came over his face. He was the same height as Larkin, but he still managed to look down his nose at him as he spoke.

Larkin bit back his annoyance. "So what would make it a great plan?"

"Well, I'm glad that you asked," Vic said, "because you've come to the right place for great plans."

Em rolled her eyes. "If you want to steal things," she said. "And get caught." She raised her eyebrows at him. "Every time."

"Well," Vic said, ignoring his sister's remarks, "we are stealing Larkin's friends away from The Scourge." The air grew thick with Vic's superiority. He turned back to Larkin. "I should be the one in the woods with Breckin. I guarantee I'm faster than you are. Besides, your friends will come away with you a lot quicker than they'd come away with two strangers, and I don't want Em in that cabin any longer than necessary."

Larkin wanted to toss the plan back in Vic's smug face. He also wanted to be the one to take on the dangerous task, to save the day.

But he remembered what Adelessa had said about understanding what was important. Saving his friends was first on the list. And this arrogant boy had come up with a better plan to save Ariana and Noll than he had.

He was supposed to be on the road to wisdom. When would he learn? He had to stop trying to always be the hero. That sort of thinking had him waving his sword at chipmunks and nearly blowing their chance to save Kavenland by falling into the river. Even now, if Vic hadn't held him back, he'd undoubtedly be a captive of The Scourge, too, no matter what his daydream said.

He swallowed. A great lump of humility worked its way slowly down his throat.

"You're right," he said to Vic. "Your plan is better."

Vic preened like a cat. Larkin was surprised he didn't lick his paws and scratch behind his ears.

Larkin told them what he thought would be the best course of action. Vic nodded. He refused the ointment. "I don't care if The Scourge sees me or not," he said. "He won't catch me."

Breckin also refused the offer of the ointment. "I won't need it. But I warn you—we won't be able to fool him for long. Maybe half an hour or so. We'll lead him the opposite way you're going, so double that. You'll have an hour to get as far away as you can."

"Thanks," Larkin said. He hoped it would be enough.

Vic looked for a long time at Em. The superiority had oozed out of him like air from a balloon. It was clear that he didn't relish his role now that his plan was about to be put into action. He licked his lips, but when he spoke, the words sounded drier to Larkin than his aunt's day-old chicken.

"See you later, Em. Be careful," he implored. Then he and Breckin headed into the woods to the right of the cottage. As he watched them go, Larkin shook his head. He had no idea what to make of Vic. He'd never met anyone quite like him before.

Larkin became aware of Em standing at his shoulder. "A lot of that bragging stuff is just an act," she said. She turned to face Larkin. "He'll do everything he can to help us."

Larkin hoped so. So far, Vic had struck Larkin as sneaky and untrustworthy. He shrugged and rummaged into his pack. He pulled out the jar of ointment. "Let's give them a few minutes before we put this on," he said.

"Ok."

Larkin gathered up Ariana's bow and Noll's sword from The Forest floor. He was trying to figure out how to ask Em a question. Finally, he just decided to ask it.

He cleared his throat. "Why do you have a letter as your name and a number on your shirt? Is it something girls have to do in your world?"

Em looked baffled for a minute, then let out a laugh. "No, it's nothing like that. My name is Emily. Everyone calls me 'Em' for short. And this number?" she added, pointing down to her shirt. "We have a game called 'football' in our world. Men put on padding and helmets and run into each other. They all wear numbers so that we can tell them apart."

"Sounds like jousting," Larkin said.

"Without the horses and spears," Em pointed out.

Larkin thought about it. The game sounded like fun. He'd like to hear more about it. Of course, he'd want to make sure Noll was on his side in a game like that.

"Vic's prized possession is a number 21 jersey," Em said, "but that's from a sport called baseball."

Larkin wanted to hear more about both games, but not now. He looked out toward where Vic and Breckin had walked. There was no sign of them.

"I think that's enough time," he said. "Let's put the ointment on and see if we can rescue my friends.

Em took the jar and began applying the mixture. She slowly began to disappear. Larkin rubbed it all over himself as well.

"I can't really see you," he said after he'd finished. "Can you see me?"

"No."

"Reach your hand out." Larkin reached his out as well. He waved it around until he felt her hand. He grabbed it. It was small and dry, and it clasped his firmly.

"Let's go," she said.

Larkin slung Ariana's bow over his shoulder and grabbed Noll's sword in his free hand.

They walked through the door in the vine wall and across the field. Larkin could see the massive figure of The Scourge pacing back and forth in the window. He heard his thunderous voice as he and Em tiptoed toward the edge of the cabin.

"Do you think you can outsmart me?" The Scourge roared. "No one outsmarts me, ever."

"But it's true," Noll stammered. "We've been invaded."

"Kavenland has no enemies," The Scourge bellowed back. "That was taken care of long ago."

"They're from the Archipelago," Ariana answered in a firm voice.

"The...what?" The Scourge said. His voice came out in a raspy whisper.

"The Archipelago," Ariana said.

"No," The Scourge answered in a voice that sounded like sandpaper being rubbed over a rusty pipe. "It can't be."

Larkin leaned down to where he guessed Em's ear might be.

"Ready?" he asked.

She squeezed his hand.

"Ready."

Larkin freed his hand, took a deep breath, and cupped his hands over his mouth.

"Hey, Scourge!" he yelled, loud enough to be heard by The Scourge in the cabin and by Vic in The Forest. "You missed one."

He ducked back behind the cabin.

"Invaders from the Archipelago, huh?" roared The Scourge. "You almost had me. Once I saw you with a Gwyllion, I knew you were here to rob me. You will pay for your impertinence."

Larkin heard the door open, and The Scourge rushed out. Just as he did, Vic, as planned, yelled from deep in The Forest.

"Yoo-hoo, Scourgey-poo! Come and get me!"

The Scourge raced by them. "Sounded much closer," he muttered to himself as he whisked past.

As soon as The Scourge was out of sight, Larkin and Em raced back around the corner and toward the door. He pulled a rag from his back pocket and began rubbing the ointment off himself as he vaulted up the steps and pushed open the door.

"Larkin!" Ariana shouted in surprise.

"Shhhh!" he cautioned. "Let's get you out of here."

He pulled a knife from his sack and sawed away the rope that bound her to the chair. Em worked on untying Lila's binds. Once Larkin freed Ariana and handed over her bow, he made his way over to Noll. He carefully cut Noll's binds and returned his sword while Em finished with Lila.

"Let's go!" Larkin said. "Out the door and into the woods on the right."

Larkin held the door and waved everyone through. As they dashed out, Larkin glanced quickly around the inside of the cottage. His eyes fell on a silver shield that leaned against the wall.

It was huge—taller and much wider than Larkin. It gleamed and glinted in the spare light of the cottage. It had ornate carvings around its circumference. It was beautiful, as much a work of art as an object of war.

"Larkin!" Ariana said.

"Right," he muttered to himself. He sprinted out the door, tearing after the group making its way into the woods.

"How did you..." Noll began, but Larkin cut him off.

"I'll get you caught up. But first, we need Lila's help. Lila, Breckin is with another of our companions drawing off The Scourge. But as soon as The Scourge realizes you've escaped, he'll come after us. Can you lay down a few false paths that will slow him down?"

"And no tricks this time?" Ariana cut in.

Lila nodded, then said under her breath, "I can't believe that Breckin actually found help."

As they followed Lila through The Forest, Larkin and Em rubbed the last of Gurn's ointment off their bodies and clothes. Larkin introduced Em to Ariana and Noll as they ran. He quickly explained that she could talk with cats and dogs and that she was from a different world.

"What?" Ariana exclaimed. "That's incredible!"

"Let's save it for later," Larkin said between breaths.

A half hour later, huffing and puffing, Larkin motioned for them to slow to a walk.

"You're alive!" Ariana said and wrapped Larkin in a hug that almost knocked him down. She stepped back and gave him a short punch to the chest.

"Oof!" Larkin said.

"Only you," Noll said as he shook his head.

Larkin stared at the ground for a moment, then he looked back up at his friends. "I'm sorry for everything," he said. "I was angry and jealous. It's my fault that we got separated and my fault that you were captured by The Scourge."

Ariana slapped him on the shoulder. "You? Jealous?" She shook her head. "No way. Tense from leading us through The Forest? Sure. A little grouchier than usual?" She looked at Noll. He smiled back at her. "That's why we pulled that trick with Gurn. Good thing we did, too, because you used his ointment to rescue us. And besides, if we hadn't gotten separated, we'd all be prisoners of The Scourge right now. All in all," she concluded, "it's worked out for the best."

"Where is Gurn?" Larkin asked. They took a moment to explain all that had happened since they'd been separated. Larkin's heart lurched when they told him that Gurn's wife had been among the Nisser who'd grown weak and disappeared.

But he also recognized what Gurn's absence meant to them now.

It meant that navigating the rest of The Forest was up to him and his friends.

Larkin told Ariana and Noll briefly about what had happened to him since he fell into the Flumyn.

"The Hudenpole?" Noll said in wonder. He slowed to a stop and gazed wistfully into the distance. "I wish I'd seen them."

Larkin wasn't so sure about that.

"The Hudenpole said it would take us a week to get to Rockhaven," he informed his friends. "Thanks to Em and her brother, we know that the invasion has hit Laketown, too."

Ariana let out a low whistle. "And that means that there's no other way to get word to Rockhaven except from us," she said.

"Will a week be too late?" Noll asked.

Larkin shrugged. "It's going to be close," he said. "Assuming there are no other setbacks."

Noll handed Larkin back his sword, which The Scourge hadn't bothered to take away. "I found this on the riverbank."

Larkin thanked him and fastened the sword around his waist. Noll had hung his head and hadn't quite met Larkin's eyes as he spoke. Coming out on the losing end of a fight—even with The Scourge—bothered Noll, Larkin could see. Larkin hoped that his friend's fragile self-confidence wouldn't be damaged.

"I'm glad you've caught up," Lila said, "and thank you for rescuing me, but I think we'd better keep going. The Scourge can move a lot faster than we can, and we can't trick him forever. I don't think he's going to be merciful if he finds us. He won't like being outwitted."

Ariana lowered her voice. "No one outwits me," she said, imitating The Scourge as well as she could. "I'm The Scourge." She bristled. "He's about as friendly as a thousand angry hornets. He's the rudest, most ornery person I've ever been around."

"The scariest, too," Noll added.

Larkin smiled at Ariana's impersonation, but it also gave him something to think about as they jogged along. He compiled in his head what he knew about The Scourge, and he began to have an idea about the mystery surrounding who The Scourge might really be.

Finally, an hour or so after the rescue, Larkin suggested that they slow down again.

"Vic and Breckin have to circle around to find us. We need to give them a chance to catch up," Larkin explained. He turned to Lila.

"Breckin was helpful," he informed her.

Lila snorted.

"He seemed...childlike," Larkin offered.

"A good description," Lila agreed. "And he's one of the better ones. When humans came through The Forest in the old days, I'd sometimes hear them talk about how great it was to be a child. 'Childlike wonder,' they'd say. 'Simpler times.' Well, I know all about simpler times. I'm Queen of the Simpletons."

"If it's really that bad, why don't you give up?" Ariana asked.

Lila let out a sigh.

"They need me," she said. "They really are like children, and sometimes that's good. But sometimes it's bad. Most young children think only of themselves. It's not until they grow a little older that they realize that the world extends beyond them and that they need to think about others. Most of the Gwyllions are stuck in that selfish age forever and are incapable of thinking about anything but their own needs. They need someone to look after them. That's me."

"Sounds more like a nanny than a queen," Noll offered.

Lila was about to answer when they heard something behind them. Vic and Breckin burst through the underbrush.

"The Scourge is coming!" Vic said, breathlessly. "And he's not in a good mood."

Chapter Sixteen
Ariana–The Forest

Ariana had her bow in her hand and an arrow pointed at the boy before she even realized that she'd moved. Larkin put his hand on her arm and gently lowered it.

"It's Vic," he said. "Em's brother—the boy I told you about."

The boy was bent over double, and his chest heaved in and out. His long, dark hair hung down and obscured his face. Rivulets of sweat dripped off him and splashed onto The Forest floor. Em walked over to him and laid her hand on his back.

"Is he close?" she asked.

The boy nodded his head and stood up. He put his hands on his hips, arched his back, and sucked in lungsful of air.

"I can't believe how fast he is," he said between gasps. "That's the fastest I've run in my life, and he's not far behind." He wiped his hand across his forehead. "I'm sorry," he said. "Breckin and I did the best we could."

"What do we do now?" Noll asked.

Ariana felt a quick twinge of pity for Noll. He was never the most confident of boys, and now that his gift of size and strength had been easily beaten by The Scourge, he had a slump-shouldered, hangdog demeanor about him.

As for herself, she felt as if a great weight had been lifted from her shoulders, a weight she hadn't even fully realized she'd been carrying. The weight was the guilt she'd had for not being able to protect Larkin from Scrofa the boar. But Larkin was safe after all. It was incredible. She felt as if she could walk on a cloud. Then she frowned as she remembered their current predicament. Being treed by a giant boar was probably better than being chased by The Scourge.

Larkin turned to Lila and Breckin. "Can you delay him?"

Lila shrugged her tiny shoulders. "I'm not sure how much more we can do," she said.

"I told you," Breckin added, "that The Scourge won't be fooled by us for long."

Vic raised his head up. He looked at Em and raised an eyebrow. "Should we split up?" he asked.

Split up? Ariana thought. Why would they do that?

Em gave a brief, almost imperceptible shake of her head.

"I think it would be best if we stuck together," Larkin said slowly. "The Scourge is faster than us, and I have no doubt that he'd have an easy time picking us off in small groups. Of course," he added, "he's also stronger than us, and I don't think there's much chance we could take him even if we banded together. There doesn't appear to be a good choice."

Ariana's foot tapped The Forest floor impatiently. She was all for making a stand.

"Well," Em said quietly, "we don't have to make a decision right now. The only thing we have to do now is to keep moving."

"I agree," Larkin said.

"But what about us?" Breckin asked.

"We'll keep trying to help," Lila answered sharply.

"But you're safe now," Breckin said, puzzled. "Why don't we just run away?"

Lila slapped her palm to her forehead. "We're going to try to help them because they helped me," she said.

Breckin looked doubtful.

"Just do it," Lila said through gritted teeth. "You lead the way." She turned to Larkin. "Follow him and I'll bring up the rear. Maybe I can delay The Scourge a little."

They set off at a fast jog, following Breckin through the underbrush. The Forest's canopy harnessed the heat like an oven. The leaves hung limp in the still air as Ariana wiped the sweat out of her eyes.

She wasn't sure how long they could keep up this pace. Ariana wasn't worried about herself. Heat or no heat, she could run at this pace all day. In fact, they were moving quite a bit slower than she would be if she were on her own.

Vic seemed the same way. She noticed that he'd regained his wind and moved effortlessly on the path that Breckin laid down for them. Larkin was ok, too. But Noll's legs looked heavy, and Em labored to keep up. Vic noticed it, too, and swung her up onto his back, despite her protests.

"Just for a bit," he grunted, and ran on. Even with his sister on his back, Vic ran easily, and Ariana realized that she couldn't even hear his footsteps on the dry floor of The Forest.

A few minutes later, Ariana heard something else—a voice she'd hoped to never hear again.

"There's no sense in running! I will track you down!" It was The Scourge, and though his voice sounded distant, Ariana knew that he would quickly close the gap between them.

Ariana looked over at Larkin. She couldn't believe that he'd survived, found them, and rescued them. But what did it matter?

"Let's stop and fight!" she called to Larkin.

"Keep running!" Larkin answered. "Let's not fight until we have to."

The group picked up its pace. Ariana heard Noll's legs thud heavily into the ground. She looked over her shoulder. It looked like he was running in mud.

And the sounds of The Scourge grew rapidly closer.

Ariana could hear him shouting.

She could hear him crashing through the underbrush.

He almost had them.

It was the sound of impending doom. Any minute now, The Scourge would be upon them.

Then Ariana heard a sound that she didn't expect to hear. In fact, she couldn't think of a sound she would expect to hear less out here in the middle of The Forest. She was almost convinced that she'd imagined it when she heard the sound again.

"Woof!"

Ariana looked up in amazement to see a dog galloping straight toward them. Vic stopped running and Em climbed off his back.

The dog slid to a stop in front of Em, tail thumping. She dropped to her knees and threw her arms around it.

"Canis!"

Chapter Seventeen
Em—The Forest

Em gave herself over to the grainy wet licks and nuzzles of Canis for a wonderful moment. Then she held him at arm's length.

"We're in trouble," she told him.

"Follow me," he said.

"Let's go!" Em yelled to the others. "We have to follow Canis!"

"The dog?" Noll asked between huffs and puffs.

"Trust her," said Larkin.

"Go!" said Vic.

Canis bolted off. Em and the others followed. The sounds of The Scourge's pursuit were closer than ever.

"I've almost got you!" he bellowed.

Em looked up ahead. They were at the base of a mountain.

But that was impossible. There had been no sign of it as they raced through The Forest. And they couldn't have missed it. It was huge.

Ahead of her, Larkin stopped dead in his tracks and gaped up at it.

Up ahead, Canis disappeared around a boulder. Ariana, Vic, and Noll raced past Larkin. Em stopped beside him and grabbed his arm. "We have to go, Larkin!" she said. Behind her, Lila gave Larkin a small shove in the back of the leg.

"Keep going," she said, panting. "Breckin and I are going to leave now. You'll be safe if you hurry."

Em and Larkin stumbled forward after the others.

"Larkin!" she heard Lila call out. The boy looked back over his shoulder.

"The Gwyllions are in your debt! Thank you!"

And with that, Lila and Breckin scurried back into The Forest.

Em and Larkin turned around and sprinted after their companions. Em could hear the cursing and shouting of The Scourge behind him.

"I've got you now!" The Scourge yelled, just as Em rounded the boulder. A little way ahead, the others were making their way up a narrow, wooded path. A few feet behind, she could hear The Scourge as he pounded after them. Any moment now, and he'd be upon them.

"Where did you go?" he roared. There was a pause, as if something had dawned on The Scourge.

"No!" The Scourge bellowed in rage. His voice suddenly seemed to be coming from underneath Em and from very far away. "It can't be! Don't think you've seen the last of me! I will hunt you down."

And then the voice faded. Em whirled around. The Scourge was gone. All Em heard was her own ragged breathing and the sound of birds chirping. She and Larkin rushed to catch up with their companions and Canis.

"I think we're safe from The Scourge now," Larkin called up to them. They turned around, their necks craning and their eyes searching. Then Em saw their shoulders relax as she and Larkin approached.

"What just happened?" asked Ariana.

"I don't know," Larkin said with a helpless shrug. "One minute he was right behind us, and the next minute it was as if we'd floated away from him somehow. And where did this mountain come from?"

No one answered. He turned to Em in wonder. "I assume you know this dog?"

Em smiled. "This is Canis," she said. "He led us out of Laketown and into The Forest."

"Aww, isn't he cute!" said Ariana. She dropped to her knees and scratched him behind his ears.

Em could already tell that Vic thought the same thing about Ariana—that she was pretty cute. Em figured his eyes must hurt from fighting so hard not to stare at her.

Ariana popped up to her feet. "I hope that was ok," she said to Em. "I don't know how to deal with a dog that you can talk to. I mean, do they still like to be scratched and petted? I would think so. I mean, if it feels good to a normal dog, why wouldn't it feel good to Canis? Although I guess it's not so much that Canis can talk with you as it is that you can talk with him." She frowned. "Right? I mean, not the talking part, but right that he'd still want to be petted?"

Em felt her face break into a wide grin.

"I think you can treat him like any other dog," she said. As if to accentuate the point, Canis rubbed his flanks against Ariana's legs, almost knocking her over.

"I guess I should introduce you guys," Larkin said to Vic. "This is Ariana," he said, and Em stifled a smile as Vic's eyes darted all over Ariana's pretty face, never quite meeting her eyes, "and this is Noll."

"Nice to meet you," Noll said in a friendly voice. He clapped a huge hand on Vic's shoulder, and Vic's knees sagged.

"Well," Larkin said, "I guess you should lead the way, Em. It's Canis who bailed us out, and he seems to know where we're going."

Canis wagged his tail and trotted off. Em turned to follow, and Ariana fell in beside her.

"So Larkin says you're from a different world? What's it like? How did you wind up here? Why is your name a letter, and why are you wearing a number on your shirt? And you met Adelessa? And it's amazing that you can talk with cats and dogs. That must be so cool!"

Em laughed. Ariana's exuberance was disarming. She felt a faint flicker in her heart. She realized that her constant companion—the ache of loneliness in her chest—had softened just a little.

Could Larkin, Ariana, and Noll really be this accepting?

Kids in her world seemed to be quick to judge. Oh, sometimes a kid would be ok to her one-on-one, but when another kid came around, all that changed.

"Have you ever noticed," she asked Vic once, "how kids can be decent when it's just two of you, but pretty awful when they get in a crowd?"

"Only about a million times," he'd muttered.

Em had almost winced a few minutes ago, sure that a scornful blow of dismissal would land from Larkin or one of his friends now that they'd been reunited with each other.

But it hadn't.

They seemed—nice.

Em answered Ariana. She explained how they'd come to Kavenland—leaving out Vic's theft of the golden comb—how they'd fled the invasion of Laketown, and how they'd met Larkin. Em realized that she was talking more than normal, but it didn't really feel strange.

"Incredible!" Ariana said.

Em looked back at Vic to make sure that he was okay. Vic and the other boys had been catching up on the events that had brought them all together, but Em could tell that Vic was distracted. She followed his gaze and saw what had distracted him.

Ariana.

Em smiled to herself. Ariana turned around to see what Em was looking at, and her gaze stopped at Vic. Vic quickly blushed and looked away.

For the next several minutes, Em watched, amused, as Vic and Ariana kept glancing at each other, never quite making eye contact. Em had never seen Vic act this way.

Ariana nudged Em and jerked her head back in Vic's direction.

"So, he's your brother?" she asked.

"Yes," Em answered.

Ariana leaned toward her. "He's kind of cute," she whispered.

"I think he thinks the same about you," Em replied. Ariana gave another darting glance backward.

"How can you tell?" she asked. "Every time I sneak a glance at him, he looks away and starts staring at his shoes."

"That's how I can tell," Em said. She looked back at Vic again. His face turned the color of a cherry. Em smiled, but that smile quickly turned into a frown.

It was too bad that Vic and Larkin didn't seem to like each other. That might get uncomfortable if they spent much time together. She felt herself trusting Larkin and his friends, but Vic didn't trust anyone. She understood why. Still, reasons or not, Vic's distrust of Larkin wouldn't make things any less awkward.

Up ahead, Canis had come to a stop and sat facing them. His back was to a sheer cliff. A tunnel loomed behind him. Em looked at him, nodded, then turned to the others.

"Canis says that the tunnel is an entryway to Baedyn's Valley," Em said.

"What?" Noll exclaimed. "Did he say 'Baedyn'?"

"Who's Baedyn?" Vic asked.

"One of the Ancients," Noll said in awe. "I didn't know any of them still existed."

Silence fell over the companions.

"What's going on?" Noll finally asked. He spread his arms wide. "Why are we together? Are there others like us?" His face colored slightly. "Sorry, Larkin...uh...I..."

Larkin squirmed. "No, no, it's fine," he said. "Adelessa says that I have a sort of special power." Em saw a tinge of color burn his cheeks. He looked down. "I smell things," he said.

Ariana wrinkled her nose.

"You smell things?"

"That's what Adelessa says my power is. She says that it'll help lead me to wisdom somehow."

She grinned and gave Larkin a short jab to the shoulder. "I told you you were special!"

Larkin rubbed the spot Ariana had socked. "Adelessa also told me," he said, "that there were two others." He gestured with his head. "I don't think that there's any question that she meant Em and Vic. But I think we might be it. In all Kavenland, I think there's just the five of us."

"And two of us aren't even from here," Vic pointed out.

"Adelessa says our ancestors are from here, though," Em countered.

"Really?" Larkin said.

Em opened her mouth to tell them about the golden comb and how Adelessa said it came from Kavenland, but Vic cleared his throat. Em looked at him, and he gave his head a short, sharp shake.

"Yes," Em said instead to Larkin. "At least, that's what she told us."

Noll stared off to the side. Ariana folded an arm across her stomach, rested the other arm on it, and dropped her chin into her palm. Larkin gazed up at the sky and stroked his jaw.

"What does all of this mean?" Noll asked. "What are we supposed to do? And why are there only five of us?"

Larkin shrugged. "Why are there five of us at all?" He gestured to each of them as he spoke. "Why can Em talk to cats and dogs? Why can Vic run so fast and so lightly? Why can any of us do what we can do?" His gaze rested on Em. "What do you think, Em?"

She tapped her forefinger on her lips. Em thought it was interesting that Larkin had asked for her opinion. It seemed clear that he was the leader of the three kids from Kavenland and that he was used to making the decisions for them. Perhaps it had something to do with his seeking wisdom, though Em didn't think she had anything particularly wise to add. Still, she gave it her best shot.

"Maybe it has something to do with this invasion," she said. "Can it really be a coincidence that we've all met now, in the middle of a war, and that we've met in the one place in your country that no one ever goes?"

"I think you're right," Ariana said. "I don't know how or why, but we're somehow all in this together."

"And think of what we've done and what we've seen," Noll added. His face looked young to Em—a child's face sitting on top of an enormous body. "The Nisser, The Scourge, Gwyllions, the Hudenpole." A wistful look came over his face. "What were the Hudenpole like?"

"They're really tall," Larkin said, looking at Noll from head to foot, "about as tall as you. They're thin and very quiet and very…" He searched for a word. He raised his hands hopelessly. "'Honest' is the only word I can come up with." Larkin's eyes rested on Em.

"I think that's a good word," she said. "I don't think you could lie to them if you tried."

Larkin nodded. "I agree. And they told us some interesting things. They said that humans ravaged The Forest and that we would have ruined the woods altogether if Sendina hadn't put a stop to it. They came up with an agreement that we should leave The Forest to them. That was the first reason no one ever went into The Forest. The Scourge became the second."

Noll let out a low whistle. "They didn't teach us *that* in school," he said.

"They didn't teach us about how badly we treated the Nisser, either," Larkin observed. "And speaking of things they didn't teach us in school, I have an idea about The Scourge, too."

He was interrupted by a bark. Em knelt beside Canis and patted the back of his head. She looked at Larkin apologetically.

"Canis says that Baedyn is waiting for us," she said.

"The Scourge can wait," he answered. "Lead on."

Canis turned and padded through the tunnel. Em and the others followed. It was pitch dark and cool. Em reached out and found that her fingertips could just touch the smooth walls on either side. She reached up but couldn't touch the ceiling. She hoped that Noll could walk through without bumping his head.

They'd only been walking for a couple of minutes when Em saw a dim light ahead. The light grew brighter as they neared the end of the tunnel. Em blinked and shielded her eyes as she stepped out. As her eyes adjusted, she stopped short.

She gazed out at the most beautiful place she'd ever seen.

In front of her were rolling green hills, woods of towering pines and oaks, and clusters of white birch and sycamores. In between were vast meadows dotted with herds of animals grazing on long grasses. Wildflowers bloomed everywhere, supplying vibrant blues and purples and oranges. The land in front of her was completely encircled by a high cliff way in the distance. Far to her right, a waterfall poured down into the Valley. Beyond the cliffs were snow-capped mountains. White puffy clouds hung lazily in the sky, and a bright yellow sun breathed warmth into her body.

Em had never seen anything like this place. At the same time, though, it was oddly familiar.

The rest of the companions came up behind her. They silently took in the awesome sight of the Valley. Em saw Larkin inhaling deeply through his nose. His face wrinkled up in surprise. Em wondered if he smelled something different than flowers and grass.

Ariana came beside her and flung her arms out wide. "This place is incredible!"

"Thank you," said a voice. And then, suddenly, where the voice had been, a body appeared. It was that of a very tall man—taller even than The Scourge, Em guessed—with a long flowing beard. He was dressed in white and carried a large oaken staff. Animals of all shapes and sizes surrounded him. Canis bounded past Em and up to the tall man, feet prancing and tail wagging.

"My name is Baedyn," said the man, as he reached down to scratch Canis behind his ears. "Which of you are Em and Vic?"

Em stepped forward. Vic glanced at her, hesitated, then moved to her side.

Baedyn nodded. "Welcome," he said, then widened his gaze to take in the others.

"You are the first humans to enter my Valley in many, many years." He frowned. "I wanted to let you in, but I didn't think I'd be able to. Under normal circumstances, you would not have been allowed here. Perhaps it is Em. Perhaps it is something else like this attack. Birds and other animals have been flooding into my Valley for days now, telling me of the invasion. Canis has told me of your flight and has vouched for your character. At least, for Em's character." He turned to Vic, who lowered his eyes and scuffed at the ground. Baedyn chuckled softly, a sound that wrapped around Em like a favorite blanket. "He vouched for you, too, Vic, though he wasn't sure about you at first."

Vic raised his head, though not quite enough to look Baedyn in the eye.

"You are safe now," he said. He asked Em to walk with him. "Follow us," he said to the others.

As she walked beside the towering figure of Baedyn, Em again felt a sense of déjà vu, this one so strong that it made her dizzy. She searched her mind for what it was, but it was like grasping at a handful of fog.

She turned her attention back to her surroundings. Animals frolicked about. Some were familiar, like deer, beaver, and fox.

One made her gasp.

Some people were moved by art, others by architecture, others by mountains or canyons. But the animal that galloped toward them was the most beautiful thing Em had ever seen. At first, she thought it was a chestnut-colored horse. But when the creature turned its head to the side, Em saw that it had a long, golden horn protruding from its head.

"It's a unicorn!" Em gasped.

Baedyn smiled at her. He walked over and patted the unicorn's neck.

"Yes," he said. "There are just a few remaining, and they all live here with me. Come, Em, and be the first human in a thousand years to lay your hands upon a unicorn."

Em approached slowly. The unicorn tossed its mane and reared back to stand on its hindlegs. It spoke to Baedyn in a language that was strange to Em.

"This is Nebb," Baedyn said, "and Nebb, this is Em. Em, can you understand Nebb?"

The unicorn spoke to Em. Em's shoulders slumped, and she shook her head.

"I feel like I can almost understand her." She felt a deep pang of disappointment.

Baedyn gently rested a huge hand on her shoulder. "I'm sorry," he said. "Perhaps, given time, you and Nebb will be able to talk." He frowned, and deep crevices lined his leathery face. "Perhaps time is the key," he mused. "Perhaps this gift of yours comes out when the time is right. When it is most necessary."

Em's mind flashed back to her last birthday. Her parents had just died. Vic was still working at his after-school job. She'd gone into the little dirt yard behind their house. She'd tucked her legs up under her chin and cried. She felt so lonely. A neighborhood tabby named Bella had rubbed up against her.

"I wish you could understand me," Em had said.

"Yes," Bella replied, "sometimes you just need someone to talk to."

It had taken a moment before Em realized that she'd understood Bella. It changed everything for her. She'd always felt a close bond to cats and dogs—way more than with people. But in the few months since that day, cats and dogs had been her constant companions.

Em thought about Baedyn's words. When she'd needed a companion most, Bella had been there. In her brief conversations with Larkin and the others, she understood that Ariana's ferocity only came out when she was protecting others. Maybe, in time—or at the right time—she would understand all animals, like unicorns and foxes and birds and raccoons.

She certainly hoped so.

Em felt Nebb's muscles ripple as she ran her hand down the unicorn's neck.

"We don't have any unicorns in my world," Em said. "I wish we did."

Nebb looked at Baedyn, and Em followed her gaze. Baedyn looked out over the Valley. His face slowly changed. The twinkle in his eyes and the smile at the edge of his lips vanished. It was like a violent storm that blew in and chased the sun and the blue sky away.

"The story of the unicorn in Kavenland is a deplorable one. One of the noblest of all animals, hunted into near extinction by humans." Baedyn spat out the last word, as if he were trying to clear a sour taste from his mouth. Then the anger ran away from his face, and it was replaced by an expression so sorrowful that Em felt a lump in her throat. Baedyn turned to address the others.

"The unicorn was too smart to be easily captured, and too wild to be tamed when it was," he said. "Humans couldn't force it to be a donkey or a plow horse. They couldn't understand it, so they sought to destroy it."

His voice dropped so low that Em had to strain to hear him. "They hunted the unicorns for sport." He rubbed Nebb's flank and shook his head slowly. "For sport," he repeated softly. "They killed them and cut off their horns to mount above their fireplaces, and they left their bodies on the ground to rot where they'd shot them full of arrows."

"But I've never seen a unicorn horn," Larkin said. "I didn't even know unicorns had ever really existed."

"You can see for yourself that they do," Baedyn answered. "As for the horns, they aren't like those of a stag or an elk. They're living things, and they decay and turn to dust soon after the unicorn dies." He shook his head, and his face turned red with anger. "Stupid. Killed for no reason except sport. What a waste."

He stroked the unicorn's head. "The last few unicorns made it to my Valley. They're safe here, and they will never leave again."

His hand dropped to his side, and he once again gazed into the distance.

"Other animals weren't so lucky." He pointed at an odd-looking creature. It was tall, with the beak and feet of a chicken or turkey, a long neck, and a big, round body. It looked at Baedyn, flapped its enormous wings, then dropped its head and began eating the grass at its feet.

"The Didi bird," Baedyn said. "The last of its kind. He has no mate. When he dies, the Didi bird will be gone forever, hunted to extinction for food. I was too late to save them, just like I was too late to save various pigeons and wildcats and other animals that humans eradicated from Kavenland."

He turned back to the companions with a sad smile.

"You're not here for a history lesson," he said. "Come. It will be dark soon." Em said good-bye to Nebb and followed Baedyn with the others.

Soon, the heavy feeling that Baedyn's story had laid upon Em lifted a little. She looked around. The animals had dispersed. They apparently didn't find the five human visitors to be terribly interesting. There were birds everywhere, though, and butterflies darted in and out of the wildflowers. The Valley felt warm and magical. Once again, the feeling that she knew this place tugged at a corner of Em's mind, even though she knew it was impossible.

Of course she'd never been here. She and Vic had only been in this *world* for a few days.

They soon came to a cabin. Flowers sprung from boxes at the windows, and a huge sycamore burst through the moss-covered roof.

Baedyn held open the door and motioned them inside. The cabin was composed of one large room with the sycamore tree in the middle. A small kitchen and a fireplace stood in the far corner. To her left, underneath a window, stood a lectern, and on it, the biggest book that Em had ever seen.

"It's the natural history of Kavenland," Baedyn said, as if anticipating Em's question. "It's all the animal and plant life that I have observed for thousands of years. I'm still learning and still writing, although," he frowned, "I don't suppose anyone will ever read it."

"You must know more about those things than anyone in the history of Kavenland," Noll said. "It would be a shame if you couldn't find a way to share it."

"Think of all the good it could do," Larkin said. "Our history is always told from our perspective. But I've learned things about the Nisser and the Hudenpole and even the Hill People that I never knew. We could learn things from the perspective of animals like the unicorn."

A light of hope flickered in Baedyn's eyes, but it just as quickly dimmed.

"Follow me," he ordered.

He strode out the door and the others followed.

He swept his arms over the view in front of them. The sun was sending its last burnt orange rays across the purple and red sky. Flocks of birds settled into trees, butterflies landed on flowers and closed their wings, and herds of animals settled down in the thick fields. Em felt the sting of true beauty in her heart and the sweet sadness of evening in her soul. Baedyn glanced down at her.

"Beautiful, isn't it," he said, in a low rich voice. Em nodded. Baedyn smiled down at her, then his smile ran away as he looked at the others.

"And what would humans do?" he said, bitterness lashing at his words as they floated about in the still evening air. "Plow it, tame it, chop it down, hunt it down. Always seeking to subdue their surroundings." He looked sharply at Noll and Larkin. "Why won't I pass my knowledge on? 'Knowledge is power,' you say. Humans would subvert the knowledge I gave you. You would use the knowledge of the animal against it to gain the upper hand. Because everything with humans is about gaining the upper hand."

"I don't understand," Vic said. "Em and I aren't from here. Noll said you were an Ancient, but I don't understand what that means." He looked around at the others before addressing Baedyn again. "You look just like us, only a lot bigger. You talk about humans, but you're human, too, aren't you?"

"Am I?" Baedyn asked. Then, where he'd been standing, there appeared a huge, dark figure with one leg and one eye in the middle of its vast forehead. "AM I?" the giant roared. Em recoiled in fear. The giant disappeared, and in its place was a rainbow of colors so dazzling that the companions had to shield their eyes and look away. "Am I?" said a voice that sounded so joyful that Em cried out in pleasure. Then the rainbow was gone, and they heard a voice whisper, "Am I?" The question was borne on the breeze and surrounded them, filling all space, so they could hear nothing else.

Em looked at the others. They had wide eyes and open mouths. She looked left and right, and up and down, but she saw no sign of their host.

Then Baedyn reappeared in front of them, a slight smile on his face.

"Not so human after all, am I?" he said, with laughter in his voice.

"But what are you, then?" Vic asked.

Baedyn pursed his lips. "What am I?" he muttered to himself. He looked out over the heads of the companions. "What am I?" he said again and cast his gaze around the Valley. His eyes took on a faraway look. He seemed to Em to be looking back in time.

"You can call me a shepherd," he said finally. "The animals have no one to speak on their behalf, so I have been there to care for them. The rivers and the trees used to talk to me, too, but their tongues have gone silent." He smiled sadly. "They used to be friends of mine."

Ariana stood open-mouthed. "The rivers and trees were your friends?"

Baedyn nodded. "There was Meliades, who looked after the trees. She was quiet and serious. Then there was Nayas." Baedyn's features softened. "She was sheer joy and energy, bounding through her waters from one end of Kavenland to the other. No, we may look like you, but we Ancients are not and were not human."

Baedyn stopped talking. It was so quiet that Em might have heard a butterfly's wings beating.

"What happened?" she asked.

"Sendina decided that the age of humans had come to Kavenland. The Ancients were told to withdraw or leave. Meliades left Kavenland, and Nayas..." He paused for a long moment, a wistful look on his face. "Her endless cycle from the mountain streams to the ocean and back has ended. She is stuck in one place now, and her joy has turned to a dangerous resentment and bitterness. There were others who were scattered by Sendina as well."

He let out a sigh that was so long and deep that leaves rustled in the trees. "I know that Kavenland was once a place of beauty and promise. Much has changed, though there is still hope."

No one said anything. Em felt a sadness so heavy that she was surprised she could stand up under its weight.

"Yes," Baedyn said, "I withdrew to this Valley with the animals, and I pledged not to leave it. By my agreement with Sendina long ago, my Valley was sealed to humans as well." He pursed his lip and stroked his beard. "I'm not sure how you found my Valley, come to think of it. It must mean something, but I'm not sure what that is."

The companions fell silent. Finally, Larkin spoke up.

"Whatever the reason is," he said, "it saved our lives, and I think I can speak for my friends when I say we thank you. But we need to get word to Rockhaven. Will you help us?"

Crickets had begun their nightly symphony, but they suddenly grew quiet. No owls hooted. No mockingbirds sang. Even the wind had died down. It was as if the entire Valley held its breath, waiting for Baedyn's answer. He frowned in an expression that Em knew well. It was an expression that said, "Well, I'd help you if I could, but..."

But a memory pushed Baedyn's expression from her mind as clearly as if someone had thrown a cup of icy water in her face. The foggy feeling of déjà vu that had dogged her since she entered Baedyn's Valley cleared, because Em suddenly knew exactly where she'd seen Baedyn's Valley before.

"This is the place that Adelessa showed me," she said.

Baedyn stopped and turned around. "What's that?" he asked. "What did you say?"

"Adelessa came to our world through the Door in the Stone. She threatened Vic and me, but she also showed us what could happen if we followed her into this world. As soon as we got here, though, we couldn't remember what she'd showed us." She gestured around her. "But now I remember. This is what she showed me."

Baedyn's forehead furrowed, and he pursed his lips.

"Interesting," he said. "I haven't seen little Adelessa in years."

Vic arched an eyebrow and looked at Em. "*Little* Adelessa?" he whispered.

"I wonder how she's doing," Baedyn continued. "And she showed you this Valley. Interesting. Perhaps she had something to do with you finding your way here."

He clasped his hands behind his back and looked down at the companions.

"What do you know of Adelessa?"

"I know she's old," Larkin offered.

"And she had a sister who died a thousand years ago," Vic said. Em noticed that he and Larkin were still doing their best to avoid acknowledging each other.

"I feel like she guided us on this mission to get to Rockhaven," Larkin added, "and I know that she was hoping that Em and Vic would join Ariana, Noll, and me."

Baedyn's head tilted to one side. "Hmm," he said. "I won't say any more. When she's ready to tell you her story, I'm sure she will. In the meantime, the fact that Adelessa has helped you makes me even more sure of the answer to your question."

Em had forgotten what the question was.

"Yes," Baedyn said. "I will help you."

Chapter Eighteen
Noll–The Forest

Baedyn made them a dinner of oats and honey and vegetables. Noll had been thinking all day about what Baedyn had said to Em when she couldn't talk with the unicorn—that maybe the ability to talk with animals other than cats and dogs would come to Em when she needed it most.

But what about his own massive strength and size? He tried to drive his humiliating thoughts away, but they kept swirling around in his head.

He'd been easily bested by The Scourge. He'd been swept off his feet with one arm, pinned to the vine wall, trundled into the cottage, tied to a chair and interrogated, and there was nothing he could do about any of it. He'd been intimidated, he knew. His ears and face burned warm and red, and he noticed that he'd crumpled his napkin in his fist.

He'd never been bold like Larkin or fearless like Ariana. What good was his huge size and enormous strength if he couldn't even put up a decent fight?

His mind went further back to when they'd first entered The Forest, and he'd cowered from a noise that had turned out to be a chipmunk.

A chipmunk.

Noll felt his shoulders sag. He sought familiar ground to escape his feelings.

There were times in his life when he'd done that by daydreaming about The Protectors or other mythical and legendary beings in Kavenland. Now he'd walked among some of them. He smiled at the thought. And he'd met kids from a different world. That was something that had never entered his mind before.

The boy, Vic, had some rakish charm and was good-looking, but he wasn't really Noll's type. Noll thought back to Bogdan, the other boy who had apprenticed at the blacksmith's shop with Noll. Bogdan was more his style. He was kind and funny and he looked you in the eye when he talked. He wished he'd had the courage to let him know how he felt, but every time Bogdan was around, his palms got sweaty, and his throat seemed to shrink so that he couldn't talk.

As for Vic, he looked at Noll the same way that everyone did except Larkin and Ariana. Vic had seen Noll's immense size, and he'd edged away, as if all Noll wanted to do with his great size was crush somebody. Noll was used to it—the audible gasps, the eyes that grew wide, the furtive glances—but that didn't mean he liked it.

Not that Vic didn't have courage. He'd proven that with the part he played in the rescue of Noll and Ariana. It took a lot of guts to use yourself as bait for The Scourge.

Em, on the other hand, treated Noll like he was any other kid. He liked that. She seemed to trust that he must be okay if he was with Larkin. And maybe that was the big difference between the two. Maybe he and his friends would have to earn Vic's trust.

He looked down at his dinner. Noll usually had a huge appetite, but now he pushed his food around with his spoon.

He peeled his eyes from his plate, and when he looked up, he saw that Baedyn was staring at him. He spoke in a quiet voice that only Noll heard—or perhaps he didn't speak aloud at all, but Noll heard him, nonetheless.

"We will talk later," Baedyn's voice said. "For now, enjoy your companions."

Noll blinked. When he glanced around, he noticed that some of the shyness that everybody had initially felt had begun to melt away. Ariana told the story of Farmer McNatt's broken fence, embellishing it a little so that everyone laughed. Vic loosened up a little. He told the story of being in a race in school called a 'cross country' race. He got off to a big lead, but he missed a turn in the woods, and practically ran across the country before they found him, an hour later, drenched in sweat and wandering around on a back road. Vic walked around with a confident air, so it surprised Noll when he mostly kept his head down as he started to tell the story. Soon, though, Ariana and Noll's laughs emboldened him, and he made a little more eye contact by the time he finished.

Especially with Ariana, Noll noticed.

Noll also noticed that Larkin had tried to keep a straight face during Vic's story, although a smile broke through on occasion before Larkin could stop it. Noll wondered about the coolness between his best friend and Vic. He wasn't sure why Larkin didn't like Vic, but it was clear he didn't. That was odd. Larkin usually found something good in everybody.

Afterward, Baedyn arranged pillows on the floor and scrounged some blankets for them. Noll thought he would have trouble sleeping in this strange place with people he'd just met, but he hadn't slept in two days. He was asleep before he'd known he'd laid down.

He woke before the others. His stomach rumbled. The smell of pancakes being cooked in butter wafted across the room and tickled the inside of his nostrils. Dust particles danced in a shaft of light that shone through the front window. Outside, birds whistled and chirped and sang. It seemed to Noll that they sang with all their hearts, thrilled to greet another day.

He knew how they felt. The sharp edges of his deep disappointment at his performance against The Scourge seemed to have been rounded into something more bearable by Baedyn's assurance last night that they would talk. Now here he was lying with fingers locked behind his head on a stack of pillows in Baedyn's cottage.

Baedyn! One of the Ancients! It was like he'd woken up in one of the stories he loved so much. He'd met the mysterious Adelessa. He'd kept the company of Gurn of the Nisser. He'd met Gwyllions. He'd been a captive of The Scourge.

He shuddered slightly at the last memory. It wasn't a warm one. Still, he had met The Scourge and survived.

His head lolled to one side, and he saw Baedyn busily making breakfast. He rolled over as quietly as he could and tiptoed over to the kitchen area.

"Could you use some help?" he asked Baedyn.

"No, but I could use the company. It's been a millennium since I've seen any humans."

"Do you miss seeing us?" Noll asked, as he carefully sat on one of the large milk cans that served as a makeshift chair. "Humans, I mean."

Baedyn took so long to answer that Noll wasn't sure if he'd heard his question. Finally, the old man let out a long sigh.

"Yes, I think I do," he said. "Each animal has its own personality, you know. Some deer, for example, might be a little bolder or a little more inquisitive than others. But all of them will run away if challenged by a predator."

Noll hadn't ever really thought of animals—except maybe cats and dogs—having distinct personalities, but it made sense.

"Humans, on the other hand," Baedyn continued, "can be completely unpredictable. The Hudenpole see mostly the worst in humans, I think. They see that humans can be mean and vindictive, something animals aren't. An animal will fight for a reason. Humans can fight over anything—or nothing. Humans can be nice to you one minute and cruel to you the next, as it suits their own selfish purposes. They will lie and steal." He cast a quick glance at the sleeping form of Vic when he said this last word, though Noll wasn't sure why. "They will even kill each other."

Baedyn shook his great shaggy head before continuing.

"But they will also show compassion and love. They will laugh and cry. They will say things that make you stop and think or shake your head. Humans are...*interesting*, I'd say. That's what I miss."

Noll thought about his own experiences. He loved his mom, and she loved him. He and Larkin and Ariana were all best friends, and they supported each other's strengths and weaknesses without question.

But he also thought about his great, hulking size and how it made him an outcast. Nobody bothered to find out that he was just like them in so many ways.

And just when being big might really come in handy—just when it might have been worth being teased for all those years—he'd been thoroughly beaten by The Scourge.

A sudden absence of light interrupted Noll's thoughts. He looked up to see that Baedyn was standing over him.

"The deer accepts that he is fast," Baedyn said in a quiet voice. "The bear accepts that he is strong. Why don't you accept that you are big?"

"It makes me different," Noll said after a moment. "I just want to be like all the other kids."

"How terribly boring that would be," Baedyn said. He pursed his lips. "One deer must always be the fastest. One bear must always be the strongest. They don't fit in with the others—they rise above them."

"But being the biggest didn't help against The Scourge," Noll said.

"I can think of only one other in the history of Kavenland who might have beaten The Scourge, and that's Beredor."

Noll's eyes widened.

"Yes," said Baedyn, "I knew Beredor. But you are not Beredor, for which I am thankful."

Noll wanted to ask what he meant, but Baedyn held up a hand to cut him off.

"I am not interested in discussing Beredor or The Scourge," the Ancient said. "I am much more interested in you. You are still young. When all is finished, perhaps you will be stronger than both. Who can say?"

He put his hand on Noll's shoulder and squeezed. "I can see that you have wonder and joy in your heart. Make sure you never lose them."

"I wish other kids saw me that way."

"Larkin and Ariana do. And they strike me as exceptionally good judges of character. You can't worry about what others think of you because you can't control it." He shrugged his shoulders. "Just be yourself. That will be good enough for the people that matter."

Noll hoped that was true.

"And I'm sorry," Baedyn continued, "terribly sorry—that you and your friends have had to take on such a big task at such a young age. But you have been given your size and strength for a reason. Do not turn from who you are. Embrace it. Strength will flow from there. Use that strength to fight for yourself and your friends."

Baedyn dropped his hand to his side. He eased away and began to put pancakes onto plates. Noll thought about the Ancient's words as he looked over at Larkin, rubbing his eyes now and sitting up, and at Ariana, who bounced out of bed like there was a spring underneath her. She socked him playfully in the arm as she swung into a chair. Noll smiled. Warmth spread through him, and he felt a small seed of resolve plant itself in his stomach.

"Time is of the essence," Baedyn announced, as the others piled around the breakfast table. He slid plates of pancakes in front of everybody. "Eat up and then pack your things."

Noll and the others ate hurriedly.

"Leave the dishes behind. I'll clean them up later," Baedyn instructed after everyone had eaten. He grabbed a walking stick and strode out the door. Noll and the others followed.

"Mr. Baedyn," Ariana asked, "would it be possible to stay for a day, rest up, explore the Valley, then head out on our mission? Surely, we could spare one day?"

Baedyn pursed his lips.

"Hmm," he said to himself. "Against the rules. Shouldn't even be here now, really." He cocked his head to one side. "It's my Valley, though, isn't it?" When he moved his eyes back to the companions, his face looked younger to Noll than it had before.

"I could allow you to do that, yes," he said, "but know this. Time doesn't move in the same way here as it does in the rest of Kavenland. It is of no consequence here in the way it is outside of this Valley. Yes, things are born, and things die, as happens everywhere. But there's no notion of 'later' or 'tomorrow' or 'next week.' There's only now. And because of that, you'd see things that you've been too busy to notice, and you would experience life in a completely different way than you ever have. But if I left you a day to enjoy the Valley, you might leave only to find that a week had passed in the outside world, or a month, or even years. It is the way of it for those who live their lives totally immersed in the moment. I won't tell you that it's a better way to live your life, although," he added with a smile, "I think it is."

Noll looked at the others. He saw Larkin shake his head slowly. "Your offer is generous," he told Baedyn, "and a big part of me wants to say 'yes,' but I can't." He looked at Ariana and Noll before he returned his gaze to Baedyn. "Our friends and families are beyond your Valley, fighting for their lives against some evil force that has invaded Kavenland. I could never truly enjoy your Valley with that on my mind. We must get through to Rockhaven. We are our country's last hope, especially now that Laketown has been invaded, too."

Noll nodded. As great as the Valley was, he agreed with Larkin, especially now that Vic had told them of the invasion at Laketown. They had no time to spare. Baedyn, meanwhile, laid a gentle hand on Em's shoulder.

"Child," he said. "Humans have not been allowed in my Valley for over a thousand years. It is not entirely by my choice that you are banned from my borders. You and your friends are different, though. To them, I have extended the invitation to spend a day. To you and your brother, I extend the invitation to stay forever.

"Canis has spoken very highly of you. He says you are unlike any other human he's ever known. I've seen that for myself in the short time you've been with me. If you were to stay, I feel sure that you would be able to talk to all the animals in time. I think you would be happy here."

Em's face shone. Her mouth opened slightly, and she looked about in wonder. But then her mouth closed again, and her slender jaw set. She stared at Vic and shook her head slowly.

"Something has brought the five of us together," she said quietly. "I don't know what it is. I don't think any of us does." She looked around at the Valley, as if trying to burn every detail into her memory forever. Then she locked eyes with Larkin.

"I'll go with you," she said. Noll felt a wave of sorrow for Em. He'd only known her for a brief time, but it was clear that if any human ever belonged here, and would ever be truly happy here, it was Em.

Larkin hadn't taken his eyes off Em. Noll was sure that Larkin must be thinking the same thing he was. Finally, he gave a brief movement of his head.

"I know how hard this is, Em. But we'll be glad to have you with us."

Noll shot a quick glance at Vic, who looked disappointed at Em's decision. Noll had the feeling that Vic would desert them without a second thought. He also wondered why Baedyn had looked at Vic when he talked about people who stole things. And even with the laughter they all shared last night, things between Larkin and Vic hadn't seemed to warm up, either. Noll hoped that wasn't going to be a problem if they continued on together.

Em, meanwhile, was rubbing the corners of her eyes with the heels of her hands. When she lowered her hands, Noll saw that her eyes were red and wet. She looked up at Baedyn. "Thank you for your offer. I hope Canis can stay. I think he belongs here. I think Vic and I belong out there."

Baedyn looked at her for a long while before answering. "Canis is welcome here," he said with a nod. "And now, I will take you to the edge of my lands. I'll also tell you this: the Valley moves. It's never in the same place twice."

Noll thought about how the mountain had appeared out of nowhere and how The Scourge seemed unable to see it or them. He shook his head in amazement once again.

"I've moved the Valley so that you'll exit within a day's journey of Rockhaven. By traveling through my land, you've saved several days of travel. It might allow you to get to Rockhaven in time to warn them of the attack. But it also means you'll have to cross the Lake of Despair."

Noll gulped. He wasn't sure why, but the way Baedyn said 'Lake of Despair' made him shiver.

"Don't touch the water," Baedyn continued, "and don't go in it for any reason. The queen of the lake is a sorceress of an ancient time." Baedyn looked away, his eyes wistful. "An old friend who's grown bitter and angry." His eyes regained focus, and he looked at the companions with a stern expression. "Don't even look at the water if you can help it. She'll know your weaknesses. She'll try to bend you to her will. If you do fall in or even touch the water, get to shore, and get out of sight of the lake as soon as possible. Her power doesn't extend beyond its borders."

This was sounding worse and worse, Noll thought. First The Scourge, and now this scary sounding queen.

He halted the march of his insecure thoughts. He looked at Larkin and Ariana. They would do anything for him. He would do anything for them, too.

His backbone stiffened. Baedyn was right. If for nothing else, he needed to embrace his size to help his friends.

"I'll give you a boat," Baedyn went on. "Go directly across the water, by the shortest route, and you'll be on your way to Rockhaven. It's not much further now."

"It sounds like we're really going to do this," Ariana said. "I mean, it sounded like a big adventure when we were starting out, and then, for the longest time, it seemed that all the grownups who say kids these days are no good were right, and that we were going to fail."

"Do grownups say that in this world, too?" Vic asked.

"Why?" Baedyn grumbled under his breath as he poked around through the underbrush. Noll could just make out what the Ancient was saying. "Why do humans say this about their own children, every generation? A deer, a bear, a skunk, a bird—all animals grow up to take their rightful place in the world. None think they're inferior to their parents or grandparents. None are told that their generation is too weak."

Baedyn straightened up and looked at the companions.

"You seem too young to have this much responsibility thrust upon you. But if you share it among five people, the burden should be lighter. Not light. But lighter."

Baedyn rummaged around in the weeds. He was talking to himself again. "Now, where is that boat?" Noll heard him say.

"Sir," Larkin interrupted, "there's been something bothering me. When I first entered your Valley, I smelled a deep sense of contentment. And yet I sensed a danger, too. But it felt like a danger that's somehow far away."

Noll remembered seeing Larkin sniffing the air with a funny look on his face. Now he saw Baedyn look at Larkin shrewdly.

"The contentment you feel is very real," he answered, "for this is a place in great harmony and balance. But the danger you feel is very real as well, and it's closer than you might think. There may come a time when humans cut too deeply into the world around them. If that happens, the seas will rise, and the lands will sink beneath their waves.

"The Scourge is dangerous, and the Hudenpole can be dangerous. These invaders from the Archipelago are dangerous, too. But those are the dangers of the present. They can be overcome.

"The danger you feel here is a warning. It's the danger that could happen to our world if humans push too far. That danger has no cure. That danger is forever."

"Yup," Vic muttered. "That sounds like our world, too."

Em lifted her head up for the first time since she'd turned down Baedyn's invitation to stay.

"Our world is a lot different than yours, but Vic's right," she said. "We have wars and famine and the threat of our planet growing too warm. And yet the people that have caused a lot of those problems seem to think it's our generation that's flawed."

Baedyn grunted in what sounded like agreement as he pushed aside some more weeds.

Ariana said to Larkin, "And you sensed all of that. See! That sense of smell is pretty cool after all, isn't it?"

"Yeah, it's great," Larkin said with a roll of his eyes. "Maybe I can sniff the invasion away."

"Blow your nose and see what happens," Ariana offered with a laugh.

Baedyn stood up. "Here it is!" he exclaimed. He pulled a long boat out from under a tree with one hand. He beckoned Noll to him. Noll bent down, picked up the boat and swung it easily over his shoulder. Baedyn then handed the paddles to the other four.

"Follow the path directly ahead of you," he said. "It won't take long. Off you go."

He shooed them down the path.

Noll took two steps then felt the urge to turn around. He wasn't sure if he wanted one final look at that magical land or if he just wanted to thank the Ancient. But when he turned around, all he saw behind him was The Forest.

Baedyn and his Valley were gone.

Chapter Nineteen
Vic–The Forest

Vic Blake, dashing figure of mystery and intrigue, felt his palms itch.

He thought about Larkin's ointment that made people invisible. He'd love to get his hands on it. With his quiet footfalls and Larkin's gunk, there'd be no stopping him. His amazing feats of daring would be on the lips of all the backward losers in this world.

He'd be a legend as he moved from town to town, robbing the rich and giving to the poor.

Ok, so he'd give some to the poor. The rest he'd keep for himself and Em.

They'd be rich. After the life he and Em had lived so far, that would be nice.

The voice inside him—the one that had warned him about stealing the teacher's mug and that had told him not to be so rude to others—had grown faint. But it was still loud enough to chase the daydream of stolen riches away.

He thought back to the way Baedyn had looked right at him last night when he'd glanced around the old man's cabin looking for something to swipe. His eyes had met Baedyn's. The old man was staring right at him. Vic felt the blood rush to his face as he took a sudden interest in an oven mitt that sat on Baedyn's counter. Maybe Canis had told Baedyn that Vic was stealing things when they'd met in Laketown.

Or maybe it was something else. What had Noll called him? An 'Ancient'? Maybe he could read minds or something, like Adelessa and the Hudenpole.

What a weird world this was.

Now they were headed for some place called The Lake of Despair that was ruled by some sort of wicked queen. Baedyn told them not to look into the water, but Vic wondered what harm it could possibly do. He shrugged. What was he going to steal out of a lake anyway--seaweed?

He didn't figure this looney of the lake was worth getting nervous over.

Vic looked ahead of them. If anyone *could* make him nervous, it would be Noll. He was absolutely enormous. Vic figured he might be able to lift one side of the canoe off the ground if he put his back into it, but Noll had tossed the canoe onto his shoulder and was walking along as if it weighed nothing at all.

"I've never seen anyone that big or strong," Em whispered. "Not even close."

"Me, neither," Vic answered.

"He seems really nice, though. I'm glad he's with us."

Vic grunted. Noll was all right, he figured. The five of them had even had some laughs last night in Baedyn's cottage. He wondered if he could talk Noll into coming back with him and Em through the Door in the Stone when all this was over. Of course not, he realized, but he allowed himself to fantasize for a moment what it would be like having Noll as his wingman back in their world. All those kids who'd made fun of him over the years would sink to their knees and grovel for forgiveness. Maybe Vic would grant it, and maybe he wouldn't.

He realized a grin had come over his face, and he quickly banished it. He had to think about the here and now, and Vic was worried about his sister. Not about her being all buddy-buddy with Larkin, though he didn't care much for that.

No, it was Em's decision to stay with the kids that concerned Vic. Her shoulders were hunched, and her feet dragged. She looked like she was carrying a weight a lot heavier than the canoe Noll was toting.

"I know that was hard not staying in Baedyn's Valley," Vic told her. "I somehow think you made the right decision, though." Actually, he didn't, but there was nothing they could do about it now. It was the perfect place for Em, and he felt bad for her. He didn't care that much about it himself but hanging out with Em in

Baedyn's Valley sounded better than getting involved in a war in this crazy place, even if Baedyn did seem a few bricks short of a full load. Still, Vic wanted to cheer Em up.

She squeezed his hand and continued to walk beside him. Vic turned his eyes forward again. Larkin walked behind Noll with his eyes focused straight ahead. He was deep in thought. He was the leader of the three. There was no question about that.

And now he was trying to steal Em away from him. He made a little face as he talked to himself in a caricature of Larkins's voice. "Why do *you* think we're together, Em?" "Oh, too *bad* you can't stay here with Baedyn, Em!"

Phony baloney, Vic thought. Larkin just wanted to be the center of attention.

Vic figured that Larkin was one of those kids who always thought he was right because the world was easy for him. He thought about the story of Farmer McNatt that Ariana had told. Vic thought that Ariana and Noll had been smart to run away, and that Larkin had been a sucker to go back and admit that he'd broken the mean old man's fence.

Of course, it had worked out well for Larkin. Vic's jaw tightened. Things always worked out for kids like Larkin.

Ariana walked behind Larkin. She'd tied most of her thick hair back in a ponytail, and it swung back and forth as she walked. Back and forth. Back and forth. Back and forth.

Em nudged him in the ribs.

"She's pretty, isn't she?" Em said.

He remembered Ariana tumbling out of the vine wall and rolling to her feet with an arrow pointed at The Scourge.

"She's pretty, all right," he answered. "Pretty fierce."

Em grinned at him.

"What?" Vic demanded. But Em just shook her head and kept walking. At least her feet had stopped scuffing along the trail, Vic thought.

A brief time later, Em tugged at his sleeve. "Vic," she whispered, "you should apologize to Larkin."

"Apologize?" he gargled out, almost choking on the word. "What for?"

"You haven't been very nice to him." He started to speak but she raised her hand. "He saved our lives, Vic."

"Yeah, well we saved his friends' lives, too, thanks to my plan." He glanced up. The other kids were far enough ahead that they couldn't overhear them. He wagged his finger at Em. "Him saving us with the Hudenpole was easy. Besides, he needed us. Mark my words—if things get tough and it's him or me...well, I can bet who he'll choose."

Em threw her hands up and kept walking. Vic looked ahead at the others.

He suddenly recalled Adelessa connecting with his mind and sharing something with him. He seemed to think it had to do with Larkin and the others, but he couldn't put a finger on what it was. It was frustrating. It was like a dream that gave you a certain feeling but that you couldn't remember anything about when you woke up.

It took them an hour to work their way down the side of the mountain. Below them, the lake sparkled as it stretched long and slender to their north. It didn't look to Vic as if rowing the boat across its narrow girth would take very long. Then it would be down the slope on the far side of the lake, out of The Forest, and into Rockhaven.

For the first time in days, they had a path out of The Forest. And for the first time since they'd entered The Forest, the path seemed clear and easy. It was what lay on the other end of the path that concerned Vic. He didn't relish getting tangled up in some war. They wouldn't make kids fight, though—right?

Up ahead, Noll swung the canoe down and placed it by the water's edge. Vic looked around. The lake was ringed by mountains on both sides, although there was a natural dip on the far shore. That was where they would go.

They reached the shore of the lake where a stream flowed into it. The stream wasn't large, but by years of erosion, it had cut a wide swath through the mountains. It went straight east for miles, back in the direction they'd come from.

Noll slid the front of the boat into the water, and Vic and Larkin set the paddles inside. They all remembered Baedyn's warnings about the queen of the lake. They were trying to figure out the best way to get in and push off without anyone setting foot in the water when they heard a small noise coming from Ariana.

She was looking up the long stream bed, her hand above her eyes to shield the sun.

"Oh, no!" Ariana exclaimed. "The Scourge has found us. He's coming, fast!"

Vic followed her gaze. He was puzzled.

"I don't see anything," he said.

But Larkin and Noll were already moving.

"If Ariana says she sees something, she sees something," Larkin said. "We have to go—now!"

Larkin edged the canoe forward so that most of it was in the lake. "I'll steady the boat. Remember—don't touch the water! Noll, you get in first. Good. Now the rest of you get in and grab your paddle. On three, I'll push from shore and jump in, and you push off the bottom with your paddles at the same time. Here we go. One, two, three."

They did as they were instructed, and when Larkin jumped in, Vic and the others pushed with their oars. Vic could feel the bottom of the boat grating along the rocks of the lake. For a sickening moment, he thought they were going to be stuck, but then the boat slid free, and they drifted out into the lake.

"Careful now," Larkin cautioned. They all settled into the boat's bottom and started paddling as fast as they could. They were little more than a quarter of the way across the lake when Vic heard a voice yelling.

"I told you I'd find you!" he thundered. "And now you will pay!"

Vic risked a look over his shoulder and instantly wished he hadn't.

It was The Scourge. He plunged into the lake after them.

"Row!" yelled Larkin, but Noll had already started to heave with two oars. The boat leapt forward at a speed that amazed Vic, but when he looked back, he felt sick.

The Scourge was gaining on them. His face was a storm cloud of anger. Whatever ill effects the Lake of Despair might have on them didn't appear to translate to The Scourge. He pulled out his sword and held it above his head.

"You cannot escape!" he bellowed. "You thought you could make a fool of me? You will soon pay the price for your insolence!"

Vic pulled on his oar as hard and as fast as he could. His muscles felt like they were on fire and his breath came in ragged pants. Even so, The Scourge was getting closer. Then, to Vic's amazement, Larkin stood up in the boat to address The Scourge

"I can smell your anger," he said. "But I sense something else. You're disappointed in yourself."

The Scourge slowed for a moment to consider this accusation. But then he shook his great, shaggy head and started forward again.

"What do you know of me?" he snarled.

"I know you never killed people who wandered into The Forest. I know you didn't eat babies who were supposedly left as sacrifices to you. I know that because I know who you really are. And that means I know what you're supposed to do. And this isn't it. I know it, and you know it, too."

The Scourge stopped in his tracks. There was a look of bewilderment on his face.

"You should be ashamed of yourself," Larkin added.

"What...? How...?" The Scourge started to say.

"I'll come find you when we're finished," Larkin said, "but we must get to Rockhaven. The invasion really is from The Archipelago. Kynwas leads it. You know what that means better than I do."

"Kynwas," The Scourge whispered, his hoarse voice carrying across the water. Then louder, he repeated it. "Kynwas!" Finally, his thunderous voice echoed between the mountains. "Kynwas! I will destroy you!" Then he turned and waded quickly back to shore. The last Vic saw of him, he was sprinting back down the stream bed.

Noll stopped rowing. Everyone stared at Larkin, their mouths agape.

Everyone except Vic.

He looked past Larkin and saw something glittering at the bottom of the lake. Something else flashed next to it.

Vic rubbed his eyes. The bottom of the lake was filled with gold and rubies and diamonds. He leaned forward to get a closer look.

"How did you do that?" Vic heard Noll ask Larkin. Noll's voice sounded far away. Another voice sounded closer. It was a woman's voice, and it came as part challenge and part invitation.

"Come, master thief," the voice said, "do you think you can steal the world's greatest riches from the world's mightiest queen?"

"It started with something Adelessa told me," Vic heard Larkin say, but his voice seemed even farther away than Noll's.

"Come," said the woman's voice. "Come, see if you can take what belongs to me."

Vic reached his hand toward the water. Had someone warned him against doing that? He didn't know and he didn't care. Those sorts of rules didn't apply to someone like Vic.

He plunged his hand into the water to see if he could reach the jewels on the bottom of the lake.

"Vic!" he heard Em's voice say from a million miles away.

And then he felt the lake pull him into its depths. Vic was startled, but he regained his senses and swam toward the bottom. He reached his hand toward a glittering emerald and wrapped his hand around it. It was huge. He opened his hand to look at it, but all he saw was a muddy stone sitting in the palm of his hand.

"Fool!" the woman's voice said. The voice came from his right. A beautiful mermaid swam in front of him. She had a golden crown on her head.

"You didn't think it would be that easy, did you?" she said in a mocking tone.

Vic's chest puffed out. No one made a fool of Vic Blake. No one. He'd rob this queen blind.

"The real riches are this way, if you think you can get them," the queen said.

Vic was vaguely aware that something was wrong. Was all the air out of his lungs? He didn't care. He began to swim after the mermaid when he felt himself yanked upward, back out of the water and onto the bottom of the boat.

He choked and gasped as he looked up at Noll's face peering down at him. He rolled over and wretched and coughed. He wheezed for breath, and sucked droplets of water back into his lungs. His throat burned. He thought, for a moment, that he might die, until his rasps finally brought in clean breaths of air.

Larkin, also wet, was lying next to him.

"Are you ok?" Noll bawled at Vic.

Vic nodded his head. But then a great craving came over him. He had to go back into the lake! All that gold, all those jewels, just waiting for him to take them.

He bolted up and scrambled for the side of the boat. He was almost over it and back into the water when he felt someone grab the back of his shirt.

"No, you don't!" said Noll.

Next to him, Larkin let out a wail. "I must save the queen!" he proclaimed. "She's a damsel in distress! Only I can save her from certain death!"

"Oh, brother," Vic heard Noll mutter. Without letting go of Vic, Noll reached out and yanked Larkin away from the edge of the boat. He pinned Vic and Larkin to the bottom of the boat.

"Ariana, Em, can you get me some rope to tie these two up?

Vic heard some scrambling around, then he was flipped onto his stomach. He struggled with all his might. He had to get back into the lake! He needed to steal those priceless jewels! He felt rope bite into his ankles. He jerked around, but it didn't help. Soon, his legs and arms were immobilized.

"Noooo!" he protested. He thought hard. "There's enough for everyone, I swear. I'll steal it from the queen and share it with all of you. The queen is rich. Let me go and we'll all be rich beyond your wildest dreams!"

"She's not rich," Larkin said from beside him. Vic moved his chin around and saw that Larkin was tied up next to him. His head thrashed from side to side, and little flecks of spittle erupted from his mouth. "She's poor! Her father died and left her destitute. Bad men are coming for her! Only I can help! You must let me go!"

"Can you two stand watch?" Noll said to Ariana and Em. The girls nodded. Vic heard Noll grunt, then he heard the oars splash into the water, and then the boat began to move again.

"Em!" Vic said. "Em! Em! You have to cut me loose." His voice dropped. "I can steal it all, Em. We'll never be poor again. Just let me go!"

Em turned her head away.

"Em! Em! Please!"

Next to him, Vic heard Larkin pleading with Ariana to be returned to the lake. She said nothing to him in reply.

Vic's head began to feel feverish. The blue sky circled above him, faster and hazier until he shut his eyes.

When he opened them back up, he found that he was lying on his back on the ground. His wrists and his ankles were still bound.

"What happened?" he asked. "Where am I?"

"You're out of the boat and away from the lake," Em said. A moment later, Vic saw Noll walking toward them with Larkin flung over his shoulder. He set him down beside Vic.

"Can we untie you now?" Noll asked. "You won't go running back toward the lake?"

Vic shuddered. "No chance of that," he said. "I was about to drown when...when..."

"When Larkin and Noll pulled you out of the lake," Em finished. "Noll grabbed Larkin's ankles as Larkin laid over the side of the boat and into the lake. Once Larkin got a hold of you, Noll pulled you both out of the water."

Vic felt Noll tugging at his knots while he listened. Ariana loosened Larkin's ties at the same time. When he was free, Vic sat up and rubbed the raw spots on his wrists and ankles.

"It was Larkin's plan," Noll said. "He had to think quickly. He was afraid that if he jumped into the lake, something bad would happen to him."

"It did," Larkin said quietly. "It brought out the worst in me. It was another test, and I failed it again, just like I did with Scrofa when I fell into the river."

Vic looked at Larkin, open-mouthed. Vic knew that it was his own fault that he'd almost gotten them both killed. Larkin had just risked his life to save Vic's, and yet here Larkin was, acting as if he was the one who had done something wrong. What made this boy tick?

Vic felt a door open inside of his soul. Guilt and self-loathing seeped out. He wallowed around in it. It was unpleasant.

He'd misjudged Larkin terribly, he realized now. When they'd first met, Vic predicted that Larkin was the kind of boy who would never apologize—moments before he did, in fact, apologize. He'd save their lives with the Hudenpole. In return, Vic had given Larkin no reason to trust him or like him, which was why Larkin always addressed Em and never Vic. Vic had told Em that Larkin would choose himself over Vic if things got dangerous, but Larkin had just proved him wrong about that, too. Vic flicked his eyes toward him. A look of irritation and disgust was stitched on Larkin's face. Vic couldn't blame him for being angry.

Vic's face buzzed and he felt it turn pink. He had to come clean. He had to tell them the truth about himself, and if he didn't do it now, he was afraid he never would.

He opened his mouth. No words came out. He closed it again.

He just couldn't do it. He realized suddenly that he wanted these kids to like him. What would Larkin and the others think of him if he told the truth?

Vic cleared his throat. He had to speak up.

"I," he started to say, but Ariana raised her hand to silence him.

"Oh, no," she said in a hoarse whisper.

"What?" Larkin asked.

"Not this," she whispered. "Not when we're so close to Rockhaven."

"What is it?" Vic asked, but as he did, he heard a howl that made his legs feel like they were made of pudding.

"Wolves!" Ariana shouted. "Run!"

Chapter Twenty
Larkin–The Forest

The five companions scrambled down the slope. Larkin was in the lead. The howls of the pursuing Wolves sent shivers down his spine and spurred him on. He looked ahead and caught glimpses of great fields that were visible through the trees. They were that close to getting out of The Forest and completing their mission of warning Rockhaven of the invasion, but it looked like they weren't going to make it.

He looked back again and was horrified by what he saw. Em had stopped in her tracks halfway down the hill. She turned slowly and walked back toward the sound of the Wolves.

"Em!" Larkin screamed out.

But Em kept walking.

Larkin dug his heels into the hillside and ground to a stop. The thought flashed through his mind: Em or Rockhaven?

By the time he'd stopped sliding, he'd decided. He ran back up the hill after Em. The others turned, realized what was happening, and followed him. Ariana nocked an arrow into her bow, while Larkin and Noll drew their swords. Vic picked up a large rock to arm himself.

They hadn't yet reached her when the first Wolves burst onto the scene.

"Em!" Vic half-yelled and half-sobbed.

But to Larkin's amazement, the lead Wolf skidded to a halt in front of Em as the other Wolves fanned around them in a semi-circle. The lead Wolf was gray and huge, the size of a pony. It looked at Em in curiosity. Time seemed to stand still. Then, the Wolf turned to the others and growled while Em turned to her companions and spoke.

"This is Talullah. She is the queen of the Wolves. I could hear what she was thinking as she was charging down the hill. She's worried about her son. He's deathly sick. It sounds like some kind of infection. I've told her that I think I can help."

"Em!" Vic said, his voice hoarse and strangled. "I thought you could only talk with cats and dogs."

She shrugged. "Me, too," she answered. "But Baedyn said that I might be able to talk to other animals in a time of need. I thought he meant a time of need for me." She motioned her head toward the Wolves. "But this is a time of need for them."

The other Wolves began growling a little, but Talullah gave a short, sharp bark, and they sat back on their haunches and waited. Em and Talullah faced each other, and a tense silence prevailed. Finally, Em spoke.

"I'm going back with Talullah. The rest of you should go on to Rockhaven. The Wolves won't follow you."

"I'm not letting you go alone!" Vic cried.

Em turned back to face Talullah and the unnatural silence returned for a moment. Both Em and Talullah looked at Vic. Everyone then turned to look at Larkin. The decision was being left to him. He felt the same way he'd felt outside The Scourge's cabin, when he'd agreed to let Vic take the riskier job—like a great invisible hand was pushing down on him. He'd never realized that leadership could be such a burden, especially when lives were at stake. He wished he could be sure that he was making the right choice. He nodded slightly at Em.

"I don't like splitting up," Larkin said. "My heart says we should all go with Em, but my head says we can't delay our task any longer."

"I'll go with her," Vic croaked.

Larkin didn't care much for Vic, but he had to admit that the boy had some guts. And he didn't blame him for being afraid. The Wolves' teeth were the length of carving knives. He nodded and turned to Em.

"We must get word to Rockhaven. I trust you and your instincts, Em. If the Wolves will allow Vic to go with you, and if they'll allow us safe passage out of The Forest, then I think we have to split up for now."

Em leaned into the giant she-Wolf until their heads almost touched, then she addressed her companions.

"Talullah says you can come, Vic. She'll escort us back to the edge of The Forest when we're done." Em turned to Larkin. "She'll allow you safe passage out of The Forest. When Vic and I are finished, we'll find you in Rockhaven."

"Em, are you sure?" Ariana said. "I mean, it's all well and good that you can talk to them, and I guess you can add them now to the list of animals—cats, dogs, and Wolves—that you can talk with, and we believe in you, but..." She looked the Wolves up and down. "They're awfully big. And their teeth are huge."

"I think we'll be fine," Em said. She saw Larkin's uneasiness and stepped toward him. She got on her tip toes and whispered in his ear, "It's going to be all right. Thanks for trying to defend me. And thanks for trusting me." She turned to her brother. "Come on, Vic," she said.

Larkin felt a pang as he watched them go with the Wolves. He shuddered at the thought of what the giant Wolves would have done if they'd caught up with them. He realized that Em had saved their lives, but now she was risking her own. He wondered if he'd ever see her and Vic again. He'd grown fond of Em in the short time he'd gotten to know her.

He didn't wish any ill will on Vic, but Larkin admitted to himself that he didn't care at all if he ever saw the boy again.

He also knew that he, Ariana, and Noll had to carry out their original task—to try to warn Rockhaven of the attack upon Kavenland. There were a lot of people counting on them.

The whole country, in fact.

Still, he knew Ariana and Noll felt the same way he did about seeing Em and Vic walk away with the Wolves. The three friends carried on in silence, each with their misgivings as they headed down the hill and—for the first time in what seemed like ages—

stepped out of The Forest. They stopped and looked around at the open fields and the open sky.

"We made it," Noll said. He shook his head. "I thought you were crazy to suggest it, Larkin, but we made it."

"And now all we have to do now is get to Rockhaven and warn Sir Alymer," Ariana said.

Her nose wrinkled. "I sure hope Em and Vic are going to be ok. Em sounded like she knew what she was doing."

"I agree," Noll said. "I have faith in her."

Larkin nodded. He did, too.

The Great Road lay just in front of them and ran to their right along The Forest and up to Rockhaven. On the other side of the Great Road was a vast plain of farmland, with scattered houses and barns. These fields fed most of the southern and western parts of Kavenland, Larkin remembered from his school lessons.

They stepped onto the Great Road. They walked for a couple of hours until they crested a rise in the road, then they stopped in their tracks.

Before them stood Rockhaven, and behind it, far in the distance, the snow-capped peaks of the mountains. A massive wall, some fifty feet high, stretched in a great arc from the impenetrable hills to their left across the plain to join the hills that tumbled out of The Forest up ahead and to their right. Larkin had heard that Rockhaven was unassailable, and now he could believe it. It was said that the hills surrounding the city could not be traversed by an army. A siege seemed the only way to defeat Rockhaven. Even then, the people of Rockhaven could harvest the fields and wait behind their walls for a year or more before hunger drew them out.

A breeze blew down from Rockhaven and across the plains. On it, Larkin could smell a chilling black treachery and a pale red despair.

Larkin stopped in his tracks. He realized that he had to stop ignoring these smells.

"What is it?" Ariana asked.

Larkin wasn't sure. This new odor now gave him a sense of foreboding, despite the sunshine and blue skies. Was it Tallulah's despair about her son? Was Vic up to some sort of treachery?

"Let's keep going," Noll suggested. Larkin reluctantly walked on, but the sense that something was wrong grew inside of him. He was about to speak up when Ariana interrupted his thoughts.

"It looks like we got here just in time," she said. "And it was just as you feared, Larkin—no one else got through to warn Sir Aylmer."

"You're right," Noll agreed. "The farmers we walked by seemed to have no sense of urgency. Wouldn't they all be working to get their crops inside the walls if Sir Alymer knew an attack was coming? And look at the walls. I don't see any banners raised or any activity indicating that they're getting ready for a fight."

"Here comes some activity now," Ariana said. Her hands shielded the setting sun as she peered toward the castle. "And it looks like trouble."

Larkin couldn't see as well as Ariana—no one could—but as a band of riders grew closer, fear clutched his heart.

At the head of the group that made its way toward them was a tall man with silver hair.

Larkin was suddenly sure that the cause of the treachery and despair he'd smelled was coming straight at them. He wished he'd reacted the moment he'd taken in those smells. If they'd run back into The Forest then, maybe they wouldn't have been spotted from Rockhaven. Now, they were on foot and badly outnumbered.

He'd failed again.

A surge of anger swept through him. His right hand went to the hilt of his sword. Next to him, Noll growled and pulled out his sword. Ariana already had her bow out and was pointing it from one rider to the next as they circled around the three friends.

But Larkin realized that fighting was fruitless. They were on foot, and the riders on horseback had them outnumbered ten to one. He cautioned his friends to lower their weapons.

The man with the silver hair reined in his horse and sneered down at them.

"What have we here?" he said with contempt. "Three vagabond travelers, barely of age. What could bring you to Rockhaven?"

"Our business is with Sir Alymer," Larkin said.

Before he could say anything else, the man reached to his side and flicked out a long whip. It caught Larkin sharply on his left cheek. He blinked and raised his hand to his face. He felt blood, warm and sticky on his fingers.

"A boy should act with better manners when addressing a superior," the man said.

"And when I see one, I will," Larkin retorted.

The silver-haired man snarled at him, then he seemed to reconsider. "So you want to speak to Alymer? We can arrange that."

He gestured to one of the men and a rider-less horse was brought forward.

"Put your weapons away," he said to his men. He got down from his horse, grabbed Larkin by the front of his shirt with one hand, and lifted him up as if he weighed no more than a small child. For a surprised moment, Larkin's arms and legs flailed, and then he was dropped roughly into the saddle. The silver-haired man then turned to Ariana.

"My lady," he said, bowing mockingly and taking a step toward her.

"I'll get up myself," she said. The man looked at Noll as Ariana scrambled up behind Larkin.

"Whoa-ho," he said. "We have a big one here. Better get him his own ride." He gestured toward a small pony, which was brought forth.

"I'll walk," said Noll defiantly.

"You'll ride," said the silver-haired man. He reached for his whip. Noll, with a look of fierce determination on his face, crouched into a fighting stance.

"Noll!" said Larkin.

Noll looked at Larkin, looked around at the men crowded around them, and reluctantly sheathed his sword. He climbed on the pony, an angry and sour look on his face, as the silver-haired man laughed derisively. Noll's feet dragged the ground on either side of the small animal which lurched under Noll's weight. Larkin thought that Noll might cower in humiliation, but he sat tall in the saddle, a look of defiance smoldering on his face like a pot of water about to boil over.

The silver-haired man jumped on his horse and rode away. The companions, surrounded by the other riders, were herded along after him. They soon passed through the gate and into the city of Rockhaven. It had grown dark, and there was little activity on the streets. A short time later, they reached the castle and dismounted. They were hustled through the massive front doors, and the silver-haired man led them quickly through corridors and down two flights of stairs.

"Where are you taking us?" Ariana demanded.

The silver-haired man grunted but said nothing. The companions were half-pushed down a short corridor, the sharp points of swords stuck in their backs. The silver-haired man stopped in front of a large oaken door and reached for a key ring that hung on the wall. He separated out a large key, which he slipped into the lock.

"What are you doing?" Noll asked sharply, but as the door swung open into the hallway, the trio was quickly shoved through the doorway and into a dark room. They stumbled forward and before they could turn around, the door closed behind them. Larkin heard the lock close with a metallic clang.

Thoughts rushed through Larkin's head in the darkness. They'd survived so much to reach Rockhaven—The Forest, Scrofa, the Hudenpole, the Scourge, the lake, and the Wolves.

But none of that mattered now.

They were prisoners.

He'd failed.

Chapter Twenty-One
Em–The Forest

As they walked back through The Forest, Em reached out slowly and put her hand on Talullah's shoulder. Some of the Wolves seemed to have accepted her presence, but Em could feel tension among a few others. They weren't talking, but many of them were looking at the biggest Wolf other than Talullah. That Wolf bared his fangs at Em.

It wasn't a smile.

Streaks of saliva made his teeth glisten in the late afternoon sun. The hair on the back of his neck bristled.

Vic sidled up to Em. "These Wolves give me the creeps," he whispered. "My goosebumps have goosebumps."

Em looked at Talullah, then turned back to her brother.

"Talullah says you walk as quietly as a Wolf," she said. But then she beckoned for Vic to lean toward her. She lowered her voice, and said into his ear, "Don't show fear."

"But I *am* afraid," Vic croaked. "Look at the size of the teeth on that mean-looking one! His incisors are longer than my hand!"

"I know that it's hard, but the more scared we are, the more the other Wolves will rally around him. He doesn't trust us."

"I feel the same way about him."

"Try not to think about it," Em said. Vic had plenty of courage, she knew, but he didn't understand animals like she did. True, the big Wolf and his followers might rip them to shreds. But showing fear was the worst thing they could do right now.

After a few minutes, Talullah halted and turned to face her.

"I'm going to talk with the other Wolves," she communicated with Em. "We are close to our home. Many Wolves will not like me bringing you there. They think that if you escape, you'll bring back more men to try to kill us."

"We won't do that," Em said. "I promise you that I will do everything I can to save your son, and that I won't betray your trust in me."

"I believe you," Talullah answered, "but it may be that I am blinded by the desperation I feel for my son." She sat on her haunches, but even in that position, she was taller than Vic. "Still, my instinct says to believe you."

Talullah nodded her huge head and turned to address the other Wolves while Em filled in Vic about what the queen of the Wolves had told her.

Vic took a deep, shaky breath. "Great," he muttered underneath his breath. "I hope you know what you're doing."

"Me, too," Em replied. She pulled him down so that she could whisper in his ear. "You do realize that we were probably not going to outrun the Wolves, don't you?" She let go of him. "Well," she added, "you might have been fast enough, but the rest of us wouldn't have made it."

"I never would have left you behind," he said.

She patted his arm. "I know."

"And I would have stayed with you in Baedyn's Valley," Vic added.

Faster than she thought possible, water sprung to Em's eyes. Saying no to Baedyn's Valley was the hardest thing that Em had ever done in her life. Her heart had told her that she belonged there. Or most of it had.

She could live with animals all her life. But she knew Vic wouldn't be happy there. Despite all the rejections he'd suffered, he still wanted and needed to be accepted by other people. That would never happen in Baedyn's Valley.

Besides, she was enjoying the company of other people for the first time in her life. She felt a warmth inside her, like snow melting on a spring day. Every instinct told her that Larkin, Ariana, and Noll were good kids. She just hoped that Vic would let down his defenses long enough to see that for himself.

Talullah called Em over. "The Wolves would like to know what you were doing in The Forest. Frankly, I'd like to hear about that myself."

Em pursed her lips. She decided to leave out the part where Vic and she were from a different world.

"Kavenland has been invaded," she said. "We entered The Forest from Laketown in the company of a dog named Canis. We met up with three others from the north of Kavenland. That's who you saw us with. We were in the Valley of Baedyn, and he thought enough of our mission that he allowed us to pass through his lands."

The Wolves glanced at each other at the mention of Baedyn's name. Em addressed them all when she continued.

"We hope that you'll allow us to rejoin our friends once we've helped your queen's son. I know that you don't trust humans, and I don't blame you for that. I can only tell you that my brother and I mean you no harm."

The Wolves muttered to themselves. As they did, Vic beckoned her over.

"Em," he whispered hoarsely. "What makes you think you can heal this Wolf?"

"I still have the herbs and medicine that the Hudenpole gave me," she answered. "I don't see why they wouldn't work on a Wolf as well as they did on my foot."

Vic's mouth dropped open. "You're risking our lives on that?"

"I think it will work," Em said.

"Great," Vic muttered. "That's just great."

As they talked, some of the Wolves paced back and forth and growled at Em and Vic. The big, unfriendly Wolf approached Talullah. They touched their heads for a minute or two before Talullah padded over to Em.

"That is Ridgely," she said. "He is my son's best friend. He has spoken for the Wolves who don't like your presence. He's agreed to allow you into our lair." Talullah's voice trailed off, but Em thought she understood what Ridgely's condition for granting them safe passage back out of The Forest might be.

"If I'm successful, I think they'll let us go," Em told Vic.

"And if you're not?"

Em tried to keep all expressions from her face as she looked back at him. He shuddered.

"Death by Wolf," he said with a gasp. "Definitely not the way I want to go."

Em had no argument with that.

They followed the Wolves in silence. As dusk settled, they walked into the center of a large clearing, surrounded by jutting rocks on three sides. Em could see caves within the rock walls, with the largest straight ahead of them. Talullah led them to that cave. Ridgely stopped outside. Em approached him, but she didn't make physical contact with him as she had with Talullah. Ridgely let out a low growl, but then quieted down. Em held a brief exchange with him, then turned away and followed Talullah inside.

"What was that all about?" Vic whispered.

"I'll tell you later," Em whispered back.

In the far end of the cave lay the biggest Wolf that Em had yet seen. It gave off a fetid odor. Flecks of foam were on its lips and its head lolled from side to side. High on its muscular left foreleg was a weeping open wound. It let out a weak growl as Em walked toward it. Em beckoned to Vic.

"This is much worse than I'd feared," she confided to him. "Can you get the cup out of your pack?"

Vic obliged, though Em saw his hands shake as he pulled the cup from his bag. Talullah spoke, and Em turned back to Vic.

"The injured Wolf is Fangmeer, Talullah's son and the heir apparent as King of the Wolves. He was wounded a week ago, and the gash on his leg has become infected. There was talk of removing it."

Vic shuddered. "Amputation by Wolf," he said in a choked voice.

"Fangmeer refused," Em continued. "He's weak and feverish and failing quickly. Had we been here the day he was injured, I think that healing the wound would have been easy with the medicine I was given by the Hudenpole. But I don't know whether Fangmeer is too far gone now."

Vic gulped. "If it's too late for Fangmeer, that means it might be too late for us, too."

Em didn't answer. She sensed again that showing fear was unwise, even if Vic was right. Of course, there was plenty to be afraid of, but she tried to block it out of her mind.

Em took the cup from Vic and poured some water into the bottom. She added the mixture she'd been given by the Hudenpole and ground it into a paste. She looked at Fangmeer.

"I want you to know," she said, "that this is going to hurt. Snapping at me will do no good for either of us."

She took a deep breath and knelt in front of him. She scooped out the paste from the cup, paused for a moment, then exhaled and lathered the paste over the awful wound.

Fangmeer bolted up and let out a bellow of pain. The force of his roar blew back Em's hair as wet saliva flew into her face. His breath had the sort of awful, sour smell that attracted buzzards and bugs. His jaws snapped inches from Em's face, and for a moment, she thought he might bite her head off.

But he settled back, grimaced, and let out small huffs of pain through gritted teeth. Em felt his huge muscles tense and spasm, but she worked slowly, making sure that the entire wound was covered. Finally, she stood up and looked at Talullah.

"I've done all that I can. He needs to rest. We'll come back and check on him in the morning."

Ridgely led them to the center of the clearing, and they lay down to sleep. Em stared up at the strange constellations in the sky and thought about home for the first time since Adelessa led them through the Door in the Stone.

She didn't miss it.

She didn't miss kids making fun of her, even though it didn't bother her nearly as much as it used to, and being an outcast didn't bother her nearly as much as it bothered Vic. She had come to realize that no one else should have the power to make her feel bad about herself. It could be hard in school, where she didn't have any real friends. But she had Vic, and she had cats and dogs, and that had to be enough for her.

It was different here. She'd seen and done more things in a few days in Kavenland than she had in her whole life back home. It was strange and scary and wonderful all at once. Besides, she liked Larkin, Ariana, and Noll. They hadn't judged her. They'd accepted her and her ability to talk with animals. She didn't have to hide who she was.

She thought she and Vic could fit in here.

Em decided that she was happy that they'd come.

Of course, she'd be happier if the medicine worked on Fangmeer.

"Do you think we could slip away from here?" Vic asked, as if reading this last thought.

"Not a chance," she said. "I'll bet Ridgely has his supporters watching us all night. I don't think trying to escape would help our chances of living through the night."

Vic let out a long sigh. He rolled over and tried to get to sleep. Em looked back up at the sky.

The next thing she knew, something hard was pressing into her rib cage. She looked up to see the giant snout of Ridgely poking into her. The early morning rays of sun spilled a halo around his great head.

"You have been summoned," he said. He put his paw on Vic's shoulder and shook him awake. Vic bolted up like he'd sat on a thumbtack. He looked around wildly until he made eye contact with Em. He swallowed and licked his lips.

"I hope your medicine worked," he said.

Em nodded in reply. She did, too.

They followed Ridgely over to Talullah' cave. As before, Ridgely stopped outside, and Em and Vic entered.

Em let out breath she hadn't realized she'd been holding. She could see immediately that Fangmeer was better. The foam was gone from his mouth. The wound had closed completely, and it no longer oozed. The massive Wolf sat up as Em approached him.

"Thank you," he said. "I can feel that your medicine has healed me."

"You're welcome."

"Will you please send Ridgely in? I'll talk with you more after I talk with him."

Em motioned for Vic to follow her. She told Ridgely that Fangmeer wanted to see him, and the huge Wolf brushed past them. They moved toward the large clearing. Vic paced anxiously, while Em wandered around with her hands behind her back. She didn't see any other Wolves, but she sensed they were being watched.

Vic sidled over to her.

"What did Ridgley say to you yesterday before we went into Fangmeer's cave?" he asked.

"He told me that I'd better heal the prince," she answered. "He also told me that he didn't think that I would."

"Cheerful," Vic grumbled.

After a few minutes, Em looked up to see Ridgely slowly wander out of Fangmeer's cave with his head bowed. Another Wolf trotted over to Em and Vic.

"Fangmeer will see you now," he said. They followed him across the clearing. The Wolf stopped outside of the cave and stepped aside for Em and Vic to enter.

Em and Vic walked quietly back into the cave. Fangmeer moved his head in the direction of his mother, so Em and Vic went to Talullah first.

"I give you the thanks of a queen," Talullah said, "but more importantly, I give you the thanks of a mother."

She leaned forward and licked Em. As gentle as Talullah tried to be, her tongue still felt like a wet wire brush being scraped across her face. Even so, it was wonderful.

"It's been a great honor to do you a service," Em said. She felt, for some reason, that she needed to be formal, so she curtsied. She nudged Vic, who bowed awkwardly. Talullah barked out a short laugh that she tried to turn into a cough.

They turned to Fangmeer.

"Thank you," Fangmeer said. "You have saved my life."

Em translated for Vic as Fangmeer continued.

"Ridgely and I were hunting a week ago. We brought down several bucks. I told Ridgely that I would stay behind to guard the food, and that he should run back here to get help."

Talullah padded over and laid a great paw on her son's shoulder. "He did this, even though the rule is that Wolves must never travel alone."

Fangmeer craned his neck to meet his mother's gaze.

"My decision was arrogant," he said. "A mistake I will never make again." He turned back at Em and continued.

"While Ridgely was gone, four White Bears emerged and challenged me for the food," he said. "I fought them off for as long as I could. I was wounded, and I would have certainly been killed, but Ridgely arrived back just in time. He sank his fangs into the biggest Bear. The other Wolves attacked, and the White Bears ran away."

Talullah's eyes flicked toward the entrance of the cave before they settled back on Em and Vic.

"Ridgely has a sad history," she said quietly. "His parents went raiding in the fields outside of Rockhaven when he was just a cub," she said. "It's a dangerous job, and one Wolves won't do unless it's a time of great famine. His parents were killed by farmers who were protecting their livestock. Ridgely has hated humans ever since."

"He's asked for my forgiveness for the incident with the White Bears," Fangmeer said. "I've tried to tell them that he saved my life, but he doesn't see it that way. Instead, he blames himself for leaving me alone. So I've told him I will forgive him under two conditions: first, that he forgives humans. His parents were doing what Wolves do, and the humans were doing what humans do."

He paused and smiled.

"What is the second condition?" Em asked.

"That Ridgely gives you a ride to Rockhaven. You will move much faster with him than you would on you own."

"Thank you," Em said.

"Thank you, Em," Fangmeer said. "I owe you my life. If you should ever need us, the Wolves are in your debt. Now, I'm sure you're eager to rejoin your friends in Rockhaven, so Ridgely will give you a ride to the edge of The Forest." His lips curled up in another smile. "You'll be the first humans to ever ride a Wolf. It's a small price to pay for the debt I still owe you."

With nothing more to be said, Em led Vic out of the cave. Ridgely loped over to them and sat on his haunches in front of Em.

"You've saved him," Ridgely said. He slowly lowered his great, shaggy head toward Em. He rested his forehead gently on hers. Em felt a glow so warm that she got goosebumps.

"You've saved me, too," he told her. "Thank you."

She threw her arms around his neck. "You're welcome," she whispered in his ear.

"I'm sorry for the way I treated you," Ridgely said. He looked away as he spoke. "When my parents were killed, Talullah took me in and raised me as a son. I thought until this morning that Fangmeer would die, and that I was responsible for his death. He is my best friend, and he is like a brother to me."

"I understand," she whispered back. "My brother is my best friend, too."

"Please tell your brother that I admire his courage," Ridgely said. "He stayed with you even though he knew he could die. He has the heart of a Wolf."

"Yes," Em agreed, "he does. I only wish he realized it."

She stepped over to her brother and told Vic what Ridgely had said.

Vic looked at Em, then back at Ridgely. "Uh, thanks, Ridgely. Or Mr. Ridgely, or...uh...thanks."

Ridgely let out a noise that sounded like a chainsaw starting. Vic leaned into Em.

"Did he just laugh at me? First a dog and now the Wolves? I'm the comedy hit of Kavenland's animal kingdom!"

Em bit back a smile and turned to Ridgely. He smiled back, with his great, wet teeth, and laid down on his stomach.

"You will be safe," Ridgley said. "You may not see them, but Wolves will be accompanying us throughout our journey. Come."

Em glided over to him as if on a current of air. Beside her, Vic's shoulders sagged, and he dragged himself over to the great Wolf. Now that they were out of immediate danger, the weight of Vic's encounter with the queen of the Lake had settled upon him, Em saw. They climbed on Ridgely's back, and he trotted off quickly and quietly. Em could feel the Wolf's powerful muscles beneath her, and Ridgely moved as lightly as if there was no one on him at all.

A feeling of euphoria washed over Em. Her senses tingled, and she felt more alive than she ever had in her life. In the last three days, she'd met Baedyn and petted a unicorn. Then, she'd been able to perform a service for Wolves that were the size of small horses. Now she was riding one, and they were on their way to meet three interesting kids who she liked and who seemed to like her, too. Her only worry was her brother.

Vic had been acting cocky the whole time they'd been here. It was his defense mechanism. She knew Vic wanted to feel accepted, but she also knew that he had to accept himself first.

"It's OK, Vic," she said.

"What's OK?"

"All of it. I understand that you don't want to trust Larkin." Vic didn't want to trust anyone. "I know why, too." A long series of Vic being rejected by kids scurried before her eyes. Those kids were too scared to buck the popular kids who made fun of Vic's clothes and their house, or too shortsighted to see what she saw in him and what Ridgely saw in him. "But if you don't trust anyone, you're going to wind up alone and lonely."

And maybe a hardened thief, Em thought. That would be bad, too. She wanted the Vic she knew, not the Vic he thought he had to be.

It was one of the reasons that she was glad they'd come through the Door in the Stone. Em was afraid that Vic was starting to enjoy stealing things back in their world. She understood the desperate need for attention that had started him down that path, but he was outgrowing the childish reasons for being a thief. She knew he'd stolen things to keep them alive, too, but there wasn't any need for that anymore, either.

She wanted him to be the Vic that he was when it was just the two of them together, not the Vic that he too often showed to the rest of the world. Going through The Door in the Stone could give them both the fresh start they needed.

"Ridgely's right, you know," Em told him. "You do have the heart of a Wolf."

Vic harumphed, but Em could tell that he was secretly pleased by the comment.

They rode in silence for a while. "We should be at Rockhaven well before nightfall," Ridgely eventually told her.

Em could tell that they were moving at a little different angle than they'd been going with Larkin, Noll, and Ariana, and she guessed that Ridgely must be taking them on a more direct line to Rockhaven. Em wished the ride could go on forever, but it wasn't long before Ridgely came to a stop.

"We're here," he said. They were just a yard or two inside The Forest. Em could see the great wall that stretched from the tumbling rocks to their right, across the floor of the Valley, and to the foot of the high, craggy hills on the other side. It dwarfed the wall they'd seen in Laketown. The Valley was at its narrowest point here and fanned out to the left, where farms and long rows of crops stood in wide fields.

All they had to do now was cross the field in front of them, approach the gate, and find Larkin and the others.

Ridgely let out a small noise.

"What is it?" Em asked.

Ridgely stared at the castle. "Larkin and the others should have been here by now," he said, "and yet there's no sign that Rockhaven is preparing for an attack. The walls should be garrisoned, and people should be working feverishly in the fields to get the crops harvested and inside the city walls." He turned to Em.

"There's something wrong."

Em translated for Vic. He groaned.

"Now what?" he said.

"There's another way in, a way that's unguarded," Ridgely said. "We'll have to move further up into the hills, and it'll be dark before we get there."

He paused and shook his huge head as if something had just occurred to him. As he spoke to Em, she felt Vic's anxiety as he stood by her shoulder. What Ridgely said made perfect sense, and it also made Em's stomach drop.

"You're right," she said to Ridgely.

"Wait," Vic said. "Right about what? What are you talking about?"

When Em spoke again, her words sounded small to her own ears. They sounded as empty as she suddenly felt.

"Ridgely says that if the alarm hasn't sounded, it can only mean one thing for Larkin, Ariana, and Noll."

"And what's that?" Vic asked.

"That they're in big trouble."

Chapter Twenty-Two
Noll–Rockhaven

Noll reached the door moments after he heard the lock click shut.

"Let us out!" he yelled, as he hammered on the door. "We must get word to Sir Alymer! Rockhaven is in grave danger! Kavenland is in grave danger!"

There was no reply. All he heard was footsteps retreating down the corridor. His forehead sank into the wooden door. Was it possible that they'd come all the way across their country, that they'd reached their destination, and that it wasn't enough?

Noll shuffled a few steps back, lowered his shoulder, and ran at the door. He rammed into it with everything he had.

The door didn't budge. Noll staggered backward and fell to the ground.

He thought of their village in flames, of the evil Kynwas killing the tanner and his two sons. He thought about everything they'd been through to get to their destination. He wondered if it would all end here, on this hard-packed dirt floor in a dungeon in Rockhaven. Noll felt frustration and anger surge through his body. He leapt up, let out a yell, and beat on the door until his hands grew raw and sore.

"Unbelievable," said Ariana. She strode up beside Noll and kicked at the door in irritation. "With all that we survived in The Forest, to have come all this way, and now we've failed."

"It's my fault," Larkin said. "Coming through The Forest was my idea. I talked you into leaving our families and friends behind for this fools' errand."

"And what errand was that?" a voice asked from the darkness.

Noll froze. Beside him, Larkin tensed. Ariana took a step forward.

"Who's there?" she demanded of the voice in the dark.

Noll stepped past her toward the voice the darkness. "Who are you?" he roared. "What do you want? Why didn't you say something when we were thrown in here?"

There was a grunt and the sound of a man getting up from the murky recesses of the dungeon room. He hobbled toward them. When he stopped in the dim light of the doorway, Noll saw that his ankles were bound, and his hands were tied behind his back. His sheer size surprised Noll. The man was almost as big as he was.

A few days ago, Noll might have tried to make himself seem smaller. Now, though, he stood his ground and stood up to his full height. The man's eyes shot up as he looked at him.

"Well," he said. "I'm guessing you're not from around here." His eyes darted to Ariana and Larkin and then back to Noll. "From your clothes, I'd say you look like northerners."

Larkin stepped forward. "You're Sir Alymer, aren't you?"

"Yes," the man answered. "I'm Alymer. And who are you? And what is this errand you were on? How is Kavenland in great danger? And what the devil do you mean by surviving The Forest?"

Larkin introduced himself and his friends. Noll and Ariana sawed through Sir Alymer's binds with their swords as Larkin filled him in on what had happened, beginning with the invasion of the Archipelagans in the north, their conversation with Adelessa, and their journey through The Forest to warn Rockhaven. He told him about meeting up with Em and Vic and learning of the invasion of Laketown. He left out Gurn, the Hudenpole, The Scourge, and Baedyn, as well as the fact that Vic and Em weren't from their world. Noll thought that was smart, because as he listened, even Noll had a tough time believing what Larkin did tell Alymer, and he'd experienced it all.

"And where are these other two from Laketown?" Alymer asked after thanking Noll and Ariana.

"Still in The Forest," Larkin answered.

As Sir Alymer rubbed his wrists and ankles, he narrowed his gaze at Larkin.

"It's part of my job to know when someone speaks the truth and when someone lies," he said, then muttered under his breath, "though I was deceived myself recently." He spoke up again. "Your story rings of the truth," he said, looking at the others before his eyes settled back on Larkin, "though perhaps not the whole truth," he added, raising an eyebrow.

Noll saw Larkin's cheeks flush, but before he could aid his friend, Ariana stepped forward.

"I'm glad you believe us, Sir Alymer, but if you'll forgive me, it doesn't seem like that does us much good, since we're locked up in this dungeon. I mean, we could be circus performers or traveling bards or the last of The Protectors, and it wouldn't really matter. The problem is out there," she said, pointing to the door, "and we're stuck in here, on the wrong side of that door, if you see what I mean."

Sir Alymer nodded glumly. "You're right." He strode to the door and rapped his knuckles against it. "Eight inches thick," he said. "Re-enforced on the outside. No handle on the inside. The strongest padlock the greatest steelmakers in Rockhaven could forge. Beredor himself couldn't break through that door."

"But how did you wind up in here?" Noll asked.

"I was tricked by a scoundrel and betrayed by a friend," he answered. Sir Alymer slapped the palm of his hand against the door. The noise echoed throughout the room. He turned back to face Noll and his friends.

"Did you meet Grydyl," he continued. "Silver-haired fellow?"

Noll and his friends nodded.

"He came here about a year ago," Sir Alymer continued. "I never cared for him, and my wife couldn't stand him. But he became friends with Roderick, my lifelong best friend. Roderick took over many of my duties running Rockhaven after my wife died."

A cloud of anguish crossed over Sir Alymer's face. Then his expression hardened.

"After I finished grieving, I thanked Roderick for his service. But it's clear that Roderick enjoyed his taste of power and decided to grab it for himself. He and Grydyl threw me in this dungeon a week ago."

Noll looked at Larkin. So did Ariana. Larkin stroked his lips with his forefingers.

"It seems to me that this invasion has been well thought out," he said slowly. "Adelessa told me that the Archipelago has been planning this attack for centuries. The hardest part of Kavenland to get to would be here in the south, and your stronghold would be the toughest to attack. But what if they didn't have to attack? What if Grydyl came here from the Archipelago a year ago with the aim of overthrowing you? Then the gates would be flung open to the invaders because they'd be opened from the inside. And if that plan didn't work, they have another army marching here from their invasion of Laketown. "

Sir Alymer nodded. "You're a very sharp young man," he said. "It does makes perfect, diabolical sense," Sir Alymer said. He paused.

"And it also means that if we can't get out of this dungeon, Kavenland is doomed."

Chapter Twenty-Three
Vic–The Forest and Rockhaven

Ridgely carried Em and Vic back through The Forest with Rockhaven off to their left. It soon disappeared from view as the Wolf picked his way up the jutting cliffs and rugged hills that made up the natural defense on this side of the city. The hills seemed to Vic to be insurmountable.

But Ridgely kept finding draws and gullies that allowed him to climb higher. As they neared the summit, the trees grew shorter and shorter, and at the top, there were no trees at all. Light faded as they looked down at Rockhaven far below. They dismounted from Ridgely to give him a break from the long climb, but he soon indicated to Em that they should get back on. As they did, Vic could see the outline of two other Wolves behind them, keeping watch. He shook his head in wonder. Yesterday, he was terrified of being ripped to shreds by a giant Wolf. Now he was riding one with others close by, and he'd never felt safer in his life.

The climb down the other side of the steep cliffs, though, was frightening. Vic was sure there was no way down, and he could understand why Rockhaven had been built where it was and why the people felt secure inside their massive front wall and the tumbling cliffs that encircled the city. He sunk his hands deep into Ridgely's fur and clenched tightly. Ridgely let out a low growl.

"You're gripping too hard," Em told him. "Ridgely promises that you won't fall."

In a few short days, Vic realized, he'd gone from questioning his sister's sanity to trusting completely her ability to communicate with animals, so he forced himself to relax his grip. Ridgely was amazingly surefooted as he bounded down the steep face of the rock. Trees began to reappear, though they were sparser on this side of the cliffs, growing up as they did from the tiniest of flat spaces. He couldn't help but compare them to himself, clinging to life under less-than-ideal conditions.

Finally, Ridgely leapt down into a steep trench filled with round stones. Em quickly translated from Ridgely.

"This is where the water runs off from the hills in the springtime. There's a wall ahead that was built by the people of Rockhaven many years ago, and a small hole in the wall that allows the water in. They store the water in a great underground well and use it all summer long. The hole is heavily grated on both sides of the wall, so there's no getting through that way."

She paused, and Ridgely made some more guttural noises. Em nodded and translated.

"The wall dips down near the trench and is only about ten feet high. It might be guarded during an invasion, although it doesn't seem likely that an army could get down here."

Vic agreed with that. As sure-footed as he was, he wouldn't have wanted to climb down here on his own. An entire army could never do it.

The big Wolf stopped parallel to the wall. Em climbed off for a moment and threw her arms around the great Wolf's neck. "Thank you," she said in a voice muffled by Ridgely's fur. As she climbed back on, Vic swore he saw the Wolf's teeth bare in a smile.

Once Em was back up beside him, Vic knelt on Ridgely's back, and Em stood up slowly on his shoulders, using the wall for support. Then Vic stood up as well, with one hand steadying the back of Em's legs and the other groping for the wall. His legs shook from the weight and the awkwardness, and a bead of sweat trickled down his forehead.

Then, suddenly, the weight was gone.

"I'm on top of the wall," Em whispered.

Vic looked up. Em lay flat on the wall with her arm stretched down. "Can you reach me?"

Vic reached up. His fingertips brushed against Em's outstretched hand. "All I'd do is drag you off the wall," Vic said A thought sprang to mind.

"I'm going to jump on three," he said. "Can you ask Ridgely to help?"

Em spoke to the Wolf and moved out of the way. Then she counted off. "One." Vic flexed his knees. "Two." The huge Wolf crouched and arched his back. "Three!" Ridgely straightened up fast and Vic jumped. He was catapulted much higher and further than he'd thought he would be. He cartwheeled his arms and legs in panic. He had a brief glance at the city, and for a moment, he was sure that he was going to sail clear over the wall to the other side. But the wall was wide, and he landed on it with a thump that knocked the wind out of him.

"Made it," he grunted.

"I can see that," Em said with amusement in her voice. She looked back down at Ridgely.

"Thank you!" she said in a loud whisper. Vic peered down through the darkness. He saw moonlight glint off white teeth. One more Wolf joke at his expense. Then he saw a flash or two of movement, and Ridgely was gone.

They collected themselves for a moment. Then Vic looked down on the Rockhaven side of the wall and saw a lane whose houses ended some 15 feet or so from the wall. The lane stretched toward the castle in the distance. Candles still burned in the windows of many of the homes, giving the city a soft glow. He guessed that it was about nine o'clock. He thought that he might be able to leap onto one of the houses, trusting that his landing would be quiet enough to go unnoticed. He could help Em climb down the wall, and they could search for Larkin, Ariana, and Noll.

But then he had a strong impulse.

Larkin, Ariana, and Noll wanted to save Kavenland, but their motivation was different from the one he and Em had. The other kids were fighting for their loving families, snug houses, and regular meals. It sounded like it was worth fighting for, maybe even dying for.

But he and Em had only come to Kavenland because they were forced to. What he and Em wanted was what Larkin and the others had. His hand went to the gold comb that was still in his pocket. Adelessa had said it was worth far more in this world than in their world.

He and Em could have a new life here. He thought of his bad parents who drank too much and cared too little for him and Em. He thought of not fitting in with the other kids back home. This was their chance to start over.

He could sell the comb. Rockhaven was a big place. Surely, he and Em could slip away and start a new life here with the money they got. He'd been thinking about leaving the others behind all along, but events had conspired against that idea. Now was their chance. What did it matter to them which side won the war?

Besides, he feared what Larkin and his friends thought of him, and what they would think of him if he told them what type of person he was. Better to avoid another heartbreak and simply disappear. It would be easier that way.

But was running away from his problems again what he really wanted? It was when they'd first arrived in Kavenland, and he'd been running away in his mind ever since they'd gotten here. But he himself had been the cause of the problems here, he realized. It was he who'd treated Larkin badly ever since they'd met, not the other way around. He'd had a chance to come clean after the incident in the lake, but he hadn't spoken up quickly enough.

Suddenly, those images were crowded aside, and the vision that Adelessa had first shown him in their own house came back to him. He saw himself and Em with the others walking through The Forest. He saw them together in Baedyn's cottage. He saw warmth and caring in the faces of Larkin, Ariana, and Noll. Em had sensed it first, he now realized, and that was a big reason why she'd turned down the offer to stay in Baedyn's Valley.

Yes, they'd only known the others for a couple of days, but they'd already saved each other's lives. They'd already built a bond that Vic hadn't felt with anyone, ever, except Em.

He recognized that he was afraid, but it wasn't this war that he was afraid of.

He felt the familiar acid ball in his stomach. It tried to spread. It tried to remind him that kids like him didn't have friends, that to trust anyone else was to be a fool. Trust was the road that led to heartbreak and disappointment.

He gritted his teeth. Images of Chip Newhart and the other mean kids at school sprang to mind. In desperate hope, he'd put his trust in them time after time, but that trust had been misplaced. He was afraid to trust anyone again.

He didn't know what to think.

He didn't know what to do.

"I'm sorry I brought us here, Em," he whispered.

She squeezed his hand. "I'm not," she said firmly.

"But don't you wish we could go back to the way it was in our world before I stole that stupid comb?" he asked.

"No."

"If Adelessa showed up right now and offered to take us back through the Door in the Stone, you wouldn't want to go?"

She shook her head. "I like it better here. For both of us." She rested her hand on his shoulder. "I don't want you to be a thief, but I'm glad you stole that comb, because it got us here."

Vic didn't realize the burden of guilt he'd been carrying since Adelessa had taken them through the Door in the Stone. It was his fault that Adelessa had the leverage to make them follow her. It was his theft of the comb that had upended their lives. But Em's words made it feel as if a mountain had slid off his shoulders. She was happier here. He felt lighter.

The other guilt was there—the guilt of how terrible he'd been to Larkin. For now, he felt energized by it. He would use it as fuel to help Larkin and his friends in any way he could.

Maybe he didn't have to run away here to start a new life. Larkin, Ariana, and Noll seemed willing to accept him for who he was as long as he treated them the same way.

"Are you ready to find the others?" Em asked him.

Vic felt a surge go through him. He recognized it as resolve. It jolted him the same way that something had when he'd decided to rob the jewelry store back home. But that resolve was frayed at the edges. This resolve was icy hot and strong and full.

"I guess at the very least," he said, "I owe Larkin an apology." He gestured to the house closest to the wall.

"I'm going to jump onto that house. You know how light I can be on my feet. Then I'll climb down, circle back to the bottom of the wall, and help you down."

Vic walked along the top of the wall until he was even with the nearest house, took a deep breath and leapt. He landed softly, caught himself with his hands as he sprawled forward, and scrambled off the roof. He jogged back to the wall. Em turned around, held the top of the wall with her fingers, and walked down the wall until her legs were completely stretched out. She looked down at Vic, he nodded, and she let go.

Vic half caught her, and half broke her fall. They tumbled to the ground, got up, dusted themselves off, and headed down the street toward the castle in the distance. They'd agreed that that was the place to go. Vic hoped that they'd soon have a good laugh with their new friends about the steps they'd taken to sneak into Rockhaven.

He doubted it, though.

Ridgley was right. There definitely seemed to be something wrong.

If Rockhaven knew that an invading army was advancing on them, there would surely be some more activity than this. The streets were dark and quiet. Too dark and too quiet.

"Meow!" a cat screeched loudly.

Vic stiffened as if he'd been jabbed by a cattle prod. Em knelt down beside the cat. "Have you heard anything unusual?" she asked it.

The cat purred and rubbed itself against Em. Em shook her head at Vic.

"Nothing," she said. She thanked the cat, and they continued, sticking to the shadows as they got closer to the castle.

They stopped at the edge of a great square with the castle on the other side looming above them in the darkness. As Vic pondered what they should do next, a man in fine robes strode purposefully across the square, followed closely by two other men. All three had swords hanging from their belts. The man in the nice clothes had a grim look on his face.

Vic nudged Em. "Looks like they're heading into the castle."

Crouched over and using the darkness as cover, they followed the three men, stopping at the bottom of the wide steps that climbed to a set of massive double doors. Two sentries, standing casually outside the doors, drew themselves up to attention as the men approached.

"Sir Dryndar!" one of the guards said. "It's quite late, sir."

"Pressing business," said the man in the fine clothes. "I need to see Roderick and Grydyl right away." His manner was crisp and authoritative. The sentries bowed.

"Of course, sir. Wait in the front hall, and we'll get them for you."

"Get ready!" Vic whispered to Em. The huge doors swung open, and with all eyes on Sir Dryndar as he marched forward, Vic and Em glided up the stairs and slipped inside the castle doors. They were in a large, dimly lit room. Vic grabbed Em's hand and led her into a corner. One sentry went to fetch Roderick and Grydyl, while the other closed the front doors then came back and stood in the middle of the room with Sir Dryndar and his two attendants. Dryndar paced briskly in a small line, back and forth.

A few moments later, a huge man with silver hair appeared, trailed by the sentry. Vic remembered the silver-haired men leading the invasion of Laketown when he, Em, and Canis had been running through the streets. Vic felt his skin crawl. The silver-haired man looked coolly down at Dryndar and gave a curt bow. "Sir Dryndar," he murmured. He dismissed the two sentries with a casual flick of his wrist. He watched them leave, then addressed Dryndar.

"What can I do for you at this late hour?" he said, with what appeared to Vic to be a trace of annoyance.

"Kavenland has been attacked. A large army will be here within a day or two."

The silver-haired man flinched but recovered quickly. "And how did you come about this information?"

"A farmer working my fields escaped from the attackers and made his way to me. He said another farmer was with him and came here to warn you. Is that true?"

"No one has come to me with this information. Are you sure of this man? Surely you don't know every peasant who works your fields?"

"He's not a peasant, as if that mattered. He's a farmer, and his family has worked in my family's fields honorably for generations. I can vouch for the man."

"Well, it's certainly too bad that Sir Alymer hasn't returned from his hunting trip yet. However, as you know, Sir Roderick has taken his place in many affairs and has been staying here at the castle in his absence." He clapped his hands, and two men emerged from the shadows. "Get the conservatory ready and have someone fetch Sir Roderick," he commanded. The two men left the room.

He turned back to Dryndar and asked, "Can you tell me anything about this invading force?"

"No, only that it IS, in fact, an invading force. It's been a thousand years since we've fought a war. And if they're this far south, they must have already taken Laketown and possibly Glensworth, too. If King Tenney has had the courage to leave his stronghold," he muttered to himself. "But there's no sense in saying all of this twice, Grydyl. Someone needs to get word to Alymer and bring him back here, and I have to talk with Roderick. Now!"

The silver-haired man looked unruffled. "I'm sure Roderick will be in the conservatory soon. There's no point in getting there before he does. Have you sounded the alarm, told anyone else of this news?"

Dryndar shook his head with exasperation. "There was no time. I came here immediately."

Grydyl nodded his head. "You acted wisely. Everything must be all set in the conservatory by now. This way." He walked through an open doorway at the far end of the room. Dryndar and his two attendants followed.

"Come on!" Vic whispered, and they trailed silently behind the party.

They got through the doorway just in time to see the group ahead of them turn a corner. Vic and Em tiptoed forward and peeked around it. They watched as Grydyl opened a door for Dryndar and his attendants and followed them inside. Vic and Em advanced cautiously toward the room. They heard a muffled cry, the sounds of a scuffle, and then silence. Vic looked at Em. Without speaking, they dashed back down the hall and hid behind a suit of armor. A moment later, Dryndar and his men were dragged away down the hall.

"Where should we take them?" one of the men asked Grydyl. "With the farmer?" So the other farmer had gotten there after all, thought Vic. "Or with Alymer and the three young ones from last night?"

Em clutched Vic's shoulder.

"With the farmer," Grydyl answered. "I'm not sure what Alymer and Dryndar can do together tied up in a dungeon cell, but it's best to be safe and keep them apart. Quickly now," he added. "We don't want them waking up."

Vic and Em crept out from behind the suit of armor. Up ahead, the three groups of men carried their unconscious burdens down a flight of stairs. Grydyl was watching their progress when a tall, proud-looking man appeared from a side corridor.

"Grydyl," he said, "what do we have here?"

Vic and Em froze. Vic thought for a moment that the man was talking about them, but neither of the men glanced back down the hallway. Vic was a bit surprised that Grydyl took on an obsequious manner.

"Sir Roderick," he said, bowing deeply. "A small disturbance is all. Dryndar and two of his men showed up. They know of the invasion. They've been dealt with and are being taken to the dungeon."

"Does anyone else know of the invasion?" Roderick asked sharply.

"Dryndar says no."

"More loose ends."

"If you'd allow me some more permanent solutions, there'd be fewer loose ends."

Roderick shook his head. "We've already talked about this. When the Archipelagans make me the regent of Rockhaven, it'll be easier to rule if I don't have blood on my hands, especially the blood of someone as popular as Alymer."

"As you command," Grydyl answered, bowing again.

Roderick gave a curt nod and walked briskly away. Grydyl's servile expression changed into a sneer at Roderick's back.

"Regent of Rockhaven?" he muttered under his breath. "We wouldn't let you rule a henhouse." Then the silver-haired giant strode away in the opposite direction from Roderick.

Vic leaned toward Em and whispered, "Let's go!"

Em nodded. They moved down the hall. Vic held his breath as he peered around the corner and down the stairs where the guards had dragged Dryndar and the others.

He didn't see anyone. He exhaled.

"All clear," he whispered.

They tiptoed down to the first landing. Long hallways stretched in either direction. Most of the doors were closed. One was open. Light spilled out into the corridor, and Vic could hear the voices of men.

"I'll bet a silver and two bronze," one voice said.

"Roll the dice," said another.

Other men laughed and whooped and cheered.

Vic motioned for Em to follow him down the second flight of stairs.

What would they find when they got to the bottom? Would other guards be there or not? He reached the bottom and peeked around the corner. He went limp with relief.

The guards were nowhere in sight, and a set of keys hung from a hook on the wall.

Several huge doors stood on each side of the hallway. Vic removed the keys. His hands were slick with sweat, and he almost dropped the keys. They clanged together like a windchime. Vic swore under his breath. He whirled around, expecting to see a squad of armed guards sprinting down the stairs.

Nobody came.

Vic turned his attention back to the doors. When he turned the key in the first lock it made a dreadful "click," and the door seemed to make as much noise as a Steelers' crowd after a touchdown as it swung open on its rusty hinges, but it still wasn't loud enough to summon the guards.

The room was empty.

"We don't know what's behind any of these doors," Em said between gritted teeth. "It could be Dryndar. It could be Larkin and the others. It might be some murderer for all we know."

Vic nodded. The same thoughts had occurred to him.

He pulled open another door as quietly as he could, although he still winced at the sound. He moved quietly into the dark room, but before he could take another step, he was whisked off his feet, and a hand was clapped over his mouth.

Chapter Twenty-Four
Larkin–Rockhaven

As soon as they heard the key groan in the lock, Sir Alymer motioned for everyone to be quiet. He waved them over to stand behind where the door would open. He quickly gestured and mimed what he wanted them to do.

When the door opened and a figure stepped cautiously inside, Noll grabbed him, and Alymer, Larkin, and Ariana rushed out into the hall.

As they did, they nearly stumbled over a second person.

Larkin stopped.

"Em!" he cried out in surprise. He instantly cringed at how loud he'd said it. Inside the dungeon room, he heard Noll's voice.

"Vic!"

Ariana seized Em by the shoulders. "Em!" she exclaimed in a loud whisper. "Vic! How in the world did you find us?" She swung her head back and forth before her eyes settled on Vic. "Not that I mind, of course. I mean, we weren't getting out of here without you. This is Sir Alymer, by the way. He's the one we came to find to warn about the attack, although, of course, we didn't expect to find him down here when we were captured last night. It's amazing, by the way, how long a day seems when you're cooped up in a dungeon." She turned to Em. "What happened with the Wolves? What were they like? Did you heal the queen's son? What..."

Sir Alymer raised his hand. "I'm assuming that these are your two friends who stayed behind in The Forest?" he asked. Larkin nodded. "I'm sure we all have a lot of questions," Alymer continued with a nod to Ariana, "but they'll have to wait. Right now, we must get out of here."

He turned his attention back to Em and Vic. "Can you tell me anything about our situation?"

Vic quickly recounted how they'd followed Dryndar inside and how he and his two men had been ambushed, knocked unconscious, and dragged into one of the other dungeon rooms. He also told him that both Grydyl and Roderick knew all about the invasion.

As he spoke, Larkin looked at Vic closely. He seemed different somehow. The furtiveness was gone. He made eye contact as he spoke.

Larkin remembered what he'd thought when Vic and Em had left with the Wolves.

He'd hoped that he'd never see Vic again.

He'd never been happier to be wrong in his life.

Alymer nodded as Vic finished talking. "It seems that this coup has been managed with just Grydyl, Roderick, and a handful of soldiers loyal to Roderick," he mused. "That should make things easier, even if I'm not sure who in the castle I can trust. We'll need to get to the top of the stairs as quietly as possible. Can you swing those swords you're carrying?" he asked Larkin and Noll.

Larkin nodded. He looked at Noll. His mouth slashed a grim line across his face. He nodded firmly. Noll's determined expression made Larkin feel an inch or two taller.

"Not good odds," Alymer continued. "If we added the men in the dungeons that would even things up a little. But it sounds like they'll be in no condition to fight. I hate to do this, but let's leave them behind for now. Avoiding a confrontation is our best bet, anyway."

With that, Alymer guided the companions out the door and up the stairs. They reached the top and moved swiftly and quietly toward the front of the castle. Alymer led them across the great room and into another hallway. He came to a door, opened it, and ushered everyone inside.

"The armory," he said. He grabbed shields for Larkin and Noll and a sword and shield for himself. He opened a drawer, pulled out a piece of paper, and scrawled something on it. He placed it in an envelope and stamped it shut with a seal.

"What about us?" Ariana said, gesturing to Vic and Em as well. "I want to stay and fight!"

"I admire your spirit, but hopefully there won't be any fighting yet. You can help in another way. I need you to get word to a man named Fergus who's loyal to me." He handed the envelope to Ariana. She was fuming as she snatched it from his hand.

"Give him this," Sir Alymer continued. "He's not more than five minutes from here, but the way is filled with twists and turns. Each of you needs to memorize a small part of it. If you're successful," he added, looking straight at Ariana, "you'll be back here in no time with an army behind you. If you fail, nothing that we can do here will matter. Follow me."

He made Ariana, Vic, and Em repeat the directions back to him one-by-one as he led them to a side entrance of the castle.

"Good. Fergus is a good man. I don't need to tell you that he must raise as many of his men as he can and return here as fast as possible. Good luck," he added, and ushered them out the door.

He turned back to Larkin and Noll.

"Come with me. I need to find Roderick and put a stop to this."

Alymer led Larkin and Noll back down the hallway and across the great room. He opened some doors but found only empty rooms behind them. Larkin counted the minutes. He figured his friends had left ten minutes ago. Five minutes to find Fergus, a few minutes for him to gather his men and get armed, and another five minutes or so to reach the castle.

Adrenaline coursed through his body, and a jumble of thoughts whirled around his head like a tornado. Were they really going to have to fight? Part of him hoped that help would arrive before the trouble started. But then he thought of Kynwas and the silver-haired men who'd burned their village up north. He remembered his vow of revenge. His mind grew sharp and focused.

They entered the hall that led to the dungeon stairs. Two men strode toward them. Larkin immediately recognized Grydyl as the man who'd left a welt below his eye with the whip. He thought the other man must be Roderick.

"Alymer!" the man gasped.

"Roderick, my old friend," Alymer replied, with irony and bitterness in his voice. "Didn't expect to see me, did you?"

If Grydyl was surprised to see Alymer, he didn't show it. He turned to his companion. It was clear who was in charge. "Go get the guards, Roderick," he said. Roderick immediately turned around and fled down the stairs.

Alymer turned calmly to Noll and Larkin. "Go down this hallway to the left," he said quietly. "Take two rights, and you'll be behind Grydyl and back at the top of the stairs. Hold off the guards as long as you can. Help should arrive soon.

"Grydyl," he then said, turning back to the silver-haired man, "I take no pleasure in killing. But with you, I'll make an exception."

Larkin and Noll tore down the corridors and came up behind Grydyl a few moments later. The silver-haired man and Alymer had pulled their swords and walked toward each other. Down below, they could hear Roderick rousing the soldiers. It wouldn't be long before they were streaming up the stairway. Larkin looked up at Noll.

If Vic had changed in the last couple of days, so had Noll. When Larkin had awoken in Baedyn's cabin, Noll and the Ancient had been talking. Noll had stood straighter and walked more purposefully since that time. Larkin clapped his hand on his friend's shoulder.

"I know it hasn't always been easy being the biggest," he said. "But it sure could come in handy now."

Noll's eyes gleamed and a malicious grin spread across his face. He unsheathed his sword and glared down the stairs. Larkin heard a clash of swords behind them and took a quick glance at Alymer and Grydyl. As big and strong as Alymer was, the silver-haired man was bigger and appeared to be pressing the attack. Larkin thought about rushing to Alymer's aid, but when he turned back, he saw Roderick charging up the stairs with six guards behind him. Several steps below them, Roderick came to an abrupt halt as he noticed Larkin and Noll for the first time.

"Well," he said, sneering. "What do we have here? A couple of boys defending Sir Alymer?"

Larkin's throat felt very, very dry. He hoped he sounded more certain than he felt as he spoke.

"We're of age," he said.

"Not for much longer," Roderick threatened. "Run away, boys, and let the grownups settle things."

"The only thing that will be 'settling'," Noll snarled, "will be your head at the bottom of these stairs."

Roderick paused.

But it was a brief pause.

"Very well!" he growled.

Roderick and his men drew their swords and charged up at Larkin and Noll.

Chapter Twenty-Five
Ariana–Rockhaven

Ariana was furious. She didn't want to run an errand. She wanted a chance to redeem herself. She wanted to protect Larkin and Noll.

She wanted to fight.

But as they ran through the twisting streets of Rockhaven, Ariana began to understand why all three of them were needed.

"Second left!" Em called out. They raced around the corner.

"First right!" Em said, and they sprinted up a small lane.

After three more quick lefts and rights, it was Vic's turn to call out the directions. Then it was Ariana's turn. And she realized that Sir Alymer had been right. They were only five minutes from the castle, but they must have taken ten different turns. There was no way one person, or even two, could have memorized the directions.

It didn't make her any less agitated, though.

"Is this it?" Vic asked, as he slowed to a stop in front of a large home. Ariana brushed past him and began pounding on the door.

"Wake up!" she yelled. "Sir Alymer needs you. Now!"

A couple of moments later, the door was flung open, and a large man with a long red beard and heavy shoulders stood glaring down at them. His ample stomach strained against his night shirt as if it were the vanguard of a one-man army.

Ariana thrust the envelope at him. "Read this note!" she said.

Fergus rubbed his eyes as he opened the envelope with a thick finger. "Couldn't this wait until morning?" he groused.

Ariana threw her head back in exasperation and pointed her arm to where she thought the castle was. "Roderick and Grydyl have staged a coup. Sir Alymer needs you right now!"

Fergus shook his great shaggy head and let out a roar.

"Grydyl! That slick, silver-haired..." He sputtered and ran out of words. 'Wait here!" he commanded.

He disappeared inside the house. Ariana heard some yelling, and soon a thin man scurried out, darted between them, and hustled down the road. Fergus then re-appeared, a sword at his waist, stuffing his nightshirt into a pair of pants.

"Let's go!" he bawled. Ariana and the others tore off but stopped when they heard Fergus holler from well behind them.

"Whoa, whoa, there, young jackrabbits! I'm not built for speed." He lumbered up behind them, already breathing hard. "Besides, I sent my butler off to get help. We're likely to need more than just us if there's been a coup. Now," he continued between huffs and puffs, "can someone tell me what's going on?"

Ariana blew a hard breath out. Vic stepped in front of her and explained what had happened. Ariana noticed that as he talked, he kept walking to hurry Fergus back the way they'd come.

Fergus reminded Ariana of a big bear. He was large and hairy, and he grumbled and snorted as Vic told him what they knew. By the time they reached the castle, the big man was red-faced—and not just because of the exertion of being pushed along faster than he would have liked.

All around them, soldiers streamed up streets and alleyways and converged in front of Fergus. Ariana guessed that there were at least fifty of them. She glanced at Fergus, then back at the castle, then back at Fergus again. But she wasn't the only one who was impatient.

"Men," Fergus shouted, "Sir Alymer is under attack. Two boys are in there with him. Anyone else you see inside is probably an enemy. Let's go!"

Fergus clumped up the steps. Ariana and the others followed with the rest of the men.

"Open the doors!" Fergus ordered, and the two guards on duty moved quickly to obey. "Sir Alymer is in danger. Come with us or be branded traitors," he ordered. Ariana saw the men glance at each other as they whisked past and then fall in behind them.

They hurtled into a large room. Two new guards sprang toward them, swords raised but dropped them when they saw they were outnumbered.

Fergus motioned for some of his men to search the rest of the castle. They sprinted away as he grabbed one of the captured guards by the collar.

"Where is Sir Alymer!" he demanded. He shook the man so hard that Ariana wasn't sure if the man could answer. But before he could try, a huge, silver-haired man burst into the room. He dashed past Fergus, knocked over two of his men, and ran for the open doors.

It was Grydyl, and he was going to escape.

This was the man who had imprisoned Larkin, Noll, and herself.

This was the man who'd put Kavenland's last chance to defeat the invaders in danger.

Ariana felt a bonfire light inside her. She'd felt surges like this in the past, but it had never been this strong before.

She had to protect her friends.

She had to protect her country.

She leapt forward and ran at the man. He turned and leered at her. He lashed at her with his fist, but she ducked under it and hit him in the stomach. His muscles were like iron, but he made a satisfying grunt of pain. He stepped back and swung his sword at her in a silver blur. She slid underneath it and kicked at his ankles. His legs were like tree trunks, but he still stumbled. Then he turned and ran toward the door.

Ariana sprung to her feet, cried out, and toppled back to the floor. Her ankle screamed in pain. She looked up to see the silver-haired man bounding toward the door.

Then someone dashed past her. It was Vic. He flung himself on Grydyl's back. The silver-haired man staggered, off balance, and crashed into the wall. Vic hung on, his arm around the man's throat, but the man backed him into the wall hard, twice. Vic's grip slackened, and he slipped to the floor.

But Ariana and Vic had slowed Grydyl enough. He was surrounded before he could escape. Ariana limped toward him. Vic weaved unsteadily to his feet. Ariana was sure that the fight would be brief, and that the silver-haired man would be overpowered, but Grydyl fought like a wild man. Two of Fergus' men slumped to the floor and two more flew back as if they'd been hit by a battering ram. Ariana thought for a moment that the silver-haired man would break free, but Fergus and six others finally subdued him, bound his ankles and wrists, and stuffed a gag in his mouth.

From somewhere else in the castle, they heard a commotion, then quiet. Fergus tied a long rope around Grydyl's ankles, grabbed the end of the rope, and began dragging him toward where they'd heard the sound. The rest of his men followed.

Em came to Ariana's side. Ariana flexed her foot and rolled her ankle around. She hobbled a few steps, grimaced, and leaned toward Em. The fire within her had cooled, and she felt exhausted.

"Thanks," she said through gritted teeth.

Em looked back at her, wide-eyed. "That was amazing," she said. "It took a dozen men to bring him down, and you might have done it yourself if you hadn't hurt your ankle."

Ariana shrugged. "It's just something that overcomes me when people or things that I care about are threatened." She looked down at her new friend. "Not as awesome as hanging out with a bunch of enormous Wolves. I can't wait to hear all about it."

Vic made his way toward them rubbing the back of his head.

"Nice work," Ariana said. "Grydyl would have gotten away if you hadn't jumped on him."

He nodded, then winced in pain as he rubbed the back of his head.

"Now what?" he asked. His eyes looked a little glassy and unfocused.

"Now we find Larkin and Noll," Ariana answered. "And hope," she added, crossing her fingers for luck, "that they didn't run into Roderick or Grydyl."

Chapter Twenty-Six
Larkin–Rockhaven

arkin was scared, but only for a moment. After that, there wasn't time.

Roderick and his men yelled and ran up the steps. Larkin and Noll shoved at them with their shields, using their advantageous position from the top of the steps to push down on their attackers. Roderick stumbled and fell back into the men behind him. After that, Larkin and Noll swung their swords furiously, if inexpertly. Larkin tried to tell himself to remember his lessons with his uncle, but it was hard to do when the fighting began.

Their shields proved to me more useful, and Larkin was glad Alymer had gotten them out of the armory. He and Noll used them to ram down at the men as they came up the stairs. One of the guards nearly broke through, but Noll grabbed him with his free hand and hurled him back down the stairs and into the advancing soldiers. Several of them lost their balance and fell backward.

They regrouped on the landing below. Larkin heard himself panting. In the distance, he could hear the clashing of steel and the exertions of Sir Alymer and Grydyl. He had no idea which of them was winning, but he didn't dare turn around to look.

He did cast a quick look at Noll. His friend stood tall and erect. He stared down at the soldiers, and Larkin's eyes followed his. One of the men lay crumpled on the landing. Larkin could see his chest rise and fall slightly. The man had been knocked unconscious. One man clutched at his side, and when he drew his hands back, Larkin could see that they dripped with blood. Another man stood against the wall. He moaned and rocked back and forth holding onto his arm, which stuck out at an odd and unnatural angle.

There were still several men left, however.

"Charge!" Roderick yelled and leapt back up the stairs. The remaining men followed him. Noll and Larkin flailed away, stabbing, kicking, and pushing with their shields. Larkin felt a short, sharp pain in his forearm, but he kept on shoving and thrashing away. Between the yelling of the men, and the clashing and clattering sound of metal against metal, and the blood rushing in his ears, it was all a lot louder than Larkin expected.

But above their din came another noise from somewhere else in the castle. A voice that sounded like Sir Alymer's shouted "In here!" Suddenly others were at their side, and Roderick and his men were throwing down their swords. Larkin and Noll staggered back, helped by friendly hands which patted them on the back and voices that congratulated them. His adrenaline siphoned out of him, and Larkin sagged against a wall. His body ached, and he could feel the sting of a cut on his arm. He looked at it. It wasn't anything serious. Noll was covered with blood, but his smile stretched wide and confident across his broad face.

"Well," he said to Larkin. "We did it."

Larkin managed to smile back. His first real fight. He hadn't run and he hadn't died. He sheathed his sword and looked down at his hands. They trembled. He wondered if being in fights would ever get any easier.

There was some final commotion toward the front of the castle and then a relative quiet. A large red-headed man appeared down the hall, dragging Grydyl behind him, bound and gagged. Several soldiers staggered behind them. One clutched an arm, another gasped for air. Larkin spotted Vic. He was rubbing the back of his head with one hand and holding onto Em with the other. He looked unsteady. Ariana had her arm thrown around Em's shoulder. She walked with a pronounced limp.

Larkin and Noll rushed to their friends.

"What happened?" Larkin asked. Ariana quickly told of their dash through Rockhaven to get Fergus and of the capture of Grydyl. Larkin filled them in on their fight at the top of the stairs.

They turned around as Roderick and his men were brought forward, and Alymer began talking with the red-haired man.

"Fergus!" Alymer exclaimed. "You arrived just in time. And not just to save us tonight, though I thank you most heartily for that," he said with a grin. His face grew serious again. "These younger ones," he continued, pointing at Larkin, Noll, Vic, Ariana, and Em, "arrived at my cell, where I've been held captive for the last week. They rescued me and came with an extraordinary story of Kavenland being invaded by an army from the Archipelago."

"What?" Fergus bellowed, but before he could continue, Alymer raised his hand.

"I know it sounds fantastic, but I believe them. Roderick and Grydyl plotted to overthrow me. Thanks to my five new friends, that part of their plan has failed. But Larkin thinks they have a second part to their plan—a back-up in case the coup failed. He thinks that an invasion is still coming. I think he's right. The invaders can't be more than a day or two away. There's no time to lose."

Larkin noticed that Grydyl had been squirming on the floor. He could see now that he'd loosened his gag and sat up.

"You fool, Roderick! You weak fool! This is why I told you to kill him." He looked at Alymer. "Just like I killed your wife," he spat. He looked around at everyone in the hall, head moving wildly from one face to another. "You will all still die. We've been waiting for this moment for centuries. Our father was sneered at in Kavenland, but the time for his revenge has arrived."

"What did you say about killing my wife?" Alymer asked in a hoarse whisper.

"Oh, yes," said Grydyl proudly. "I poisoned her at your anniversary feast. I knew it would make you weak and vulnerable. You're all weak and vulnerable. If Roderick had killed you, our armies would have walked through open gates, unopposed...'

Grydyl's diatribe was ended by the back of Alymer's hand crashing across his mouth. Blood and spit flew as his head spun to the side, and though Larkin was sure the blow must have hurt terribly, Grydyl turned back with a smile.

"You will die," he said. "You will all die."

Alymer reached for his sword, but then stepped back. "Yes, I shall die," he said through gritted teeth. "We'll all die. But not today and not by your army." He looked at one of his guards. "Gag him, make sure he's bound tightly, and throw him in the dungeons with Roderick and their followers."

"Weak!" Grydyl taunted, as the soldier walked toward him. "You're too weak to even kill the man who killed your wife!"

"No," Alymer answered quietly. "I'm too strong to do it." He looked down at his hand. "I never should have struck you." He looked back at Grydyl. "We have laws here, and those laws must be obeyed, even by those in power. That's what true strength is. What would be weak would be taking the law into my own hands and killing you, as much as I'd like to right now."

He turned away as the men dragged their prisoners off. He beckoned for Larkin and his friends to come forward. He looked at Vic and Ariana.

"How are you feeling?"

Vic managed an unconvincing smile.

"Okay," he said.

Ariana grimaced and nodded. "Fine," she said.

"They're heroes!" Fergus bellowed. "That scoundrel Grydyl ran past me and knocked over two of my men. If it wasn't for them, Grydyl would have gotten away."

Larkin wasn't surprised at all that Ariana had acted. He turned his attention to Vic. The boy smiled shyly back at him. Larkin reached out his hand.

"Thanks for saving us," he whispered.

Vic took his hand and shook it. "I owed you," he whispered back.

"If Grydyl had escaped," Alymer continued, "he could have warned the invaders that we know about their attack. They thought they would have the element of surprise. Now we do."

Alymer gestured to Larkin and the rest of his friends.

"Thanks to the five of you," he said, "we have a chance to save Kavenland."

Chapter Twenty-Seven
Vic–Rockhaven

Vic should have slept soundly.

His head was propped up on two down pillows. A thick cover was pulled up under his chin. His body felt like it had been enveloped by the mattress, which was somehow soft and firm at the same time. It was nothing like his thin, lumpy mattress back home, on the other side of the Door in the Stone.

But guilt had robbed him of sleep as surely as he'd robbed Mr. Zipkoff's jewelry store of the gold comb that was in his fist. Every time he'd touched down into sleep, guilt and insecurity wrenched him awake.

He needed to tell Larkin and the others that it was his theft that had brought him and Em to their world.

He wasn't sure how the other kids would take it when he confessed, but he knew that he had to tell them the truth.

He had to.

But finding the time to do it was hard.

He got up. At the foot of his bed were his clothes, washed and pressed. Noll was already dressed. He stretched, his shoulders looking like boulders as he rolled his head around his massive neck. He looked down at Vic's clothes, and his head tilted to one side. He reached down and held something up between his fingers, arm outstretched.

"What are these?" he asked Vic.

Vic felt his face turn crimson. He hopped out of bed and snatched his underwear out of Noll's hands.

"They're called 'tighty whiteys' in my world," he said. He started to get dressed. Noll stopped and sniffed the air.

"Bacon!" he exclaimed. A third bed had been dragged into the room late last night, and Vic watched as Larkin rubbed his eyes and swung his legs out of bed.

"C'mon, c'mon," Noll urged as Larkin tugged his clothes on. "Follow me," Noll said, and tapped the side of his nose. He grinned at Vic. "We can leave the important smells to Larkin. When it comes to food, though, I'm your guy."

Vic and the others followed Noll. Vic should have been famished, but his stomach was unsettled, and the thought of food made him queasy.

They stepped into the hallway and ran into Ariana and Em. Ariana walked without a limp.

"I used some of the poultice I got from the Hudenpole on Ariana's ankle," Em said. "How's your head?" she asked Vic.

Vic ran his fingers over the spot that Grydyl had rammed into the wall. Em had put some of the poultice there, too. Now there wasn't even a bump. The cut on Larkin's arm had closed as well.

"Score another one for the Hudenpole," Vic said.

Em put her arm around Vic's shoulder and whispered in his ear.

"Can you believe this place?" she asked.

Vic shook his head, but he couldn't speak. Words stuck in his throat like he'd swallowed a huge spoonful of peanut butter.

"This way, I think," Noll said. The huge boy walked with confidence down a long hallway. As they neared the end, a woman bustled out of a swinging door, carrying an armful of bread loaves. She stopped when she saw them.

"You must be our guests," the woman said. "On to the dining room, then." Noll winked at his friends and tapped the side of his nose as they followed her down the hall.

"You have to be half-starved," the woman continued. She ushered them into a large room. Several others were eating around a long table, among them Sir Alymer, who looked tired. But he beamed when he saw the companions.

"Our young heroes!" he said and beckoned for them to be seated.

They sat down to eat. Between mouthfuls, Larkin asked Alymer what would happen next.

"Thanks to you five," he answered, "we've been able to spend the night getting ready for the invasion. All the houses are sending soldiers, and we're assembling an army outside the walls. We'll set out shortly, find the enemy, and attack.

"You've earned a spot with the army, but I want you with a reserve force behind the forward lines. I hope we won't need you. You've all done enough to try to save us."

Ariana scowled and looked ready to say something, but Alymer didn't seem to notice.

"A few of my advisors said we should stay behind our walls," he continued. "But it sounds like much of Kavenland has been overrun. How could we hide here in safety when the rest of our country is in danger? We must meet the enemy and destroy it."

He pushed back from the table, wiped his mouth, and got up to go.

"Get yourselves fitted in the armory, and I'll see you outside."

Vic watched Sir Alymer go. He looked around at the tapestries and paintings that hung on the walls. He took in the great marble fireplace at one end of the room, and the elaborate woodwork of the chairs that they all sat upon.

Vic had daydreamed about being rich. He'd fantasized about comfortable beds and heaping plates of food. It surrounded him now, but he couldn't enjoy his experience.

Guilt filled him up and left no room for any other emotion.

How was he going to be able to tell Larkin and the others who he really was? He glanced at Larkin, calm and in control, and Noll, strong and focused, and Ariana.

Ariana...

Ariana...

Em nudged him in the ribs. She rolled her eyes. He only turned a little pink as he looked away.

After breakfast, and after he and Em had armed themselves for the coming battle, Vic and the companions stepped through the castle's great doors and were met with a deafening clamor. It was clear that word of the attack had spread through the night.

"Daddy!" said a young girl, throwing her arms around a man's leg and hanging on fiercely. Her mother wiped a tear from her eye and pulled the girl away.

Merchants bustled through the crowd handing out food.

"An army can't live on steel," a man said, and stuffed loaves of bread into their sacks.

"When we first came to this world," Em reminded Vic in a whisper, "you were stealing loaves of bread so we could eat. Now they're giving them to us for free."

Vic nodded as he continued to take in the scene around him.

A woman in an apron held her son at arm's length. He couldn't have been much older than Vic. The boy tried to push away, but the woman pulled him close. He finally wrestled himself free, embarrassed, tugging up his pants that were weighed down by the cumbersome sword at his side as he joined the throng of men who were gathering outside the city walls.

Men were forming into lines. Off to his left, Vic watched as a stream of people trudged up the Great Road toward the castle. They looked stunned as they filed past him and into the city of Rockhaven. He could imagine their last few days—the gathering of loved ones and a few possessions, leaving everything else behind, and the fear of invaders behind them and an uncertain future in front of them.

It was a sobering reminder that they'd arrived just in time.

"I can't believe all of this is happening so fast!" Noll observed.

"Yeah," Ariana added, "and we need to be up front so we can fight for these people, not stuffed somewhere in the back of the army." She stamped her foot on the ground. "They might as well throw us back in that dungeon room." Her face had a storm cloud look that made Vic want to edge back a half step.

They were still trying to figure out exactly where they should be going when they saw a large, bearded man striding toward them. It was Fergus. He clapped a paw on Noll's shoulder.

"Will you look at the size of this one!" he exclaimed. "I thought my eyes were playing tricks on me last night, but I can see they weren't. You're the biggest person I've ever seen!" He lowered his voice and leaned in. "Alymer wants you in the rearguard, but I've seen you fight." He winked at Vic and Ariana. "You'll want to be up by me, where the action is. I've got a special place for you in my ranks. I'll come get you in a few minutes." He leaned back, smiled, then strode away.

Vic swallowed hard. He looked at Ariana, whose eyes shone with excitement. Larkin looked unruffled. Em had her usual placid expression. Noll looked ferocious.

"Sounds good to me," he growled.

Something had changed in the large boy, Vic thought. He could swear that Noll had grown another few inches in the past couple of days.

Soon, the lines of soldiers were assembled with their backs to the castle. An officer guided the companions to their place in the ranks. Alymer rode on horseback out in front of the army.

"Men of Rockhaven!" he proclaimed. "We haven't met an attack on these shores in a thousand years. Invaders from the Archipelago have come to take what is ours. We will not let them have it. We did not ask for this fight, but we will not run from it!"

A large roar went up. Fergus appeared at their side.

"Now!" he said and whisked them away. They'd gone from the rear of the formation to the front, along the left side of the army, which had already begun to move forward.

Larkin caught his eye. Vic looked back at him. Larkin shrugged and smiled.

"Our next adventure, huh?" Larkin said.

Vic tried to smile back. He hoped it convinced Larkin.

Vic remembered seeing a statue of Atlas, the figure from Greek mythology who had to carry the entire world on his back. Now that the army was moving, Vic's guilt had returned, and it made him feel like he was struggling under a similar weight.

Fergus, meanwhile, kept remarking on Noll's size. "Why, I'm a big man, by all accounts. But you must have been bigger than me when you were eight!" He let out a hearty guffaw and slapped Noll on the back.

As they marched, Vic did his best not to think about his mounting guilt and the coming fight. Instead, he turned his attention to the refugees trudging past them up the Great Road. If they could defeat the invaders, all these people would be safe. If they couldn't, it wouldn't matter if the refugees reached the castle or not.

Ahead of him, Ariana was showing Em how to use the bow and arrow she'd selected from the armory. Em was getting the hang of it. After a few minutes, though, she said something to Ariana and slipped away toward the Great Road. Ariana slowed down to join Vic and Larkin. The three of them walked together in silence. There wasn't much to say.

Em reappeared at Vic's elbow.

"I've been talking with the horses and the donkeys from the refugees," she began.

"Wow!" Ariana interrupted her. "First dogs and cats and then the Wolves and now this! You can talk with horses and donkeys! Too bad you couldn't talk to that unicorn. I'll bet you could now. When this is over, maybe we can try to get back to Baedyn's Valley. It would be amazing to talk with a unicorn. Of course, if that never happens, there are still plenty of other animals. There are badgers and raccoons and skunks..." She wrinkled her nose. "Would you even want to talk to a skunk?" she asked no one in particular.

Larkin cleared his throat. "You were saying?" he said to Em. His brow furrowed as he concentrated on her words.

"They say the invading army is moving very fast," Em told him. "They say it's being led by more of the silver-haired men."

Vic groaned. He reflexively rubbed the back of his head, even though Em's poultice had removed the pain and the swelling. Grydyl had tossed him aside and knocked down several men as if he were a bowling ball and they were the pins. Vic remembered the group of silver-haired men that had easily cut through the

Laketown defenses, and he hoped there weren't too many of them up ahead.

All day long, as the army continued its march, men with grimy faces and grim expressions straggled toward them and joined their ranks. These were the men, badly outnumbered, who'd already fought the invaders to give the refugees time to make it to Rockhaven. Vic wondered how many of the fighters hadn't survived.

The companions ate dinner that night a little apart from the others. They collapsed more than fell asleep, but Vic tossed and turned again, unable to get a deep and restful sleep.

They got up early. It was still dark, with a faint glow appearing over the horizon. They hunched over their breakfast. They didn't say much. Vic figured they were worrying about the coming fight. He looked around at them. He'd never had this kind of companionship. He didn't want to lose it. He could envision telling Larkin and the others how he and Em had come here. He could envision them getting up silently with their plates and walking away, like kids would do when he'd sit down with them at a lunchroom table.

He didn't want that feeling of rejection. He didn't want that humiliation.

He didn't want that loneliness.

But he also knew that he couldn't have friendships based on half-truths and lies.

He cleared his throat.

"I'm a thief," he said. "I steal things."

Larkin cocked his head to one side. Noll stopped with a spoon halfway to his mouth. Ariana stared at him. He looked at her, then he looked away.

"It was my fault that Larkin and I almost drowned in the Lake of Despair," he continued. "I saw gold and jewels at the bottom of the lake. I knew I wasn't supposed to go in, but my greed got the best of me. It's my fault. In fact, we'd still be back in our world if I hadn't stolen something I shouldn't have. Adelessa used it to blackmail Em and me to come here through the Door in the Stone."

Nobody said anything. Vic felt empty, like his insides had been sucked out by a vacuum cleaner.

"I'm sorry," he said. He hunched his shoulders, ready for the stinging blows of rejection that he knew would follow.

No one spoke for a moment. It was Noll who broke the silence.

"I still think there's a reason that we're all together," he said. "Whether you stole something in your world or not, you and Em are still meant to be here."

"And if you hadn't stolen something and come to our world," Larkin added, "Ariana and Noll would still be the prisoners of The Scourge."

"Exactly," Ariana said. "And even if we'd escaped, we'd still be in that dungeon with Sir Alymer if it wasn't for you and Em."

Vic glanced up at her. He expected to see a look of loathing on her face. What he saw was a look of appraisal, as if Ariana were trying to figure out what this new information about Vic meant.

Vic reached into his pocket. His hand closed over the gold comb. He pulled his fist out of his pocket. He unclenched his fingers. The comb glittered in the semi-darkness. Vic realized that it was brighter here than it was on the other side of the Door in the Stone.

"This is what I stole," he said. The others leaned forward to examine it in the predawn light.

"It's beautiful," Ariana said. The others murmured in agreement.

"It looks just the way I remembered it," said a startling, clear voice from the darkness, "even though I haven't seen it in over a thousand years."

Chapter Twenty-Eight
Vic–Adelessa's Story

"Adelessa!" Larkin said.

As she stepped toward them, Vic looked at her and rubbed his eyes.

The woman standing in front of him looked completely different than the one he and Em had met in their living room on the other side of the Door in the Stone.

He rubbed his eyes and looked at her again.

He saw an ordinary-looking woman.

Strange. When he'd seen her a couple of weeks ago, she was the most hideous thing he'd ever laid eyes upon.

He had no idea why she'd changed so much.

He slipped the comb back into his pocket and sat down with the others. They were looking at her expectantly.

Adelessa let out a long, shaky sigh as she sat among them. She stared at the ground for so long that Vic wasn't sure if she'd come there to tell them something or not.

She finally spoke.

"I will tell you what I think you need to know about why Kavenland is in the mess it's in. I've told some of this to Larkin, but I'll fill you all in on some other details now." She picked up a stick and scratched it absently along the ground. Then she tossed the stick aside.

"I must take the blame for a lot of Kavenland's problems," she began. "It's a guilt I've had to live with for over a thousand years."

Vic started. Ever since the incident with the queen of the Lake of Despair, he couldn't sleep, he couldn't eat, and he couldn't look anyone in the eye. He'd felt so alone and so miserable.

That had been the effect of a few days of guilt gnawing away at his insides.

Adelessa was talking about feeling guilty for three hundred and sixty-five *thousand* days.

The burden of that guilt must have been crushing. He felt a deep and sudden sympathy for her.

"Let me tell you briefly what happened," Adelessa said. "It was over a thousand years ago when Sendina found out that two of the Ancients had come together and had a baby. That had been forbidden by Sendina. The Ancients kept it a secret from her until their son had become a young man."

Vic held a hand up. "I'm sorry to interrupt," he said, "but who exactly is Sendina? The Hudenpole told us a little about her, but not much."

"I'm sorry," Adelessa said, "of course you and Em don't know who she was. Sendina was the creator of Kavenland. Everything that is here—the mountains and meadows, The Forest and the fields, the rivers and the lakes, are because of her."

Vic looked at Larkin, then Noll, then Ariana. Adelessa was talking matter-of-factly about a deity of some sort, and none of them batted an eye. He felt light-headed.

"So where was I?" Adelessa asked.

"Two of the Ancients had a forbidden child," Em said.

"Yes," Adelessa said. "A boy. And when she found out, Sendina was furious. Sendina thought that the offspring of two Ancients could upset the balance she had made in Kavenland. She banished the young man from Kavenland and ordered the Ancients to either leave Kavenland or withdraw from all contact with humans or Hudenpole."

"That's when Baedyn went to his Valley, wasn't it?" Em asked.

"Yes," Adelessa replied. "And the other Ancients went their own ways, though where they went isn't important now. What is important is that the son of the Ancients left Kavenland, but when he did, he took Tyndella with him."

"You told me about that," Larkin said. "You said that Tyndella was the most beautiful woman Kavenland has ever seen."

"That's right," Adelessa answered.

"But why was her leaving such a concern to you?" Noll asked.

"Because Tyndella was my sister."

No one spoke. The sounds from the rest of the army camp receded into the distance. Even the wind seemed to be holding its breath.

"I'd been ignoring her, you see," Adelessa continued. "She only cared about her beauty after Sendina presented us with a choice of gifts." She looked at Vic as she spoke, and his hand went automatically into his pocket and closed over the golden comb. She gave him an almost imperceptible nod before continuing.

"One morning, Sendina called Tyndella and I to her. She had laid out four items on a table. There was a sword, a harp, a pendant, and a golden hair comb."

Every head swung toward Vic. Em's eyes widened. Noll's mouth dropped open. Larkin shook his head in wonder. Vic felt his face flush and grow warm.

"Is it the same comb that Vic just showed us?" Ariana asked.

"Yes." Adelessa said. "How it came to Vic and Em's world is another story, though you'll learn how that was even possible in just a moment. Where was I?"

"The four items on the table," Vic said. He preferred the attention be back on Adelessa as quickly as possible. He couldn't believe that he'd been carrying around some ancient relic in his pocket. And to think, he'd once pawned it to Mr. Zipkoff back in Pittsburgh for four hundred dollars.

Adelessa continued.

"Sendina told us that each of the four items had magical powers. The owner of the sword would be the greatest warrior in Kavenland, and the owner of the harp would write songs and stories that would make people laugh and cry and fall in love and which would be sung and told forever." She looked back down at the ground again. "As the elder daughter, I had first choice, and I almost chose the harp. A day hasn't gone by in the last thousand years that I haven't wished that I had. Maybe then everything would have been different." She shook her head curtly. "But I didn't. I chose the pendant instead."

She reached inside her shirt and held out the pendant so that Vic and the others could see it. It was a simple necklace with a large emerald at the end of it. Once each of the companions had seen it, Adelessa tucked it away again.

"After I chose the pendant," she continued, "which would give its wearer insight and knowledge, Tyndella chose the golden comb, as I knew she would. The comb would make its wearer the most beautiful and envied being in Kavenland. I begged Tyndella not to take it. She was already so beautiful. But she snatched it up as soon as I had chosen the pendant."

Adelessa looked at the companions with a pleading expression that surprised Vic, but which he recognized. She wanted to explain her actions. She wanted forgiveness from the five kids sitting around her. It was the same way he'd felt when he confessed to the others just before Adelessa had arrived.

"I wanted to know why the sun rose and set," she said, "and how rocks were formed, and where the wind went when it stopped blowing, and why flowers bloomed, and rain came down, and streams flowed." She dropped her head. "Tyndella and I had been so close. But we grew apart. All she wanted to do was stop and admire her reflection in every pool and pond we passed by. She was worshiped and loved by all for her beauty. And when the son of the Ancients came to her and flattered her and wooed her, she fell in love with him. When he was banished by Sendina, Tyndella stole away with him, and they rode east, away from Kavenland forever."

Vic knew without asking who she was talking about. "That son was Kynwas," he stated.

"Yes," Adelessa answered. "A loathsome, horrible being. He was haughty and cruel, and he was despised by everyone who knew him. Everyone except Tyndella. He left, swearing revenge upon Kavenland for banishing him and for not loving him."

"The Hudenpole told us that Sendina sat on the edge of Kavenland and wept for forty years, and that her tears became the sea," Em said.

"The eastern sea, yes," Adelessa confirmed.

"Sendina was Tyndella's mother, wasn't she?" Noll asked suddenly.

Vic looked at him, puzzled. The others did, too.

Noll threw his massive arms out wide. "That was how my mom reacted when I told her that I was going to go with Larkin and Ariana across The Forest. She cried. She said she could cry a river because she was afraid she'd never see me again."

Adelessa sat stock still for a moment, then slowly moved her head up and down.

"Which means that Sendina was your mother, too," Vic said to Adelessa.

Adelessa nodded again.

"Oh my gosh," Ariana said.

No one spoke for a moment. Finally, Adelessa continued her story.

"The flooding caused by Sendina's tears raised islands in the middle of the sea," she said.

"The Archipelago," Noll said.

"Yes," Adelessa agreed. "Scrubby land with few trees or vegetation. Over the years, sailors were blown off course and wrecked there. They were forced to stay because there were no trees to mend their ships. And so the population in the Archipelago grew. Then, many years after Kynwas had stolen Tyndella away, the Protectors got restless and sailed east."

"And the Protectors were?" Vic asked.

"The Protectors were the children of the Ancients and humans. Sendina had allowed those unions, right up until she learned about Kynwas. After that, she banished the Ancients, and all such unions stopped. There were fifty Protectors, and they had strengths and abilities far beyond regular humans. One of Sendina's final acts was to call on those fifty to protect Kavenland."

Noll's eyes shone with excitement. "And they did!" he said. "They fulfilled their duties. They beat the Frost Giants of the north and repelled the invasion from the Southern Isles."

Adelessa looked sad. She muttered under her breath. Vic could hear her, but he wasn't sure the other kids could.

"Heroes," she said. "How do you tell kids that heroes have their faults just like everyone else? Who am I to shatter illusions? But they must know the truth."

She cleared her throat and spoke so that everyone could hear. "I've told this part to Larkin already. The Protectors did some good things until Beredor got bored. Sendina had wanted them to stay in Kavenland to protect the country, but Beredor led the Protectors—those who hadn't been killed in the fights you just mentioned, Noll—east, to the end of the world, where they were decimated by the Stone Giants. A few survived and tried to sail back to Kavenland. They were blown off course and landed in the Archipelago. They had brought chests of gold and silver and cedar seeds—Kavenland's most precious resources—to trade with whomever they met."

She let out another long breath.

"They met the wrong person. Kynwas killed the Protectors. He took their ships. He planted the cedar seeds and built ships of his own. The people of the Archipelago multiplied. Tyndella died many years ago, but before she did, she and Kynwas had offspring—the silver-haired beings you've encountered. And now Kynwas has brought war upon Kavenland as an act of revenge."

"Just before you left me last time," Larkin said, "you told me there was a prophecy."

"Let me go back a few steps," Adelessa said. "When Sendina found out that Tyndella was gone she was beside herself with grief. After she cried for forty years, her anger grew great. She knocked down swaths of trees, stopped the winds, and clawed at the hills and mountains. She tore so deeply into the fabric of Kavenland that she opened pathways to other worlds. That's how the Nisser came to this world and how your ancestors," she gestured toward Vic and Em, "left Kavenland to get to your world."

"Through the Door in the Stone," Em said.

"Through the Door in the Stone," Adelessa agreed, "with the comb. After her rage, Sendina called me to her and told me of her prophecy for Kavenland. She told me that others had or would get other pieces of the prophecy, too. This is what she told me:

The five with their powers like those from the past
Will bring peace to Kavenland's shores at last.

"After she spoke her final words to me, she told me good-bye, and she floated up to the night sky, where she became the moon. Every day for a thousand years, I've been searching for five people with special powers who would fulfill my mother's vision."

"So," Em said, "your sister ran off with a terrible person, your mom left to become the moon, and it's up to you to try to clean everything up?"

"And you've spent a thousand years searching for the five people who might help you do that," Vic added.

Adelessa gave a small nod.

Ariana shook her head slowly. "I think that's the saddest story I've ever heard," she said.

"Well," Adelessa said, "I didn't tell the story to make you sad. I told you so that you would know who it is you're fighting against and why I wanted the five of you to come together."

"And you think we're the five that the prophecy speaks about?" Vic said.

"I do," Adelessa said. "But you can never be sure about prophecies, and I only have a piece of one. Is it the beginning of the prophecy, or the end? Will the five start a conflict or will they end one? I don't know. Does Kynwas have a piece of the prophecy, too, and think he's being guided to a certain victory because of it? Does he have the same prophecy I do and thinks *he* knows who the five are? Or did Sendina not speak with him at all, and he is only being guided by hatred?" She shrugged. "I don't know the answer to any of those questions."

That brought another silence to the companions. Vic thought about the implications. Maybe, somehow, he and his sister and three other kids were going to play a key part in bringing peace to Kavenland.

Or maybe, more likely, some ancient god-like figure and four of his huge sons were the five the prophecy talked about, and they were going to bring peace to Kavenland by destroying it with their awesome power.

As if on cue, a trumpet burst forth and shattered the silence.

"Battle stations!' a voice cried out. "We're under attack!"

Chapter Twenty-Nine
The Battle

Larkin's heart thumped in his chest as he and the companions sprinted to their stations.

A breeze blew down the hill to their east and across the Kavenland army. The breeze bore scents of bright red danger and a bruised yellow deceit.

The danger was obvious. In the distance, a large army was spilling over a hill and descending toward the Kavenland army. All around him, Larkin saw Kavenland soldiers staggering forward, tucking nightshirts into pants, strapping on swords as they ran, and flinging hands up to shield their eyes from the sun which rose directly behind the attacking enemy.

Larkin wasn't sure what the deceit could possibly mean, but there wasn't time to think about it now.

"How did we get surprised?" a man next to Larkin asked. "What happened to our sentries?"

"Yes," repeated another, "why is this happening?"

A few other voices joined in the chorus of complaints.

"Silence!" bellowed Fergus. "Our sentries must have been captured, probably by those wretched, sniveling Hill People. They've caught us by surprise, and they'll be on us any moment. Leave the 'why' and 'what happened' for later and get ready to fight now!"

Fergus strode up and down in front of the men in his command. He bawled out words of encouragement at the top of his lungs, but Larkin found it hard to concentrate. It seemed to him as if Fergus' voice was coming from underwater, drowned out by the blood rushing in his ears. He looked to his left. The man next to him fidgeted, and his Adam's apple bobbed up and down. The man to his right shouted and raised his sword with a flourish. Further down the line, another man had dropped to his knees and appeared to Larkin to be praying.

Larkin made eye contact with Vic. Vic gave him a quick nod. Larkin glanced at Noll. His giant friend was listening and reacting to every word Fergus said. His face was etched into furrows of total focus. Next to him, Ariana swept her dark hair away from her eyes. She stood on the balls of her feet and leaned forward as if into a great wind. Larkin hoped she didn't range too far out in front of the rest of the army when the fighting began.

Larkin looked past Fergus's shoulder and saw the attackers in the distance running toward the Kavenland army. He realized, suddenly, that this was his first real battle. He and Noll had fought a few men in Alymer's castle, but this was going to be different.

Vastly different.

~~*~~

Fergus clapped a hand on Noll's shoulder.

"No one will ever question your courage, lad," Fergus said quietly, "but I've had second thoughts. I think it might be best if you and your friends stayed in reserve for now."

Noll let out a low growl. He thought back to the embarrassment he'd felt in the encounter with The Scourge. He snorted. Ariana had actually called for him to stand behind her and let her do the fighting!

Those days were over. That embarrassment he'd felt had since hardened into resolve. He'd been battle-tested in the fight against Roderick and his men at the top of the castle stairs.

The people of his country needed to be protected.

He needed to protect them.

He rolled his neck. He hefted up his shield and pulled out his sword.

"I'm not going anywhere," he snarled.

~~*~~

The day was already warm, but it felt to Vic that a squadron of ice-covered spiders was running over every inch of his body.

He saw the silver-haired men on horseback bearing down on them. He remembered the carnage they'd left behind in Laketown and shuddered.

He'd prefer to steer clear of them in the fight that was coming.

Sprinkled throughout the army that advanced toward them were groups of shaggy-haired men and women with worn leather shields. They whooped and hollered. They brandished axes and thrust long spears into the air. They looked like the men who'd chased him and Em in The Forest. Vic figured they must be the Hill People. He tried to swallow but found that his mouth was completely dry.

He hoped he didn't run into the Hill People, either.

He felt a rising sense of panic. What was he doing in this strange world with a sword strapped around his waist? What was he doing with all these grown men in the front line of an army? Even worse, what was Em doing here? He looked down at her. She kept adjusting the helmet she'd gotten in Rockhaven. It tilted and slipped down over her face. She pushed it back. It perched on the back of her head for a moment before it slipped backward, and the strap slid over her chin and caught on the bottom of her nose.

"Em," he said. "Go back with the horses. See if you can learn anything from them or...or...or from the birds or something."

She snorted out a laugh.

"Please!" Vic begged. "This is no place for you."

She held his eyes for a long moment. "You're right," she finally said. "You'd spend the whole time worrying about me, and that would be dangerous for you."

He let out a breath as he watched her work her way back toward the rear of the army. Then he examined his own emotions. The world seemed out of focus, like he was looking at it through the wrong end of a pair of binoculars. The sweat on his forehead felt cool and damp in the warm air. He looked down at his hands. They trembled.

Then he thought of the bullies who'd taken his backpack at school. There were six of them, but he still burned with shame at the thought of running away from them. He set his jaw. Never again, he vowed.

~~*~~

Em understood Vic's concerns, but she also knew she didn't want to stand by idly while he and their new friends took all the risks.

She headed for the paddock. She thought she might be able to offer some help with the horses. There weren't that many of them—fifty, maybe a few more.

When Em arrived at the enclosure, all the horses were still there. Alymer and the other leaders must not have had time to retrieve their horses.

Em looked across the field. The Archipelagan army was already surging down the hill. They had 15 or so men on horseback. Em saw the riders' silver hair glinting in the early morning sunlight. That was bad. They would have the upper hand in the battle to come.

Em walked among the horses. Some bucked and whinnied. Others stood calmly. Em figured that the soldiers on both sides had emotions that were similar.

She talked with the horses, who were surprised that she could communicate with them. She patted some, talked soothingly to others, and all the time had one thought on her mind.

What could she do to help?

~~*~~

As she stood next to her friends waiting for the battle to begin, Ariana thought about the refugees who had trudged up the Great Road toward Rockhaven. It made her think back to her villagers up north. She remembered their faces—expressions of terror, numbness, and uncertainty as they fled their homes. She thought of the huge old man eviscerating the tanner and his two sons—friends of hers. Her friends and their dad were dead.

She hadn't been able to protect them.

Her village was a heap of charred wood and wreckage.

She hadn't been able to protect Fieldstone from Kynwas.

Larkin had vowed to destroy him. Larkin was right. Kynwas had to be stopped. He had to be defeated.

As the Archipelagan army swept down the hill and raced toward them, Ariana felt her teeth clench. She reached back for her quiver, fitted an arrow, and waited for the call to action.

~~*~~

Larkin rose onto his toes then settled back on his heels. His hands clenched and unclenched. The battle was moments away.

He looked ahead of him. He saw that there were more of the enemy coming down on his right, on the opposite side of the field from where he and his friends were stationed with Fergus. Larkin grasped the strategy immediately. If the attackers could turn the Kavenland flank, they could push the army into a position with only The Forest at its back. Nobody in Kavenland would flee into The Forest. They would be pinned down, and any retreat would be cut off. Larkin saw the large figure of Sir Alymer motioning soldiers to his right. Men hustled to get to that side of the battlefield. Larkin realized that Sir Alymer had seen the exact same threat that he'd noticed from the attacking enemy.

He also noticed that Sir Alymer was on foot. Yesterday, he and several other men had been on horseback, but they must not have had time to mount up this morning. That would be a disadvantage when they had to confront the silver-haired men.

Larkin reflected, briefly, about all the times he'd fantasized about being in a battle. He remembered the war games that he had played with Noll, Ariana, and Ariana's brothers.

But this wasn't a game.

His heart hammered in his chest.

He pulled out his sword and gripped it tight.

~~*~~

"Archers!" Fergus roared. A man shouldered past Vic and nocked an arrow in his bow. Ariana was on the other side of Vic, and she began shooting arrow after arrow. He couldn't believe how quickly she could shoot and reload. He swung his eyes forward and saw some of the men from the Archipelago stumble and fall. But they kept charging, and before he knew it, Ariana had slung her quiver and bow back over her shoulder and drawn out her sword. He looked around. Everyone in the Kavenland ranks had pulled out their swords, too.

Soldiers on both sides were running forward now and yelling. Vic didn't remember deciding to run, but found he was sprinting ahead. He didn't remember drawing his sword, either, but it was in his hand. For some reason, one of the Archipelagans stared right at him as the two armies collided. The man screamed and made straight for him. He drew back his sword and swung it as Vic raised his shield. Vic blocked the blow, but the force it knocked him down.

A thought flashed through Vic's head: the ground seemed like a dangerous place to be. You couldn't defend yourself, and you might get trampled. He scrambled to his feet, but the man was gone. Whether he'd been killed or swept away by the tide of the battle, Vic wasn't sure.

He drew a deep breath. He needed to wade into the battle. He needed to fight for his new friends.

~~*~~

As the armies rushed toward each other, Ariana, sword in hand, did the one thing she never thought she would do.

She froze.

She swung her head from one side of the battlefield to the other. She felt the familiar welling inside her that infused her with strength from the ends of her fingers to the tips of her toes. She was ready to protect.

But there were so many.

How could she possibly protect them all?

Her strength seemed to drain away. She felt powerless.

Her mind raced, but she willed it to slow down. As her thoughts calmed, she realized that what she wanted to do so desperately simply couldn't be done.

She couldn't stop every kid from being bullied. She couldn't stop all of the strong from picking on all of the weak. As much as she wanted to, she couldn't right every wrong in the world.

She couldn't protect every soldier in the Kavenland army.

But, she reflected, as the strength coursed back through her veins again, she could still do a lot.

She sprinted forward, looking for her friends in the chaos of the fight.

~~*~~

The armies collided. The sun rose behind the invaders, making it hard for the Kavenlanders to see. Larkin glanced at his friends. He saw alarm in Vic's eyes. Noll had a grim look on his face as he advanced into the ranks of the attackers. He didn't see Ariana, but he figured she was probably halfway through the Archipelagan army by now.

Larkin tried to tamp down his panic as he squinted into the sun. He felt like he was fighting blind. He saw a flash of steel and raised his shield. A blow crashed against it and sent him reeling. Larkin flailed back with his sword. It was like fighting a shadow. He ducked behind his shield just as another blow fell. He staggered under its weight and jabbed with his sword. It stung and reverberated in his hand as an Archipelagan soldier whacked it. It was all Larkin could do to hang onto it.

Around him, some of the Kavenlanders had already had enough and were running away. Larkin had to fight back the urge to drop his sword and follow them to safety.

~~*~~

Noll felt an icy anger burning in his stomach.

The Kavenland army was being pushed back. They were blinded, squinting into the morning sun, and they were dispirited by the fury of the early-morning surprise attack.

"Stay and fight!" he bellowed, as he slashed his way through the Archipelagan attackers. "We must hold the line until the sun gets overhead. Once we can see, we'll be able to counter-attack."

Noll had to show his compatriots that they could win. They just had to get through the next hour or two.

But it looked like they might not make it. The right side of the Kavenland army was being bent back in their direction. It was the Hill People leading the charge for the invaders. They pressed forward, howling and screaming. The Kavenland army folded in before them.

Larkin and Vic stayed beside him, but the ranks of men around them diminished as soldiers slipped away toward the rear of the army. Noll saw their faces. They looked frightened and beaten.

"They're devils!" one man shouted. "Those silver-haired men are unnatural."

"They can't be defeated!" another man echoed. "They could beat our whole army by themselves."

"The Hill People are too much for us," another said in a shaky voice. "If they can't stab you, they'll bite and kick. How can we beat someone who hates us so much?"

"Quiet!" Fergus bellowed above the din. "Re-form. It's the invaders or The Forest. Re-form!"

Noll glanced over his shoulder. Men were lining up to the rear. Behind them was the Great Road and then The Forest. To his right, the line stretched in a ragged diagonal across the plain. Above, the sun had moved almost overhead.

Noll wasn't sure how much longer the Kavenland army could hold out. They were on the verge of being routed.

Noll caught a brief glimpse of Sir Alymer, fighting in the middle of the battlefield and issuing orders to the men on the right flank.

"Fall back behind the line!" he ordered. "Get ready for a new attack!"

To his left, Noll saw Fergus swinging and thrusting his sword, surrounded by enemy soldiers. Noll fought his way over to the big man, and the two of them drove the attackers back.

"Thank you, lad," Fergus said. "I wish we had ten more like you. I'm afraid we're losing the fight."

"We have to do something!" Noll said.

"Like what?" Fergus asked.

Noll told him.

~~*~~

Ariana dashed about from one companion to the next. When two men started flailing at Larkin, she jumped in and evened the odds. After those men fell back from the ferocity of her attack, she moved on to help Vic and Noll.

But as she moved forward, she passed others who were moving away from the enemy. Their chests heaved and their feet dragged, and their heads hung as they worked their way to the rear of the Kavenland army. Their fear and fatigue seemed to spread like contagion. The man next to her set his shield and sword on the ground and slipped away. In the distance, Ariana could see a handful of other Kavenland soldiers slinking south down the Great Road.

The silver-haired men had been doing much of the damage for the Archipelagans. While soldiers on both sides were getting tired, the silver-haired men seemed fresh. They roared in triumph and swung their swords with astonishing power and effect. Wide swaths of men fell around them, dead or wounded.

Ariana felt a lump in her throat. Was the future of her country going to be decided here, today, on this battlefield? Was Kavenland going to be defeated by these cruel and unnatural silver-haired men?

No, she thought. She couldn't allow that to happen. She had to help protect her country.

Fergus was fighting like a madman. The merry twinkle in his eyes was gone. His mouth carved a grim line underneath the blood and grime that caked his face. Noll joined him, and after a brief flurry, she saw Noll grab the big man and pull him close. He said something urgently in his ear. Fergus listened and nodded.

As long as they had fighters like Noll and Fergus, and Larkin and Vic, and Sir Alymer, Ariana thought, Kavenland still had hope.

Ariana saw a flash of activity over to her right. Ariana gasped in horror Sir Alymer and a large group of soldiers had been separated from the rest of the Kavenland army. The Archipelagans almost had them surrounded. Ariana tried to fight her way over to them, but it looked to be a lost cause.

Sir Alymer and his men were going to be cut to ribbons.

~~*~~

Em had discarded her helmet and worked her way among the horses until she learned that Clover, the mare of Sir Alymer, was their leader.

"If I open the paddock gate," she asked Clover, "can you make sure that none of the horses run off?"

Clover assured her that she would. "Climb up," she urged Em.

"But I've never ridden a horse," Em protested.

Clover snorted.

"Who better to teach you than a horse?" she said. She knelt, and Em scrambled onto her back. When the horse stood up, Em felt a very, very long way from the ground.

"Squeeze with your thighs," Clover instructed. "Not that hard. There. That's better. Use your thighs and your calves. Don't grab the bridle. I'll take you wherever you want to go. If we start to gallop, you can grab my mane, but don't pull."

Em thought she was going to fall off a few times, but she began to get the hang of it as Clover coaxed and ushered the horses out of the paddock. Em could feel the horse's muscles and power beneath her. It began to feel less like she was on a roller coaster at Kennywood amusement park in Pittsburgh and more like she was working with a strong and intelligent companion as Clover walked her over to the top of a small crest.

What Em saw sickened her. The Kavenland army was being routed. She could make out Noll in the center of the army, striking broad, heavy blows with his sword. He was easy to spot. Em couldn't see Vic, Larkin, or Ariana.

She had to trust that they were ok.

She had to.

"Look!" said Clover. "A little right of center. It's Alymer. He's in trouble!"

Em scanned the field until she could make out Alymer. Like Noll, he was taller than almost anybody else. He and his men fought back-to-back, completely surrounded by enemy soldiers.

"What can we do?" Clover whinnied.

"Get the other horses around us!" Em commanded.

"Got it!" Clover said.

The horse spun this way and that, with Em clinging desperately to her mane. The other horses surrounded them, flanks rubbing against each other, nickering and snorting in fear and excitement.

"Clover, tell them to stay in a tight formation, and charge!"

Clover leapt forward. Em leaned out over her neck. She felt the air blow her hair back. Her eyes squinted and teared up as they tore across the open ground. Em looked back. All the other horses were right behind them, bunched together and bearing down on the soldiers attacking Sir Alymer.

Clover barely slowed down as she crashed into one of the Hill People. The man was flattened. Clover rose up on her back legs and let out a whinny of triumph. Em hung on as Clover came down hard on another soldier. All around her, surprised fighters from the Archipelagan army were being trampled by the herd of horses that she and Clover had led into the battle.

Those who weren't flattened ran away in terror and confusion at this unexpected attack.

A large cheer went up from the Kavenland army.

Sir Alymer had been saved.

They still had hope.

~~*~~

Em had saved the day, Noll saw.

Sir Alymer strode across the field and took his place at the front of the Kavenland army. Would he call for them to stand their ground, Noll wondered? Or would he want to retreat now when there still might be a chance to escape down the Great Road?

"Bring up the rearguard!" Alymer yelled. "The rest of you—charge! For Kavenland!"

The men around him moved forward, but not, it seemed, with any great enthusiasm. Noll looked at Fergus.

"Now!" he shouted. Fergus nodded and let out a great roar. Noll sheathed his sword and charged for the nearest silver-haired man on horseback. Fergus was on his heels.

"Noll!" Larkin shouted from behind him. "What are you doing?"

The silver-haired man saw Noll coming. He raised his sword up and swung a mighty blow at Noll's head. Noll threw up his shield and turned aside the powerful stroke. With his free hand, he reached up and grabbed the silver-haired man by the belt. He hauled him off the horse, and Fergus finished him with a mighty blow from his sword.

Another cheer went up from the Kavenland army. The soldiers who'd been advancing slowly now quickened their pace. The Archipelagan army seemed dismayed by the death of one of their leaders. Their men began to look around, as if waiting for someone to take control. No one did, and their lines began to waver. The Kavenlanders who had trudged back under the morning's onslaught now stood tall and confident, and they rushed toward the faltering enemy.

Larkin caught up with Noll.

"You are crazy!" he said.

Noll felt his face split into a jack-o'-lantern smile that had no mirth in it.

"Let's go finish these guys," he growled.

~~*~~

Vic felt his chest swell with pride at what Em had done.

She and Noll had completely turned the tide of the battle.

As the Kavenland army advanced, Vic gripped his sword firmly and adjusted the strap on his shield. He squared his shoulders and strode into the fray, ducking in and out between soldiers. His sword was more like a long knife, a weapon which Larkin had recommended to him. It was an excellent choice. He stabbed a thigh here and an arm there. It was hard to get a clean shot on anyone. They had their shields up, as he did, and it dawned on him that they didn't want to be stabbed any more than he did.

Whenever a sword swung at him, Vic found he could get out of the way easily. His quickness was serving him well to attack and defend.

He couldn't see more than a few feet in front of him. All around him, men swung their swords and pushed with their shields. Some swore and screamed in pain, and some yelled in triumph.

The ground underneath Vic was soon churned up and the footing became less steady. It was slick in spots with pools of blood and the entrails of dead and dying men. The stench was horrific. The metallic scent of blood was mixed with the innards of men that leaked through gaping wounds and spilled onto the muddy ground. Vic tried to ignore that as well as the howls of anguish that rent the air. He had to stay alert, and lucky, to avoid being like one of those men who were wounded or dying. The thought flashed through his mind that the stories of heroic battles he'd read in school never mentioned the ghastly smells and sounds, nor the desperation to stay alive that Vic felt. He knew others around him felt it, too.

He caught a brief glimpse of Larkin in the swirl of bodies. He was hammering away at one of the invaders. Vic tried to fight his way over to help him, but he couldn't get through the press of bodies.

He saw Noll's towering form moving steadily forward. His sword glinted in the sunlight as he brought it up and crashed it down. Fergus strode next to him, and the Archipelagan army gave way before them.

Soon Vic realized that the Kavenland army was winning the battle. Vic stepped over dead bodies and moved forward and to the right. Others around him were doing the same. The Archipelagans were still fighting, but they were doing it while moving backward.

Suddenly, a surge came back at him. The men in front of him were knocked aside. A lone Kavenland soldier stood in front of Vic, but a sword flashed through the air, and the man's head rolled and landed at Vic's feet. Vic recoiled and staggered backwards. One of the huge, silver-haired men dismounted from his horse and stood in front of him.

Vic glanced around desperately. He had nowhere to run. He would have to rely upon his quickness. He went into a crouch and gripped his sword tighter. The silver-haired man looked at him with contempt.

"This is the only one who will dare stand before me?" he said to no one in particular. "A mere boy?"

The man swung his sword at Vic's head. He was much faster than the others he'd faced that day, and Vic ducked just in time. He felt the whoosh of the sword as it passed over his head. He was going to roll out of the way when the man's shield swung up from the other direction and hit him in the chest. It felt like he'd been kicked by a mule. Vic sagged to the ground and gasped for breath. The wind was knocked out of him. He knew that if he didn't move, he would die, but his body wouldn't respond.

The silver-haired man sneered at him and raised his sword. Vic turned his head away. He saw a silver blur out of the corner of his eye as the sword descended toward him.

Then he heard a clash just a few inches from his head. When he turned his head back around, he saw Ariana drive the silver-haired man's sword aside. A surprised look came over the silver-haired man's face. Then, when he saw his attacker, his eyes grew hooded, and he looked down at Ariana with disdain.

"A girl?" he sneered. "Shall I play with you like a cat with a mouse, or kill you quickly?"

Ariana responded by lunging at him. She stuck her sword into his upper arm. The man howled, leapt back, and scowled at her. He slashed his sword at her head, and she ducked out of the way. Then his shield came up. Vic saw that it was the same attack the silver-haired man had used on him. He watched in horror, waiting for the blow that was sure to knock her off her feet.

But the blow never landed. Ariana spun in a tight circle around the shield as it moved past her. She crouched down and exploded upward, plunging her sword into the exposed side of the silver-haired man. She drove it deeper into him. He let out a gasp and toppled over, dead.

Ariana put her foot onto the man's chest and tugged her sword free. She looked at Vic.

"Are you okay?" she asked. Her black curly hair whipped around in the breeze. She looked fierce and powerful.

Vic bobbed his head.

"Thanks," he gasped.

Ariana nodded once, turned, and threw herself back into the battle.

Vic staggered to his feet and ran after her.

~~*~~

Larkin had been to the ocean once when he was younger. He remembered standing in thigh-deep water at high tide. The waves crashed against him, forcing him back, and then the undertow flowed back and dragged him forward.

The early afternoon felt like that. Every time the Archipelagan army surged forward, the Kavenland army hurled them back. Larkin stabbed and pushed. A face, horrible and twisted, appeared in front of him. Larkin didn't have room to swing his sword, so he crashed his fist into the face, and the face disappeared. Behind him, a few feet away, Ariana and Vic fought one of the silver-haired men. The man's sword flashed and blazed, but Ariana and Vic ducked and swung back. Alymer bolted forward with a roar and shoved his sword into the chest of the silver-haired man. The man collapsed to the ground. The Archipelagans who'd been fighting around him ran away. The Kavenlanders ran after them.

As the afternoon wore on, the tide turned, and the Kavenlanders began to methodically push the Archipelagan army back. The whole battlefield began to drift away from the Great Road and The Forest and toward the far-right end of the great plain. Soon, Larkin could tell, the Archipelagans would have to retreat. Kavenland was going to win.

The ranks were thin on the left flank. Fergus had yelled for his troops to hold their ground, but he himself had chased the retreating Archipelagan army and many had followed him, eager to join in the rout.

Larkin had stayed a little behind this last surge. He was sure that something was wrong.

He remembered the bruised yellow deceit that he'd smelled that morning, and he thought back to the other emotions he'd smelled since he first became aware of his gift.

He thought with shame about the scent of pride and envy he'd smelled when he tried to single-handedly save everyone from Scrofa the boar. It had been his own pride and envy, and he'd ignored it, leading to nearly disastrous results. Power, treachery, and despair had come to him when they'd left The Forest and headed for Rockhaven. He hadn't acted on that, either, and he, Ariana, and Noll had been captured by Grydyl.

He'd been embarrassed by his gift. He'd thought it was lame. He'd ignored it, but hadn't that just been his pride coming out in a different way?

The clamor of battle drifted away into the distance. Larkin stood alone. For the first time since his gift had become apparent to him, he gave himself over fully to it. The scent of deceit returned, and it was overwhelming. Larkin thought about what had happened and how it might affect what was going to happen next.

Most of the Kavenland soldiers hadn't had time to eat before the attack came that morning. They'd fought, squinting into the sun, on empty stomachs, against an army coming downhill. They'd been at a disadvantage all day.

They were exhausted.

Larkin had a moment of clarity that allowed him to understand the deceit he'd smelled. He felt sure that he now grasped the enemy's true strategy. The entire attack today had been a deception. It had all led to this moment.

He looked up and saw Vic approaching. The boy waved his hand in greeting. His face showed conflicting emotions of fatigue and elation, like warding off a chilly day by wrapping up underneath a favorite blanket.

Larkin understood, because he felt it too. They'd been surrounded by danger and death all day, and they'd survived. It felt good to be alive.

But more than that, Larkin felt troubled. Vic started to say something, but when he saw Larkin's face, he stopped.

"What's wrong?" he asked.

"I think we've been duped," Larkin answered. He pointed across the large field. Way in the distance, he saw Noll walking slowly their way. Em plodded next to him on horseback, and Ariana walked beside her. Behind them was the rest of the Kavenland army, some clashing with the few remaining Archipelagan troops still on the battlefield, and others swaggering around in the throes of victory.

"All our soldiers are over there," Larkin said. "Most of the Archipelagans have retreated. Maybe they're resting up right now."

Vic's eyes narrowed. "Resting up for what? What are you saying?"

"I'm saying that this is the perfect time for the Archipelagans to hit us hard and fast with a counterattack. What if the first attack had been designed to wear us down and draw us away from the Great Road?"

Vic turned his head to look back at the Kavenland army.

"So you're saying that Sir Alymer and our entire Kavenland army have been deceived?"

Larkin nodded.

"And that the real attack is about to begin?" Vic added.

"I'm afraid so," Larkin answered. "Imagine the Archipelagans plunging down the Great Road with some fresh troops led by more of those silver-haired monsters. There's no one over here to stop them. This whole flank is unprotected. They could easily get behind our army."

Vic let out a low gasp. "They'd have us encircled," he said in a hoarse whisper. "They'd be able to cut us to bits."

"Exactly," Larkin said. "The battle—and the war—would be over. This army is Kavenland's only hope."

Even as he spoke, Larkin's mind leapt forward to a terrible future. He saw the silver-haired men doing here in the south what they'd done to Fieldstone—burning and killing and looting. He saw his friends and family in the north, hopeless without help from Sir Alymer, throwing down their swords and being taken prisoner. He saw that evil monster who'd destroyed his village, Kynwas, reigning supreme over a people he hated. There would be nothing in Kavenland then but misery, fear, and death.

Larkin's fists bunched up at the thought.

"We have to stop them," he said firmly.

Vic glanced up the Great Road and back at Larkin.

"You see it, don't you?" Larkin asked.

"Yes," Vic answered, "I do. It's a brilliant and devious plan." He scratched his head. "How in the world did you figure it out?"

Larkin felt a flush come over his face. When they'd been planning to rescue Ariana and Noll from The Scourge, Vic had sneered at Larkin's gift of smell. It was one of several instances that the boy from the other side of the Door in the Stone had grated on his nerves.

But a lot had changed since then—for both of them. Larkin swallowed his embarrassment.

"I could smell deceit in the air this morning," he said. "It's even stronger now."

Vic looked him in the eye and gave a curt nod.

"That's good enough for me," he said. "Let's go warn Sir Alymer and the others."

Larkin shook his head.

"You're much faster than me," he said. "I'd only slow you down. You get word to Alymer, and I'll see what I can do here."

Vic pursed his lips. "You're right," he said. "That is a better plan. I'll be back as fast as I can." He tore off. Larkin was amazed at his speed. He figured that Vic would reach Sir Alymer by the time he himself got into position.

Larkin turned and started running toward the Great Road.

"Follow me!" he shouted, as he ran past the few stragglers on this side of the battlefield. "There's a fresh attack coming!"

A few jogged after him half-heartedly, while the others just watched as he darted away.

Larkin reached the Great Road. He didn't have long to wait.

A half dozen of the silver-haired men galloped over the hill and down the Great Road, headed straight for him. A band of soldiers followed behind them.

Larkin heard something and looked quickly over to his right. Em was coming to his aid, charging across the battlefield on her huge stallion with Ariana, Vic, and Noll in hot pursuit. Sir Alymer was at the head of a group of soldiers sprinting toward him as well, but Larkin could see that no one would reach him in time. He let out a deep breath. He realized how exhausted he was. His shield hung heavy at his left side. With his last bit of strength, he heaved it up, drew his sword, and waited for the silver-haired men riding directly at him.

They were fifty feet away and closing fast.

Suddenly, a huge figure in white emerged like a whirlwind from The Forest in front of Larkin. The figure hurled himself into one of the silver-haired men on horseback. The horse reared and the silver-haired man fell off. He scrambled to his feet and sneered, but the figure in white brought his sword around in a blur and beheaded the man in a single stroke. The other five silver-haired men dismounted and raced forward to attack the enormous figure in white. They swung their swords at him in huge, hard strokes, but the figure in white parried their thrusts aside. He stepped back, tilted his head toward the sky, and let out a thunderous roar. Then, with a speed that Larkin could hardly believe, he counterattacked. One of the silver-haired men let out a horrible wail and fell dead. The others turned and ran away, with the figure in white in pursuit.

Em and the other companions all arrived at Larkin's position at the same time. They dashed up the Great Road toward the panicked Archipelagan army. Em was balanced perfectly on her horse and shot arrows at the bewildered Archipelagans. The lessons she'd gotten from Ariana appeared to be paying off. Larkin had felt exhausted just a few moments before, but the adrenaline of the chase pumped through his body. He and the other companions swung their swords with renewed vigor. In a few moments, the reinforcements led by Sir Alymer swarmed up behind them. The Archipelagan army wavered for a moment, then broke and fled.

Instead of the Kavenland army having its flank collapsed in the surprise attack, it was the Archipelagans' flank being rolled up. Panic ensued in their ranks across the Valley, and the Archipelagans began to run away. The Kavenlanders wanted to pursue them, but Sir Alymer held them back.

"It's getting dark, and we don't know what lies over that rise. It's too risky, and our army is worn out. But we fought well. If we'd lost, Rockhaven would have fallen, and with it, all of the south. But Rockhaven has been spared, and as long as Rockhaven stands, Kavenland has hope."

Ariana and Vic walked back to Larkin. Em dismounted from her horse and joined them. Noll sauntered over, swept the back of his hand over his blood and mud-streaked forehead, and smiled broadly.

"It's not so bad being big after all," he announced. Larkin and the others grinned. Larkin reached out and gripped Vic's hand. Vic shook it, looked him in the eye, and gave a brief nod of his head.

Larkin turned to Ariana. Her brown eyes flashed in the waning sunlight. Her face and arms were streaked with grime and blood. She gave him a short jab to his chest.

"Good job, Larkin."

Em gently squeezed his forearm.

"You did it," she said, quietly.

"We did it," he answered. He glanced around at the Kavenland army. Men were still letting out whoops of joy and relief. He drew his focus back to his friends. "The five of us did it."

Ariana pulled out her sword and thrust it up at an angle. "To the five of us!" she exclaimed. The rest of them pulled their swords and crossed them with Ariana's.

"To the five of us!" they said.

Larkin heard a noise behind him. He turned to see Sir Alymer coming toward them. They lowered their swords and made room for him.

Sir Alymer stepped into their midst. He clapped his hand on Noll's shoulder and nodded at the others. He smiled broadly at Larkin.

"Larkin," he continued, "you've come to our rescue once again. First, you surmised that this army was coming. We would still be in Rockhaven otherwise, and we would have been completely surprised by their attack. And today, we would have lost if you hadn't spotted their counterattack." He scratched his head. "Something's puzzling me, though."

He cocked his head to one side and looked at Larkin quizzically.

"Any idea who that was who came crashing out of the woods?" he asked. "He saved your life, and he helped save the day."

Larkin nodded.

"He's been known for centuries as The Scourge," he said. He glanced at his friends. When his eyes met Noll's, he smiled, then he looked back at Sir Alymer.

"His real name, though, is Galeran the Great."

Chapter Thirty
After Battle

This was every daydream Larkin ever had, and at first, the adulation was wonderful. Sir Alymer pounded him on the back and told everyone in earshot what his quick thinking had done. At the victory dinner after the battle, Alymer raised a toast to Larkin and his friends. Fergus came by, then others, and soon everybody wanted to treat him like a hero.

"Three cheers for Larkin!" Fergus hollered above the clanking of dishes and the laughter and singing of the celebration.

The soldiers cheered, banged their tankards on the table, and chanted in unison. "Lar-kin! Lar-kin! Lar-kin!"

Larkin squirmed. He began to feel hot and uncomfortable. As soon as the attention went somewhere else, he slipped outside the huge tent.

He stood for a moment breathing in the night air. A scent of home seemed to waft across the plains, and for the first time since he'd left, he thought about his aunt and uncle's small farm. He'd wanted so desperately to leave it, to have a great adventure. He'd had one, but he'd also seen the destruction and death that war brought.

He heard footsteps behind him, and he looked back to see a huge figure walking toward him.

It was The Scourge. Or rather, it was Galeran.

He towered over Larkin with the usual scowl on his face. Larkin realized he'd taken a step back as the former Scourge approached.

"You were right," Galeran rasped in his coarse voice. "I was ashamed of myself. I'm back, although I don't really want to be around other people right now. Eight hundred years of solitude is a hard habit to break."

"You saved my life," Larkin said.

"And you saved mine," Galeran replied, "by restoring me to who I was born to be. I'm ready to be a Protector again. I've told Sir Alymer that I'll be nearby, in The Forest, ready to help when needed. Maybe I can undo some of the problems that I helped to create."

Larkin realized he was holding his breath. Was Galeran talking about the trip the Protectors made to the Archipelago? Adelessa had told Larkin and his friends that story, but Galeran didn't know that. Maybe that was it. Or was there something else? Larkin thought, for a moment, that his childhood hero was about to take him into his confidence with some great secret.

But the moment passed. Galeran thrust out his hand. Larkin, surprised, shook it. Galeran's enormous hand folded over Larkin's. Then the last of the mighty Protectors spun on his heel and strode into The Forest without looking back.

Larkin shook his head. He didn't think his day could get any more surreal.

He was wrong.

A small figure in a tattered traveling cloak approached him. As she drew nearer, he recognized her.

"Adelessa," he said.

"Well done," she said.

When he'd seen her that morning with his friends before the battle, he'd seen her for the first time as a beautiful woman. He hoped it meant that he'd grown as a person.

They stood side by side in silence. He was content to look up at the stars for a while, but he guessed that Adelessa wasn't here by chance.

He looked at her expectantly. A slight smile spread across her face.

"Yes, you're right. I have something to tell you. But I have something to ask you as well."

Larkin waited in silence.

"How did you know that The Scourge was Galeran?"

Larkin gathered his thoughts for a moment before answering.

"When you first told me about this invasion, back in The Forest, you said that there was a surviving ship from the Protectors' ill-fated trip to the Archipelago. That's when the story of The Scourge appearing in Kavenland begins. When I saw him, I couldn't believe how big he was. No regular human could be that big—not even Noll. The only person I've seen who's that big is Kynwas."

He stopped. Kynwas was still out there. Larkin's breathing grew rapid and shallow. He forced himself to slow down before continuing.

"The Scourge claimed to Ariana and Noll that he'd never been outwitted, and Galeran has always been described as the smartest of the Protectors. There were other clues, like the incredible craftsmanship of his shield and sword. I'm not an expert, but they reminded me of the story about the great blacksmith, Helidix, who'd made swords and shields for the Protectors before they battled the Frost Giants."

"Those are a lot of clues, but nothing decisive," Adelessa said.

"I know," Larkin said. "What really tied it together for me was his bitterness. I could smell it. I'm not sure why he lives in The Forest or how he became The Scourge. Did he have survivor's guilt after all the other Protectors died, and so he decided to go to The Forest by choice? Or maybe he wanted to take power and was defeated. Maybe someone was afraid he would try and banished him first. Maybe they made up a bunch of stories about him—like him killing travelers and eating babies—so that everyone would be afraid of him."

Adelessa nodded slowly. "Your last idea is the closest to the truth. Remember, Sendina had ascended to the sky. All the Protectors except one were dead. A man with great ambition made Galeran out to be The Scourge—a monster who threatened the very safety of Kavenland. Ridiculous, of course. But the man had great charisma. His followers begged him to take control to save them from this threat, the threat he himself had invented. He pretended to be reluctant, but, of course, full power was what he'd wanted from the start. His name was Tendemus, and he became Kavenland's first king."

Larkin remembered being envious that Gurn was over three hundred years old. He imagined himself as a hero then, using that three hundred years to perform great deeds and build his own legend. But Galeran had been a real hero, and he'd been rejected. Larkin shuddered at the thought of the anger and resentment that must have eaten at him like a cancer for the better part of a millennium.

"That must have been a long 800 years for him," he said.

Adelessa nodded.

"It may be a while before his anger cools, Larkin, but you've done him—

and Kavenland—a wonderful service. He can be a great ally in the fighting still to come."

"It's still hard to imagine that The Scourge is Galeran," Larkin said with a shake of his head. "The most evil creature in the history of Kavenland turns out to be one its greatest heroes."

"Good and bad can be hard to tell apart sometimes, even in the same person. I'm certain that you see me in a different way than Vic, and yet I'm still Adelessa, with all of my good sides and all of my faults."

She put her hands behind her back and rocked back and forth from her toes to her heels.

"Tell me," she said, "what made you run to the Great Road at the end of the battle? Was it your desire to be a hero?"

Larkin shook his head.

"No," he said. "I finally understood that I had to embrace my gift. I smelled the deceit and saw what they were going to do and..." He shrugged.

"And you ran to the road."

"Yes."

"The actions of a hero," Adelessa said, "are usually performed when someone is doing the right thing, not when they're trying to be a hero."

Larkin thought about that. Vic volunteering for the hardest job at the cottage of The Scourge. Em going with the Wolves then riding to the rescue in the battle. Noll at the top of the stairs. Ariana saving Vic's life in the battle. All those actions were heroic. None of them came from any of his friends trying to be a hero.

Something troubled Larkin as he remembered the deeds of his friends.

"Do you know why there were only five of us in Kavenland who have these special abilities?" he asked.

Adelessa shook her head slowly. "I don't. I am only basing my thoughts on what the prophecy tells me."

"Or what you think it tells you," Larkin countered.

"Yes," Adelessa answered.

Larkin looked at the ground. He thought about The Protectors. Even if Adelessa was right, and the prophecy was about him and his friends, there was a significant difference between fifty half-gods and five kids. A long silence followed. Adelessa ended it by clearing her throat. "To answer your question, the best I can think of is that there were fifty Protectors, and now there are five of you. Perhaps there is some symmetry there."

"But how can five of us expect to take the place of fifty of them?"

"No one's asked you to take their place," Adelessa answered. "But I think there is one big reason that the Protectors ultimately failed." Her eyes glazed over slightly, as if they were focused on events from long ago.

"They were immensely powerful. They had every strength and every advantage they could have. But they acted as fifty separate entities. Galeran tried to talk sense into Beredor, but Beredor never listened, even though they were best friends. None of them listened to each other. All the Protectors thought more of the individual glory that they could win for themselves than of doing what was best for Kavenland."

Her eyes refocused. "They were asked to protect Kavenland. Ultimately, they couldn't."

"But if fifty Protectors with all of their powers couldn't save Kavenland, how can five kids be expected to?"

Adelessa's voice grew soft. "But don't you see?" she asked. "You already have."

Larkin blinked several times. He hadn't thought about it like that.

"Now," Adelessa continued, "I did come here to tell you something. I didn't want to tell you before the battle, because I didn't want to distract you."

Larkin looked at her expectantly.

"Your villagers are safe for now. Your aunt and uncle, Ariana's parents, Noll's mother, your friends, and your neighbors—they have been joined by others in the north, and they have slowed the enemy's march. They have bought themselves time, and I'm sure that Alymer is coming up with a plan to come to their aid."

Larkin breathed out a long sigh of relief as he tilted his head back to the night sky. They were still alive. There was still hope for them.

"And what about your mission to King Tenney?" he asked. "Is he going to help?"

Adelessa frowned. "I have been sidetracked, and I haven't made it to Glensworth yet. My guess is that King Tenney's waiting to see which side he thinks will win before he commits. He cares only for himself and his own power. Perhaps after today's win he'll join the fight. But I have my doubts."

She clapped her hands together. "But that's something for others to worry about on another day. Enjoy this night. You and your friends have earned it."

"*Especially* my friends," Larkin said.

Adelessa met his gaze with a questioning look. Larkin looked away and back up at the stars and the familiar constellations they formed. He spotted his favorite, The Rider—a woman riding a unicorn which moved in an opposite direction to all the other stars as it charged its way from west to east through the nighttime sky.

"It's the others who deserve all the credit," he said. "I've always daydreamed about being a hero. I tried to be a hero against Scrofa and failed. Even the queen of the Lake of Despair mocked my desire to be a hero. It was the others who did the hardest parts. They're the heroes."

Adelessa pursed her lips. "There were enough challenges for everyone to play their part. But every group needs a leader, and you led the others." Her mouth formed a thin, serious line across her face. "And remember this: there is no end to what you can accomplish when the risks and the credit are shared equally among friends. Just ask the last of The Protectors.

"And think about what happened when you became separated. Ariana and Noll were captured by The Scourge—or Galeran, as we should call him now. You were captured by the Hudenpole, and the three of you were imprisoned by Grydyl. But look what happened when you worked together. Everyone's strengths came out, and you saved Kavenland."

"But did we really succeed?" Larkin asked. "Kynwas is still alive."

"Your mission wasn't to stop Kynwas,' Adelessa answered. "Your mission was to cross The Forest and get word to Alymer. Against all odds, you did that. And maybe a great deal more," she mused to herself. "Now come."

She walked Larkin over to the tent.

"Enjoy your friends," she said, as she pulled aside the tent flap to let him in, "and enjoy your victory. In life, both are worth savoring."

Vic looked up to see Larkin walk into the tent. He caught a glimpse of Adelessa behind him before she disappeared into the night. She'd changed appearances even since this morning. He shook his head as Larkin sat down beside him.

"I don't get the whole Adelessa thing," Vic said. "She's gone from hideous to plain looking to...well, I'd call her beautiful." He looked over at Em. She shrugged.

"She's always looked the same to me," she said.

"If you see her differently," Larkin said to Vic, "I think that's because you've changed, not because she has."

Vic wasn't sure what that meant, but he did think that he'd changed. He imagined himself back home. He wondered if this new version of himself would have an easier time making friends. But Adelessa hadn't offered him and Em the chance to go back through the Door in the Stone yet.

Besides, he had friends here now. He'd never had that before. He looked over at Noll—big and friendly and curious. And, if Vic wasn't mistaken, Noll was curious about a certain person right now.

Noll was looking at a boy who sat near Fergus. The boy had been glancing Noll's way all night.

Noll thought again about Bogdan, the boy back in Fieldstone who he'd been too shy to talk to. He'd been shy about a lot of things back then. He'd tried to hide from his size, but he wasn't hiding anymore.

He hated the attention he used to get because it was for all the wrong reasons. It meant he didn't fit in. But he loved the attention he was getting now. Fergus had bellowed out the story all night of how they'd charged and defeated the silver-haired man. When the people in the tent talked to Noll now, it was with awe and wonder.

Maybe what Baedyn had told him was true. Maybe he did need to embrace being different from everyone else.

It was funny. He knew that Larkin loved the stories of The Protectors because he wanted to be a hero. Now he was, and he clearly felt uncomfortable with it. He'd slipped outside, but Noll was glad to see that his friend had come back into the tent.

Noll had no intention of leaving. He was having too much fun.

He decided to stare right at the boy who sat near Fergus. When the boy looked his way again, Noll locked eyes with him. The boy looked down shyly, then looked back up at Noll. Noll felt a nudge in his ribs.

"Well, don't just sit there—go talk to him," Ariana said.

"I think I just might," Noll said, without taking his eyes off the boy. He got up and walked toward him.

Ariana watched him go. She loved seeing her friend have this much confidence. Their recent adventures had changed him.

She hoped she'd learned something, too. It made her happy to protect those that she could, but it made her sad to think that she couldn't protect everybody all the time. She was going to have to learn to live with that.

She glanced sideways at Vic. Sometimes Vic seemed to have a lot of confidence and sometimes he didn't. There was definitely more trust in his eyes, though. She nodded to herself.

Trust was one of those things you had to have, right? She crinkled her forehead. I mean, if you don't have it, what kind of person are you? You need to be able to trust others. You need to be able to trust yourself. Do you do the right thing when no one's looking? Had Vic come that far? He said he was a thief. But that was before. Or was it? What if...

Ariana felt a tug on her sleeve. She turned to see Em, her head tilted to one side, a puzzled look on her face.

Ariana laughed. "Was I off somewhere in my own mind again? That happens. Sometimes I get a thought, and I chase after it like it's a rabbit on the run. It bounces here and there—my thoughts, I mean, not the rabbit, although if I was continuing the analogy..."

Em smiled as Ariana prattled on. She thought Ariana might be the nicest girl she'd ever met. And after watching her fight, Em was glad to be on her side.

She and Vic had been through so much since Adelessa had met them back in their world, she thought. There were times at first that she wished they hadn't followed Adelessa, but Em was glad now. She felt accepted here—and not just by the animals. There was Ariana, Noll, and Larkin. Larkin made everything look so effortless and so easy. She wondered if he'd always been that way, or whether what had happened to all of them had changed him as much as it had changed her and Vic.

She looked at her brother. He kept sneaking glances at Ariana. Ariana was still talking about rabbits. Em gently squeezed Vic's arm.

"Are you glad now that we followed Adelessa through the Door in the Stone?" she asked.

Vic thought for a moment. Kavenland was very much like what Adelessa had said it could be. He and Em weren't just accepted here, they were even considered heroes.

And Vic felt better about himself, too, and he realized that helped him to feel better about others. And to think, it had all started with him trying to become a master thief.

He had a sudden spasm of doubt. An icy hand clenched around his heart as he thought of their future.

Yes, they liked Kavenland, but how could he and Em get by in this world? They had no money, no family, no skills, no way to make a living. Where would they live? What would they do?

Vic's head swung around in a wild panic and took in the celebration going on around him. As he did, he noticed other details. Some of the people were wearing necklaces and bracelets. They wore rings, too, their jewels flashing in the dim light of the tent. Vic thought that some of the dinner plates were made of real gold.

He reached forward and took a drink from his goblet. From the heft of the cup, he guessed it was made of solid silver.

There must be a fortune in gold and silver and jewels in this tent.

A fortune.

He daydreamed about becoming the leader of the Gwyllions. Think of it—a whole race of beings who were experts at stealing, dedicated to stealing it all for him. Vic Blake, master criminal, with an army of thieves at his disposal. Why, it would be a story for the ages.

He shook his head. His pulse slowed. He looked around again at the joyous faces gathered under the tent. He realized that everything he'd ever truly wanted—people to care for and people who cared for him—was offered to him here for free.

Sure, by staying in Kavenland, he and Em would be stepping into an unknown future. But they'd be stepping into that unknown future with each other, and with friends, and with hope.

Back home, there was nothing but loneliness waiting for them.

He'd make that trade every time. And he didn't have to steal anything to make it.

"Vic?" Em asked. "Did you hear my question?"

"Huh? Oh. Yes. Just daydreaming." He looked around the tent at Noll, Ariana, and Larkin. He pursed his lips. Then he leaned back and threw his arms over the back of his chair. He looked back at Em and gave her a wink.

"Yes, Em," he said, "I am glad we came."

Acknowledgements

Years ago, Kevin Smith suggested that I write for younger readers. It rang true. Thank you, Kevin—it's been a wonderful first few steps on what I hope is a long journey! His encouragement helped me, as did the encouragement of my early readers: Pete Peterson; Penny Armstrong; my sisters, Susie and Wesley; and my sister-in-law, Debb Mullet. I'd like to thank editors Lina Rivera (show, don't tell!), Rachel Saula (your belief in this story gave me belief—thank you!), and Carolyn Grace (thank you for providing me with the final and necessary details to finish the story!). At various stages, all three helped me bring *The Door in the Stone* to its current form.

I'd like to thank my excellent agent, Uwe Stender. He has been a steady supporter throughout the long process of publishing *The Door in the Stone*. This book would not be in your hands without him.

Thank you to some excellent authors who helped me toward the end of the journey, especially Leslie Tall Manning and Cori Wamsley.

Special thanks to my son, Schaefer, and my wife, Meg, whose patience and encouragement for the project were vital. Meg's marketing skills and tech savvy are also well-beyond anything I can conceive. Thank you! And I'd like to thank my daughter, illustrator, and critic, Cooper Saturn King.

About the Author

Rob King has ambled through life with one foot in a fantasy world, one foot in the sports world, and his head firmly in the clouds. When he was young, he played sports (especially football and baseball) and read books that took him to imaginary worlds where good and evil battled amidst strange and wonderful creatures. But he had to grow up. Now he covers sports (especially the Steelers and Pirates) and writes books that take readers to imaginary worlds where good and evil battle amidst strange and wonderful creatures. You can learn more about Kavenland and the upcoming books in the series at robkingauthor.com.